SWEET SENSATIONS

At ease now, Megan finished her unwrapping. The rich scent of chocolate wafted toward him as, with a triumphant smile, she raised the blossom of crumpled wax paper and offered him its contents.

"If you can't decide, I'll choose one for you," Megan offered. She examined the chocolate pieces cupped in her hand, as though deliberating which would taste sweetest, then selected one. She held the bite of fudge aloft, poised a few inches from his mouth. "Open up."

The surprising intimacy of her suggestion was enough for his lips to part on their own. Gabriel did as she asked, watching with his mouth open and waiting as she brought the morsel of fudge closer. Its heady aroma teased his senses, sparking a hunger he hadn't been aware of until now. Anticipation stirred, making him angle his head still closer.

Slight as his movement was, Megan saw it. Her eyes widened. She stopped, their faces mere inches apart, with the treat she'd selected suspended between them. *Don't stop,* he wanted to whisper, suddenly afraid she'd realized the dangerous nature of their position and would end it too soon. *Come closer.*

Her gaze slipped to the fudge, then to his waiting mouth. He felt caressed, as surely as if she'd touched his lips already. A tremor shuddered through him, quick and harsh.

He wanted to taste *her,* not the candy. Wanted the feel of her mouth beneath his, wanted a depth of joining between them that he'd only imagined until now. . . .

Books by Lisa Plumley

OUTLAW
LAWMAN

Published by Zebra Books

LAWMAN

Lisa Plumley

Zebra Books
Kensington Publishing Corp.

http://www.zebrabooks.com

ZEBRA BOOKS are published by

Kensington Publishing Corp.
850 Third Avenue
New York, NY 10022

First Printing: October, 1999
10 9 8 7 6 5 4 3 2

Printed in the United States of America

To Charlotte Plumley,
with love and laughter
and (undoubtedly) a few tears,
and to John,
my husband and real-life hero

One

Near Tucson, Arizona Territory
September, 1882

If she could just get her corset stays pulled tightly enough, Megan Kearney figured she had an awfully good chance of achieving her dreams.

They were pretty big dreams, she'd be the first to admit. But a girl raised in the lonely, sprawling Territory of Arizona, with cactus wrens for playmates, a summertime cot beneath the stars for a cradle, and the hum of cicadas for a lullaby had to have something sweet to look forward to. For Megan, it was the chance to own her own dressmaker's shop in town. The chance to create beauty out of calico and lace and imagination. The chance to finally be safe and secure in a world of her own making.

After years of planning and saving, her opportunity had arrived—if she could only get into her best Sunday dress and get out there to meet it.

"Drat those *bizcochitos* of yours, Addie," she muttered, putting her hands to her waist. She stepped closer to the cast-off stagecoach strongbox she used as her bedroom's bureau and frowned into the looking glass propped atop it. "How am I supposed to make that dress fit now?"

Addie's gaze met hers in the mirror. "Don't ask me. I ain't the one who crammed all those goodies in your mouth."

"I couldn't help it. I was worried about this meeting." Sighing, Megan made herself stand up straighter. "Besides, you're the one who made the cookies. That's practically the same thing. They were so good, I was fairly compelled to eat them."

"That's a fine piece of logic." Grinning, Addie wrapped Megan's corset laces more securely around her capable, sturdy hands. "Why don't you try that on Mr. Webster, and see what he says about selling you his shop?"

"Don't be silly. It was difficult enough convincing him to deed me the alleyway rights and living space that go along with his mercantile. I hardly intend to discuss *bizcochitos* with a person like that."

"You go on talking that way, and you'll scare him off selling you the store altogether," Addie warned. "How many times have I got to tell you? Men don't like ladies who talk like a book."

Megan sighed. "I suppose you're right. A pretty dress probably is the best strategy."

"Ain't no supposin' about it. You listen to me, and I'll steer you right." Nodding, Addie took up the slack in the corset laces. "Now suck in your breath and quit your yappin', else you'll be walking into that fancy meetin' of yours wearing that old calico over there."

Megan eyed the faded pink dress draped tiredly over the coverlet on her bed. It looked worse than a station hand's britches after a day of drinking and carousing at the bullfights in the *presidio*. She'd never impress Mr. Jedediah Webster and his wife if she were wearing that old thing. She put a hand to her belly and breathed in as hard as she could.

"How's this?" she croaked, trying to peer over her shoulder. All she could see was Addie's gray-haired head, but judging by the way her curls waggled, she was getting ready for a vigorous tug.

"Perfect." *Yank.*

The rest of Megan's breath left her in a whoosh. Oh, well. The meeting would probably be a short one, anyway. Breathing deeply was only necessary if a body was asleep or getting ready to holler about something. She stuck both hands onto the cool, prickly adobe wall beside the looking glass and got ready for the next pull.

Yank. "Ouch!"

Why ever had she eaten all those *bizcochitos*? And what ever had possessed her to sew her new dress with an inch smaller waistline?

Vanity, she admitted to herself. *Plain and simple.* She wanted to impress the Eastern-born, city-bred Websters with her seamstress's ability and sense of style. She knew they saw her as a desert country–bumpkin, one whose nest egg of savings they were happy to take in exchange for their mercantile building, but a bumpkin, nonetheless. Everybody of consequence in town felt the same.

But not for long, Megan vowed as Addie tied up her stays and helped her button up her corset cover. She got on the rest of her underthings, then carefully lifted her new brown worsted gown from the bed. High-necked and shaped with room for an elaborate bustle, it was trimmed with black braid and jet buttons in the height of fashion.

Megan smoothed her cheek along the expensive fabric, smiling at the notion of having her own shop filled with similar fancy dresses, each one her own creation. Ladies would come from miles to own a dress like the ones she designed. A Megan Kearney original. After her dreams came true, she'd be as sophisticated as any Easterner, and twice as successful.

She would've bet her entire nest egg of savings on it, and planned to . . . just as soon as the Websters arrived.

He'd tracked criminals to sorrier, more decrepit places, but Gabriel Winter had never tailed one to anyplace more flat-out unusual than Kearney Station.

From his ridge-top vantage point behind a stand of September-dried creosote bushes, he raised his spyglass and looked over the station again. Amidst the scrub brush and cacti and mud that made up the central station yard, its flat-roofed, whitewashed adobe buildings clustered around each other for protection. A thorny *ocotillo*-rib fence wound between them, tall as the station hands working the grounds.

None were armed. To the left, one heavyset man led a pair of sorrel mares from the stables, and other hands carried equipment to and from a storage area nearby. Their voices carried to Gabriel's hiding place, borne on the same wind that carried the tang of mesquite wood-smoke across *arroyo* and flatland.

None of that was unusual. But the lengths of jade green, blue, and yellow fabric woven decoratively between the fence ribs like ladies' hair ribbons were. The borders of flowers painted above the doorways were. So were the potted cacti arranged along the archways of the Spanish-style *zaguán* that connected the main stage station with the outbuilding behind it.

Most of all, so were the pennants. From holders beside the rough planked doorways, the bright-colored flags snapped in the sunrise breeze, surprising as jewels on a mule.

Definitely a woman's touch.

Gabriel lowered his spyglass and slid it shut, smiling in spite of himself. Beauty was hard to come by in the Territory—hard to come by in life. It had been too long since he'd admired anything for its form, instead of its substance. Instead of the facts it hid or revealed.

The pursuit of truth could do that to a man, he figured. Especially a man who lived in the world of hunter and hunted, lost and found. For a minute, those painted flowers and flourishes held his imagination like nothing had in longer than he could remember.

Then Tom McMarlin crawled up beside him from the other end of the ridge, and Gabriel's mind snapped back to the task at hand.

Tracking his quarry.

"Doesn't look too damned prosperous, does it?" McMarlin muttered, parting a portion of the creosote barrier to squint toward the station. "If old man Kearney really did nab that loot, I'd say he's already pulled foot from here and hied out for greener pastures."

"Maybe." Gabriel rolled onto his back and slugged some water from his canteen. He wished it was coffee. Almost a week spent reading reconnaissance reports on the train between Chicago and Tucson had prepared him for the case, but not for the dew-damp, cold, rocky soil he'd spent sunrise on. Beneath his traveling clothes, he felt chilled to the bone.

Frowning, he wiped his mouth and screwed on the canteen cap. "But as usual, McMarlin, you're only seeing the outside."

"What the hell else am I supposed to see? We're *on* the blasted outside." He scratched a match into flame and lit a cheroot, blowing a plume of smoke toward the station.

"And that place looks one step away from dilapidation, geegaws or no."

"It's old. Not falling apart." Gabriel handed over the spyglass. "See how the whitewash looks thicker in spots? It's been redone, year after year. The roofs look solid. The grounds are cleared so the stage gets through faster; it doesn't stay that way without work."

McMarlin grunted and snapped the glass shut. "So? It ain't like their stables don't stink."

"Actually, they don't. Not like they would without so many hands keeping things mucked out. And all those men aren't working for free."

"No, they're working for a crook."

"Alleged crook."

"Alleged, my ass, you damned stickler," McMarlin said, grinning around a mouthful of cigar. "You think Joseph Kearney is as guilty as I do, or you wouldn't be here."

Gabriel grinned back at him. After years of working Pinkerton cases with Tom, McMarlin was like an older brother to him—and he knew him about as well.

"Maybe. Point is, this place is more prosperous than it looks. More prosperous than you thought at first sight." He sat up and stuffed his canteen and spyglass into his worn saddlebag. Then he passed a hand over his face and looked at McMarlin again. "You're not looking deep enough on this case, or I wouldn't *have* to be here."

McMarlin grimaced, grinding his cheroot into the rocks. He left the stub where it lay. "Is that what Pinkerton told you?"

"It's what I know."

A simple stagecoach robbery like this one should have been solved within days. McMarlin should've already had wanted posters up and a solid mark on his suspect's trail. Hell, he should've had the damned knuck in custody already. Instead, Gabriel suspected he'd spent half his assignment time whoring in Tucson and the rest of it with a bottle of whiskey in hand.

McMarlin belly-crawled back down the ridge side opposite the stage station. "You don't know your head from a horse's behind. No matter what old man Pinkerton thinks."

Gabriel almost smiled. Truth be told, part of him wanted to shuck the damned "no-fail" reputation Allan Pinkerton had bestowed on him after his first few successful cases. *Winter brings in the right man at the right time.* What started as praise had become an obligation, one harder to uphold for the thirty-two-year-old man he'd become than the cocky, twenty-year-old kid who'd earned it.

"You just keep dogging my steps, McMarlin." Grinning, he snatched up the discarded cigar stub—evidence they didn't need to leave behind of their presence there—and then followed his partner belly-first down the slope. "Maybe someday you'll get a legend of your own."

McMarlin snorted, bending to brush the dust from his fancy suit pants. Then he straightened and adjusted his tie. "I already got me a legend, with them painted ladies down on Maiden Lane. That's all the reputation I want, boy-o."

"Keep on like you are, then," Gabriel said, hefting his saddlebag over his shoulder for the trek to the *arroyo* bank where he'd picketed his horse. He scanned the ridge one last time to make sure their presence there wouldn't be detected later. "That's the only reputation you'll have."

"What the hell's that supposed to mean?"

Damn! "Nothing."

He turned toward the valley behind them, where a hazy strip of green showed the location of the *arroyo,* and started walking. McMarlin's hand stopped him within two steps.

" 'S there something I ought to know, boy-o?"

Gabriel looked at him, seeing for the first time in a long

time the differences between them. McMarlin was getting on in years. Gray lightened his sandy, close-clipped hair and beard, and the paunch beneath his expensive suit only showed how little field work he did these days. Typically, he'd dressed like a banker, armed himself like an outlaw . . . and gotten so comfortable in his place with the agency, he'd forgotten it could all vanish in an instant.

William Pinkerton, the head agent in Chicago, was close to giving McMarlin some enforced time off. The letter proving it was in Gabriel's saddlebag, wrapped in oilcloth along with the rest of the papers documenting the road agent they'd been hired to bring in. Officially, McMarlin was free to leave, and Gabriel was the head man on the case.

But standing beneath an Arizona Territory sun with the man who'd taught him all he knew about bringing in Pinkerton's most-wanted, the last thing he wanted to do was tell him that.

"Dammit, McMarlin, I can't stand here jawing all morning," Gabriel said instead. "It's a half-hour past sunup already."

"You still figuring on finding Kearney at the station?"

He jerked his head toward the cluster of buildings behind them, and Gabriel's gaze followed the motion. A stagecoach rattled in as they watched, spewing dust in its wake, and was quickly met by several of the station hands. Their Spanish-accented speech drifted toward the ridge, but the words were too faint to make out.

"I always start at the beginning. And that's it." He glanced at McMarlin. "You got a better idea?"

"Hell, yes," he answered with a good-natured grin, pulling a flask from his coat pocket. "Me and Old Orchard here'll watch your back while you're gone. Better head out, boy-o."

"Don't get too cozy," Gabriel said, going to retrieve his horse. "This won't take long."

The chase was on.

How two people had become so perfectly cantankerous in exactly the same ways, Megan couldn't imagine. But somehow, Jedediah and Mrs. Webster had managed it.

So far, she'd been forced to haggle with them over the selling price of their mercantile store, the precise boundaries specified in the alleyway rights, and the disposition of the dry goods and supplies already in inventory. Mrs. Webster clearly meant to second-guess every accord Megan had reached with her husband in their earlier meetings—in a voice so shrill, Megan's teeth ached from listening to it after the first few minutes.

If this was what was meant by wedded bliss, Megan had never been plumb happier to be a spinster.

Sighing as she listened to the Websters recite their latest demand, she reached for one of the cinnamon sugar—covered *buñuelos* from the basketful Addie had prepared. A glance from Mrs. Webster halted her hand halfway there.

A lady didn't gobble up the refreshments meant for her guests, Megan reminded herself, and raised the basket toward them, instead. "Are you sure you wouldn't like some *buñuelos*? Our station cook makes the best in the Territory."

"No, thank you," Mrs. Webster said, glancing meaningfully at the snug fit of Megan's new dress. "Although we can certainly see that *you* approve of such . . . rustic fare, my dear."

Megan felt her face heat. Before she could say anything, Jedediah spoke up, too.

"Now, now, Prudie," he told his wife. "It's not as though Miss Kearney needs to keep her figure to attract a husband—not at her advanced years." He winked and gave the basket a little shove in Megan's direction. "You go on ahead and indulge yourself."

The basket wobbled in her hand. She gritted her teeth and made herself smile calmly at them as she set it onto the scarred oak station desk.

"As it happens, I'm only twenty-eight 'advanced' years," she informed them. *And at least half of those have been spent negotiating with you.* It certainly felt like it. "Still young enough to appreciate the latest fashions"—Megan aimed an especially syrupy smile at Mrs. Webster—"and old enough to understand what it really means to bind yourself to a spouse"—another smile for Jedediah—*"forever."*

The Websters sighed and looked at their feet, separately chagrined, but united in the way they both slumped in their seats on the other side of her father's heavy stationmaster's desk.

Feeling a bit cheered, Megan sat straighter and picked up a pencil. "Now, about this provision for the living space behind the mercantile," she began, going on to press for slightly improved terms than those she'd originally agreed on . . . plus the complimentary addition of some handsomely glazed Mexican pottery she'd admired in their mercantile.

"I think you'll agree," she finished, "that such an . . . indication of goodwill is warranted here."

"I suppose," Jedediah said doubtfully.

"Very well," Mrs. Webster snapped. "Your—your good nature warrant is, of course, an indication here. Do you take us for greenhorns, fresh from the train?"

"Of course not." Megan frowned thoughtfully at the much rewritten purchase agreement on the desk, the document that would deed her Jedediah's Tucson mercantile— soon to become *her* longed-for dressmaker's shop. "But there is still the small matter of the abutment with Mr.

Meyer's establishment and its influence on the deed to be assessed. I'm sure—"

A blurred motion in the office doorway caught her eye. Addie's head appeared, vehemently shaking "no" as she pantomimed reading a book. She licked her finger and turned a pretend page, then shook her head again.

Doing her best to glare her away, Megan pulled the deed agreement closer and wrote in the addition of the pottery and the improved living-space terms. "I—I'm sure we can easily come to terms with that, though," she finished awkwardly.

Shoot, Addie had done it to her again. She'd lost the direction of her thoughts regarding the abutment when she'd seen Addie's warning. Now it was too late to let her original indignation carry her into further negotiations.

Smiling smugly, Addie pantomimed closing a book and ducked out of the doorway. Megan frowned after her. *Don't talk like a book, indeed!* How was she supposed to cope with people like the Websters, if all she could do was smile and curtsy and show off her bustle?

It was ridiculous to behave as though she hadn't a thought in her head beyond ribbons and recipes. If that was what it took to capture a husband, no wonder she'd never gotten herself one!

Aside from living in the middle of nowhere with a bunch of station hands for company and a father who spent more time at the gambling table than the dinner table, she amended. If not for Addie and the much-thumbed copies of *Godey's* brought to her by the Kearney stagecoach drivers from the Fort Lowell officers' wives, she wouldn't have had any feminine influences at all.

Across the desk, the Websters put their heads together and whispered. She took advantage of the opportunity to review the deed agreement one last time, then cleared her throat.

"It looks as though everything is in order," she said when they looked up. "Shall we sign?"

She plucked a fountain pen from its holder and held it toward Jedediah. He stared at it as though she'd suggested he eat it, rather than simply sign his name with it. Then, slowly, he leaned forward and reached for it.

Mrs. Webster jabbed him with her elbow. With a sheepish expression, he lowered his hand again.

"Ahh, we'll need to view the reimbursement before signing, Miss Kearney."

"Reimbursement?"

"The cash," Mrs. Webster clarified.

"I see."

She'd hoped to secure a cashier's check with the money at the telegraph office in Tucson before completing their transaction. Having a record of the money that changed hands would be best. After all, the entire contents of her nest egg were at risk. But as difficult as this meeting had been to arrange, and as difficult as the Websters had been to deal with, all Megan wanted to do was get it over with. A signed, witnessed receipt would have to do.

"The funds aren't a problem, are they?" Jedediah asked. "I know it's not quite in a lady's nature to deal with great sums of money."

Megan thought back on the years she'd been drawing wages as her father's bookkeeper and part-time, uncertified station manager. What did that make her, if not a lady handling great sums of money? It was fortunate she and her father had kept her financial acumen to themselves; otherwise, folks might have expected her to start wearing britches or do something equally ridiculous.

"Or perhaps you'd like to wait until your father can be present himself, to guide you?" Mrs. Webster suggested. "I've always taken my dear father's advice, right down to the question of whom I'd marry."

That explained a great deal. Suppressing a shudder at the notion of enduring a similar fate, Megan opened the desk drawer to her left and withdrew a stack of leather-bound ledgers. Their familiar, earthy scent did much to reassure her. This was her element, she reminded herself, and her home. She wouldn't allow mean-hearted people like the Websters to discourage her.

Besides, all her dreams hinged on reaching an accord with them.

"I'm afraid my father's been called away on business," she said. Called away to a Faro game, more likely. According to Addie, he'd ridden out for Tucson sometime before sunup, all afire about some "big opportunity" he meant to surprise them with. "So he won't be able to be here with us today."

"Oh, my. That's such a shame."

Megan's heart twisted. She'd never thought of it in precisely those terms before, but Mrs. Webster was right, after a fashion.

If she waited long enough for Joseph Kearney to appear and formally sanction her dressmaker's shop purchase, she'd not only be the spinster she already was, she'd be wrinkled and gray haired, to boot. As much as she loved him, her father never seemed to be around when she needed him. Today was no exception . . . and that truly was a shame.

Pride made her sit straighter. With as much composure as she could muster, Megan met Mrs. Webster's gaze head-on. "Not such a shame, madam. I've enjoyed the freedom it's allowed me."

Briskly, she plunked the ledgers onto the desktop and reached into the drawer again, feeling with her fingertips for the smooth glass canning jar that held her nest egg. The sooner they finished this, the better.

Her fingertips met cool glass. Smiling, she pulled out

the jar, keeping it below the desk so she could count its contents in private. "I'll just be a moment," she told the Websters.

"Take your time, Miss Kearney," said Jedediah.

"We want to be sure you count all those precious coppers correctly," added Mrs. Webster with a smug, haughty expression—the same expression that greeted Megan in town whenever she ventured to Tucson for fabric or lace or tinware.

Now, as always, it hurt. Why could she never muster enough defenses against those cutting looks? No matter how hard she tried, they always managed to pierce her defenses somehow.

One day such cutting looks wouldn't bother her, Megan promised herself. One day, she'd rise above them.

"You might even want to count twice," Jedediah added.

Sudden, unwanted tears of embarrassment and anger stung her eyes. She wished she'd negotiated even harder on that purchase agreement, wrangled even more favorable terms than the excellent ones she already had secured.

Her hands trembled on the jar lid, sending it clattering to the floor. Wanting nothing more than to throw her carefully counted coins and precious rolled bills right at the Websters, Megan reached inside.

And came up with nothing. Her nest egg of savings had vanished. Disappeared . . . just as quickly as the Websters themselves would, when they learned the truth.

Oh, Papa, Megan thought as she stared at the empty jar in her hands. *Whatever have you done this time?*

Two

"Stop, Miss Megan!" Addie said, reaching over to wrestle a hairbrush and comb from Megan's grasp before she could pack it. "This is the craziest notion I've heard since old Charlie took it into his head to rig parasols to the drivers' seats on all the coaches."

"It's not crazy, it's necessary." Megan packed her second-best dress atop the clothes already assembled in the open satchel on her bed, then snatched back the hairbrush and comb, stuffed them inside, and snapped her luggage closed. "Who knows how much of that nest-egg money Papa's already lost?"

"He meant well. He—he thought he'd double it. Surprise you for your birthday next month. Afore he left, Joseph told me he had a surefire system this time. One that can't be beat."

Addie folded her bony arms over her apron front and leaned against the doorjamb. Her expression said she believed everything she'd just said.

But Megan knew better.

"He always has some highfalutin', can't-miss gambling technique up his sleeve," she reminded Addie, hefting her second satchel onto the bed. "And it always works perfectly—right up until the moment he loses it all."

Addie gave her a sorrowful look. "He loves you, child."

Megan's hand fisted on the black cotton stockings she'd been about to stuff into the satchel. An image of her father's smiling, bewhiskered face rose in her mind's eye . . . then dissolved beneath a new vision of a gaming table, a haze of smoke, and Papa crying into his Levin's Park beer because he'd lost every penny of his daughter's nest egg. It was too real to be ignored.

"Awww, Addie. I love him, too."

She smoothed out the crumpled stockings and tucked them into the satchel beside her hair ribbons and the derringer she'd received from the station hands for a Christmas gift last year. She looked at the little gun again, thought better of keeping it out of reach, and slipped it into her skirt pocket instead.

"But I can't let him do this again. It's taken me two years to replace what he lost last time he found my savings. At this rate, by the time I get my dressmaker's shop, I'll be too old to see what I'm stitching."

She added a bottle of rose water and a wad of lacy handkerchiefs, then closed the satchel. "Besides, the Websters are set to head back East on Saturday's train. If I haven't gotten the money to them before then, they'll sell their mercantile to Mr. Meyer the butcher next door, and my chance will be gone."

She'd managed to hide the fact of her missing money from Jedediah and his wife, and had somehow convinced them they needed a rewritten purchase agreement, due to all the changes, before completing their transaction. With her promise to have a new contract drawn up and delivered to them later in the week, they'd left on the morning express only minutes earlier.

But Megan knew she couldn't put them off with excuses for long.

"Three days isn't much time," Addie said, coming to stand beside the bed. "What if you can't find your papa by then? You're hardly familiar with town, and—"

"I can do it."

She *had* to do it. She'd dreamed of her dressmaker's shop for so long now, dreamed of something her very own to feel proud of. Something secure to keep her safe. She couldn't give up when it was almost within reach.

Addie's gentle hand touched her shoulder. "Sheer grit might not be enough."

"I don't see why not."

With a sigh, Addie smoothed the brown worsted shoulder seam it had taken Megan a week straight to sew correctly. The shaping technique had been new and difficult to master, but in the end she'd done it.

Determination had worked then. It would work again.

"Maybe you should've told Joseph the truth, Megan," Addie went on. "Told him your plans for your shop. Maybe none of this would've happened at all."

"And maybe it would've happened even sooner." Megan shook her head and picked up her wide-brimmed traveling hat, then carried it to the looking glass. "I've got to do this on my own."

"It ain't like you're alone." In the glass, Addie's reflection twisted her apron hem. "We all would help ya if we could."

Pausing with her hat on but untied, Megan met Addie's gaze. Her fingers trembled on the wide grosgrain ribbons in her hands, making them flutter against her dress. "I know you would," she said quietly. "And I love you for it, Addie."

She turned, ribbons whirling past her shoulders. "I just plain love you for no reason at all," she said, catching Addie's spare, strong shoulders and pulling her close for a hug.

With no mother she could remember well, and a father more often afield than underfoot, she didn't know what she would've done without Addie nearby. Sniffling, Megan kept her forehead buried against Addie's familiar, crisp apron for a moment longer, then squeezed once more and stepped away.

"But I'm still heading to Tucson to bring Papa back— and my nest-egg money—and this time I won't take no for an answer."

She tied her hat ribbons beneath her chin and scrutinized the effect in the mirror, comparing it with the illustration she'd seen in the latest *Godey's* from Fort Lowell. For an ordinary straw bonnet, it looked right fine with the embellishments she'd added. The thought that she looked nice gave her the extra courage she needed to face the highbrow ladies in town—and their wagging gossips' tongues.

She pulled on her mother's old linen gloves, the only pair she'd ever owned, and turned to face Addie. "Well? How do I look?"

"Like you oughta take Mose along with you for protection," Addie answered sourly, crossing her arms again. "Them ruffians in town will take one look at you and toss you over their shoulders for Maiden Lane."

What a thrilling notion! "Do you really think so?" Megan asked, pirouetting in front of the looking glass. Her bustle swayed behind her with just the right amount of swoosh to be stylish, but . . .

"Megan! Ravishment is nothing to look forward to!"

She examined the embroidery at the wrists of her gloves and tried to look contrite. "Only if it's not done properly," she couldn't resist saying. "Why, in the French novel I read last week—"

"That's it." Addie picked up both satchels from the floor. "You're not venturing an inch from this station with notions like that in your head."

"Yes, I am." Megan grabbed a satchel and tugged. It didn't budge.

"No, ma'am." Addie tugged back. "And no more French novels, neither."

Megan tried a smile. "If you let me go, I'll bring you back some of those fine Mexican vanilla beans from the marketplace."

Addie's grasp loosened.

"You haven't had any of those since that last drummer came through, remember?"

Addie's gaze softened. "The one with that fine tinware," she murmured, clearly remembering. Nothing was dearer to Addie's heart than her cooking and baking.

"And a fresh cone of sugar," Megan said to sweeten the deal.

"Cinnamon?"

"Yes, that too." With a friendly pat, she slipped the satchel handle from Addie's left hand, then her right. Helpfully, she steered her toward the door. "Vanilla, sugar, and cinnamon. Just think of all you could make with that."

Halfway into the short hall leading to the stage station office, Addie's vision cleared. She gave Megan a sharp look, but her accompanying smile was kind. "You're a wily one," she said, shaking her finger. "You'd better take care, though. That fancy talk won't always work on folks."

"Of course not," Megan replied with a demure shrug of her shoulders. "Some people just can't be persuaded."

But about ninety-nine percent of them could, she figured—and those odds were favorable enough to suit her fine.

* * *

"If Joseph Kearney isn't here," Gabriel said tightly, "then someone else must be—someone who knows where he's gone."

Gripping his horse's reins in his fist, he scrutinized the yard of Kearney Station again before returning his gaze to the station hand who'd greeted him.

If a grunt could be called a greeting.

" 'Spect so," the man said.

Tall, blond, and well muscled as the dappled gray chomping at the bit beside him, the man put Gabriel in mind of a Swedish boxer he'd once seen in the ring in Chicago. If his taciturn responses were anything to go by, he, too, had been bashed in the head one too many times.

"When's Mr. Kearney expected back?"

The station hand muttered something unintelligible.

"Has he been gone long?"

"Can't rightly say."

Clearly, he was going to be here for a while. Swearing beneath his breath, Gabriel tried to force some patience into his voice. "Who *can* say?"

The man's eyebrows pulled together like caterpillars sneaking over the same Palo Verde branch. "What'd you say yer name was?"

"I didn't."

Gabriel led his horse to the hitching post and got the mare settled in for a long haul. When he finished, the big Swede was still standing where he'd left him.

Maybe he hadn't noticed things had changed yet.

"I need to see the man in charge," Gabriel told him. He inclined his head toward the rough adobe station building, trying not to smile anew at the pink blossoms painted over the doorway. "He in there?"

"No."

He tipped his chin toward the stables. "In there?"

"No."

He gazed over the horizon, past acres of rocky soil, creosote bushes, and prickly pear. "Out there?"

"No."

"Hmmm." Gabriel passed a hand over his face, wishing he could scrub away the weariness that had trailed him since crossing the Territory line. "Thanks for your help."

He turned and headed for the stage station office. Before he could take four steps, the hand lumbered into his path. The movement was a veritable flash of speed for an ox of a man like that.

And because of it, Gabriel knew he'd guessed correctly.

Joseph Kearney might be away from the station—or he might just want folks to think he was—but *something* important was in that office. Gabriel meant to find out what it was.

"Folks ain't allowed in there," the hand said.

Tipping back his hat brim, Gabriel took a leisurely look at the man. "Is that right?"

"Yeah."

"Why's that?"

He appeared to think on it. He got all the way to befuddled before scratching his head and giving up. "They just ain't."

Gabriel pulled back his coat, exposing the badge pinned to his vest. "Pinkerton men are."

Behind the man, Gabriel saw someone open the stage station door. A female shape stepped into the doorway, holding up one delicate, gloved hand to tip her hat brim toward the harsh sunlight. And all at once, Gabriel understood who the big man had been trying to protect.

"Get better excuses," he advised the station hand. "Or get out of the way."

Then he stepped forward to meet the woman who was about to provide his first case-solving clues.

No sooner had Megan's vision adjusted to the glare of the September sunlight than a stranger stepped from Mose's shadow and came toward her.

A drummer, she thought instantly, assessing his expensive navy suit, flashy vest, four-in-hand necktie, and shirt through expert eyes. He looked like a fashion picture in *Godey's,* and she expected he talked like a book, too.

Something in common, some traitorous part of her whispered.

She banished the thought instantly as he left Mose behind and approached the station office. She hadn't time for girlish notions of flirting with a passing peddler, however handsomely turned out he might happen to be.

He stepped closer, extending his hand in greeting. He was big, nearly as big as Mose, and good-looking, too. Beneath his hat brim, his dark-shadowed face was lit with the white slash of his smile. With it, he looked every inch the sharper, a man who could likely sell steaks to a rancher and charge him for the butchering, besides.

But despite the apparent friendliness of that smile, Megan felt a sudden urge to run. To grab the horse from Mose's hands and ride until the sunset swallowed her up.

Surely such a notion was unfounded. And the last thing she'd ever be called was a coward. Rather than run, she dug her toes into the chilly, packed station-yard dirt and stood her ground. With luck, she'd appear more composed than she felt.

He drew closer, hand still outstretched, speaking words of greeting. They flew straight past her head, chased by the lyrical huskiness of his voice. The unusual sound of it turned his words to honey, better savored than fully considered.

Lulled by the sound, she automatically slipped her hand into his to accept his handshake. The feel of his strong, warm fingers closing over hers sent unexpected shivers coursing through her, and instantly, she regretted not running while she still had the chance.

"You must be Miss Kearney." He widened that remarkable smile. "I'm here to see your father, but I'd rather do business with a pretty woman any day."

Her shivery feelings vanished. No, he didn't talk like a book, Megan amended. He talked like a flannel-mouthed Irishman out to sell her the land beneath her feet and the sky that arched over it. Only a fool would buy into the same worthless deal twice.

She'd never considered herself a fool.

"You'll find that kind of businesswoman in town," she said coolly, withdrawing her hand from his. "It's only a few hours' ride." Nodding helpfully toward Tucson, she added, "Out here, a man could get strung up for making such a suggestion to a lady."

"My apologies," the stranger said, touching a finger to his flat-brimmed hat. "I meant no offense."

"None taken."

Most men couldn't help the way they were anyway, she figured. Near as she could tell, the majority of males walked around with blinders on, thinking of nothing beyond the next drink, the next card game, the next gunfight . . . or the next woman to be taken advantage of.

If she could help it, that woman would never be her.

He lowered his hand to the gun belt strapped beneath his fancy coat. Thoughtfully, the stranger tipped up his head and took in the station office behind her, the hands working in the yard, and her new dress with equal parts interest and appraisal, like her father did when sizing up potential gaming opponents. Then, with a rapt expression, he reached past her shoulder and smoothed his fingers over the pink roses she'd painted along the door frame.

"These are beautiful." He stroked them once more, as if savoring the feel of them beneath his hand. His gaze, startlingly blue in a rather rawboned face, shifted to her. "Are you the artist?"

No one had ever admired her flowers. Mostly, folks thought painting them was a waste of time. But this man obviously did not agree. On the contrary, he stroked the painted flowers as though they were nigh irresistible—and stood so near that the warmth of his forearm teased her jaw, even through his fine wool suit.

Megan found herself inhaling the scents of tangy crushed creosote blossoms, leather, and rich tobacco that clung to his clothes . . . and telling herself that surely the breathlessness she felt owed more to her too-tight stays than any stranger's compliments.

Until she realized his expression remained intent on hers, waiting for her reply. Then there was no denying her reaction was because of him. To her knowledge, the corset had yet to be designed that could make her heart pound and her stomach lurch with excitement.

"Yes, I am. How did you—"

Mose's approach cut off the rest of her words. He shoved his huge body between her and the stranger, fixing him with a poisonous look. "I'm powerful sorry, Miss Megan, but this here man's a—"

"—about to leave, I'd say." Shaking her head in amazement, Megan looked from Mose to the stranger. Good heavens! He'd changed tactics so smoothly she hadn't even realized it. He'd recognized the error of his careless compliment and had tried another approach immediately.

Aside from herself, she'd never met anyone who'd have tried such a thing.

Whoever he was, she'd clearly underestimated him.

She looked up at him. "I'm sorry, but you can't see my father today. He's been called away from the station, and won't be returning for some time. But I'll tell him you called, Mr. . . ."

"Winter," he supplied. "Gabriel Winter."

His voice held an intriguing lilt, like a sun-warmed version of the Irish sisters' speech at San Agustín church in town. Spoken by him, his name sounded like poetry.

And she sounded like an addle-headed idiot, Megan told herself sternly. Thank heaven she hadn't uttered such a thing aloud.

"As I said, I'll tell him you were here." Gathering her full brown skirts in both hands, Megan stepped toward the station yard to have a horse saddled and brought round for her. The sooner she went after her father, the better.

"Good day, Mr. Winter," she called as she walked away. "You're welcome to some refreshments in our station kitchen before you leave. Mose will take you there, if you'd like."

"If I'd like?"

"Yes."

She turned toward him again, raising her skirt slightly higher to keep her hem out of the mud and muck littering the yard. Gabriel Winter's gaze shot to her ankles, then lingered. She felt his attention on her just as surely as if he'd reached out his hand and caressed her skin the same way he'd stroked her painted roses.

And knew she shouldn't have liked the sensation.

Much less have been thrilled to the bottoms of her sensible brogan shoes.

"Or," she added archly, assessing his broad shoulders and fit physique just as boldly, "if you prefer, you could just take your leave right now. You seem fairly well fed to me."

Either that, or most of his apparent muscle was padding tailored into his suit. As a seamstress, she'd practiced such techniques herself. Mollified by the thought of his horsehair-pillowed shoulders, Megan shut her mouth and put on her most no-nonsense expression, then shifted her attention to his face.

He was grinning. At her.

The rascal.

Her actions and words had been meant to dismiss him. Instead, he only arched his brow and asked, "Leave?"

"Yes." Was he simpleminded? "Naturally, since my father wasn't expecting you today, you can hardly think to—"

"He expected me."

Something in the way he said it made her pause. "Oh?" she asked, casually as she could.

"Yes."

It couldn't be true. She'd have known if her father was expecting a visitor, since she conducted much of the station business herself. Still, she'd underestimated Gabriel Winter once already. She didn't intend to commit the same mistake twice.

And whatever his business, it was probably best handled in private—without station hands nearby.

Megan nodded toward Mose. "It's all right, Mose. Thank you for your help."

He grinned and tugged the horse's reins he was holding closer to his chest, staring down at his big clodhopper boots. "Ain't nothin', Miss Megan."

"It was a great deal," she insisted with a smile. "But why don't you take Mollie to the stable now, and get on with your work. I'll be fine here."

Mose cast a suspicious glance at Gabriel Winter. Reluctantly, he tugged the horse nearer. "Yes'm," he muttered, taking his leave, but not before slamming his shoulder into Mr. Winter's chest as he passed.

Men. Always having to prove something.

To her amazement, the stranger didn't even sway. And, to her greater surprise, he didn't seem to feel the need to shove Mose back, either.

"Shall we talk inside?" he asked instead. He removed his hat, revealing a headful of hair thick and black as a moonless night, then gestured toward the opened stage-station doorway. "You may prefer hearing what I have to say in private."

His solicitousness surprised her. But the appreciative glance he aimed at her bustle when she moved toward the door did not. Megan stepped sideways, putting a little extra wiggle into her walk as she preceded him into the station. As near as she could tell, she might need whatever weaponry she could muster.

In her experience, a well-padded bustle could be counted upon to be effective.

Smiling, she pulled off her hat and gloves with motions leisurely enough to let her observe Gabriel Winter—hopefully, without his noticing. His tall, broad-shouldered body blocked much of the light from the doorway; then he followed her inside. His boots beat solidly on the hard-packed dirt floor as he made his way around the room, somehow managing to fill the space in a way the station hands never had. He carried a sense of authority with him as easily as he wore those citified clothes.

Her curiosity piqued, Megan finished removing her gloves, and laid them daintily across her palm the way she'd read the *Godey's* ladies did.

"Did you say my father expected you?" she asked, taking a seat behind the desk. At least there she felt more in control, however little she knew about her visitor.

Gabriel Winter nodded, still examining the room. He traced his fingers over the books shelved near the door, touched the lantern on its hook, rubbed his palm over the

pair of old ladderback chairs Jedediah and Prudie Webster
had occupied earlier. At her desk, he closed his eyes and
fairly caressed the quartz paperweight Megan kept atop
the bills of lading. It was as though the man felt as strongly
as he saw.

His eyes opened, then focused on her face with unnerving intensity. "Yes, he expected me."

Enough of this mysteriousness. "Why?" she snapped, throwing down her gloves to open the journal of express shipment records. "Do you have something to ship on the
express?"

"No, not that."

He dropped his hat atop her journal. He walked around
the side of her desk, near enough that his pantleg almost
brushed her skirts. Then, to her astonishment, Gabriel
Winter kept right on going toward the living area at the
rear of the station.

"I'm here to arrest him," he said, tossing something
over his shoulder.

She scrambled to her feet just as it landed on the desktop
with a scrape of metal on wood.

A Pinkerton agent's badge.

Things had gone from bad to worse.

Three

"Come back here this instant!"

Megan Kearney's voice preceded her to the rear of the stage station by no more than a hairsbreadth. Clear, precise, and achingly female, the sound would've been sweeter than molasses—if the lady behind it hadn't been mad enough to wake snakes. Her tone made it clear she wasn't used to being ignored.

Gabriel could see why, after noticing the way her bustle trailed her earlier. A man could follow that sweet side-to-side swoosh clear to heaven and back. For a spinster, Joseph Kearney's daughter knew how to use every feminine asset the Lord had granted.

And some He hadn't.

She barreled into the plain-furnished bedroom he'd found himself in, affording him no more than a glimpse of the room before she blocked the view with those assets of hers. The rounded flare of her hips beneath her skirt was a sight finer to look at than the old military cot, chest, and bare adobe walls behind her, and so was the rest of her.

A man couldn't help but take a second look.

"This is my father's bedroom!" she said. "Get out of here at once."

"Or what?" Gabriel asked lazily. She really was a pretty thing—if a little on the oddly dressed side. Those geegaws on her hat had been enough to send the cactus wrens toward her with thoughts of nesting on their minds. "You'll have that oversized kid you call a station hand in here to roust me out?"

"Yes!"

He shrugged. "I've put bigger men in the ground. Maybe not dumber ones, but—"

She started to tremble—with anger, he guessed, not fear.

"If you so much as lay a hand on Mose," she said, "I'll—I'll—"

Just as he'd thought, she was softhearted. Soft all over, by the looks of her. If he'd had more time, more leads on the case . . .

The case.

For all he knew, she'd helped her father pull off that damned stagecoach robbery. Reminding himself of the duty that had brought him here, Gabriel pressed his fingertips to the pale canvas tacked over the low *viga* ceiling and leaned over her.

"You'll what?"

She glared upward, taking in the way his fingertips reached the ceiling. Then she glared at him.

He grinned. Lord, but he did like a feisty woman.

"Hmmm?" he prompted.

Her big brown eyes lost some of their warmth. Her gaze narrowed, then centered on him.

Lowdown on him.

"I'll do this," she said—and kicked him in the shin.

Damnation. Pain exploded along his leg bone. Ducking, he rubbed it out, still keeping an eye on her. He wanted to know it if she took it into her head to kick him a little higher up.

"Desert women are a little different than you're used to, I guess," she said, returning his look with vinegar to spare.

Gabriel grunted. "Yeah. A city woman would've jabbed me with her parasol instead." He winced as he straightened again, this time out of kicking range. "What the hell's in those shoes?"

"Feet. Please get out."

He looked her over, gauging his chances of sweet-talking her into letting him search the place without getting crippled for his efforts.

They didn't look good.

But he had to try.

He reached inside his coat pocket and tugged out the wanted poster he'd drawn up on the train from Chicago. Based on the case file, it contained details about the stagecoach robbery, the man he sought, and the reward offered. If things went according to his plan, he wouldn't need to have it printed up and posted.

But Miss Kearney didn't know that.

"Not until you read this." Gently, he pushed the rolled-up paper into her hands.

She looked like she expected it to sit up and bite her. "Look, Agent Winter," she said, thrusting the paper toward him as though to give it back, "I was on my way to conduct some very important business in town, and I don't have time for some sharper's shenanigans. Someone has obviously misled you, if you think my father is involved in some sort of—"

"Just read it."

She strangled the poster with her fist instead, giving him a defiant glare. "No Pinkerton man has any reason to go after my father. You people hunted down the James and Younger gangs, for heaven's sake!"

Megan slapped the rolled-up wanted poster onto his chest. He clapped his hand over hers, holding it atop the paper hard enough to keep the poster from falling—hard enough to keep her from getting away.

"I suggest you devote yourself to chasing the real criminals in this Territory," she said, trying to wriggle her hand away. "Everyone knows they're common as cactus."

"And twice as prickly."

She sighed and quit struggling. "This may be funny to you, but I don't think—"

"Neither do I."

Her small hand stilled beneath his, warm enough that he could feel her heat clear through to his chest, even past the layers of paper and clothes separating them. He sensed the rounded bulk of a ring on one of her fingers, and wondered if the spinster Kearney was really as lacking in beaus as his research into her family implied.

"Then let me go and we'll both be on our way," she said, her voice crisp.

For a small woman standing up to a much larger man, Megan Kearney somehow managed to look fierce. Determined. She kept her shoulders straight, kept her gaze level on his face . . . and kept the wanted poster she refused to believe plastered against his chest while she waited for him to take the document back.

At that moment, her loyalty to her father, however mislaid, struck him as endearing as hell. Suddenly Gabriel wished he'd let McMarlin question her instead.

"This is no sharper's trick," he said. "I've got good reasons to be here. Otherwise, I'd let you head out to town and get on with your business. I'm not in the habit of making hasty judgments."

He stroked his thumb over hers, then released her hand and pressed the poster into it. "I'm sorry."

The disbelieving look she gave him did nothing to salve his conscience. As far as some folks were concerned, the Pinkertons were no better than high-paid bounty hunters. From the looks of things, Megan agreed with them.

With the air of a stable hand wanting to get the damned stalls mucked out, she dipped her head and rapidly scanned the page.

"This can't be," she muttered. With mounting confusion, she wrinkled her forehead and read it again. Then, looking wounded, she raised her head and stared toward the window. Gabriel waited. Her gaze turned distant, distracted.

Trying to think of an explanation that would prove her father's innocence somehow, he figured. It was the reaction most folks had when faced with the kind of news he'd brought. Witnessing their despair and disbelief turn to acceptance was one of the things he hated most about being an agent. It was also one of the things he'd been forced to accept early on.

"Happens all the time," he replied, hoping to take some of the sting from the news. "You couldn't have known."

She said nothing, only lowered her head and touched her fingertips to the poster. Her motions stirred the air in the room, sweetened it with the feminine scents surrounding her. Apparently, painted flowers weren't the only kind she came in contact with. She smelled like she'd rolled in a whole meadow.

Just as the contrast of blossoms drawn on dirt-streaked adobe had, the combination of sweet and tough in Megan Kearney intrigued him like nothing he'd known. He watched the play of late-morning sunlight over her features, and liked what he saw. Any honey-coated words he gave her would have truth to spare.

"In my line of work, I've seen things you would not believe, Miss Kearney," Gabriel said when she looked up from the wanted poster. "But I've never seen a woman with hair exactly the color of sugared coffee, like yours." He paused to push back a strand that had come undone from the knot at the back of her head. "And eyes like the heart of a flame."

Her jaw dropped. So did the wanted poster, to the rug at their feet. Apparently, he'd shocked her into stillness. Taking advantage, Gabriel let his gaze linger on her hair, her neck, then follow the trail of black buttons toward the ample curves of her breasts, hidden beneath her stiff-starched clothes.

"You're a right fine looker," he said softly, giving her hair one last, smooth stroke before lowering his hand. "Too bad you're a wanted man's daughter."

Too bad he wanted her himself.

He couldn't think about that. Not with a case at hand. But it had silenced her well enough, and that would have to do. He couldn't afford to turn mush-hearted now.

Putting behind thoughts of wanting for wanted, Gabriel surveyed the room and decided the chest was the most likely hiding place for the stolen money he sought. With an ache of regret he didn't care to consider, he went first to the scratched wooden trunk at the foot of the cot.

He didn't expect to find the loot stored in such an accessible place, but the criminals he'd tracked had done stupider things in the past. It wasn't his practice to overlook any potential lead. Bending to one knee on the soft rag rug, he peered closely at the latch.

"Too bad you're insane!" she cried.

Ahhh. She'd recovered.

With a rush of displaced air that smelled of soap and

sage, Megan Kearney came toward him. Before she could
reach him, he grabbed for the cold iron latch, wrenched
it upward ... and felt the whole chest shudder as she
heaved herself on top of it, rear end first.

It slammed shut.

"And you're the one calling me insane?" he asked.

"Yes."

Looking indisputably *un*convinced of her father's guilt,
and extremely satisfied with the loud thunk the lid had
made when it came crashing down, she glared at him from
her perch on top of it. "You can't look in here, you—
you—*madman!*"

"Madman?" Gabriel watched her blow a wisp of hair
from her eyes, and fought the urge to grin. "I've been
called worse."

"I'll just bet you have."

He shrugged.

She narrowed her eyes, transforming them from the
warm, caramel brown he'd admired earlier into something
a shade darker—and miles more dangerous. Nothing
appealed to him more than a woman with grit, a woman
with the courage of her convictions and the gumption to
back them up.

"Unfortunately," she said with a toss of her head, "whatever it was, it wasn't nearly bad enough to describe a man
like you."

"Probably not." He shrugged and flipped her scratchy
brown skirt hem out of the way, then wedged his fingers
along the lid's seam and tried to lift it. It rose an inch ...
a little more—then the little hellion bounced harder.

"Youch!" He snatched his fingers back, narrowly missing
having seven or eight of them crushed flatter than her
station hand Mose's head. "Careful. This is official business."

"It's official bunk! My father hasn't done anything."

"Ma'am, as you read on that poster, somebody stole ten thousand dollars from a Kearney express shipment last month. If that's what you call bunk, you've got a mighty sobering idea of what's a crime and what's not."

Her expression turned serious. Then defiant.

"Well, since *we* haven't had any thefts reported, and *you're* chasing the wrong man, it's still bunk," she said. "But I guess a common trespasser like yourself wouldn't care about things like what's right and wrong."

Ahh, yet another tactic. An accusation, followed by a change of subject. *If you don't have the answers, change the questions.* His estimation of Megan Kearney went up a notch.

"Trespasser, hmmm? I've heard that around here, a man could get strung up for such a thing," Gabriel said, echoing her earlier remark. "Even one who has a pretty daughter to hide behind."

With a murderous look, she flung something small and shiny at his head. He ducked just in time to hear it ping against the wall and drop to the floor.

His Pinkerton badge. He left it where it lay and caught hold of her wrists instead, meaning to haul her off the trunk lid by force. Instead, the incredible sensation of having so much softness in his grasp stopped him before he could move. Warm and pliant, her skin felt like silk beneath his callused fingertips.

Like warm *outlaw's* silk, Gabriel reminded himself. He couldn't afford to be swayed by distractions, even ones packaged as prettily as Megan Kearney.

"You're wrong. I care a lot about what's right and wrong," he said. "Most agents do."

"Humph. How do I know that thing's even real?" she asked, jerking her chin toward his badge.

He tightened his hold on her wrists. "It's real."

Her chin didn't lower, and her behind didn't budge,

but her gaze lowered to the sight of his big, tanned hands wrapped around her slender wrists. He saw her eyelashes flutter, like she was surprised at the sight, and then her gaze met his again.

"Let go of me," she said.

He murmured a refusal, mentally bracing himself for the screaming and struggling—and inevitable victory—that would come next. A hundred-odd pounds worth of woman wasn't keeping him from searching that chest, and it was high time he made that much clear.

Her cool, measuring glance told him she understood. Just to be sure, Gabriel stroked his thumbs over the delicate insides of her forearms and warned, "If I have to move you forcibly off there myself, I will."

Megan gave him an odd half-smile, then opened her mouth to suck in a gulp of air. Resigned to the need to haul her off the chest and get to work searching, Gabriel braced himself to release her wrists in time to muffle her scream.

Instead, something seemed to occur to her. Megan stopped in midbreath and cocked her head at him, eyebrows arched. "You really don't care if I scream, do you?"

"Nope."

Her forehead wrinkled in apparent puzzlement. She looked at him a moment longer.

Her breath came out in a whoosh. "Isn't that against the rules?"

"There's only one rule to tracking outlaws."

Her eyebrows lifted in question.

"Find them before they find you, and get out alive."

"Oh." Her gaze softened.

His shifted to her lips . . . and they'd softened, too. They looked full, slightly downturned at the corners. Kissable. *I'll be damned. . . .*

"That's the saddest thing I've heard all year," she murmured.

Something feathery touched his palm. Her fingers, caressing the pad of his thumb. Gabriel arched his hand without thinking, allowing her greater access to stroke him. Maybe he'd judged her unfairly. The sins of the father weren't necessarily those of the daughter. . . .

She spoke, crooning something about softness and release. He was too engrossed in watching her lips form the words to notice exactly what they were, probably something about dresses or babies or cooking, all those things women cared about to the exclusion of everything else. In his experience, there was nothing a woman wouldn't sacrifice for the sake of home, hearth, and family.

Family, family . . . . The notion sparked something in him, some sense of warning, but it came too late to be heeded. Her hands worked magic on his palms, his fingers, the scars lacing the backs of his hands. God, how long had it been since a woman had touched him like that?

He couldn't remember. But he wanted more.

"However," she said, suddenly and quite clearly, "I still won't let you search my father's things. So you might as well leave." With a triumphant look, she tightened both hands on the trunk lid, making it plain that lifting her would mean lifting the trunk, too, because she wasn't letting go.

Wasn't letting go with her free hands.

How the hell? Somehow, she'd gotten loose. She'd also gotten a firmer grip on the trunk beneath her, one designed, by the looks of it, to be damned well immovable.

Gabriel shook his head. Her face came into focus, faintly freckled, slightly square jawed, and pretty as a picture— even *with* the smirk she had on it.

"Next time," she advised, "try not to get yourself all worked up over a lady's"—she paused delicately, lingering over the next word to choose, then gave him a smug little smile—"feminine charms, if you're planning on detaining her. I do believe you're your own worst enemy in that regard, Mr. Winter."

He'd be damned. He'd half-expected all his glib talk about her hair and her eyes and her fine woman's figure to turn her wrathy, like it had outside in the station yard. Instead, she'd stood there, listening calmly, and used it to ambush him with later! Little Miss Megan had finagled a way to freedom with his own loose talk for a cover.

Aside from himself, he'd never met anyone who'd have tried such a thing.

Obviously, he'd underestimated her.

It wasn't a mistake he meant to make twice.

So Gabriel tried another tactic instead. Getting to his feet, he hooked both thumbs in his gun belt and looked down at her. "I'm authorized to take you into custody, if necessary."

She flinched, realizing how far in over her head she was, he'd wager. Protecting a potential road agent couldn't be easy. To his admiration, she recovered quickly.

"Now, why would you want to do something like that?" she asked, clasping her hands in her lap and gazing up at him sweetly. "I swear, Agent Winter, you must have more important things to do than be concerned with a harmless female like me."

She fluttered her eyelashes, then added, "Isn't that right?"

The overall effect was like being walloped to death with a feather pillow. It didn't hurt much while it was happening, but in the end, you still wound up six feet under. Not many people successfully misled him, and he didn't intend for a woman like Megan Kearney to be the first, no matter how much she batted her eyelashes and petted his hands.

He'd handled rock-hard criminals in the past. He could handle her, too.

"No, it's not right," he said, leaning over her. "I'll drag your pretty little conniving self all the way back to the Pinkerton office in Chicago, if that's what it takes."

"Conniving! I'll have you know—"

"Yes, conniving. You probably can't help it, though." He slipped his hands to her shoulders, feeling her tremble beneath his palms—with fury, probably. "Like father, like daughter."

"My father's no crook!" she yelled, trying to wriggle her shoulders out of his grasp. "Let go of me."

"Gladly." He held her tighter, then hauled her off the chest and deposited her in the middle of the rug. She lunged to reclaim her place on the chest, but Gabriel got there first.

"Next time you try to stop a man from doing something, Miss Kearney," he advised as he undid the latch, "you might consider doing a little less posing."

Pausing to gaze pointedly at the hands she'd folded so demurely across her lap, he leaned his elbow on the chest lid and smirked up at her. "I do believe you're your own worst enemy in that regard."

With an unintelligible sound of frustration, she rushed toward him. "You can't search that. It's a violation of privacy. I'll—I'll—" her chin jerked upward, a pious attitude in search of a target—"I'll report you to Mr. Pinkerton."

"He already knows." Gabriel lifted the lid.

She shot it a despairing glance. "You've got the wrong man!"

"That remains to be seen."

He scanned the chest's contents, taking in a jumble of fabric, bottles, and folded papers. Strange items for a station master to keep stored. He picked up a leather-bound ledger and stood facing her, absently running his thumb along the book's cracked binding.

"Criminals behave in predictable ways, Miss Kearney. That's how we track them. How we catch them."

"I don't believe you. My father never acted criminally in his life. He's not that kind of man."

He looked up. She stood silhouetted in brightness and shadow, smack in a shaft of light from the window behind her. Silently she hugged her arms over her chest and stared at the floor, motionless but for the steady stroke of her thumbs on her brown-clad elbows. For a woman—hell, for anybody—she seemed remarkably self-contained. Controlled.

But that small restless movement of her thumbs spoke volumes, and Gabriel was a listening kind of man. That irrepressible gesture told him all he needed to know.

Megan Kearney was worried. Even if it didn't show on her face, even if she argued her father's innocence from now till next Sunday, she had doubts. And she was thinking them over. He wanted to be there for the conclusions she reached.

He moved closer, then tipped her chin up with his hand. "You don't have to believe me. You only have to believe the evidence."

She jerked away. "You won't find any. Not as long as I'm around."

"You've hidden it that well? I'm impressed."

"You mustn't have very high standards, then. There was nothing to hide."

"I'd rather ask your father about that. When will he be back?"

Her mouth turned down at the corners. "With luck, not until you've pulled foot back to wherever you came from. An accusation like this would kill him."

She looked like she believed it. Gabriel couldn't afford to. "Thieving's a dangerous occupation."

Megan bit her lower lip, giving him a speculative look. "Will you at least agree not to search the station until you've spoken with my father? I'm sure he can straighten this out, if you'll only—"

"No." Gabriel flipped open the musty ledger in his hand, scanning the rows of neatly penciled entries.

Her hands flattened over them, obscuring the yellowing pages. "If you search this place now, the station hands will see you!" she pleaded. "It's only a skip and a jump from there to them figuring out what my father's accused of."

"Crime doesn't pay." Blithely, Gabriel spread his fingers over hers and moved them aside.

"Neither does a stage station, if the hands up and leave. How long do you think they'd work for a crook?"

"Depends on what kind of men they are. I've seen plenty who'd light fires for the devil himself, if the pay was good enough."

"Present company included, I expect?"

He grinned up at her. Megan Kearney didn't quit, he'd give her that. "I don't know yet. Been playing with matches lately?"

"I meant you."

"I know." He closed the ledger, cradling it in the crook of his arm while he scrutinized the other items in the chest. What was in those packets of folded papers? Gabriel reached for one.

Megan stuck her body in the way. About six inches from his nose, her breasts swayed with the movement. It was either grab them and find out exactly how devilish she could be, or lower his hands and look at the folded papers later, after she'd moved aside. Regretfully, he clasped both hands on the ledger and held it against his thighs.

"Every man cares what folks say about him," she said,

straightening. "So must you. Do you want to be known as the agent who brought in the wrong man?"

"I won't be." *Winter brings in the right man at the right time.* "I never have been."

"There's a first time for everything," she pointed out, nudging the chest lid closed with her hip.

"I'm searching that."

"Of course you are."

Briskly, she took his elbow and led him toward the door, her manner at once cheerful and determined. She'd hatched a new plan, Gabriel figured, and realized he looked forward to discovering what her quick mind had come up with almost as much as he savored the tantalizing brush of her body against his.

There were worse ways for a man to investigate a case than tailing a woman like Megan.

"But," she continued, "I'd like it very much if you'd *stop* searching. In fact—"

They squeezed together, chest to chest, through the narrow hallway and emerged in the chill of the station office, a route as deliberate as any trap he'd laid for Pinkerton's most-wanted.

"—what do you suppose it would take to persuade you to postpone your search?"

That brought him up short. A deal? Or a bribe?

Gabriel stared down at her, taking in the way her face tilted expectantly toward his, the way her lips pouted slightly while she waited for his answer, and drew the only conclusion that seemed reasonable.

"If you're offering yourself in trade, sugar," he said, feeling his pulse quicken at the notion, "I couldn't rightly decide without tasting a sample."

Four

Gabriel heard Megan's quick, indrawn breath, felt her take a jerky step backward. He pressed closer and cupped her jaw in his hand, waiting to see if she'd struggle or back down. Instead, she held herself still at his touch, watching him warily.

He nodded his approval, stroking his thumb over her earlobe and down the side of her neck. "But if you taste as good on the inside as you look on the outside . . . well, sugar, a little compromise does have its way of keeping things rolling along."

"It certainly does," she agreed, keeping her gaze on his face. She looked like a kitten considering its first lick of cream, like a half-wild creature tamed with a touch. "Provided it's done the right way, of course."

Chuckling, Gabriel let her lead him a little further across the room, closer to the wall behind her. The unabashed curiosity in her gaze lured him as surely as did the warmth of her skin beneath his fingers—maybe even more.

"I'll do it right," he promised. Gently, he flexed his fingers at the nape of her neck, tilting her head in preparation for a kiss. "I'm a thorough kind of man."

"Mmmm." She reached the rough-dabbed stucco wall at her back, carried there by the teasing, backward dance she'd been doing ever since they'd stepped together into the station office, and a smile flickered over her face. Retreat now was impossible—for both of them—and that smile of hers said Megan knew it.

"So I gather," she said. "You've already got both arms *thoroughly* on the job."

He did. He'd wrapped his free arm around her waist halfway across the rough-hewn room. Now, Gabriel used it to drag her a little closer, so her back arched away from the wall.

"Although a lesser man might've been content with using only one arm," she teased, laughter lighting her eyes. "Do women often wriggle away from you in situations like . . . this one?"

He stared at her. What had become of the starch and spice miss who'd met him in the station yard with Mose? Of the fiery woman who'd protested her father's innocence? This lighthearted side of Megan was one he hadn't seen before, and it intrigued him all the more, even knowing she was likely laying a trap for him again. To be on the safe side he widened his stance, keeping his shins safe from surprise attacks.

"I don't know," Gabriel said, smiling. "I haven't had all that many offers like . . . this one."

Anticipation roughened his voice, lent an edge to the words he'd never meant to reveal. Needing to regain control, he lowered his face enough that her minty breath mingled with his, and added, "I don't like leaving things to chance."

Slowly, gently, he brushed his lips over hers. Her mouth

was the most tender heat imaginable. It tasted of softness, hinted at innumerable textures meant to be touched and explored and savored. With a murmured sound of wanting, Gabriel kissed her again, so lightly that he ended the contact even as she leaned forward for more.

Sighing, she swayed into his chest, making her breasts rub against his vest front. She felt like a piece of heaven wrapped in wool and black beads, and he couldn't help wondering about the womanly body beneath all those fuss-fancy clothes. What would it be like to cup her breasts in his hands, weigh their silken heaviness in his palms, watch her nipples pucker into tight peaks against his fingertips?

"There's no chance in a kiss like that one," Megan whispered, keeping her eyes closed as she pressed her cheek to his shoulder. "Luckily for you, I'm an appreciating kind of woman."

Touching her that way would be like holding sunshine in his grasp, Gabriel decided. Hot enough to burn his hands, too brilliant to capture for long . . . impossible to keep.

And impossible to trust. Much as he wanted to believe appreciation was all that lay behind Megan's sweet-sounding words, he hadn't forgotten her earlier proposition.

Neither, he figured, had she.

Question was, how far would she go to get what she wanted?

"Sugar," he said, stroking her hair, "that's just the beginning."

Grinning, he couldn't keep from tracing his fingertips over her pink-tinted cheeks. *He'd* put the blush on that smooth skin of hers. Lord, if only such softness didn't house a scheming mind. "But it's not enough to take me off the case."

Her eyes opened. She seemed startled. "What did you say?"

"Or make a deal with you," Gabriel went on, letting his hands fall aside as she shoved herself away from his chest. Her retreat told him she'd heard him loud and clear. "No matter how nicely you kiss."

Her eyes narrowed. "You beast! You—"

"Truth be told," he interrupted, "your instincts were right." Almost against his will, he admired that quality in her. "Most operatives use self-interest like yours to help build their cases."

She cast him a measuring glance. "But not you?"

"Depends on the potential gain."

"I offered you plenty of gain."

"Interesting way of putting it."

Her blush deepened. So did the urge he felt to drag her back into his arms and finish what she'd started. Was the woman wilier than he'd thought, or just plain too innocent to know when she was setting up bonfires?

"You don't even know where my father is," Megan said, ducking away from the wall. "You told me so yourself."

He hadn't, but her assumption was understandable enough. He'd asked when Joseph Kearney would return to the station, not where he'd gone. Experience had taught him, though, that most people heard what they thought would be said, not the actual words. Usually, it worked in Gabriel's favor. It might this time, too.

"Do you know where he is?"

"I wouldn't betray him by telling you if I did." A few agitated steps took her to the window, where she stood, looking out over the station yard just long enough for Gabriel to realize she was about to play her last card—and didn't want to.

"There are other agents on this case, other men looking for your father," he said. "They're not all like me—"

"You mean some of them have compassion?" She whirled from the window to face him. "This station is my family's lifeblood. It's the food in our mouths, my father's dream, and the livelihood of the men in that yard. You can't rip that apart with your wrongheaded threats and accusations. I won't let you."

"You can't stop me."

"You're wrong," she said stubbornly.

"Sugar, I've tailed men over more miles than you'll see in two lifetimes. Arrested them and brought them to justice from fourteen states and half as many territories."

He paused, moved closer, and tucked back that same wayward hair of hers, letting the back of his knuckles linger on Megan's cheek. "Your father can't run far enough to escape me, and you can't beat me."

She raised her head. "Show me the evidence you have."

"No."

"Tell me what proves my father's implicated in the robbery."

"No." He pulled his watch from his vest pocket and flipped the timepiece open. "I take it your station has accommodations for travelers?"

Her mouth dropped open. "You intend to stay?"

"For as long as it takes to search the place. Or until your father returns, whichever comes first."

"But that might—"

"Take days? That's fine with me. I'm a patient man."

"You can't stay here!"

"You don't have accommodations, then? All I need is a place to sleep and a—"

"I can think of a suitable place for you."

He grinned. "I'll just bet you can."

"Go to blazes, Mr. Winter!"

"I've been there and back," he said, retrieving his hat from the desktop and shoving it onto his head again. "But I'm obliged for the invitation, all the same."

He turned toward the open doorway.

"Wait!" she cried, rushing to the door right behind him.

She reached past his arm and slammed the door, shutting out the sounds in the station yard. The metallic clank of horses' harnesses faded, muted along with the voices of the stage handlers and drivers.

"What for?"

Her shoulders heaved, straightened, but she didn't face him. "Please," Megan said. "I—I—"

Hell. She was going to cry. A woman's last weepy damned resort. She'd probably tell him it was because of him, too, when it was plain as warts on a bullfrog her father was the real trouble.

"I can't stand the thought of . . . Oh, p-please leave my father alone!" she begged in a choked voice.

Her back was to him, so he couldn't see her face. But Gabriel heard the catch in her voice caused by held-in sobs, saw her fumbling around in her skirt pocket for something, and knew he was as defenseless as the next poor knuck in the face of a weeping woman.

He shoved his handkerchief toward her. "Now, hold on a minute," he murmured. "There's no call to cry on account of the no-goods in the world. They sure as hell aren't crying for the likes of you."

"I—I'm sorry," she sobbed.

Now he had her apologizing for crying! She might as well just apologize for being a woman and be done with it. Near as he could tell, it wasn't like a female could help turning on the waterworks. Obviously she was too distraught even to take his handkerchief. He doubted she'd even noticed it, she was getting so worked up. Gabriel felt like hell.

"There's no need to apologize," he said. "You haven't done anything wrong."

Suddenly Megan turned. He was startled to glimpse,

despite her reddened cheeks and watery eyes, a smart-alecky smile on her face.

"Not yet, I haven't," she said, jerking her fisted hand upward, to about waist height. "And if you leave now, I won't have to."

The derringer in her hand jerked upward again as she took aim at his chest. "Please leave."

Five

Gabriel Winter's dumbfounded gaze swept from Megan's derringer to her face. "Darlin', you're not the type to plug an outright criminal with that peashooter of yours, much less a lawman."

He was right. She'd be a fool to admit it, though. With a little luck—and a little harmless brandishing of her weapon—he'd be just distracted enough to forget about pursuing her father. At least for a short while. If saving Papa and safeguarding Kearney Station meant offering herself to Agent Winter as a temporary diversion . . . well, that's just what she'd do.

"Maybe." Megan wrinkled her nose, as though considering what he'd said. "*If* a lawman's really what you are, that is."

Privately, she had her doubts. Any man who could use his blarney-kissed Irish brogue to feed a woman sweet words about her hair and her eyes and her figure, who could suggest a wildly improper trade of favors for secrets and then kiss her to near swooning moments later, had a wide streak of elemental deviltry in his character, lawman or no.

It wouldn't do to let down her guard around him. Megan kept her weapon steady. This was a man who could not be trusted.

Not that she'd been anywhere close to doing so, Megan assured herself as she sharpened her focus on his roguish face, waiting for whatever he'd do next. If she'd forgotten herself for an instant or two, that was only because he'd forced her to play every role she could think of to try to stop him from searching the station. It certainly had nothing to do with the shocking feel of his arms holding her close, his hands stroking her hair, his mouth meeting hers in a kiss so gentle, so tantalizing. . . .

She grabbed hold of her wayward thoughts and steeled her resolve. Too much lay at stake here to risk being distracted, and she'd need all her wits to deal with the challenge Gabriel Winter presented.

How was she to stop him from searching the station— preferably without getting herself arrested in the process?

She still couldn't believe none of the methods she'd tried earlier had worked. Even tears hadn't been enough to soften him, and she hadn't thought to find a man alive who'd remain unmoved by a woman's tears. Agent Winter's heart must be as cold as his name implied.

The realization was enough to kindle fresh terror inside her. This time, it was just possible she'd bitten off a greater challenge than she could chew. Megan steadied her gun with hands gone suddenly damp and trembling, and did her best to assume an air of nonchalance.

"In any case, Agent Winter, you must know that crooked lawmen roll through this territory as often as tumbleweeds do. So even if what you say is true, I—"

"It's true." He stepped closer. "I am a lawman, clear to the last inch."

Involuntarily, she checked the truth of his statement. The civilized polish of his city slicker's wool suit and clean-shaven jaw suggested a businessman more than anything else. But the low-slung heft of his gun belt and the cynical steel in his gaze told another story. It was the latter Megan was inclined toward believing.

He really was a lawman. One intent on locking her father in irons and dragging him to jail for a crime he couldn't possibly have committed. Dear Lord. She had to do something to stop him. The havoc Agent Winter could wreak at Kearney Station with his wrongheaded investigation was terrifying.

"And an honest lawman, at that," Gabriel went on, dropping his gaze to her derringer, "one with half a mind to take you in right along with your father. It's a dangerous woman who'd draw a weapon on a Pinkerton man—no matter how wee a one it might be."

Summoning all the bravado she could, Megan smiled past the hammering of her heart and looked him up and down. "Pshaw, Mr. Winter. You don't seem so very wee to me."

His answering smile looked deadly—and miles more charming than it had a right to be, given the circumstances. Caught beneath its influence, she could almost believe he was a man who'd lock an innocent woman in jail. Most certainly, she could believe he was a man who'd give his lady prisoner a scorching good-bye kiss . . . Only moments before turning the key.

The cad.

"Is there always a double meaning to your words, Miss Kearney? Or might it be possible someday to believe what you say?"

"I doubt very much you believe in anything or anyone."

Gabriel's eyes narrowed. "I believe in facts."

"I've already given you those," Megan said. "My father was not involved in any wrongdoing. So if you'd kindly leave before your presence here causes any more ruckus—"

"No."

Despite the threat of her derringer, he moved closer. Either she didn't seem menacing enough to keep him away, or he was too fearless to heed her warning. She sensed the ready strength in his shoulders, felt the warmth of his body near hers, and started trembling anew. Desperate measures were in order.

Megan attempted a sneer, like the ones the Easterners wore when they stepped off the stage and glimpsed The Great Desert for the first time. As meanly as she could, she said, "I already asked you once to leave, Mr. Winter. I'm not asking again."

Unfortunately, he seemed unimpressed.

"I'm not leaving here until I'm finished." His bemused smile was enough to get her dander up, all on its own. "And I'm a long sight from being finished with you."

Her thoughts whirled. Trapped between the door at her back and the solid, implacable man at her front, Megan did the only thing that seemed reasonable.

She raised her gun higher.

He spared it a glance. Nothing more. An instant later, Gabriel brought his big hand up to cradle the back of her neck in his palm, and the searing heat of his skin was almost enough to make her drop the derringer without a single thought.

Holding her breath, Megan looked up into a face shadowed with hard-won experience. For a man not much older than she was, Gabriel Winter seemed remarkably cynical. His features called nothing to mind so strongly as danger, and the angle of his jaw, the sharp edge of his nose, and the predatory gleam in his eyes did nothing to dispel that impression.

However civilized the trappings he wore, Gabriel Winter was nonetheless a hunter. One who would not rest until he'd taken what he'd come to find.

She had the sudden, panic-stricken fear he had come to find her.

As though he'd guessed her fear, he increased the pressure of his fingertips against her nape and tilted her head toward his. The other quality agent Winter possessed in abundance was masculine assurance, and he was plainly unafraid to use it.

"If my presence here is too much for you," he said, "I'd advise you to lay down your weapon right now. Otherwise, you'll find yourself with more of me than you can handle."

Megan figured she already had more of him than she could handle. She almost admitted it aloud. After all, his unexpected arrival at the station had already forced her into sweet-talking, kissing, and desperate measures the likes of which she'd never tried before.

And the likes of which would have worked on almost anyone else, she felt sure. Drat the man and his stubborn, wily ways!

She needed time to think. She needed time to plan. She needed distance from the impossible-to-ignore masculinity of a man with her father's ruination on his mind . . . and the back of her neck in his hand. Gently, he thrummed his fingers over her skin, teased the fine hairs at her nape, stroked her as though he hadn't anything better to do in the world than sample the feel of her beneath his fingers.

And watch her with the eyes of a hawk.

"Understand?" he asked.

She understood. Understood he wasn't leaving the station unless she found a way to make him, somehow. Blast it.

In answer, Megan jerked her head upward, trying to free herself from his grasp. She found the impulse as impossible to resist as it was useless. Although he took his hand from her neck, hers was a temporary victory at best, and she knew it. She could no more escape the war of wills that had begun between them than she could snap her fingers and have her father magically reappear at the station with her nest-egg money safely in hand.

She almost cried out at the thought. What chance did she have to regain her savings, her chance for a future, now? With only three days until the Websters left Tucson for good, a father gone missing, and a relentless, silver-tongued Pinkerton man to keep track of, it looked as though her dressmaker's shop dream was about to slip from her grasp for the last time.

It would be years, maybe many years, before another affordable shop came available to buy. Whatever else happened, she could not let this Pinkerton man delay her. Neither could she let him ruin her papa's life and livelihood by openly accusing him of something he couldn't possibly have done. Somehow, she had to find her father, recover her savings, and get away with both before Agent Winter realized what she was up to.

With that thought in mind, Megan glared up at her unwelcome guest. If she left for Tucson to find her father as she'd planned, he'd surely search the station, with or without her consent. It would throw the place into an uproar. Somehow, she had to draw him away from here. But how?

Would he believe she'd had a sudden change of heart? Probably not.

"Do I understand?" She repeated his question, hating the shakiness in her voice even as she lay her free hand dramatically over her heart. "My goodness, Agent Winter. You can't possibly mean you would take *me* into custody!

Not for something so inconsequential as ordering you off my land."

"With a firearm for persuasion."

She shrugged and gave him her sweetest smile. "I find it increases a man's attention span."

His gaze flickered over her, taking in her upswept hair, her dress, and her shoes just visible beneath her hem. Leisurely, he lengthened his perusal to include the flare of her long brown skirts, then took his time following her bodice's trail of jet buttons upward to her face.

The rascal grinned. "I expect you manage to keep a man's attention," he said. "With or without a peashooter handy."

His quicksilver smile, coupled with the heat in his eyes and the apparent sincerity in his voice, would surely have set another, more gullible woman to swooning on the spot. She knew better than to listen. Never had a man spoken such niceties to plain Megan Kearney. She prided herself on being practical enough not to hope for them.

At least she had until now.

"You flatter me, Agent Winter." *Concentrate,* she ordered herself. Was he falling for her tactic? "That must be how I knew you'd never arrest a lady like me, not even for pulling out this little old derringer of mine. Why, I've never even heard of such a thing."

"I have."

He was falling for it! "Oh, my. You don't mean . . . ?"

She let her voice trail off, and did her best to pack a goodly dose of trepidation into the stare she gave him. Deliberately getting herself arrested was a desperate means of making Agent Winter leave the station, to be sure. But Megan felt fairly certain she could elude him once they'd set out on the road to the jail in Tucson. The way to town was as familiar as her own dress patterns to her—but not to him.

She blinked sorrowfully up at him and whispered, "Jail? For me? You can't mean it."

His gaze darkened, turning his eyes a deeper, lonelier blue.

"Oh, but I do," he said. "I'd arrest you now, if I thought you could really pull that trigger."

Despair tugged at her. He hadn't believed her threat at all! At this rate, she'd never get him away from the station.

"But I could pull the trigger! You might not believe it, but I can be mean as all get-out when provoked. Ask anyone. Ask—"

He grinned. His hand covered hers, eased her fingers' desperate clench on the cold metal protection of her derringer. "No, you couldn't."

"I could! You shouldn't judge a book by its cover, Agent Winter. I'm snake-mean sometimes. You should see—"

"I can see," he interrupted. "And I only needed one look at this place—and at the behemoth out there in the yard, watching out for you—to know that's not true."

He must mean Mose. Whatever could simple, sweet Mose have said to the Pinkerton man to make him think such a thing?

She couldn't give up. *Wouldn't.* "But I—"

He stopped her. "You're about as mean as a day-old kitten, sugar." One by one, Gabriel pried her fingers loose from her weapon, even as his next words washed over her with deadly seriousness. "But let me warn you right now, if I find out you're involved in my case, I will take you in. And I'll turn the key to lock you up myself."

Visions of the scandalous good-bye kiss she'd imagined earlier whirled through her mind. Combined with the memory of the kiss he'd already given her, it was almost enough to set her tingling anew.

A person would think she wanted him to kiss her again, or something. Megan gave herself a shake and tried not

to think about the fact that his hands still covered hers—
and with a touch as tender as that of a man come courting
the woman he fancied, too.

She'd bet a man like Gabriel Winter didn't bother with
courting anyone. She'd bet a man like he was just took
what he wanted. Suddenly, she wasn't at all sure that if she
found herself in such a position, she could refuse him
anything.

A ridiculous notion, of course, Megan told herself. Surely
she had more fortitude, more discipline, than that.

"If you're involved in this robbery," he went on, "I'll
find out. And then I'll find *you*. And it won't matter that
you're a woman."

She couldn't keep back the shiver that crept up her
spine at his words. But she could help what she did about
it, Megan vowed. Never let it be said that she'd abandoned
her family, or the station hands who depended on her, in
their time of need. The last thing she meant to do was let
Gabriel Winter ride roughshod over their lives.

"Would it matter if I were innocent?" she asked, lifting
her chin.

"If you were innocent"—He slipped her derringer from
her hand and removed its bullets, dropping them into
his palm as he spoke—"then I would know it. I've never
brought in the wrong man."

He returned her gun with a small, aggravatingly gentle-
manlike bow. "Or the wrong woman."

"How can you be sure?"

"I'm sure."

Her chin came up another notch. "I believe you're confusing arrogance with certainty, Agent Winter."

"Well said, coming from a woman who's confusing
affection with innocence." He paused, shook his head.
"For your sake, I wish you could love your father enough
to excuse his crimes. But you can't."

"I won't need to. He is innocent."

Gabriel frowned and turned toward the window, stepping far enough from her to draw back the edge of the curtains and gaze into the yard beyond. The rigid set of his wide shoulders looked fearsome, but something in the tilt of his head suggested he hadn't fully decided about the case at hand.

That possibility was one Megan couldn't afford to pass up. She didn't care if she was grasping at straws. She wanted to be the one to convince him—in her father's favor.

"Joseph Kearney has never done a single thing to regret in his life." *Except maybe disappear on an occasional gambling junket with his daughter's savings,* her conscience jibed. "Certainly nothing that would warrant having Pinkerton men on his trail. You must believe me. He's an innocent man. I just know it!"

"Based on what?"

His tone was deceptively mild. The stern set of his handsome face as he turned to her was anything but.

"You say he's innocent. Based on what?" Gabriel repeated.

"B—based on belief, of course," Megan stammered, taken aback at the bleakness she glimpsed in his expression. Whatever had put the wintery chill in this man's eyes had wounded him, too deeply for words. "I believe it's true, with all my heart."

Gabriel thumbed up his hat brim. From beneath its shadows, he studied her. "You'd take something like this on faith?"

"Of course. What else is there?"

He studied her a moment longer. "Then you're a bigger fool than I thought."

Her, a fool? Simply for believing in her own father's innocence? Megan didn't know whether to be shocked, insulted, or saddened that he was so disillusioned as to think such a thing in the first place.

Before she could decide, he turned. Briskly, he surveyed the room, and his gaze lit on the two satchels and the parasol she'd stacked in one corner of the station office in preparation for her travels to Tucson. He nodded toward them.

"You'll be wanting to bring those, I'd imagine. We'll leave in an hour."

"Leave? But I . . . no!"

His mocking smile caught her off-guard. "Don't make me waste time drawing up matching father-and-daughter wanted posters, sugar."

Shock glued her feet to the floorboards. *"You're arresting me?"*

Gabriel's eyebrows rose. "Not yet. Trusting someone isn't a crime. Just foolhardy."

He pulled down his hat and reached for the doorknob, keeping one hand on the gun belt beneath his fine suit as though expecting her to make some desperate, doomed attempt to escape him. Megan knew better.

She'd elude him later, if necessary, when the odds were better suited to her favor.

"That's why I'm not trusting you," he went on, "I'm telling you. You're going with me to find your father. And, if need be, you're going to help me do it. Ought to be no better bait to a devoted father than a daughter in need, wouldn't you say?"

Perhaps . . . for any father but her own. As Mrs. Webster had so cruelly pointed out earlier, Joseph Kearney didn't quite measure up to the ideal of a doting papa.

"I'd say you're a beast!"

"No, a realist." He had the audacity to wink. "Although the two might look the same to you, just at the moment. You'll come 'round in the end, I'll wager."

"And turn out like you? Sweet heaven, I hope not."

He shrugged. "Beyond the first prick, it's kinder to see things the way they really are."

With a powerful sweep of his arm, he opened the door. The sounds of the latest stage pulling away in the distance, men working, and birdsong from the pair of cactus wrens nesting nearby rushed inside on a choking drift of dust and autumn sunlight.

In the midst of it all, Gabriel Winter stood on the threshold with his back to her and his arms folded, as though deciding which outbuilding to search first, which station hand to begin the questioning with. His whole manner bespoke authority.

And Megan understood a threat when she saw one.

"You can't really expect me to help you!" she cried. "I'm the last person who'd want to see you bring in my father."

"That's why I'm not leaving you here."

Unreasonable, unexpected tears came to her eyes. She'd always managed to bring folks around to her way of thinking, especially when it mattered. With the Websters. The station hands. Her papa. Addie. What was so different about Gabriel Winter? How, when she most needed to outreason, outtalk, and outmaneuver a Pinkerton man, had she suddenly lost her ability to do it?

Addie's words came heartbreakingly to mind. *You'd better take care,* she'd said. *That fancy talk won't always work on folks.*

Blast it, it could and it would. Megan wasn't beaten yet.

"I'm not leaving you unguarded," Gabriel said, facing her at last, "to run and warn your father the minute I ride beyond sight of the station."

He laughed, with an uncommon lack of humor, and passed a hand wearily over his face. "Or should I say, the minute I turn my back on you. You're a wily one, sugar."

"Only when I need to be." Like she'd need to be in order to keep an eye on him, while he tried to trap her poor papa. "Only when my back's up against a wall, like it is now."

This time his laughter was genuine. "You backed yourself into that wall, if I remember aright. I only kept you company beside it."

That he had done—and more. The memory of her body arching away from the wall as his arms pulled her closer brought new heat to Megan's cheeks . . . and strengthened her resolve. Gabriel might have the upper hand for the moment, but she'd managed somehow to lead him in the direction *she'd* set at least once before. She could do it again.

Amazingly, a part of her almost looked forward to the challenge.

"Be that as it may," she told him coolly, mimicking his crossed-arm pose, "things have a way of changing quickly here in the Territory. As a city man, of course—from Chicago, didn't you say?—I don't expect you'd know about something like that. You'll see soon enough, I suppose."

"I suppose I will. I have no trouble seeing what's right in front of me."

As though in demonstration, Gabriel's shuttered gaze lowered to her bosom. Gradually, his attention moved to her waist and hips, which he leisurely examined before raising his gaze to meet hers again. She should have been shocked by such an intimate appraisal. She *was* shocked. But it wasn't because of his improper behavior. It was because of the frank appreciation in his gaze that followed it.

"Exactly what do you think you're doing?" she snapped.

He smiled into her eyes. "I should think that would be obvious enough, even to someone like you."

Someone like her? What was that supposed to mean? Bewildered, affronted, and more than a little embarrassed to be the subject of such intense scrutiny, Megan drew up her shoulders and faced him straight on.

"Well!" she said in her snootiest tone, copied directly from the ladies in town, "I hadn't figured you for a dress-making connoisseur, Agent Winter, but—"

"I wasn't looking at your dress."

In the face of his outright lie, her composure deserted her. "Yes, you were. I saw you!"

Gabriel's smile widened. "Whenever possible, I prefer to work from the facts. Your dress is all that stands between them and me."

Just as she realized what he'd meant, he stepped into the sunlight of the stage-station yard and turned to her. "I'd hate to draw up that wanted poster wrong, darlin'." He tipped his hat. "We ride out in less than an hour."

Six

She's likely the daughter of a thief, Gabriel reminded himself as he rode beside Megan Kearney into the dusty streets of Tucson late that afternoon. *And far too wily to be trusted.*

Not that he'd been tempted to trust her. At least not beyond the first moment she'd batted those sad brown eyes at him and invited him to a necktie party on his own behalf, just for suggesting he'd like to do business with a pretty woman. If that hadn't been warning enough of her true nature, her aiming a firearm at the lapels of his favorite suit would have been.

Plain as the saddle beneath him, Megan Kearney was desperate to prove her no-good, gone-missing father innocent. However unworthy the damned knuck was. And in Gabriel's estimation, dangerous usually rode in on desperate, sooner or later. He meant to be ready when it closed in on the woman beside him.

Until then, he'd stick as tight to her side as the twin satchels and frilly parasol she'd insisted on lashing to her sidesaddle for the trip to town. They bounced as she rode, flopping up and down in concert with the close-curved brown bustle on her dress. For a woman reportedly raised in the West, Gabriel noticed, Megan rode remarkably poorly.

In an effort to accommodate her, he slowed his horse to a walk as they neared the center of the *presidio*. Here, wood and water vendors filled the streets, driving their goods-laden mules between freight wagons and pedestrians as they plied their wares in English and Spanish and occasionally in Chinese.

Speaking loudly enough to be heard amidst their sing-song calls and the rattle of a stage passing nearby, he turned to his unwilling companion and asked, "How long have you lived in the Territory?"

From beneath the wide straw brim of her geegaw-bedecked hat, she gave him a surly look. "Long enough to know that innocent men don't always go free around these parts, especially once word gets around and vigilante justice takes up the case."

As a punch to his sense of integrity, her reply found its mark. Nevertheless, he kept his voice calm. She'd realize the truth soon enough—if she hadn't begun to already. Facts didn't lie.

"A long while, then," he said mildly.

"It's only seemed so since this morning."

Gabriel frowned and guided his horse past a group of Indian women carrying earthen *ollas* toward the center of town. Several cowboys rode past, spewing dust from their horses' hooves. On either side of the packed-dirt main street, whitewashed adobe shops and saloons squatted side by side, almost identical in their flat roofs and peeled-log *ramadas*. Given the warm autumn weather, the meager shade they cast felt welcome as a cold drink of well water.

Even so, the shadows they rode through weren't half as

cooling as the chilly demeanor of a woman who thought she'd been wronged. He cast a sideways glance at the daughter of his likeliest suspect, and all but shivered at her schoolmarm's posture and tight-lipped survey of the people and buildings surrounding them. She didn't want to be here.

Especially with him.

That made them even, Gabriel figured. He didn't want to need her here. But he did. And until the case was solved, he'd have to make the best of it. After nightfall, he'd track down McMarlin and send him to follow up on the search of Kearney Station he'd been forced to postpone. In the meantime, he'd have to do his damnedest to thaw out Miss Megan Kearney.

He searched his mind for a neutral topic of conversation, something he could use to take some of the starch out of her expression. Once he'd found one, Gabriel turned his most charming smile in her direction.

"A woman like you must have several beaus here in town," he remarked. "If I stop to kiss you again"—he snagged her mare's reins in his hand and halted their progress beneath the shelter of a newspaper office's *ramada*—"will someone be riding out from behind one of these sun-baked buildings to avenge your honor?"

Her startled gaze met his. As though sensing her unease, her horse skittered sideways, forcing him to draw the animal closer—along with its rider.

Turning her face quickly away, Megan raised her chin. He doubted she realized the provocative way the gesture lengthened the vulnerable column of her neck. Or the way it loosened the prissy, high-buttoned collar of her dress, revealing the telltale flicker of her pulse beating wildly at her throat.

Gabriel did. And vowed to remember.

"Avenge my honor? Only if I'm lucky," she said. A hint of

pink stained her cheeks as she added, "If I'm exceptionally fortunate, one of them will challenge you to a duel—"

"Ahh. You're a romantic, then?"

"—and win."

Undoubtedly pleased with the notion of her Pinkerton captor gunned down in the midst of the busy street, Megan snatched back her mount's reins and started forward again.

In the bustle of Tucson's main thoroughfare, it would be easy to lose sight of her. In all likelihood, that was what she'd intended, and with his wounded male pride for an excuse, to boot. He'd say one thing for her, she possessed resourcefulness to spare.

Intrigued far more than he felt willing to admit, Gabriel followed her. He wended his way past ladies out for a stroll in white dresses, *sombrero*-wearing men, solitary riders, and enough buckboard wagons to clog the streets, keeping Megan's ramrod-stiff, brown wool–covered back in his line of sight until he drew up beside her horse once more.

Casually, he rested his hands atop his saddle horn, clasping the reins loosely as he glanced at her. "You've a cruel mouth on you, Megan Kearney. Did no one ever tell you you'll catch more flies with honey than with vinegar?"

She seemed unsurprised to find him beside her again. "Actually, I've caught more pests than I ever wanted. My trouble is getting rid of them afterward." Giving him a pointed glance, she sat even straighter in her saddle. "No matter what I do, they just keep buzzing around me."

"I'm wounded." He adopted a hound dog–sad expression to prove it.

She shrugged. Heartless to the end . . . except when backed up against a wall, with amusement in her eyes and her body trembling in his arms. Memories—unwanted memories—of the soft, tentative touch of her lips chased away his notions of teasing her further.

"Wounded and wrong," Gabriel went on. "To my recollection, sugar, your mouth wasn't cruel at all."

Her flush deepened. "I'll be sure to remedy that next time."

"I'm glad to hear there'll be one."

With surprise, he realized it was true. He wanted to kiss her, long and often. Fast and hard. Sweet and slowly. Her fiery defense of her family hinted at a passion she could hardly deny. Could he unleash it in other, less dangerous ways?

"One what?" she asked.

"A next time to find out if that mouth of yours is as honeyed as I remember."

"Oh!" With gloved hands, Megan twisted her mare's reins tighter. She nibbled her lower lip, her teeth white in a face gone deep pink with embarrassment. "Well. I'll have you know, Agent Winter, that my mouth is most certainly not . . . not . . . what you said."

Her sudden shyness was as endearing as it was unexpected. Would he never understand the twists and turns of this woman's mind?

Gabriel grinned. "A bite might serve to convince me."

Watching the play of her lips and teeth, bedeviled by the memory of her freely given kiss, he thought about it some more and changed his mind. "But then again, it might have exactly the opposite effect. Would you care to try it out when we reach our hotel, darlin'?"

Her head jerked upward. A magnificent feat, Gabriel reckoned, considering the probable weight of her hat.

"Perhaps," she said archly, "if it's a kiss *good-bye*."

A quick, hunted expression crossed her face. Even as he wondered at its cause, it vanished. In its place, somehow Megan mustered the necessary vinegar to deliver him a thin, wholly counterfeit smile.

"Do you have any other questions for me, Agent Winter, or shall we agree to behave like the enemies we are?"

If they did, he'd never learn anything from her about the running of Kearney Station, the hands who worked there . . . or her father's suspicious absence. Somehow, he'd have to cajole her into cooperating with him. Or, at the least, he'd have to convince her not to deliberately sabotage his robbery investigation.

A fool's errand, to be sure.

He'd be better served to continue his investigation as planned, tracking Joseph Kearney as quickly as possible. But he couldn't leave a wild card like Megan unaccounted for while he did.

Somehow, he'd have to keep her beside him, use what she knew, and bring her father to justice in the end—just as he'd been hired to do. His livelihood, and his reputation, depended on it.

Winter brings in the right man at the right time.

He smiled at her. "I'd rather not be your enemy, sugar."

"I'm afraid it's too late for that." She spurred her horse harder.

Gabriel followed, frowning in thought. The way to charm Miss Megan evidently wasn't tied to either flattery or hints at her sought-after status. Unusual, compared with most of the ladies he knew. Given what he'd learned of her so far, he shouldn't have been surprised at that. But it left him at a loss as to what to try next. A gesture of goodwill?

They neared the Cosmopolitan, the two-storied, balconied hotel of adobe and wood where he'd planned to headquarter his fellow Pinkerton agents in the field and himself in his search for the thief. He'd booked a room there while fresh from the train. It would be simple enough, he reckoned, to engage an additional room for his prickly feminine guest.

And simpler still to have her share his.

Too bad she'd never agree. Shoving that enticing thought from his mind, Gabriel spied a fruit vendor on the street corner nearest them, and brought his horse around in that direction instead. As long as the two of them were the unabashed enemies she'd claimed, he'd sooner goad her into cold-blooded murder than he would persuade her into something so warmhearted as sharing his room.

Regardless of how much they'd enjoy the latter.

With a wry grin for the thought, Gabriel stopped beside the fruit vendor's wooden cart and examined the melons, oranges, and lemons piled atop it. With a quizzical look, his companion stopped, too.

"And as a matter of fact," he told her, "I do have one more question for you."

Bending from his saddle, he exchanged a coin for one of the man's vibrant oranges. With that accomplished, he straightened and held the fruit toward Megan. "Would you mind so very much calling me Gabriel?" he asked softly.

Her eyebrows rose. In the silence that fell between them, she looked from the orange in his hand to his face. Something akin to regret filled her expression.

"Why?"

"Why?" Puzzled, he kept his hand extended toward her. Had she no liking for gifts, either? "Because you say 'Agent Winter' as though my name is something you'd like to scrape from your shoe. I'd rather you call me Gabriel."

"Oh." She frowned and looked downward, consumed, to all appearances, with an overriding interest in the drape of her skirt over her bent knee. Drawing an unsteady breath, she pleated the folds of fabric in her gloved hands, but made no move to accept his gift . . . or to honor his request.

It seemed she *would* mind calling him by his given name.

Very much.

Damned stubborn female.

The awkwardness between them grew, and the orange in Gabriel's palm felt heavier with each passing moment. Giving it to her had been a stupid idea in a day filled to brimming with several just like it.

Maybe he'd lost his knack for detective work. Sure as hell, he'd lost his taste for the plain meanness it often called for. After years of living on the road, days like this— and obstacles like Megan Kearney—made him long for nothing more than laying down the life he'd known as an agent and starting over someplace new.

But he'd be damned if he'd start over with a losing record.

He had to solve this case. The sooner the better.

"Perhaps 'Agent Go-To-The-Devil' would be more to your liking then?" Gabriel conjured a smile to hide his ridiculous caring about what she called him, and how she did it, at all. He tossed the orange into the air, caught it, and repeated the motion. " 'Course, something a shade less heated might be more befitting a lady's sensibilities. Agent Chowderhead, Agent Halfwit . . . Am I getting close to something you might agree with, Miss Kearney?"

He chanced a look at her. Quickly, she ducked her head, but the motion couldn't conceal the silly smile on her face.

"Miss Kearney?" he prodded. He couldn't have explained the ridiculous pleasure he felt at having made her smile, and he didn't want to try. "I can see you don't care for oranges, but I know you're capable of expressing your opinion."

In answer, she leaned a bit from her sidesaddle and reached to catch the orange in midair. Gabriel snatched it back, and she gave him a quelling look.

"Actually, I'm partial to 'Agent Chowderhead,' " she said. The sassy smile on her face was a sight to behold.

"I thought you might be."

"But I'm willing to settle on Gabriel," Megan went on, her expression sobering, "if that's what you'd prefer."

Her voice was soft, filled either with the apology he found himself hoping for . . . or with the guile he'd come to expect from her. The sweet sound of it could have lulled a lesser man into underestimating her talent for distraction.

Luckily, Gabriel counted himself the wiser since meeting her this morning.

"And," she went on, "if you'll agree to call me Megan in return. I'd like it very much if you would."

He gave her a doubtful, sideways look. Deftly, he flipped the orange upward, rolled it over the back of his hand, and turned his palm to cup the fruit and complete the trick.

He offered it to her. "I will. Megan it is."

Her fingers curved over the orange, touched and joined briefly with his. In that instant, he wished her gloves away. He wished for the feel of her bare skin on his, even in an area so small as their hands, and knew his dealings with her could demand more than he'd bargained for. Far more.

Or offer just as much.

Anticipation flowed through him, hot as the sun overhead and just as impossible to extinguish. He wanted her. If the sudden, reflexive tightening of her hand on his meant anything at all, Megan felt the same. Her awareness of it showed in her eyes when she looked up at him. It sounded in the breathlessness in her voice when she spoke.

"Thank you. Very much."

Damn, but she gave over her thanks like another woman would have invited a man upstairs. Sweetly. Seductively. Too bad it would likely wind up costing him just as much, in the end.

For now, he didn't care.

"You're welcome. No need to thank me, though."

They'd reached an accord. It ought to have been enough, at least for a start. But Gabriel had never been a settling kind of man. Motioning for her to follow, he set his horse into motion toward the two-story, balconied haven of the Cosmopolitan hotel.

"After all, I reckon being on familiar terms with each other will be mighty useful," he said, nodding toward the hotel's whitewashed adobe façade and distinctive sign, "once we're inside . . . sharing our room."

Seven

Sharing a room!

Megan still couldn't believe Gabriel Winter's scandalous suggestion—or the impossible, cocksure look the Pinkerton man had worn when he'd made it. He was too determined, too audacious, and too sure of himself by far.

Not to mention too appealing for his own good. And, if she were to be honest, her own. Never had a man paid such undivided attention to her as he had since they'd arrived in Tucson together. Never had anyone paid her such extravagant compliments, or shown such consideration for her wants and desires.

Except in the matter of their hotel room accommodations, of course, Megan amended. There, Gabriel had remained unbudgeable. She was to remain close to him—exceedingly, dangerously close to him—for the duration of their unlikely partnership.

When she'd protested, he'd pointed out quite nicely that she could always stay alone if she chose . . . in a private cell at the territorial jail. Since that would leave her father at the mercy of Gabriel Winter and all the Pinkerton men he'd assembled, Megan had felt compelled to decline his offer.

As he'd known she would. The rascal.

Sighing, Megan opened the pair of glass-fronted doors leading to the balcony of their second-story room at the Cosmopolitan. Embraced by a swirl of crisp afternoon air, she stepped outside. Almost immediately, her heart lightened.

Despite the luxury at her back, despite the man whose image and presence filled her thoughts, the world she was accustomed to living in still existed. The proof of it drifted upward on the dusty autumn breeze, made itself heard in the *clip-clopping* hoofbeats of horses and their riders passing in the streets below, and sailed past on the wings of a cactus wren sweeping toward the hotel roof.

Megan's eyes followed the bird's flight, and for a moment she wished herself as free as it was. Disasters had closed in on her from all sides. This time, she feared, quick thinking and fast talking might not be enough.

But what else did she have?

Nothing. Dispirited, she curled her fingers around the chilly scrollwork of the wrought-iron balcony rail. If she tried, perhaps she could catch a glimpse of the Websters' shop from here. Surely looking toward her future would bolster her spirits—something she badly needed to do before being called to face Agent Winter again. She'd begged a few moments of privacy when they'd arrived, citing a need to freshen up before calling on the townspeople Gabriel intended to question, but she doubted her respite would last for long.

She had to make the most of her opportunity. While nothing could cool the blush his scandalous compliments brought to her cheeks, and nothing could stop her foolish,

French novel–inspired imagination from leaping to flights of fancy at his touch, the more Megan could prepare herself for his return, the better she'd fare against him.

Sparring with Gabriel had sapped her strength. Being on guard against him had damaged her faith. And, however much she wished it weren't true, resisting the pull of his quick, charm-filled smile had challenged her heart. But she judged herself holding her own against him, at least, and that accomplishment had to count for something.

It *did* count for something. For better or worse, Megan Kearney was a woman who believed in taking action. It would be disastrous to begin doubting all she'd done so far.

Perhaps the distance she'd accomplished—however short-lived—had already made her immune to Agent Winter's rogue Irish charms, she decided optimistically. Why, he'd probably return without her even noticing his presence at all.

Immensely cheered at the thought, Megan tightened her grasp on the railing and rose up on tiptoe. The breeze stirred her skirts around her ankles, brushing worsted wool against the thin knit of her cotton stockings as she raised herself still higher by propping one foot on the lower rail. Peering south along the *presidio*'s Main Street, Megan let her gaze travel past rows of flat-roofed shops and houses, paused upon San Agustín church in the distance, then continued onward.

Was that the Websters' mercantile, there?

She stopped on a humble whitewashed building, squinting harder. It was. Someday, it would house her new dressmaker's shop, her dreams for the future—even herself, in the living quarters behind the storefront. Megan imagined herself already there, self-assured and resplendent in her *modiste's* fashionable dresses and impeccable manners, taking orders from customers eager to sample her wares.

Once there, she'd be safe. No one would be able to rouse the doubts she'd have put to rest behind braid and buttons and cunning hats. No one would be able to hurt her. She'd be done with reliance, and the ties it wound to hold her. She would be done, once and for all, with being left behind.

This time, she'd take the role of the one who left herself, and be forever beyond the reach of the fears that bedeviled her.

From so high a vantage point, the tiny shop seemed uncommonly close. *Felt* close, as though she might reach out and cup the baked adobe bricks and all they promised right in the palms of her hands.

Movement behind the mercantile captured Megan's attention and cut short her thoughts of the future. A figure dressed in black clothes and a matching hat crossed the yard with a bundle of goods in his arms. Jedediah Webster, she guessed, carrying his and his wife's belongings to their wagon parked in back and preparing for their trip to the States. She had so little time to secure their shop for her own! Only three days, and with Gabriel Winter tracking her every step . . .

She couldn't think about that now. Wouldn't. Somehow, she would find a way to clear her father's name and have the dressmaker's shop she longed for. With a sense of determination as steady as the black wrought-iron railing in her fists, Megan leaned a little further. She could drive away the uncertainty the Pinkerton man's arrival had aroused in her, just as she could bring her dream into sharper focus with a closer vantage point.

She had to.

Megan leaned, squinting once more at the shop. A longing to go there, to finish what she'd begun with the Websters and to have her future secured, pulled at her. *Why did you do it, Papa? Why now, why—*

"Megan!"

Gabriel's voice shattered her thoughts. Turning to see him charging through the entrance to their shared room destroyed her balance, as well. Thrown akilter by the sudden crash of the heavy paneled door against the wallpapered wall, by the sight of Gabriel's big body moving toward her at surprising speed, Megan wobbled sideways. With a squeal, she clutched at the railing.

Her grasp met scrollwork . . . and slid. Her midsection jabbed into the railing as she fought to steady herself, and the maze of streets and shops below her whirled. Would a fall from this height be enough to kill her? she wondered wildly. Or would it only leave her with broken limbs and less time than before to help her father, and herself?

Neither, she realized as she straightened her arms and somehow caught her balance again. She'd live to see her father's name cleared—and to tell agent Winter exactly what she thought of his bull-in-a-china-shop manners. Raising herself to her full height, Megan started to step from the railing so she could confront the man headed toward her.

Instead, his strong arms closed hard around her middle before she could speak. Her breath left her in an undignified grunt as Gabriel yanked her from her perch. With a roar of determination so fierce it made her heart pound, Gabriel lifted her against him from behind.

"No!" he bellowed. "You'll not escape it that way."

He shouldered his way backward between the balcony doors and hauled her inside. Warmer air struck her, and the room's furnishings jogged by in a jumble as he carried her beyond the lace-curtained windows, past the marble-topped bureau and the cluster of traveling satchels piled beside it, past the potted palm and horsehair settee, all the way to—

The bed. Its white, tufted counterpane rose at the edge

of her vision, and in that instant Megan realized his intent. Squirming against his iron hold, she yelled for all she was worth.

"Let me go!" she demanded. "Have you lost your mind?"

The rest of the words she'd meant to speak flew from her thoughts as she felt herself lifted, higher than before. He'd ascended the step stool used to clamber into the fancy, four-poster hotel bed. Megan wriggled harder, twisting and arching in his arms, but Gabriel's strength surrounded her. It made her struggles useless and her cries as ineffective as shouts into the wind.

She sailed downward. Her body struck the bed hard enough to make the counterpane and down-filled mattress billow at her sides, temporarily blinding her with their snowy thickness.

"Be still!" he growled.

Was he insane? Momentarily stunned, Megan told herself he couldn't really mean to throw her onto the bed and simply ravish her with no warning at all, could he? Agent Winter was a lawman, a self-professed man of truth. Surely his baser instincts were under stricter control than those of the average cowboy or rustler or station hand in town for an afternoon's carousing.

The impact of Gabriel's hard, wool-clad body following hers onto the mattress squashed those hopes. Caught beneath his taut muscles and unforgiving strength, Megan remembered how easily he had overpowered her at the balcony railing, and knew that in this instance at least, she was beaten.

For now.

"I won't let you do it," he said. "Christ, but if I'd been a step or two later—"

His voice choked to a stop, strangled by whatever impulse tightened his long-fingered grasp on her wrists, as well.

Panting, Megan arched her neck and looked from side to side, taking in his sun-browned hands gripping her arms long enough to confirm with her eyes what her mind already knew.

Gabriel Winter was a man as untrustworthy as she'd suspected from the start. She'd do well to remember that in the future.

"If you had been a step or two later, I wouldn't be lying here," she felt compelled to point out, "with you! And I'd be glad of it."

Frustration assailed her. What in heaven's name was he about? What kind of man would assault her this way and then regret aloud the fact that he'd done it too slowly for his liking?

Megan prided herself on her ability to understand people, including the station hands, drivers, and businessmen she came into contact with daily. But Gabriel Winter confounded her. If she lived to be a thousand, it wouldn't be time enough to comprehend the workings of his mind.

"*Glad of it?*" His head bowed. "Dear God, not again," he whispered.

"Again? But I'd only just—"

"Yes, and come too close, at that!" His interruption came fierce and unguarded, his brogue strengthened by the force of his emotions. "I said you were a wily one, Megan Kearney, and I knew it to be true. From the moment I first laid eyes on you in that station yard, I knew you were as uncommon to me as the rest of this damned Territory. But I wouldn't have pegged you for this."

"For what?"

His passing mention of the very unfamiliarity she'd surmised—and now knew—he held with Arizona Territory and its people intrigued her. Reassured her, too. But this wasn't the time to explore what might be her only advantage against him. Plain and true, Gabriel Winter wasn't making sense, and the feeling of being two thoughts behind him in their dealings unsettled her more than Megan wanted to admit.

Needing to get to the base of his reasoning, she returned to what he'd said before without waiting for an answer to her question.

"There's nothing wily in looking out over the city," she told him, trying to imagine what he'd seen when he'd come into the room and glimpsed her at the balcony railing. "Nothing uncommon or strange in looking toward release from the—"

His gaze sharpened. Megan saw his interest and snapped her mouth closed. However flap-jawed an agent he might be, nothing demanded that she confide her plans for the future in him. Indeed, it would be wiser not to. If Gabriel Winter learned of her missing nest-egg money, learned of her father's role in its disappearance, that would only incriminate Papa more.

Striving to seem indifferent—no easy task, given the unexpected stimulation of being sandwiched between the cradling mattress at her back and the hot, wholly unyielding Pinkerton man at her front—Megan gazed up at him.

Sweet mercy, but he was a handsome man! His face held angles and experience too hard edged to be called beautiful. But just for a moment, she glimpsed the goodness beneath the grit Gabriel Winter showed to the world around him, and that peek inside him was enough to entrance her. Breath held, Megan stared more boldly, and then reality returned.

Despite her earlier hopes, she hadn't magically become immune to his charms. The realization kindled something close to panic inside her, a sensation very like the way she used to feel as a child, twirling round and round the station yard until she came up dizzy.

At least then it had been a-purpose.

"Go on," he said, his voice a rumble she felt clear through the clothes that separated them.

Go on with what? her despairing mind wondered. And then she remembered.

"In, in looking toward release from the . . . stifling air of the hotel," Megan countered, doing her best to ignore Gabriel's raised eyebrows and skeptical expression. She wished her hands were free to flutter before her face, fan-like, and bolster her excuse. "I swan, they must never air out these rooms. It's nigh sweltering in here, and only a few minutes past noon, at that."

His gaze bored into hers, deep blue and filled with a tumult of emotions Megan couldn't begin to name. *Lust,* a part of her whispered, but some hidden part of her nearly hoped for more.

"Deny it all you want," he said, stone-faced. "I'll go on believing the truth of what I saw."

"And what did you see?"

She felt his body tense against hers, every muscle rigid with remembrance or restraint . . . or deceit, Megan warned herself. Turning softhearted over Gabriel Winter would only endanger her further.

But gazing up at the lines of weariness bracketing his mouth, at the darkness shadowing the eyes she'd admired so much upon meeting him, she did feel softhearted. Stupidly, Megan wished herself free of his grasp, if only to hold him in her arms instead. Despite her wariness, she couldn't help wanting to ease him. Nor could she help wanting to know what he'd been about in dragging her from the railing by force.

"What did you see, Gabriel?" she asked again. "When I stood at the balcony before?"

His haunted gaze met hers. He bowed his head, showing her the shining midnight of his hair falling near to his suit collar . . . and, in sharp, unknowing contrast, the pale skin at the nape of his neck where he'd been shielded from the sun.

"I saw my past," he said.

The rasp in his voice warned her his past was nothing he remembered fondly. Nothing he spoke of willingly. And then Gabriel blinked, and whatever ghosts of the past he carried vanished with the gesture.

"You were ready to jump, Megan. Don't deny it again." His hand caressed her cheek, and his breath feathered past her hair with a gentleness that surprised her as much as his words did. "Rather than admit the truth that's in front of you, the truth about your father, you were ready to jump to escape it."

Her mouth fell open. "You thought I was"—sweet heaven, she could barely bring herself to say it aloud!— "was about to *jump* from the balcony?"

Were he not so deadly serious, the very notion would have made her laugh. She, give up her life for the sake of an accusation that most certainly couldn't be true?

"If I were broken so easily as that, I'd never have survived beyond girlhood." *Or beyond all that had come on its heels.* "No, Agent Winter, I wasn't—"

"You wouldn't be the first," he said solemnly.

Or the first he'd stopped from taking such a desperate measure, Megan guessed, and the knowledge that Gabriel had thought he was saving her life just now cast a brighter light on all he'd done.

"And I'll wager you wouldn't be the last," he went on. "No one wants to believe the worst of the people they love."

"Fortunately for me, I do not."

She wriggled experimentally, succeeded only in wedging herself more firmly beneath the weight of his chest and thighs, and stilled to catch her breath. Mercy, the man must have been born straight from the mouth of a quarry, to be so hard everywhere!

"Fortunately for you," Megan added, searching for another strategy to free herself, or at least to put more than a shadow's width between them, "I tend not to believe the worst of the people I don't love, as well."

"Maybe you should, when the proof is all around you."

"I wouldn't begin to know how."

"Then it's time you learned." His words were rough. But the steady caress of his thumb against her temple told another, gentler tale—one that came from the heart, not the mind. Aloud, he said, "Denial can't hold back the truth. No more than you could hold me back when I brought you inside."

He'd halted her, not defeated her. She couldn't let him think he'd won already. "I could have! If only I—"

"No. No more than you could hold me back now . . . if you had a mind to try."

Heavens! Suddenly, she tingled with awareness of her situation, caught fully beneath a man's body for the first time in all her twenty-eight spinster's years.

"I don't believe you do," he said.

"Have a mind to hold you back?" Megan did her best to give him a steely look. "Gracious, Agent Winter, you do flatter yourself. What do you think I've been trying to do these past few minutes, except get out from beneath you?"

His gaze challenged her, but it was the unexpected sweetness of his smile that jolted her heart.

"I can't say what you've been trying to do. Only what you've done. We're closer than before, thanks to all your squirming."

He was right, drat him. As though his words had made that fact truer than ever, as though they'd brought her fully alive at last, Megan's senses grew inexplicably keener.

Around her, the air filled with Gabriel's scent and her own, with the fragrances of rose water and tobacco and lingering traces of the tangy *amole* soap the maids used to launder the hotel linens. The coverlet took on a cloud softness she hadn't noticed before. The fine-spun wool of his suit sleeves rubbed over her bare wrists, and the fabric's tender abrasion only heightened all else.

She heard her own indrawn breath, and felt his chest rise against her in turn. On the fireplace mantel, the clock ticked off the moments between seeing and feeling, between awareness and whatever action their nearness would give rise to. Was this what it meant to be ravished, after all? If so . . .

If so, she could never succumb. Especially not while Gabriel Winter was her enemy. Biting her lip, Megan tried to sink into the warmth of the coverlet beneath her and escape in that way. As she'd expected, though, his body only settled more firmly on hers.

"Not that I'm complaining," he went on. "To my mind, lying still doesn't have much place in bed." Now his smile seemed surpassingly devilish, given the circumstances. "Are you hoping to see the worst—and the best—of me? You will, if you keep wiggling like that."

Panicked, Megan squirmed harder to release herself. This predicament had all the makings of the ruination of the heroine of a French novel. Despite her comments to Addie, she was in no way prepared to step between those scandalous pages herself. With a strength born of need, and hopes of dislodging Gabriel's hold long enough to scramble from beneath him, she thrust her hips toward the high, pressed-tin ceiling.

The sound that rumbled from his throat was something between a masculine moan and a half-formed plea. It froze her in place.

"If you know that's true, then let me go!" she cried.

Had he no sense at all? If her nearness pained him enough to cause the throaty, needful groan he'd just given, then why did he want to continue it?

"Let you go?"

With the practiced expertise of a man accustomed to evaluating all that came near, Gabriel took in the sight of her lying beneath him. His perusal felt soft and warm as a caress, but his flinty gaze told another story. One that mingled with the past he'd only alluded to?

"Damnation," he muttered. Briefly, his eyes flickered closed, then opened again on another curse. "If I had the brains of a jackass, I would."

Sensing an opening she might use, Megan stilled her restless squirming. "Do it then. Let me go," she urged. "You don't need me for finding my father. You have those other agents, all over the hotel, to—"

"Ahhh, but I do. I do need you."

I do need you. Gabriel was the first person she'd ever heard say so. Sadly, he only wanted her as bait to capture her father. However sugared his words might be, she couldn't afford to forget that fact.

"Pshaw, Agent Winter. You said yourself you've tracked dozens of men. Whatever could you need me for?"

"For finding the truth," he said bluntly. "For finding the facts you don't want to face any more than . . . Hell! I never should have left you here alone."

"Finding the truth? You don't believe it when it's staring you in the face. You want me for serving as your bed pillow, more likely."

Her nod indicated their ignoble sprawl atop the groaning rope-sprung mattress. Gabriel's demeanor brightened.

"Would you?"

She narrowed her gaze and added as much ice to her voice as she could. "No. And if you'll remember correctly, I *asked* you to leave me here for a few moments alone."

It was the least time she'd needed to prepare herself for him—and for facing the gossipy, mean-spirited women in town. Dealing with them was nothing Megan looked forward to.

"Leaving you alone is something I won't be doing again," Gabriel said. "From here on, we're bound as truly as convicts strung hand and foot."

"A prediction?"

"A promise."

She wanted to shiver. Doubtless, he'd meant that he wouldn't hesitate to lock her up, if it served his case to do so. But if that was so, why did untold regret linger behind Gabriel's eyes? And did that self-recrimination, so evident in the lines bracketing his mouth and brow, owe its cause to his worry over failing at his case? Or to his interest in ensuring her safety from the balcony plunge he'd thought so likely?

"Despite what you think," Megan said, addressing the last issue first, "when you did leave me alone, I wasn't about to leap to a tragic end from the balcony. My father is innocent. How can I make you believe it?"

His gaze slanted darkly over her, then settled on her mouth. "You can't."

A sigh escaped her. She'd never met anyone more resolutely determined to bypass faith for facts. Facts might change at any moment. Faith never would. Couldn't he see that?

Squinting, Megan peered up at him. She couldn't hold back a teasing smile as she said, "Up close, you seem less decrepit and aged than I hoped at first sight." *Maybe then, he would have been easier to deter.* "Tell me, then, how did you come to be so cynical?"

"Cynical?"

As though he weren't listening at all but had parroted her word, Gabriel went on staring at her mouth. She felt

his fingers smooth away a few wayward strands of hair from
her forehead, and wanted to close her eyes beneath the
good feelings his gesture aroused in her. His touch was
fair bewitching . . . and she had no defenses against it save
one.

Conversation.

"Yes, cynical. Jaded and world-weary, tired of—"

His smile touched her next. "I know what it means."

She *tsk-tsked*. "You're too young to be so cynical, Agent
Winter."

"Gabriel," he reminded her. "And I'm too experienced
not to be."

It was the saddest admission she'd ever heard. Her heart
ached at the thought of all he must have seen and done
while working to bring in Pinkerton's most sought-after
bandits. He would be bringing all that terrible knowledge
to bear on his hunt for her father, Megan knew, and her
heart ached doubly for that.

Alone, her father stood no chance against a man such
as Gabriel. But maybe with her on his side, helping to clear
his name with the time that remained, Joseph Kearney
would have a chance. Perhaps even a good one.

Summoning her courage, she asked, "Do you think that
might ever change?"

Pain flickered in his eyes, then died. "If I did, sugar, I
couldn't rightly be called a cynic, now could I?"

"I suppose not. But there's always hope, isn't there?"

He smiled outright, and his hand delved beneath her
hair to cradle the nape of her neck. Slowly, Gabriel leaned
closer, bringing the full impact of his Irish eyes and teasing
grin still nearer. His hair brushed her cheek. His face eased
sideways, beyond her vision.

His breath whispered past her ear. "Hope for you, most
surely."

Tenderly, he pressed a kiss to her ear. Megan jerked with

surprise. Her smooth jet earbobs jangled against her neck, their soft impact greater than the force of his lips ... but far less arresting.

"Lord, you taste sweet." He uncoupled her earbob from its place and kissed her again, this time in the sensitive indentation left by her jewelry. "So sweet."

Her heart turned over. Goose bumps sped clear to her toes; she felt them prickle everywhere, despite the warmth of the room and her many layers of clothing. Gabriel swept his fingers upward from her neck, tugged gently. Near her other ear came a tumbling sound, like the muted clatter of dice cupped in a gambler's palm.

Her other earbob joined the first. With more care than she would have expected from a man so large, he leaned across the dipping mattress to drop her jewelry safely onto the bedside table.

Concentrate, Megan ordered herself. His movement gave her just the opportunity she needed. However her stomach whirled at the feel of his warm lips against her skin, she couldn't wantonly lie there and hope for more.

Nor could she let his whispered endearments erase all the words he'd said just before. They confirmed what she believed of him. They gave Megan one more hope to cling to in her battle against him.

Could she turn Gabriel Winter less cynical? Make some bit of belief squeeze its way past his walled heart and mind? If she could, perhaps he'd believe the truth about her father, as well.

She had to try.

In a flurry of petticoats and brown woolen skirts, Megan seized her one opportunity to scoot from beneath the Pinkerton man's shadow. Breathless—thanks only to the blasted, too-small waistline she'd sewn into her new dress, she felt sure—she scrambled on hands and knees to the far edge of the bed.

"You could be sweet, too," she announced boldly. "With the correct sort of teaching."

Gabriel noticed she'd slipped away. Blithely, he reclined across the center of the rumpled coverlet, just beyond the place where she sat with her skirts arrayed atop her bent knees. He rolled onto his side and propped his head in his hand, seeming unconcerned with the fact that she'd escaped him.

Which showed exactly what sort of ravisher *he'd* turned out to be, Megan supposed with a surge of unwelcome disappointment.

His eyebrows rose. "What sort of teaching is that?"

Feeling unreasonably piqued, she rose and felt with her toes for the bed's step stool. Once she'd found it, she stepped from the bed and assumed what she hoped would seem a detached, professorial pose. If Gabriel respected facts more then feelings, by God, she would present her feelings as facts and beat him at his own game.

He watched her feet touch the colorfully embroidered rug, and disappointment crossed his face. "Never mind. There's nothing either of us can learn with you all the way down there, sugar."

Frowning past whatever nonsense he meant with that remark, Megan said, "I'll do the teaching here. And I'll have you know, I've discerned exactly what you need."

With satisfaction, she noticed the interest return to his expression. "You have?"

"Yes. And if you'll take my hand, I'll show you precisely what I mean."

Eight

"This is *not* exactly what I needed," Gabriel said.

And it was so far from what he'd hoped Megan meant about teaching him what he needed—*teaching him sweetness*—as to be almost laughable. Smiling despite that fact, he paused at the window of the simple yellow-painted adobe building she had led him to.

"Yes, it is," she said. "It is what you need. Or at least, a part of it."

Making a noncommittal sound, he cupped his hands at his temples and peered inside the window. All he managed to catch were glimpses of people moving amongst chairs and cloth-covered tables, flickering lamplight, and an assortment of statuary before she tugged him toward the door.

He frowned, in confusion, he told himself, not disappointment. Never that. "I hate to tell you your own city, but we could have eaten all the way across town and saved ourselves some shoe leather. Those steaks at the Congress

Hall saloon smelled mighty fine to me when we passed by there."

"And so did the *tamales* the ladies were selling in the *plaza* when we passed through there," Megan said, grinning. "I know, you told me. But nothing else is quite like this. Trust me."

Trust her? Not likely. Not as long as she insisted on shouting her father's innocence to anyone who'd stand still. But in a matter so small as this, Gabriel guessed he'd have to. After all, if his sisters and mother were any indication, women were prone to fancies like this excursion across town. Once they took a certain notion into their heads, nothing else would satisfy.

He and Megan passed beneath a fancy-lettered sign naming the place as Hop Kee's Celestial Kitchen Restaurant. Nearing the unlikely seeming red lacquered door, he reached past his companion's shoulder, dodged a low-lying feather from her smorgasbord of a hat, and pushed the door open.

"Allow me." Holding the door ajar, he doffed his own, less-embellished headgear and motioned her inside.

"Why, thank you kindly, sir." Her smile flashed. "And to think I'd begun having doubts about your status as a gentleman, after all that passed between us at the hotel."

At her words, Gabriel felt again the sweet, curved warmth of her body beneath him on the mattress, inhaled again the scents of roses and sunshine that surrounded her. Her nearness alone had the power to set his senses afire, he'd discovered. Only pure grit—and the knowledge that they were enemies still—had kept him from deliberately kindling a similar heat within Megan.

"A sliver of sunshine couldn't have passed between us, sugar. We were too close together for that."

She paused on the threshold and looked backward at him. "That's what I mean. It was hardly gentlemanly of you."

Neither were the thoughts he found himself entertaining right then. The sensual pucker and release of her lips was worthy of several moments' contemplation in itself, as was the enticing swell of her breasts, only a few breaths distant from his outstretched arm. Were her curves due to feminine trickery, like a soiled dove's padded combinations and rouged cheeks? Or were they genuine?

Sorely tempted to find out, Gabriel leaned closer into the doorway. The darkened vestibule of some Chinaman's restaurant was hardly the place to indulge his curiosity about a wanted man's daughter. But despite that fact, he felt himself drawn to touch the petal softness of Megan's mouth, to linger a little longer in the shadows with her, to sample the pleasures he might find with her . . . and to pleasure her in return.

All of which were, no doubt, exactly the distractions she'd meant to engender, he realized. He'd neatly stepped in tune with another of her double-edged maneuverings.

Damnation. It was almost enough to make him wish she'd come out with it straight, and wallop him in the shins again.

Almost.

Determined to fall for no more of her tricks, Gabriel straightened. He fisted his hand on his hat brim and said, "It was more gentlemanly than you know."

"Humph. I suppose you expect me to thank you for that?"

Her arched brows and skeptical expression said the desert would turn to snowdrifts before she'd thank him for anything—least of all holding her captive on their shared hotel-room bed.

"Thank me?" Leisurely, Gabriel took in the fit of her fussy brown dress, still slightly rumpled, despite her attempts to smooth it, and the subtle disarray of her upswept hair, only half-tamed by her hat. Both reminded him of how close he'd come to abandoning the principles that had guided him all these long years on the Pinkerton trail.

"Yes, you should," he said, and felt it to be true. He frowned. "I didn't have to let you out of that bed at all."

Thrusting her nose in the air, Megan planted her hand beside his on the door. She pushed it open a little wider. "Never mind the courtesy. I didn't realize it came with a price."

"Everything does."

It was a fact he lived with. A fact he'd never had cause to regret. But watching Megan sashay alone into Hop Kee's Celestial Restaurant, bustle swaying and chin held high as though she owned the place, Gabriel did have regrets.

He wanted her. His need for her was as real as the red-papered walls, statuary, and ornate paper lanterns surrounding him. Worse, it grew with every moment they spent together, made itself known with every shared breath they took.

But the price of having Megan would be his job. And Gabriel had no intention of paying a price so high.

Not ever.

Plainly put, he couldn't serve justice and at the same time dally with his prime suspect's daughter. He couldn't track the truth while feeding her lies. But he could—*he must*—use whatever information Megan could give him.

The trick lay in not taking advantage of her while he did.

His reputation, his livelihood, and his future all relied on tracking down the man who'd committed the robbery at Kearney Station. Surely he could do that without compromise. Although Megan might doubt he possessed the morals to do so, Gabriel knew no such uncertainties. He'd proven himself time and again.

Winter brings in the right man at the right time.

The sooner he got on with it, the better. He spied Megan
at the outskirts of the bustling dining room, hands clasped,
gazing with rapt interest at the painted menu board nailed
to the wall. Was she waiting for the proprietor? Or waiting
for Gabriel to join her before proceeding into the sea of
customer-filled tables?

Despite himself, he liked the notion of a woman waiting
for him. Liked the notion of *Megan* waiting for him. With
a hopefulness more foolish than he wanted to consider,
Gabriel made his way toward her.

All around him exotic spices perfumed the air, pungent
with spicy-sweet ginger and fresh-brewed green tea. Cutlery
clattered against plates; tea flowed into cups with greedy
swirls of sound. As he passed farther into the dining room,
the steady murmur of chattering voices grew louder, a
mixture of ambling Western speech and staccato Chinese.

For an instant, the sound threw him home to the narrow,
hilly streets of San Francisco, to the Chinatown in its midst.
Gabriel waited for homesickness to strike, waited for some
sign he was ready to go back there . . . and felt nothing.

Had he been on the trail as a Pinkerton man for so long
that the need for home couldn't touch him? Or was the
emptiness he felt only natural for a man fully grown, with
no family of his own to hold him in place?

Something told him it wasn't. He trusted that sense even
less than he did the motives behind Megan's upturned,
suddenly smiling face when she spied him approaching
her. Another plan had formed between those bejeweled
ears of hers. The open-armed greeting she gave him did
nothing to convince Gabriel otherwise.

Her gloved hands squeezed his shoulders with a trace
too much enthusiasm. "There you are! I thought you'd
left me here alone."

If he hadn't known better, he might have believed the
quaver in her smile. He might have believed she spoke

truly, and felt sorry for letting her precede him into the restaurant without an escort. But after this morning, Gabriel knew better than to believe so readily.

"And stop short of finding out what it is you think I need from this place?" He shook his head and gave her a wry twist of his lips that might have passed for a smile. "Not this Pinkerton man, darlin'. I'm not one to pass up any clues, even the nonsensical ones."

Color brightened her smooth freckled cheeks. She fluttered her eyelashes downward and, looking wounded, examined the tips of her shoes with a remarkably realistic air of betrayal. "I didn't bring you here to help you make your case against my father."

"At least not intentionally."

"Not at all!" Her head came up. This time, those lonesome brown eyes of hers flashed with more than enough ire to back up her words. "This just goes to show how much you needed to come here with me, Agent Winter—"

"Gabriel."

"—and how much you need that sweetness I told you about!"

Considering all things sweet—and better savored slowly—he skimmed his gaze over her. Damn, but she looked pretty. Too freckled and square jawed for classic beauty, but with a vitality and softness that appealed to him strongly, all the same.

"Oh, I need sweetness, all right," Gabriel said, with a smile turned genuine. "You've got me pegged there, Miss Megan."

"I'm pleased you agree."

Her curt reply seemed to close their conversation. She tapped her gloved fingers over her hair to straighten it, adjusted her hat, then drew a deep breath and sent her gaze searching over the dining room beyond them. Gabriel watched her, and couldn't help wanting more of an answer than she'd given him. Was she being deliberately coy? Or did she really not understand their differing versions of sweet and sour . . . and salvation?

He'd wager she understood him well enough.

If not now, then soon.

He looked down to find her too-contemplative gaze transferred from their surroundings to him. Ominously, Megan added, "If it's not already too late, that is."

"Too late for what?"

"You."

With that cryptic explanation, she rose on tiptoe and waved to someone over Gabriel's shoulder. He turned to see a neatly dressed Chinese man approach, wiping his hands on the apron tied around his waist, and call out to Megan.

"Miss Kearney! These old eyes must deceive me. That can't really be you, come back to Hop Kee's place after all these years."

"It is me, Mr. Kee. I haven't grown and changed all that much, have I?" Smiling, Megan fluffed out her skirts and stood straighter, as though to help bring about the answer she hoped for.

Gabriel stared in amazement. Was she really so unsure as her actions suggested? It had to be another ruse, he reasoned . . . until he noticed the way she'd drawn her lower lip between her teeth, waiting for the older man's reply.

Her obvious unease was almost enough to make him wish he hadn't mussed her dress and hair, hadn't criticized her choice of restaurants and set her on guard with jibes about how she'd brought him there to find more clues.

I thought you'd left me here alone.

For an instant, he thought of how she'd seemed to him just moments ago, with her wobbly smile and fingers clenched tight against her skirts. To his eyes, she'd seemed

genuinely afraid he had abandoned her. But the rest of
him knew that notion flew in the face of everything Gabriel
had experienced since meeting her. Brave, deceptively
clever Megan, afraid? Never.

But now she wore that same expression while she waited
for Hop Kee, as though expecting he'd find her appearance lacking. Find *her* lacking. And recognizing that fear
in her struck Gabriel deeply.

Which was the true Megan? The no-holds-barred, conniving lady sharper he'd come to know? Or the woman
poised on the edge of heartbreak he saw now?

Frowning, he stepped closer to her and turned to face
Hop Kee as he came closer. With his shoulders nearly
blocking her view, Gabriel would be ready to shield her
from Kee's disapproval. He'd be ready to soften its impact
before it could touch her . . . before it could steal the
eagerness from her eyes and the lightness from her step.

For all her scheming, squirming, and foolish readiness
to believe in her father's innocence, Megan still stood in
a Pinkerton man's care. As long as she did, Gabriel vowed,
he wouldn't allow any harm to come to her.

You could cause the most harm of all, a part of him reminded.
If Joseph Kearney turned up as guilty as Gabriel thought
he would, it would wound her far more than a restaurant
owner's rebuke. Only one of them could be right about
her father. Only one of them could win with this. Gabriel
had sworn it would be him.

Hell.

But neither he nor Megan needed to have worried over
Hop Kee. The Chinaman stopped and bowed before them
both, and Gabriel realized that this man cared nothing for
her rumpled skirts or coverlet-mussed hair. He looked
beyond such things as dresses and millinery and regal
posture—or the lack of them. The proof of his vision was

in his lined face when Kee looked at her, in his broad smile and the joyful clasp of her hands in his.

"Not so much grown, but changed in all the most beautiful ways," he announced, squeezing her hands gently. Like a doting father, he took in her appearance from shoes to hat, and sighed. "You turned out pretty fine, Miss Kearney. I always told your papa you would."

His flattery eased Gabriel's aggressive stance and at the same time brought a blush to Megan's cheeks. Her heightened color betrayed how unused she was to such compliments, however worthy of them she might be.

"Thank you," she said quietly, "but I've come to visit you, not to talk about me! I hope you've fared well, over the years. You have, haven't you?"

"Yes, yes. It hasn't been so long, after all." Kee nodded and released her hands. As though only just then noticing Gabriel stood there, he gave him a measuring look. "Except long enough for you to find a husband, I see?"

"Oh, no! Not a husband. No, no, no."

"No?" Kee's eyebrows vanished into his straight, dark hair. "Are you sure?" He looked from Megan to Gabriel, then back again. "Because the two of you seem to me like—"

"No!"

If Megan shook her head any more vehemently, she'd rattle the jumble of flowers and ribbons and dark-colored laces clean off her hat. As though realizing that fact, she edged in front of Gabriel instead, giving him a look spiked with ire when she had to jostle him and his protective shoulders aside.

"I'll never be married, Mr. Kee," she confided to her friend. "Especially not to a black-hearted, blarney-tongued, citified excuse for a—"

"—friend of the family, like me," Gabriel finished for her, grinning. Next, she'd be revealing his employment with the Pinkerton agency, and all it entailed. Most certainly, that had been her intention. He'd never learn anything about Joseph Kearney's whereabouts that way.

" 'Friend of the family'?" Megan mimicked. In the midst of straightening her hat, she stopped to gape at him. *"Friend of the family'?"*

Apparently, she couldn't get anything more past her lips than those words. *Thank God.* Taking advantage of her silence, Gabriel winked at her.

"You're right, that doesn't quite describe it, does it?" He moved nearer, letting his gun belt brush against the rose-scented drape of her skirts. "In fact, we've been even closer together than family, especially lately. Much, much . . . *much* closer."

His reminder of their sprawled union on the hotel-room bed had the effect he'd expected . . . for all of two ticks of the Celestial Kitchen clock on the restaurant wall behind her. Then Megan's voice returned.

He should have known it wouldn't take long.

Ignoring her sputter of outrage, Gabriel leaned toward Hop Kee. He grasped the other man's hand in a steady handshake as he introduced himself. "Gabriel Winter. I can't begin to tell you how welcome Miss Megan has made me feel since I've arrived here in the Territory."

"Oh, do tell, Mr. Winter." She grasped his elbow in her gloved hands and simpered. "I wouldn't mind if the whole wide world knew exactly how I feel about having you here."

As though she hadn't just insulted him, Gabriel smiled and patted the hand she'd nestled in the crook of his arm. "Isn't she something?" he asked Hop Kee. "I've never met anyone more willing to help her fellow man—"

"Right onto the next train out of town," Megan muttered from behind the gaudy fan she'd withdrawn from wherever ladies kept such things.

"—however unworthy of her assistance, and protection, that fellow man might be," he finished meaningfully.

Her dark-eyed glance from behind her fan told him Megan had understood him perfectly. And didn't like it one bit.

"Pshaw, Mr. Winter!" she said, fluttering her fan like the greatest of coquettes. "No one should presume to sit in judgment of another person's worthiness. I think we'd all agree on that score."

"Would we?"

She snapped her fan closed and gave him a stiff smile. "Of course."

"Then I must have been mistaken." Gabriel bowed slightly. "I was under the impression you'd already formed an opinion on my account." And it wasn't a favorable one.

"I—" Her stricken gaze, golden brown and widened with new insight, met his. She hadn't thought of the double standard she'd imposed. He could see it in her eyes, and in the contrite softening of her mouth. "I—I guess I never thought of it that way."

Hop Kee smiled, his face jovial and knowing beneath his skull cap. "Leave it to an Irishman to turn around your thinking. He's a persuasive one, Megan. Just like you."

Gabriel raised an eyebrow. Megan, like him? They weren't alike at all, he told himself. To Kee, he said, "However much I assure her we're all filled with charm and good humor where I come from, Miss Megan seems to believe I've been sent here to Tucson just to bedevil her."

He and the older man shared a grin. Beside them, Megan all but stamped her foot.

"Bedevil me?" she asked. "I wish it were so simple. Mr. Winter may be accustomed to keeping secrets, but I'm not. The truth is, Mr. Kee, that he's come here for one thing only."

She was putting him in an indefensible position. Chances

were good that the Chinaman knew where to find Megan's father. The last thing Gabriel needed was to scare away a potential source of information.

"And I don't understand why he doesn't just come right on out with it," Megan went on serenely. "The truth is, he really came here to—"

"—woo her."

At Gabriel's announcement, she turned a horrified look in his direction. *What?*

"Woo her and win her," he went on telling Kee. He paused to aim an especially besotted smile at Megan. She wouldn't do any more damage to his case, wouldn't reveal all his plans to track down Joseph Kearney—not if he could help it. And he damned well could. "With your blessing, of course, Mr. Kee."

"Of course!" For all appearances, Kee looked absolutely charmed. *A romantic,* Gabriel thought. All the luckier for him.

"Woo? Woo me? *Woo me.*" Megan seemed dumbstruck at the notion.

"And to do that," Gabriel went on, bending to speak with Kee, "I'll need a special table. A very private, very special table."

"I have just the one!"

A man with a mission, Kee gestured for them to follow. He wound his way between rows of customer-filled tables, past restaurant workers and exotic-looking statues, while Gabriel and Megan kept pace.

Beside him, she walked with the stiffness of a woman whose plans had gone terribly awry. "You're incorrigible," she whispered fiercely, keeping her gaze on Kee as he led them toward a distant corner of the restaurant. "Lying to my friend that way! How can I ever—"

"What makes you believe it's a lie?"

They reached their table. Upon it, evening sunlight drew

a brilliant square against a tablecloth as red as full-bodied wine. Behind it, a door swung on double hinges, set in constant motion by the passing of restaurant workers back and forth from the kitchen to the Celestial Kitchen Restaurant's bustling dining room.

Momentarily oblivious to their surroundings, Megan tugged off her gloves with trembling fingers. She drew them to rest in her palm, just as she had in the stage station office, then squared her shoulders to face him.

"Of course it's a lie!" she said, casting a cautious glance toward Hop Kee, who was busy speaking with one of the restaurant workers. "You couldn't possibly have meant it."

Gabriel shrugged. "Perhaps I've only just now come to my senses, Megan, and decided to pursue you after all."

"Pursue my father, you mean!"

"That has nothing to do with what's happening between us." Or did it? Damn, he wished he could be sure of it.

Apparently Megan harbored no such doubts. "Nothing is happening between us," she snapped, tossing her gloves onto the corner table they would share. "And nothing ever will."

He put his hand to the curve of her waist, meaning to guide her closer to her chair, and to calm her in the process. Instead, the warm, supple feel of her body beneath his fingers stayed his hand—and put a hundred doubts in his mind. Had he meant what he'd said? Or were the words only the means to an end, another way to solve his case?

"Are you sure about that?" Gabriel's gaze met hers. "Even Hop Kee could see it. He could feel it."

He traced the indentation of her waist, the alluring flare of her hip, so wonderfully round and soft beneath his hand. He tightened his fingers, wanting to draw her closer still and knowing she'd likely stomp the shine from his boots if he did.

"There is a great deal between us," he said.

"Yes. Enmity."

"Not as much as you wish." *Not as much as would be wise.* "This is something more." His brogue strengthened with the urgency he felt; even Gabriel could hear it. Powerless to stop it, he hoped she wouldn't recognize what drove him if she heard it, too. "Can't you feel it, this . . . attraction between us?"

Stillness overcame her. A small sound slipped from between Megan's lips, seconds before she glanced up at him at last. Barely more than a sigh, to Gabriel her response made all the commotion around them recede. The whole world narrowed to the woman at his side and her reaction to his question.

Defiantly, she jerked her hip sideways. Her chin came up, another sure sign of her fighting spirit. It was a quality he admired in her, despite the fact that she typically used it against him.

"If I ever do feel whatever it is you're talking about," Megan informed him airily, "then I'll be sure to extinguish it. Completely. And thoroughly. Without fail and—"

"There's no call to belabor the point. I understand." Despite himself, Gabriel grinned. To his immense surprise, she did, too. She might not want the attraction between them, but neither did she want outright war, it seemed.

Her wish for some measure of accord between them was something he'd need to encourage, if he were to gain any ground with his case. It wasn't likely she'd help him, as long as she saw him as an enemy to be bested. Could he encourage an alliance between them?

He had to try. Not because he wanted her, Gabriel assured himself, but because he wanted to finish this. Needed to finish this. Soon.

"And if I were to pursue you, all the same?" he asked quietly.

She examined his vest with more absorption than the

plain dark garment warranted, all but memorizing the fabric's taper from his chest to the gun belt he'd strapped beneath his suit coat. She said nothing.

"Or woo you?" he coaxed, unable to keep back the renewed smile that flickered over his face at the old-fashioned language. There was nothing funny about his intentions, though, or his interest in her, however unwise it was. "What then, Megan?"

"You—you're teasing me," she protested. She lifted her gaze from his chest to his face, and the glitter of tears in her eyes was enough to steal his breath. "Because of Mr. Kee. You're only saying these things to flatter me, to—"

"Hop Kee is still busy with his employee. He can't even hear us."

"But—"

"But I'm telling you truly," Gabriel interrupted, beset with an urge to kiss the downward turn from her lips. Would she taste as hot and honeyed as before? "You're a very desirable woman, Megan."

Her lips parted. He glimpsed a new light in her eyes, a kindling of something uncommonly rare. Uncommonly beautiful. Then as suddenly as it had appeared, it vanished. In its place came the kind of wariness he'd come to expect from her, along with a goodly dose of starch.

It pained him to see it, and even more to hear it come from her mouth.

"I don't believe you. And I don't trust you," she said. "And no quantity of Irish charm will be enough to make me forget it. Do you think me stupid enough to fall into every trap you set for me?"

Lord, but she could let fly a meaner barb than any woman he'd met. And now that he'd glimpsed the tender side to her, somehow those spiky words of hers stung even deeper than before.

"I could ask the same of you." Gabriel noticed Mr. Kee

finishing his conversation with the worker, and leaned slightly forward to add, "Since you've been trying to lure me into a fair share of traps since I got here."

"Traps? I don't know what you mean."

"Don't you?"

"No! But if it's too uncomfortable for you here in the Territory, perhaps you ought to take your leave."

"Not until I've finished the job I came here to do. I intend to win. I always do."

Hop Kee's approach left her little room to argue, and Megan knew it. She flounced into her chair at the table, teeth set in determination, and struggled to seat herself closer. The sound of ripped fabric announced the difficulty she had in doing so.

With a feminine growl of frustration, she tried again.

"Allow me." Gabriel bent over her, sensing both her trembling and her resentment of his help. He didn't care for either one. The last thing he'd do was stand by while a lady did everything but turn herself upside down, just to take a meal.

Arms flanking her sides, he grasped the chair's edges in both hands. Her warmth washed over him, tempting him to find some excuse to linger there, some reason to prolong the contact between them. He could find none, save wanting to. That would never be enough.

When he did move the chair forward, his motion inadvertently stirred the air between them. It became a rosy wash of fragrance so pure Gabriel had to close his eyes against it. Was he mad, to surround himself with the essence of her?

Surely he was, but not for long. "Don't fight me," he said. "It will only make things harder for us both."

He saw her eyes close, briefly. When she opened them again, the golden light he'd seen before in her gaze was undiminished. "I have to."

Hop Kee's approach cut short whatever reply Gabriel could have made. The Chinaman clapped his hands together and surveyed their table—and Megan's seated position beside it—with obvious pleasure.

"You like this one?" he asked. "I think it is the special one you wanted."

"This table looks perfect," Gabriel said, putting on a smile. If Megan's rapt expression was anything to go by, she thought so, too—not that he could waste time wondering over her change of mood. Neither could he delay his true reasons for being there any longer.

With that in mind, he offered Kee another handshake, and an invitation. "Can you join us for a few minutes? With so much news to catch up on, I've about worn poor Megan's voice clean through, and we haven't even gotten to talking about her father. I was hoping you could tell me how Joseph's been faring these last few years."

Nine

"Defeated again," Megan announced, eyeing Gabriel over the table they shared. "A person would think you'd get tired of hearing the same old things about my father, and not believing them."

"It's not a question of believing," he said quietly. "It's a question of finding out the truth." He smoothed his fingers over the rich red tablecloth, then brought them to the side of his teacup in an absentminded caress. "Obviously, this wasn't the place to find it."

"Obviously."

A small sense of giddiness burbled up inside her. One meal and too much conversation later, the Pinkerton man still wasn't any closer to tracking down her father than he'd been when he walked in—even after all his questions. She couldn't help but feel a little vindicated.

Her father was innocent, blast it! Somehow, she'd prove it, too. But to do so, she had to gain some measure of

Gabriel's trust, something she wasn't likely to do without first softening the cynical bent of his thoughts.

So far, doing *that* had proved more difficult than she'd envisioned. Gabriel had remained unmoved by her friend Hop Kee's jovial presence and lively conversation. He'd been unimpressed by the elegance of the Celestial Kitchen's red-and-gilt dining room. And he hadn't loosed the frown from his face for the past half-hour or more.

How could that be? She'd felt sure this place held at least a fragment of the magic that would sweeten him up. Over her years of cherished visits there, Megan had certainly never come to Hop Kee's restaurant and failed to leave feeling happier than before.

She wrinkled her nose at the undeniable conclusion. Her adversary was clearly cut from a different—and far tougher—bolt of fabric than she was.

Well, she'd just have to work harder. There was nothing honest labor and quick thinking couldn't get for her, including her own way with Gabriel Winter. Megan considered him, wondering how best to turn their situation to her advantage.

With that same scowl firmly in place, Gabriel sat across from her and stared into his cup of green tea, just as he'd done since Hop Kee had departed for the kitchens. Light from the paper lantern above their table illuminated his features, highlighting the handsome, surly angles of his face and throat. Even more so than the late-afternoon sunlight shining through the wood-framed window beside them, it wove gleaming blue-black highlights in his loose dark hair, and emphasized the strength in his wide, suit coat–covered shoulders.

It also cast more light than she wanted on her own behavior.

This went beyond mere strategizing, Megan realized with chagrin. She was only one gesture short of propping her

chin on her hand and sighing over the man like a girl just
out of short skirts! What was the matter with her, mooning
over the appearance of an uncompromising, icicle-hearted
lawman like Agent Winter?

Really she wanted to speak to him, Megan told herself.
Maybe she'd even gloat a little longer over her success
at keeping her father's whereabouts hidden. But almost
against her will, the caressing path he made on his cup
captured her attention instead . . . and held it transfixed.

Given the striking contrast between Gabriel's big, blunt-
fingered hand and the fragile teacup, she should have
expected him to break it. Especially in his thunderous state
of mind. But it only took another slow circuit of his fingers
to convince her he would not.

Surely a touch as gentle as his could never bring the
danger she expected.

As in the office at Kearney station when touching the
books and lamps and furnishings arrayed there, Gabriel
seemed to absorb the essence of the cup in his hand.
His innate curiosity piqued hers. It made her yearn to
experience everything as deeply as he seemed to, to gather
up life by handfuls. To *know,* as closely and deeply as her
fingers and feelings and mind would allow.

Suddenly, the spinster's life she'd resigned herself to
seemed painfully empty. Wrung of its vibrancy, it lacked
texture and awareness and warmth, all things she hadn't
known she needed.

Until now.

As though the sensations that touched Gabriel could
affect her as well, Megan imagined the feel of his cup's
smooth porcelain surface in her hand. She imagined the
press of her fingertips against its unyielding delicacy,
savored the warmth of the brew inside. She inhaled as
though experiencing the tang of the tea's aroma, licked
her lips as though tasting its subtle green flavor.

Her mouth actually watered, so real did the sensations seem. When Gabriel lifted the cup to his lips, she sensed his anticipation of the goodness to come . . . and when he drank, she felt the hot slide of his mouth as though it truly had covered her own.

She shivered. Sweet heaven, what was happening to her?

Gabriel noticed. He paused with his cup in middescent, and settled his dark gaze on her. "Cold?"

Mutely, she shook her head. Had her dressmaker's shop deed depended on it, Megan couldn't have described the emotions racing through her. Excitement jumbled with terror would almost suffice, but for the sense of heady discovery she felt, too. Was this what her mother had experienced, on the long-ago day when she'd left them for good?

If it was, for the first time, Megan could almost begin to understand. How did a person begin to fight emotions like these? Her thoughts were all a tangle, and her stomach pitched with excitement far too strong to simply ignore. All she knew for sure was that cold had nothing to do with the way she'd shivered just now.

"No, I'm not cold," she croaked, fighting to show him a lighthearted smile. "My sense of impending victory is keeping me warm as toast."

"Touché." Gabriel raised his cup in a mocking salute, then smiled over its rim as he drank again.

She looked away. The last thing she wanted was to find herself bewitched anew, fascinated by the pucker of his lips as he prepared to sip, or charmed by the obvious pleasure he took in tasting. The last thing she needed was another flight of fancy, or the study of his fingers, his touch, his sensitivities.

Drat! He'd done it to her again, Megan realized. Without even drawing her gaze to his, Gabriel had somehow kept her attention as fully as if he had.

She balled her fists in her lap, filled with frustration and no small measure of confusion. The effect he had on her was almost enough to make her wish he would come up with it straight and steal another kiss outright.

As he had back at their hotel room.

Lord, you taste sweet, he'd said between one kiss and the next. *So sweet*. And she'd believed him, too. Now, remembrance of his whispered words made her shiver still harder.

His cup clattered into its saucer. "You are cold."

Baldly said, his words somehow managed to convey caring and exasperation, all in the same breath. Gabriel half-rose in his seat and shrugged out of his suit coat, then leaned over her chair to spread its protection over her shoulders.

Too surprised at his kindness to move, Megan let him tuck his coat around her. Wide-eyed, she watched as his face, slightly roughened with a half-day's growth of beard, neared hers. His chest loomed in her vision, bringing with it an intriguing mixture of scents ... leather and sharp creosote, castile soap and warm skin. Now clad above the waist in only his fine white broadcloth shirt, vest, and necktie, Gabriel suddenly seemed infinitely kinder. Impossibly intimate.

And far less threatening than she figured an avowed enemy ought to seem. In amazement, Megan felt his hands move gently over and around her, smoothing his expensive navy wool coat over her shoulders and then following the line of its empty sleeves down the length of her arms.

Her thanks were whispered from her on a shaky breath. She caught herself staring agog at Gabriel as he seated himself opposite her again, and realized she must look exactly like the witless female so many of her stage station customers first assumed her to be. Surely she was stronger than this!

He's your enemy, Megan reminded herself. *There is too much at stake to let your common sense go wandering.*

As though he'd somehow read her thoughts, Gabriel's mouth quirked upward. "You're welcome."

The cad. He'd probably planned to rattle her like this all along. She had to do something to regain the upper hand.

"My goodness, Agent Winter. You *are* a fine loser. And here I'd thought you were still brooding over Hop Kee," she said. She gave a mock-sympathetic cluck of her tongue. "I could have told you he wouldn't betray my father. Especially not to a stranger."

"It's not a betrayal to tell the truth." His gaze pinned her, overly bright and filled with all the determination of a born brawler. "And Kee doesn't know I'm a stranger."

"Pshaw. It sticks out on you like rusty pins on a dress pattern. Anyone can see you don't belong here."

"Not if you don't help clear their vision for them. Your hints about my occupation couldn't have been any bolder."

"Nor could the lies you told to hide it."

Not that he seemed so very bothered by the fact, Megan thought. Woo her, indeed! Did he think she was simple-minded? No man but Gabriel had ever called her desirable, and he was the last person she'd believe.

Across from her, Gabriel finished his tea in one long swallow, then sat back in his chair with the watchfulness he seemed to have been born with. It was unnerving to have such concentrated attention focused on her.

"I'm many things, Miss Megan," he said, "but a liar isn't one of them."

His slow smile suggested a good many of those things he claimed were sinful in nature—or at least, too wicked to be discussed in mixed company. Against all reason, curiosity rose inside her, hot and strong. What secrets had lent him that edge of danger he carried?

Whatever they were, they were no concern of hers, she reminded herself staunchly. Once she'd cleared her father's name, gotten back the money to buy the Websters' mercantile building for her own, and started in on her wondrous new life, Gabriel Winter would be nothing but a memory.

"If you were a liar, you wouldn't be likely to honestly admit it," she pointed out. "So I don't see how I can ever believe you."

"Perhaps you can't."

"Of course I can't."

But she wanted to, Megan realized with a start. She wanted to believe him, wanted an excuse not to think the worst of Agent Winter and his misguided investigation into her father's life. If she weren't careful, she'd find herself utterly off the path she'd laid for herself—no father, no dressmaker's shop, no refuge meant to keep her safe.

No dreams.

"You're wasting your breath to even discuss my believing in you," she went on. "I would be a fool if I did. You told me so yourself."

"Did I?" His lips twisted. With an expression too weary for the few years he must claim, Gabriel said, "I must have mistaken that starry-eyed faith of yours for the damned miracle you think it is."

In confusion, Megan stared at him. Was the Pinkerton man asking her to believe in him? There was no way she could, not as long as he insisted on claiming her father's guilt—and with no proof of it.

At least none that he would agree to show her.

Still, her heart had softened, enough that she recognized the wanting in his voice. And her understanding of him had strengthened, powerfully enough for Megan to act on the impulse she felt to soothe him.

Boldly, she reached across the table toward Gabriel. Keeping her palm up, she lay her hand atop the tablecloth and crooked her fingers in invitation, asking him without words to put his hand in hers.

Only his eyebrows moved in response. Their derisive tilt could hardly be called encouraging.

She did her best to talk straight through that dratted cynicism of his, all the same. After all, that was what she'd come here to do in the first place. Megan Kearney didn't quit—not even when faced with a dog-stubborn, double-dipped, suspicious rascal like Gabriel Winter.

"The miracle you want is there for the taking," she said. "All you have to do is reach for it. It's just like turning your face to the sunlight, or listening to a cactus wren sing. It's just like touching somebody. Like touching me."

All she wanted was for him to see things the way she did. For him to accept that the inexplicable did exist, and his Pinkerton bosses might have been wrong in sending him here to hunt down her father. All she wanted was a single touch, a single reason to believe he might not be as coldhearted as he seemed.

All she intended was to show him what she'd brought him here to see, and to set the stage for doing it properly.

Megan reached her hand out farther, wiggling her fingers in invitation. "It's all right," she urged. "It won't hurt you to touch me, you know. You're certainly not made of spun sugar, to melt away if I hold you too tight."

His gaze lifted, velvety and blue as a sky after sunset. Something powerful moved within its depths, something needful and aching. What had she done, what had she said, to bring about such intensity as that?

Megan searched her memory, and recalled nothing. All the same, his lingering look persisted, filled with a meaning she couldn't decipher. She could have lost herself in Gabriel's eyes, could have held his gaze forever . . . if not for knowing she had other goals to accomplish and far too little time to achieve them.

Why wouldn't he take her hand?

"I haven't any shackles hidden away in my pockets," she teased, lowering her voice still further. "Any seamstress worth her salt knows they're not in fashion this year."

His husky laughter brought a smile to her face as well. He seemed a different man when he smiled, a gentler man.

"Then I'm hopelessly outmoded," Gabriel said. "I never leave home without mine."

Wonderful, a part of her gibed. He'd be forever ready to lock up her father in irons and take him away.

"I'd say a man so well fortified has no reason to fear holding my poor tired hand." Megan waggled her fingers in blatant appeal. "Wouldn't you agree?"

He stared as though she'd lost her mind, to be baiting him so. Maybe she had. But once committed to a course of action, she'd decided she could hardly turn back.

If a simple human touch couldn't reach him, then perhaps social logic could.

"You're making a public spectacle of me, I'll have you know." It was only as she said it that she realized how prophetic her words might be, and her heart sank at the thought. Nevertheless, she plunged onward. "By morning, the gossips will be all aflutter with tales of how poor Megan Kearney threw herself at a man's head, and was cruelly rebuffed."

"Megan . . ."

Why did he hesitate? At this rate, she'd sooner charm herself than coax Gabriel to take her hand.

"What?" she asked, rather reasonably, she thought.

"I'm not one of your damned beaus," he finally blurted,

"to be charmed and petted and coaxed into doing what you want."

As if she'd had beaus to begin with. Why did he persist in speaking as though she had—and dozens of them, at that? Aloud, Megan said, "I don't see why not."

He scowled harder. "I do. And the fact that *you* don't is all the more reason why I ought to."

"You're talking in riddles."

It wasn't as if she meant to make some sort of untoward advance to him. This had nothing to do with wanting to feel his fingers brush against her skin. Nothing to do with wanting the thrilling contact of his hand clasping hers. Nothing whatsoever to do with needing to return some of the battling spirit to his soul or adding that aggravating cockiness back to his smile.

No, indeed.

This had to do with forcing a little humanity into that mean-spirited Pinkerton armor he shielded himself with, and making sure he'd recognize the truth about her father's innocence when she showed it to him later.

Gabriel reached for his flat-brimmed black hat and held it at his chest, ready to put it on. "I'm not holding your hand any more than I'm going to jump onto this table and sing 'Yankee Doodle.' Show me what you brought me here to see. Or we're leaving."

"Take my hand. Or I won't show you," Megan countered.

"You're being unreasonable."

"So are you."

He rubbed his fingers against his hat brim. Thinking, she guessed. Finally Gabriel said, "This isn't worth arguing over."

"Then do it." She nodded toward her outstretched hand. "If it's as meaningless as you say, it shouldn't bother you to touch me."

His answering stare would have sent a lesser woman under the table to hide. Luckily, Megan counted herself well fortified against it, so she stared right back and waited for his reply.

"It doesn't bother me to touch you," he said bluntly.

Was that disappointment she felt? Surely not.

Until he pounded his opinion home by adding, "I could touch you all day. All night." Gabriel lowered his voice and slowly, in a tone fraught with meaning, murmured, *"All over."*

Obviously she'd misread him, if he could taunt her with his indifference to her this way. "Fine, fine!" Megan burst out, not needing any more reminders of all the ways a man might find her lacking. "I understand."

Before she could surrender to common sense and take her arm from the table, Gabriel's large, warm hand slid over hers. With an assurance born of having her all but beg him to hold her, he threaded their fingers together and glared up at her.

"Happy?" he asked.

Slightly bedazzled by the sight of their joined hands, Megan looked up, too. She'd bested him! At least in this small way. As long as she could pile up victories, hope still remained of helping her father.

"Because you *look* downright smug," Gabriel went on, his features hardening into what she took for suspicion . . . and a goodly amount of poor sportsmanship.

She shook her head, hoping to rattle her good sense back in place. "Happy? Almost. Move your chair a little closer."

He raised his eyebrows. "Are you always this demanding?"

A gusty sigh escaped her. "Are you always this molasses slow? At this pace, I'm surprised your suspects don't pass on from old age before you ever catch up with them."

Stone-faced, Gabriel inched his chair closer. She supposed that counted as cooperation when dealing with someone like him.

Turning her wrist so her hand lay on top, she drew a deep breath. She looked at the angular lines of his profile, sent up a quick wish that she was doing the right thing in confiding in him, and then began.

"When you were a little boy," Megan said, "did you ever go someplace special with your folks? Someplace you could never have got to alone, where things were different than anywhere you'd ever been?"

She stopped to look at him, awaiting his answer. While she'd been talking, Megan saw, he'd turned their hands so his lay on top. Wanting the upper hand, of course— even literally. How typically Pinkerton of him.

He shrugged.

Undaunted, she went on. "Well, I did. And Hop Kee's was the place I'd go to. Every year, when it was time to pay taxes on the stage station, my father would bring me to town with him." A faint smile crossed her face at the memory. "My mother used to say it was the only time things at the station were really clean, when my papa and me were both gone."

Gabriel smiled, too. He stroked his thumb over the back of her hand. "She sounds like my mother."

"I doubt it," Megan said flatly. Her mother had been unlike anyone she'd ever heard of, at least, so far as she knew. And what recollections she had of Emmaline Kearney's playful nature had turned bitter long ago, with the remembrance of what had followed.

"Anyway," she went on, "one year things were especially hard. Nothing was . . . nothing was going right at the station, and I couldn't wait to get to the *presidio* and forget those troubles for a while."

It was the year her mama had left, but the last thing Megan intended was to tell him that.

"And you came here?" he asked.

Blessedly, she felt her smile return. She nodded. "Yes. The Celestial Kitchen was new then, and Mr. Kee had just come to Tucson. I'd never met a Chinaman before. When I saw the paper lanterns and the statues and the gilded mirrors from outside, I begged my papa to bring me in."

Gabriel's hand squeezed hers, offering more comfort than she would have expected. "I'll bet he couldn't refuse you much, either." His grin widened, as though his compliment held a keen-edged finish. "You probably jawed at him until he agreed. Poor man."

Megan narrowed her eyes at him. "I have half a mind to poke you in the ribs for that remark, Agent Winter. Didn't anyone ever teach you how to listen to a story?"

"No. I never cared much for fairy tales."

"Not even as a boy?" She paused, thought over what she knew of him so far, and said, "Never mind. I don't think I need to know anything quite that sad in the middle of a perfectly nice evening."

"Ignoring the truth doesn't make it any less real."

He took his hand away, leaving her missing the soothing rasp of his thumb on the back of her hand. Sharply aware of how much she'd enjoyed having him touch her, Megan folded her hands in her lap and did her best to forget the sensation.

What else could she do? It was beyond foolish to want closeness this much, especially with a man like Gabriel. Beyond reason, when she knew perfectly well no one could be relied upon to keep that closeness alive.

After a moment, he propped his elbow on the table, put his head in his hand, and asked, "Did your father bring you here, like you asked?"

His interested gaze invited her to go on with her story. Somehow, the hardness that had appeared in his expres-

sion over the notion of sharing fairy tales had disappeared,
too. *An interrogation technique, probably. Honed at the side of
Allan Pinkerton himself.* She ought to be wary, Megan knew.
But looking at the man across the table from her, she
found it hard to muster the defenses she needed.

It was funny how the tension between them could rise
and fall like this. Sparring with Gabriel Winter was like
trying to swim upstream in an *arroyo.* However much you
thought you were getting where you wanted to go, however
hard you kicked and fought and swam, you still wound up
at the same bend in the stream you'd started from.

Why hadn't the Pinkerton agency sent her a man as
placid as the waters of Silver Lake to deal with? Instead,
she had this man who seemed peaceful on the outside . . .
but on the inside, had all the tranquillity of river water
over rocks.

She gazed up at him, determined not to betray her
struggles. "No, he didn't bring me here that day. There
was a load of lumber to be brought to the station, or wagon
wheels or something—I'm not quite sure. Whatever it was,
we had to head straight back home without stopping."

Megan remembered jouncing over the miles of road
between Tucson and Kearney Station, bawling so hard
she'd nearly gotten her seven-year-old self tumbled out of
their buckboard wagon in her inattention. Her father had
snatched her back by the ruffle on her best Sunday dress,
and set her beside him again without a word of rebuke.
He'd given her his handkerchief to wipe her tears with
instead, and looked as though he'd wanted to use it himself.

She hadn't understood the reasons for his sadness then.
Now she did, and felt all the sorrier for it.

"You must have been disappointed," Gabriel remarked.

Megan glanced away from his sympathetic expression.
Her tale had turned hard enough to tell, without his pity

to cope with, too. "I was fit to be tied. For weeks I needled him, trying to make Papa go back into town and visit the Celestial Kitchen. I wanted to see it on the inside, and I wasn't going to quit until I did."

"Imagine that. You not quitting."

Sitting a little straighter, she fluttered her fan toward him. "Laugh all you want. It worked. My father brought me here only a few weeks later, and we've been coming here every year on tax day ever since."

His expression turned contemplative, as though he'd guessed there was more to the story but wasn't sure what it was. After a few minutes, Gabriel asked, "Were you satisfied, once you got inside?"

"No."

He laughed. "No? All that caterwauling for nothing?"

"Not exactly." Mimicking him, Megan propped her elbow on the table, then leaned her head against the palm of her hand. "You see, one of the station hands had a book. *The Celestial Atlas*, it was called, and it had the most wondrous pictures of constellations in it." She paused, remembering the striking images of the Gemini twins, the crab, Cassiopeia, and all the others, drawn in bold white against a night-sky black paper background. "I must have looked at that book for hours. I would have slept with it beneath my pillow, if I could have, but Addie wouldn't let me."

"Your station's cook."

It wasn't a question. Chilled to recall the many things Gabriel most likely knew about her family, Megan raised her head and got on with finishing her story. Either this would work, or it wouldn't. Either this would remind him of the goodness in the world, or not. She had to try.

"Yes. Anyway, after so long looking at that *Celestial Atlas* book, I was plumb certain there would be stars in here"—

feeling wistful, she waved her hands in the air to illustrate—
"everywhere. Just like magic."

"No. Just like the book."

Giving him a sharp-eyed look, Megan nodded. "Just like
the book," she agreed. What had made her hope he would
understand the magic, the whimsy, she'd once dreamed
of finding? "I was too young to know that sometimes 'celestial' meant a particular thing had come from China—"

"—and not necessarily the heavens."

"Yes."

He sat back in his chair. "Too bad you got the Chinaman's version of heaven, instead of a little girl's."

"That was exactly what I thought, at the time." With a
start, Megan realized he *did* comprehend part of what
she'd been hoping for, after all. Surprise uncurled inside
her, taking shape someplace beside those shivery feelings
his kiss had caused before. "But I was wrong."

Gabriel quirked his eyebrow, then absently leaned forward and picked up one of the empty porcelain rice bowls
from their table's center. He turned it in his hands, staring
down at it while he listened to her speak.

"Wrong in what way?" he asked.

"Wrong in not believing the Celestial Kitchen could be
what I wanted. Wrong in not believing that someone loved
me well enough to make it come true, somehow."

He didn't understand. She could see it in the lazy progress the delicate bowl still made from hand to hand, in
the casual bend of his head as he watched it move. Maybe
no one had ever tried stealing the heavens for Gabriel,
and that was what lent that wintery cast to his heart.

She went on. "But my father *did* love me well enough. On
the second time I came here, he and Hop Kee explained to
me that we had dined at the wrong table the time before,
and they brought me right here to this table instead."

Thumping her palms atop the smooth linen tablecloth

between them, Megan issued him her most challenging look.

He, being a Pinkerton man, and too mule-headed for his own good, only frowned. "So?"

"So this is where the heavens and China come together. And seeing it was what made me decide to always believe first—no matter how wrong everything might seem to be. *Look.*"

She reached out to touch his shoulder, gesturing with her other hand toward the ceiling. Postponing the revelation for herself, she watched Gabriel closely as he turned his face upward.

The reflection of the stars cast a glow on his image. Only cut-tin, and hand-fashioned at that, they sparkled from the ceiling directly above their table and no other. They gleamed in quantities too numerous for a little girl to count, and brought the celestial wonder she'd yearned for straight to a bachelor Chinaman's restaurant in the heart of the Tucson *presidio.*

"My papa cut out every one of them himself," Megan told Gabriel, "and he and Mr. Kee nailed them up just in time for my second visit here. They brought the heavens down to meet me."

Memories of the awe she'd felt on that long-ago day returned, and Megan made no attempt to hold them back. The tears they brought to her eyes were needful ones, no matter how bittersweet they felt today.

Across the table, Gabriel's watery image only looked upward, filled with a stillness she hadn't glimpsed before. It was impossible to tell if he felt the same magic she had.

"There are eighty-nine of them." Surreptitiously, she dabbed the tears from her eyes and sniffed. "I learned to count right in this chair, squinting up at my stars until I'd summed up every one."

Her papa had sworn she'd turn herself stone-blind

before learning to tally such high numbers all by herself. But Megan had known better. And just as long as Joseph Kearney had stayed across from her at the table, with his pipe and his cherry tobacco and his copy of the *Weekly Arizonan*, she'd had the courage to keep trying. And she'd succeeded in the end.

Just as she intended to triumph over Gabriel Winter.

Surely he couldn't remain unmoved in the face of all this. Smiling to herself, Megan transferred her gaze from the tin stars overhead to Gabriel.

"So you see? All I needed was a little faith, all along." She laid aside her fan, wishing he would say something, anything, that would reveal how her China heavens had affected him. "And now I have it. Whenever I start to feel my faith in life waver, I come here to Hop Kee's. Somehow just seeing all those stars again sets everything a little bit straighter."

She cleared her throat against the tears threatening to choke off her voice, and added, as fiercely as she could, "So what do you have to say to that, Agent Winter?"

In response, Gabriel reached across the table. He slipped his hand inside his suit coat, the same suit coat still wrapped warmly around her shoulders, and wormed his fingers around the inside pocket sewn within. Megan went dead-still, partly fearing the brush of his fingers against her, and partly anticipating it. A moment later, he took out a man's linen handkerchief.

He gave it to her, then stood. "I'd say it's too bad I didn't come here on tax day." He watched her from his position beside the table, looking darker than ever before . . . and twice as immovable. "I'd have found your father already, and not wasted all this time talking."

Shock made her fingers clench on the handkerchief he'd offered. "*What?*"

"You heard me." Hard as carved marble, he put on his

hat and held out his hand to help her from her chair. "Dry your eyes. We're leaving. I have a job to do."

Megan stared at his outstretched hand, feeling like slapping it away. Always gentlemanly, Gabriel Winter remained so—even while twisting the knife into her heart. Battered with sudden despair, she closed her eyes at the realization of what his behavior meant.

Her ploy hadn't worked. Hadn't softened him, hadn't taken an ounce from the freight wagon's weight of cynicism he carried, hadn't furthered her cause in the least. She'd revealed one of her most cherished memories to him ... and somehow, had hardened the Pinkerton man against her still further. What was she supposed to do now?

Gabriel wasn't waiting for her to decide. With an impatient exhalation of breath, he tugged her to her feet.

"Take heart, sugar," he said, oblivious to the twisted handkerchief Megan hurled at his chest. "When your papa gets there, maybe you can paste up stars in the jailhouse for him."

Ten

He should have sent McMarlin, Gabriel decided later that evening, instead of leaving him at the hotel to guard Megan Kearney.

To be sure, Carlotta Roma's house on Maiden Lane was one his old friend would appreciate. He could easily picture Tom on one of the parlor's two red velvet settees, a cigar clamped between his teeth, one fist full of whiskey and another full of money to buy up time with the ladies of the house.

That time did not come cheaply. Already, Gabriel had gone through a considerable quantity of the money he'd taken with him from the Cosmopolitan Hotel, and so far he'd only spoken with two-thirds of the ladies in question. At this rate, he'd sooner be wiring the Pinkerton office in Chicago for more money than he would be learning anything new about Joseph Kearney's whereabouts.

Wearily, he passed a hand over his face. The motion temporarily blotted out the colorful image of the fancied-up painted lady seated beside him. Unfortunately, it did nothing to diminish the powerful effect of her lavender perfume. The scent of it filled the air between them, so strongly his eyes fairly watered.

"Then you know the man I'm speaking of?" Gabriel asked her, more than ready to have their business concluded. "You've seen him here before?"

The woman, Elsa, twirled her fingers through her unbound blond hair and giggled. "Can't rightly say, darlin'. I have lots and lots of visitors, you know."

"I'm sure you do." For her benefit, he produced a smile. "Doña Carlotta told me you were one of her most popular ladies. Looking at you now, a man could certainly see why."

Her answering giggle should have stolen some of Gabriel's reluctance to cajole her into telling him what he needed to know about Kearney. It did not.

He hated this part of his work, plain and simple. Hated the deception needed to succeed in it, the subterfuge called for to drag secrets from reluctant witnesses. He'd told Doña Carlotta he was a man seeking an old partner—Joseph Kearney—to buy out his interest in a joint business venture. From all appearances, the madam had believed him.

Most likely, all her "ladies" believed him, too, including Elsa. But Gabriel could take no pride in his skillful undercover work, and he had no heart for charming yet another woman—this one only a girl. Behind her rouged and powdered features, low-cut gown, and string of gaudy paste jewels, Elsa couldn't have been more than a sweet-faced girl of fifteen years. Too young for working on her back. Too young for being misled by the likes of a Pinkerton man on a case.

Setting aside his bottle of ginger beer, Gabriel withdrew his wallet from his inside coat pocket. "I find it takes some folks a little longer than others to remember the kinds of details I need to know," he said. "I'd be obliged if you'd sit with me a while and think on it, Elsa."

"All right." Agreeably, she struck a new pose atop the settee's worn red velvet. With a hopeful air, she glanced at the clock on the mantel of the cold, ash-strewn marble fireplace beside them. "Miz Carlotta said you paid for ten minutes, so I reckon you ought to get all of them."

"Kindly put. I can see you're a woman who takes customer satisfaction seriously."

"I do." She took money seriously, too. As he'd expected, Elsa's gaze fixed on his wallet. "All my customers are satisfied," she assured him. " 'Cepting maybe the ones who get too drunk to see the deed done proper, if you follow my meaning. But that won't be a problem with you, just drinking ginger beer and all. You a teetotaler, mister?"

"No." *Just a man with a job to do, and the clear head needed to do it with.* "Just a man wanting to avoid those problems you talked about."

He winked. She giggled. The girlish sound of her laughter made him want to shove all the money he had at her, if only she'd quit working at Doña Carlotta's house—an urge about as allover impossible as the one he felt to quit working as an agent.

Working with the Pinkertons was all he'd ever known, all he really knew how to do. Gabriel had never planned for anything else. He'd never needed to.

Winter brings in the right man at the right time.

It should have been enough. Suddenly, it wasn't.

But he couldn't let it go.

Christ, no matter what it took, he would leave a clean record behind him. He'd start over someplace new, with something better than an operative's lonely life to look forward to. Just as soon as he found Joseph Kearney, and the proof he needed to document his case.

Elsa scooted closer, draping her arm along the settee's

carved cherrywood backrest. In her fingers, she dangled Gabriel's discarded bottle of ginger beer.

"In that case," she said, letting her hand travel suggestively up and down the bottle neck, "maybe I can 'courage you to stay a little longer. Sounds like you've got a theory what needs testing out."

Despite himself, he smiled at her ingenuity. It took a certain quantity of brass to approach a man like that, whether paid upfront for the task or not. "Another night, perhaps," he said. "Right now, I need to know if you've seen my friend, Mr. Kearney. It's mighty important that I find him."

Disappointment softened the rouge-reddened line of her mouth. Elsa raised her head, gazing about the parlor as though her answer might be found written on the fancy gray flocked wallpaper and ornate painted moldings.

"I don't recall if I've seen him or not," she said, taking a sullen slug of his ginger beer. "So many fellas come in and outta here . . . ."

One of them was Joseph Kearney, if the hints he'd gleaned from Hop Kee's cook at the Celestial Kitchen could be believed. His visit there after leaving Megan in McMarlin's care at their hotel had been more productive than he'd expected. Turned out, Gabriel had remembered far more of the Mandarin Chinese tongue than he'd expected.

Evidently, growing up in the shadows of opium dens had conveyed its share of lasting advantages on him.

He gazed at Elsa, taking in her crossed arms and willow-tree posture. With a woman like this, answers came only one way.

"Let's see if I can improve your memory," he said.

She gave him a suspicious look. Upon remembering what he held in his hands, though, the girl suddenly found the gumption to sit a little straighter. "I reckon my memory could use a little poke in the right direction, at that."

"I don't doubt it could."

Gabriel unfolded his wallet, absently noting the warmth it carried from being in his pocket. The same warmth must have been present earlier, too, he realized, struck by the knowledge that when he'd wrapped his coat around Megan to keep away the chill, the creased leather in his hands had spent the better part of an hour exactly where he'd thought about being.

Nestled up against the curvy warmth of her bosom.

His fingers stilled on the money he'd begun counting. Had she bewitched him, that he could sit an arm's length away from a desirable, readily available woman, and still be thinking of Megan?

Hell, no. He'd never cared much for bedding prostitutes, was all. Meeting Megan Kearney, with all her quick-stepping ways and sassy mouth and starched-over curves, had not a damned thing to do with it.

Gabriel stood, hat in hand. He threw a quantity of folded money on the low table fronting the settee, then added a card with the name of another agent at the hotel. "Leave a message for me here if you recall anything."

Overhead, the parlor's cut-glass chandelier chimed on a breath of wind, drawing Gabriel from his thoughts and firming his resolve to have this finished. He'd had all he wanted of tracking and searching . . . and battling with hardheaded women, at least for today.

From the front of Carlotta's house came the swoosh of a door opening on the surprisingly cool Territorial night. The tinny strains of a piano playing nearby grew louder, rising over the ever-present drone of cicadas. A mule brayed nearby, a dog's howl joined the chorus, and then the door closed. The room grew quiet again.

By the time he looked back at Elsa, she'd already

snatched up the money. Lips moving, she silently counted the bills he'd left, then stared up at him. "If this don't point my memory in the right direction, I don't know what will."

"See that it does."

The girl smiled and tucked the money into her bodice, sending another wave of lavender fumes upward.

Scent that strong ought to be outlawed, Gabriel thought. He refused to compare it to the subtler fragrances of roses and spice that Megan's skin carried, or to the faintly antiseptic tinge that overlaid those scents. He refused to contemplate the cockeyed pride he'd felt in identifying that smell, so uniquely hers, as the starch Miss Megan used on her crisp, high-necked dress.

And all fragrance aside, he refused to remember the shattered look on her face when he'd stared up at her China stars and pretended to feel nothing. When he'd told her he would have used her piece of little girl's heaven to capture her father quicker.

Heavyhearted, Gabriel put on his hat and went into the night. The next leg of his search lay only a few houses down Maiden Lane, past a home-sized brewery, a saloon, and a store advertising notions, patent medicines, and "lady's things." Staring at the partly shadowed gilt sign, he wondered if those "lady's things" included colognes and such.

If they did, he ought to stop on the way and buy Megan a bottle of lavender perfume. To be sure, they would both be better off if she used it.

By the time Gabriel rounded the alleyway corner leading to the back side of the Cosmopolitan Hotel, most of the lamplight inside the looming two-story building had been extinguished. Moonlight cast his shadow on the rough adobe wall beside him, and a musty-scented autumn breeze stirred his clothes as he walked on silent feet to inspect the rear of the hotel.

He couldn't shake the feeling of being followed. It had stuck with him all up and down Maiden Lane, inside a half-dozen brothels and out, and all the way to the stables a half-mile distant where he'd boarded his horse before coming here. The nagging feeling of being pursued was one a man didn't ignore.

Not if he wanted to stay alive.

Gabriel did.

Long practice had taught him a pinch of caution was worth double its effort in surprises avoided. With that in mind, and the force of habit setting his feet on a path around the hotel's grounds, he traveled the alleyway parallel to the hotel's rear.

Instinct kept him alert, and sharpened all the night sounds around him. Mice scuttled from one dark corner to the next, and the breeze pushed pages from a discarded *Arizona Citizen* across the wagon wheel–rutted dirt pathway. Overhead, the windmills that creaked incessantly to bring water to the *presidio* competed with the strains of distant saloon music and Spanish singing from the streets beyond.

He wished he had a whiskey. He wished he had a great hunk of saltwater taffy, to finish off the night with something sweet. He wished he had a soft bed waiting, piled high with enough pillows so a man could truly rest his bones without feeling like he was about to plummet clean through the mattress and onto the floor. He wished he had a woman in that bed waiting for him . . . a woman with lush brown hair and eyes shining with the reflections of a thousand cut-tin stars.

Or maybe eighty-nine.

Damnation. Thoughts like these would get him killed for sure.

Gabriel quickened his step, knowing he'd be better served to wish for something simpler. An answer to his case, a hard-certain lead to Kearney's whereabouts ... reason enough to sing, like those *troubadours* he'd heard before. Maybe the first two would lead to the third, and he'd be able to leave the Pinkerton life behind him without regrets—and without an unsolved case on his record.

The alleyway narrowed as he reached the area behind the Cosmopolitan's rear courtyard. Here, an adobe wall jutted into the pathway, its bulk intended to shelter the fountain and *Saltillo*-tiled hotel courtyard inside.

Gabriel slowed, listening hard. With its irregularly shaped wall and cover of concealing water sounds, this would be an ideal spot for an ambush. All he heard, though, were the muted sounds of water splashing into the fountain, and an accompanying feminine voice ... swearing?

"Drat those *bizcochitos!*" he heard next, followed by sounds of shoes—he surmised—scraping against something. A frustrated, feminine grunt followed, and then the night fell silent.

Only one voice he knew carried such determination, even wedded as it was to a lovely feminine form and misleadingly compliant manner. Only one woman he knew would be fool enough to scrabble around past midnight, and in the midst of the city, at that.

Megan Kearney.

Only one man he knew would look forward to the kind of homecoming that wildcat woman would offer. And Gabriel was standing in that man's boots.

Lucky him.

"Ooof!" *Drat this wall!* Slung halfway across it, Megan felt the thick adobe surface of the hotel courtyard's wall jab into her midsection for what had to be the third time straight. If she didn't hurry, the Pinkerton man would beat her inside the hotel.

And then he'd discover she'd been gone all along, despite the dapper and agreeable agent he'd left in charge of her care. Agent McMarlin couldn't have kept a dog from scratching its fleas, and the fact that he'd so readily accepted her need to take a sudden, unplanned-for, and luxuriously extended bath—*privately*—in her hotel room only proved it.

Even if it hadn't, the churchbell-loud snoring she'd heard issuing from his station outside her closed door not long after her tub of hot water had been delivered most assuredly would have. The man barely deserved his badge. In her opinion, she'd bested him easily.

Almost too easily.

Megan wished she could say the same for the blasted wall. It certainly hadn't seemed this large, or this slippery, when she'd climbed down from the balcony and clambered over it to follow Agent Winter earlier this evening. With rancor, she glared at the dark stubbled surface of her perch.

As though in answer, the wall sent a chill straight through her, one that easily penetrated the plain calico gown she'd changed into for her adventuring. *I will not wish to have Gabriel's toasty warm suit coat around my shoulders again,* she told herself staunchly. *And I will not let a pile of bricks defeat me.*

Not even if those bricks came complete with cold, mold, and the occasional pigeon dropping for decoration. She'd grown up running around the wild lands of the Arizona Territory desert, for heaven's sakes! Compared with the canyons and rocky hillsides she'd explored as a child, this measly wall was nothing.

Levering herself upward, Megan attempted to wrap her

hands around its edge and roll her body toward the beckoning safety of the hotel courtyard. Instead, she wobbled. Her locket and its chain swung forward from their hiding place inside the neckline of her dress, and clinked into the wall with an impact that made her wince. Forced to cling to the adobe like a gecko in the sun, she had to admit the obvious.

Her *bizcochito*-eating personage just wasn't up to the challenge of scaling walls and escaping from Pinkerton men. Or even escaping from one singular rogue-Irish Pinkerton man, with hardness in his gaze and a tenderness to his touch that made her shiver to recall it.

With effort, Megan shoved that remembrance from her thoughts. As someone with a two-foot wide wall to ascend, and quickly, she couldn't afford such distractions.

Besides, after all he'd said at Hop Kee's, she certainly knew better than to succumb to Gabriel Winter's heartless charm now.

And she knew as well not to let him capture her in the midst of undoing her earlier escape. She hated to think what his reaction would be. To be sure, it would involve those irons he bragged about carrying with him—and maybe even a cell at the county jail, too. For a lady! The man had no chivalry in him at all.

Goaded by visions of handcuffs and iron bars, Megan struggled harder to thrust herself up and over the wall. The worst of it was, she'd risked following Gabriel and had learned practically nothing about her papa's activities in town.

Doubtless that was because Gabriel had taken the most unlikely route possible to tracking her father. She hadn't the faintest notion why Agent Winter had insisted on visiting Doña Carlotta's house and so many others, when everyone knew respectable men like Joseph Kearney did not frequent such places.

Perhaps his activities hadn't been rigged toward tracking down her papa at all, she mused. Perhaps Gabriel had *personal* reasons for visiting Maiden Lane tonight.

Like wanting a dalliance with one of the "maidens."

Horror loosened her grip on the rough adobe she clung to. *He wouldn't!* a part of her protested, but the rest of her could all too easily picture the devilish Gabriel charming one of the ladies. He'd flatter her with compliments, all spoken with his deep, brogue-laden voice. He'd stroke her cheek, maybe curl his big gentle fingers around her nape and draw her closer for a stolen kiss. He'd look at her with that slumbrous, cat-with-cream expression in his blue-eyed gaze, and strike her breathless with the intensity it held.

Not that Megan cared one whit.

No siree. Not even half a whit.

The cad. Newly determined to best him, she dug her hands into the wide top edge of the wall and pulled. Her fingertips touched the edge, flexed . . . and then the nail on her little finger bent backward and snapped.

Squealing, Megan clutched her injured finger. Utterly unbalanced by the movement, she dropped to the alleyway below like a bucket of brass buttons shoved from a shelf.

"Ooof!" Dust billowed around her, stirred by the impact of her bottom hitting the dirt. A chill breeze whipped up the length of her stocking-clad legs, alerting her to the fact that her fall had also managed to toss her skirts in a jumble. Through tears of frustration, she glared up at the courtyard wall.

Outlined against it, bold as you please, was the shadow of a man. A very tall, very big, hat-wearing man.

Instantly, her throbbing finger vanished from her list of worries. So did the bedraggled state of her dress and the possibility of being caught by Gabriel Winter before she could return to their room and pretend to be asleep. Who but a *bandido* would be out past midnight, slinking through alleyways and preying on innocent women?

Her only possible defense was subterfuge, and Megan meant to use it. Forcing her fear-stiffened limbs to cooperate, she drew her heels beneath her body as though preparing to get up, then slumped face-first in the dirt, in her finest approximation of a dead faint.

No, just a plain garden-variety faint, she amended to herself, trying to keep her breathing steady. With luck, once the *bandido* behind her saw her collapsed on the ground, he'd skedaddle for livelier pickings straightaway.

That, or he'd peg her as an easy mark and come closer.

Filled with fear at the thought, Megan kept herself motionless and waited. Seconds later, she heard boot heels stamp across the alleyway. Her nose filled with the dust his footfalls raised, and she struggled not to sneeze. The scent of tobacco smoke drifted toward her. Sensing his nearness, she held her breath.

His shadowy bulk loomed over her. She cracked one eye open. The scuffed length of what she took for a boot trod past her nose, then stopped. Its mate joined it, as though the *bandido* stood beside her shoulder, deciding what to do with the fallen lady before him.

Megan needed no such lengthy deliberations.

Quick as she could, she snaked out her arm. She grasped a handful of trouser leg, boot, and ankle, and yanked with all her might.

The *bandido* lost his footing every bit as quickly as Mose always had, back at Kearney Station where he'd taught her this trick. With an incoherent yelp of surprise, the man smacked into the ground—no less painfully than he deserved, she felt sure—and lay momentarily motionless.

It couldn't last. Heart hammering, Megan surged to her feet and ran full bore down the alleyway. Never mind getting over the wall and eluding Agent Winter, she had bigger fish to fry now. It was almost enough to make her wish for the Pinkerton man's solid, undefeatable presence.

Almost.

Panting, she raced further. Was that the sound of footsteps following her? She couldn't stop to find out. Fearful that it was, Megan risked a backward glance over her shoulder . . . and ran straight into something hard, immovable, and undeniably human.

She shrieked, and a pair of warm strong arms closed tight around her. She'd escaped one *bandido*, only to be captured by another of his cohorts? Screaming, Megan struggled against her captor's iron grip. His hand clapped over her mouth, sealing off her screams. Seconds later, she felt herself being lifted and carried to the alleyway's darkest corner.

Her backside met cold adobe bricks. At her front, the new *bandido* pressed his body against hers with undeniable intent. His rapid-fire speech flowed over her, sounding hoarse and oddly familiar.

"Meg? Meg?" His hands roved over her, squeezing her shoulders, pulling her close, burying in the tangled mess of her hair. "Christ, I heard you scream and I couldn't get back here fast enough. What happened? Are you hurt?"

Dazed, she recognized Gabriel Winter's soothing brogue, acknowledged the blissfully familiar warmth of his hands stroking her hair back from her face. Whatever answer she might have made stuck in her throat, held there by the shock of hearing her name spoken so softly by him.

Meg, Meg. No one had ever called her that . . . and certainly not with such tenderness packed into the words. Relief, and something more she didn't dare consider, poured through her with all the sweetness of a sarsaparilla on a hot August afternoon.

"Are you hurt?" Gabriel asked again, stepping backward

a bit to take a closer look at her. "I swear, if you're hurt I—"

"It's nothing," she whispered, drawing her trembling hand to her lips. Lord, but he looked wonderful, even in the moonlight. Even in an alleyway, with a fallen *bandido* probably sneaking up behind them and danger 'round every turn. "I'm fine now."

"You're not." His gaze seared through her. "Any fool can see you've been weeping."

From the frustration of trying to escape you in time, Megan recalled, and decided to keep that revelation to herself. She didn't want to think about that now. All she wanted was a little more of the concern she'd heard in his voice, a little more of the safe feeling she'd experienced upon realizing it was Gabriel's arms that held her.

"Would you say it again?" she asked softly, unable to resist. "Would you please call me 'Meg' again, just once? I know I—"

His grasp stiffened, cutting short her words. "I never called you that."

She might have slapped him, for all the sweetness Gabriel showed her now. What was wrong with him?

"You did!" He had, and with the most beautiful bit of caring in his voice, besides. But she could hardly bring herself to ask him to say it nicely, not when he was being so intolerably stubborn about saying it at all. "You called me Meg just now, when you yanked me off the—"

"Yanked you? I kept you from running yourself full-chisel into that bakery building over there, or worse. That's what I did. You're lucky it's too late for buggy traffic."

"You're lucky I don't call out the sheriff and charge you with lewd conduct, after the way you manhandled me!"

Mad at herself and at him, Megan shoved away from the wall. Whatever had possessed her, to wish for kind words from Gabriel Winter's lips? He was her enemy, yet she continually forgot that fact. She should have known better than to ask him for anything at all.

It was disheartening to realize that, even as a spinster of twenty-eight, part of her still yearned to rely on someone other than her own lonesome self. Apparently her foolishness knew no bounds.

Feeling defensive, she looked up to see Gabriel gaping at her. His expression of disbelief didn't improve her mood.

"Lewd conduct? *Manhandled* you?" Shaking his head, he grabbed her arm and started tugging her down the alleyway in his wake. "Never mind telling me about how you're fine. I can see that for myself plain enough, since you're arguing like a fishwife. You're fine as you ever were."

Outraged, Megan jerked her arm from his grasp. *"Fish-wife?"*

"Yeah."

And the fool man seemed pleased about it, too! If she hadn't known better, she'd have sworn Gabriel savored his arguments with her. Was he mad?

He gave her an audacious smile. "Yeah," he repeated, nodding his head. "I'd say 'fishwife' about taps it."

He *was* mad. Why, everyone knew a respectable man wanted a woman who'd comply with his wishes, and never argue at all. Not being sure she could manage such a feat was one reason Megan had never pursued marriage.

The other was the fact that no man had courted her seriously, not with her father and Mose and all the other men at Kearney Station guarding the path to her door. Something about being like a sister to a dozen or so station hands tended to discourage gentleman callers. At least Megan hoped that was why they hadn't come calling.

She stopped in the middle of the wagon-wheel tracks dividing the path and put her hands to her hips, the better to glare at Agent Winter. Undaunted, he glared right back.

"You seem as though a fishwife is what you want," Megan challenged. "Fool as the notion may be."

A new grin softened Gabriel's features. "Fool to be sure. Seems I can't help myself when you come 'round."

He moved closer, then reached out his hand and tucked back a wisp of her hair. His fingers followed the curve of her ear, lingered, then lowered again. Looking into his face so near to hers, for the first time that night Megan glimpsed the weariness in his expression. Logic told her to press her advantage, maybe even escape him while she had the chance to go and warn her papa on her own.

She didn't have the heart to do so.

Especially not when Gabriel said such things to her as he had just now. *Seems I can't help myself when you come 'round.* His admission was enough to set any feminine heart aflutter. She had never felt more powerful . . . or more at risk of exposing her own mixed feelings to him.

"Then it's a good thing I still have my wits about me," Megan said, "seeing as how you've misplaced yours."

Gabriel sighed. To her surprise—surely it wasn't disappointment she felt—he didn't rise to the bait she'd tossed him. Instead, without speaking, he put his finger to the sensitive nape of her neck, then trailed it down the line of her locket's gold chain. He skimmed over her collarbone, little impeded by the open neckline of her calico dress.

Why didn't I put on something less mousy? Megan thought suddenly. Next to the ladies on Maiden Lane, she surely had all the elegance of a darned sock amidst fine embroidered silks.

But Gabriel, a man obviously more fond of the homespun in hand than fancies for sale at a price, didn't seem to care. He followed her locket's gold links still lower, setting her a-tremble with the slow surety of his touch. The subtle pressure of his hand gliding across her chest was an exquisite torture—something Megan had never in a million years expected to endure.

At last he reached the oval locket at her bosom. She felt him scoop it into his palm, felt the backs of his fingers brush over her bare skin as he cradled it.

He looked up. "I do want you," Gabriel said. " 'Twould be more than dangerous to deny it. I'm weary of fighting, and to tell you truly, more sorry for this than you'll likely believe."

"Sorry?" He was apologizing to her? Her thoughts boggled at the notion. But to be truthful with herself, more than his apology might have been at fault for that. The gentle back-and-forth contact of Gabriel's hand against the topmost slope of her bosom made all but the most rudimentary thought impossible. "Sorry for what?" she managed.

"In your shoes, I'd likely behave exactly as you have," Gabriel said, inexplicably and uselessly, when their situation couldn't possibly be reversed and his comment didn't begin to answer her question.

He rubbed his thumb over the carved flowers inlaid on her locket, then let it fall to her chest again. "But that doesn't mean I can let this go on, now does it?"

Megan wrinkled her forehead, trying mightily to make sense of his words. Seeing her confusion, he held out his hand, palm facing.

"Give me your hand."

He wanted to hold her hand? Perhaps he meant it as a prelude to an apology made on bent knee. After all that had transpired this night, she could almost believe it. There had hardly been a moment during their shared acquaintance when the Pinkerton man had failed to surprise her. Why should this moment be any different?

Already anticipating the sense of victory to come, Megan

held out her hand. "This really isn't necessary, Agent Winter. I realize you've simply done your job, and—"

"Good. I hope you'll keep that in mind."

Something heavy and cold circled her wrist. An instant later, it snapped into place, dragging her hand down with its weight. *Handcuffs.*

"No!" Ineffectually, she yanked her hand back.

Gabriel Winter's hand followed, thanks to their shared bonds. With no apparent effort at all, he pulled her hand back near his and clasped their fingers together in a mockery of affection.

"Behave," he warned, his eyes gleaming with galling amusement. "I'd hate to have to shackle those pretty ankles of yours, as well."

"You wouldn't."

His eyebrows rose. "Care to test me? I was about to go check on the fellow you clobbered"—he jerked his head toward the alleyway behind them, where the fallen *bandido's* motionless form could still be seen beside the courtyard wall—"but I could be persuaded to let the poor knuck lie there a while longer. Criminals get no pity from me."

And neither would her father, Megan knew, however innocent he must be. She brought her infuriated gaze to bear on Gabriel's face, and knew she could not let his comment pass unremarked upon, any more than she could accept his infernal manacles.

"I'm no criminal, and neither is my father." She shook her arm, feeling the awkward pull of the handcuffs, and wished she could use them to cosh Agent Winter over the head with. "These infernal things belong on the likes of him"—she nodded toward the *bandido*—"not me."

"Maybe. Or maybe not." He began walking toward the indentation in the wall that housed the fallen man, towing her along like a mutt on a leash. "But you've earned them,

I'd say, between escaping from McMarlin, tailing me through town—"

"What? I beg your pardon, but I—"

"—don't bother to lie about it." He held up his free hand to stop her automatic denial, then went on, "And assaulting men in the streets. I think you'll keep your handcuffs, at least a little longer."

Loud snoring drifted toward them as they reached the *bandido*'s temporary hideout. *At least he's alive*, Megan thought, shaken by the realization that he still hadn't moved. He must have struck his head on the courtyard wall when he'd fallen. Either that, or she'd sent him tumbling to the ground with more force than she'd thought. She'd never in her life walloped anyone so hard.

Mose would have been proud.

Gabriel stopped suddenly, forcing her to stop as well, else have her wrist yanked out of joint by the handcuffs. Glaring at them, she didn't notice at first the sudden stillness that had come over the Pinkerton man. When she did, Megan had the sense he had been standing silent for quite some time, as though waiting for her to notice something.

He nodded. "Yep, you'll be keeping your handcuffs," Gabriel repeated, staring thoughtfully at the man snoring near their feet. "I think Mr. McMarlin here will be wanting it that way."

Eleven

The refined elegance of the dining room was a point of pride at the Cosmopolitan Hotel, and when Gabriel entered it the next morning, he could see why. Immediately he felt welcomed, soothed by the familiar rustle of newspapers being read and the murmur of travelers' conversations all around him. The scents of brewed coffee and bacon sharpened his appetite, and lent a keen edge to his already prickly disposition.

He hadn't been forced to wait for a woman in years.

He was none too happy to be doing so now.

Frowning, he poured himself a cup of coffee from the silver-plated pot standing ready in the center of his table, then ordered breakfast for three—Megan, McMarlin, and himself. That accomplished, Gabriel turned his chair to better face the room's entrance. If he knew Megan Kearney, she'd take every moment he'd allocated to prepare herself for the day, and likely tack on half again as much time, too, just to prove she could. He'd never met a more vexatious female.

Or one who intrigued him more.

Damnation, but she got under his skin. At every turn she defied him. At every juncture, she tried to best him. The last opposition he'd expected to face was his suspect's spinster daughter. He didn't want to like her, but he did. Megan's determination and loyalty impressed him. Even knowing they were misplaced wasn't enough to change that.

He didn't know how long it had been since he'd believed in anything as strongly as she believed in her father's innocence.

Shaking his head, Gabriel opened his report book and propped it on his knee, then set to work penciling in an account of the work he'd done yesterday. Typically, he prepared the daily accounting required from each Pinkerton operative at night, and posted it to the Chicago office each morning. Last night, he realized as he stared at the half-filled page before him, had been the sole exception of his career.

Gabriel paused, pencil in midstroke. Was his lapse due to his growing dissatisfaction with a detective's lonely life of lost and found, hunter and hunted? Or was it because his attention had been on Megan, with her wily woman's ways and her penchant for troublemaking?

Neither, he decided. His handcuffs were at fault, along with the damned insistence he'd felt on using them. With McMarlin still sleeping off the combined effects of the lump on his head and the Irish whiskey that had allowed Megan to put it there, Gabriel had thought it prudent not to leave their suspect's daughter on the loose. Who knew what sort of havoc she'd wreak?

Undoubtedly, she'd have climbed from the window yet again, and gone to alert her father. The woman was tireless, clever ... and entirely too appealing between the clean-scented sheets of a hotel-room bed.

It had been years since he'd stayed 'til morning with a woman. Still longer since he'd spent the entire night simply sleeping with one. Something about the feel of Megan's warm, lithe body beside his, about the way she'd cuddled unknowingly against him in her sleep, left him unsettled.

Gabriel had enjoyed sharing his bed with her—even perforce—and not even McMarlin's snoring presence on the horsehair sofa just a few feet away had been enough to change that.

Neither had Megan's typically combative sleeping habits. When she'd first set to thrashing in her sleep, he'd thought her flailing arms and legs yet another ruse to earn her escape from him. Then he had suspected her moans and murmured cries a gambit to force McMarlin into intervening on her behalf. But when both had gone on past the few moments it had taken to awaken him, he had realized her restlessness was real.

As real as it was short-lived, once he'd coaxed her into his arms. Gabriel wanted to smile at the memory of Megan's body easing against his. Happy as a woman newly pleasured, she'd laid her head on his shoulder and breathed evenly once more. Possessive as a child with a favored toy, she'd spread her hand across his chest to keep him beside her, and lapsed into a deep, easy sleep.

And he, aroused as a man who'd spent years without knowing a woman's touch, had lain wakefully beside her ... hard and ready and needful.

Just as she'd planned him to, he'd wager. There was nothing he'd put past anyone who'd proved herself as sly and determined as Megan.

His scowl deepened. Refocusing on the page in his lap, Gabriel put aside thoughts of the lady for a thorough accounting of his search for the lady's father. He finished

his report, folded and sealed the pages, then slipped them
into his coat pocket for later mailing.

His fingers touched the thick folded paper already there.
The wanted poster he'd drawn on the train. Withdrawing
it, Gabriel sipped his coffee and considered his case. His
client, the foreman of a Tombstone mining outfit, had
hired Pinkerton operatives to track a missing shipment of
payroll sent special delivery on a stage that regularly passed
between the mine and Kearney Station. The strongbox
had arrived safely in Tucson several days later, but the ten
thousand dollars inside it had not.

All the evidence he'd gathered indicated theft by someone at the station. Logic suggested the man who reportedly
held the sole in-transit strongbox key, Joseph Kearney.
Circumstance pointed plainly to the same man, who'd
hotfooted it to Tucson with the money, just one step ahead
of the Pinkerton men in pursuit. If Kearney's sudden,
unexplained absence from the station wasn't a strong suggestion of guilt, Gabriel didn't know what was.

Like every other Pinkerton detective he knew, he based
his cases on a combination of experience, intuition, and
fact. The first two told him he was on the trail of the thief;
the last demanded he find proof of it.

When McMarlin left today to search the station, with
luck he would turn up Joseph Kearney's missing strongbox
key—or the original shipment instructions from the Tombstone mine foreman. Those instructions had dictated that
they be signed and included with the shipment as verifica-
tion of transit. Their absence in the strongbox implicated
Kearney as strongly as the foreman's accusing letter to the
Pinkertons had.

Somewhere, the manifests existed to prove that the stolen money had passed through Kearney's hands last. They
would be easy to find, Gabriel would wager. Harder still

would be finding the man himself, at least if yesterday's battles proved typical.

He wanted to get on with it. Filled with impatience, he looked toward the dining room's entrance again . . . and found himself nigh spellbound by the sight that greeted him there. Megan Kearney, outfitted in some sort of frothy blue dress and another of her bauble-bedecked hats, caught sight of him at the same moment and strode purposefully toward his table.

Her body, Gabriel realized as he watched, was every bit as contrary as the woman herself. Despite their buttoned-up confinement, her breasts bounced gently as she moved. Her hips swayed with an allure that should have been at odds with the stabbing progress her frilly parasol made at her side . . . but wasn't.

The vision in blue stopped at his table, bringing with her the mingled scents of rose water, hotel-provided coconut soap, and a goodly dose of dress starch. Smiling with pleasure at her arrival—surely he'd gone daft to be doing such a thing—Gabriel absently traced his fingers along the folded creases in the wanted poster lying on the table before him.

As though drawn there by his movements, Megan's gaze fell upon it. "I see you like to begin your morning's allotment of devious plotting straightaway, Agent Winter," she said. She smiled sweetly and seated herself beside him with mock companionability. "I hope it gives you indigestion."

If it did not, her quarrelsome morning mood likely would. Evidently, sleeping in irons didn't agree with her, and she intended to let him know it. Why he should care what Megan thought of him, Gabriel didn't know. All he knew was that he did—and he wanted to stop doing it.

Slowly, deliberately, he rolled the wanted poster and tucked it inside his coat pocket. "I hope it leads me to your father. Or had you forgotten I have a job to do?"

"A job?" She lifted her arched brows in mock surprise. "If tracking an innocent man like a beast, destroying his family and livelihood, and dragging his name through the mud constitutes work, then half the outlaws in this territory ought to consider themselves gainfully employed!"

"I have no doubt they do. Some of the most industrious men I've known have been criminals."

"Humph. Perhaps their influence has rubbed off on you."

Gabriel smiled. "You consider me hardworking, then?"

"No, dishonest." Megan twisted sideways to stab the hooked end of her parasol over the back of her chair, then picked up her folded linen napkin. She whipped it open, all but polishing the end of his nose in the process.

"I suppose it's not terribly surprising," she went on blithely. "A person can hardly be expected to spend all his time dealing with outlaws, and not become at least a little bit like them."

"I might say the same of you." He leaned back in his chair and folded his arms. Spoken aloud, the thought grew new roots. If Joseph Kearney were a criminal, could his daughter be innocent of that fact? "You said yourself that you and your father were close."

"Stop talking about him as though he were already gone!"

He gave her a cat-and-mouse smile. "Isn't he?"

"No," she said stubbornly. "He is not."

"Then you know where he is." Gabriel leaned forward, urging her without words to come closer as well. He lowered his voice. "Give over, Megan. Let's have this finished between us, and go on to finer things."

She looked away, as though fortifying herself against his words, his intimate tone, his cajolery. "I can't imagine what you're suggesting. And I don't need you or anyone else to tell me what to do. I'm a woman fully matured—"

"I can see that plain enough."

"—and I'll do as I like. I don't intend to rely upon anyone, Agent Winter. *Least of all you.*"

With her pronouncement finished, she raised her chin. Her spirited brown eyes dared him to oppose her. Without wanting to be, Gabriel found himself at once intrigued and aroused by her fighting spirit. No mealymouthed miss was Megan Kearney. The man who won her heart—and her body—would have to fight to claim both for his prize.

He'd also have to be daft as a post and lacking in both reason and self-preservation.

Hiding his grin, he vowed to avoid all those hazards— and to win her cooperation in spite of it. Strong-willed though she was, Megan had it in her to compromise. He knew it after last night.

Sensing her weakening, even if only a little, Gabriel pressed his advantage harder. "Tell me where to find Joseph. It's the right thing to do, the thing I would do in your place."

Her expression turned truculent. "For my father's sake, I'm glad your lack of loyalty is not contagious. I have *faith,* Agent Winter, even if you do not."

Frustration welled within him. He'd never known anyone more damned immovable, more senselessly determined to shove starry-eyed belief where it didn't belong. Didn't she understand? Faith could waver. Faith could die. Faith could vanish in a moment. *Facts never would.*

"No. What I do not have is more patience for lies," he ground out. "Where is he?"

"You can't seriously imagine I would tell *you.*"

Her killing glare ended their conversation abruptly. In an excellent imitation of a woman dining alone, Megan picked up the folded newspaper at the edge of their table and snapped it open.

Brought short by her sudden withdrawal, Gabriel stared

at the printed *Arizona Citizen* headlines facing him. The sight of them did nothing to improve his state of mind. The newspaper, the same one he'd seen before encountering Megan in the alleyway last night, only served to remind him of their meeting . . . and all that he'd said while he held her.

Meg, Meg.

He wanted to groan at the remembrance. What had possessed him? At the sound of her struggle with McMarlin, he'd been struck with a fear unlike anything he'd ever experienced. And at the feel of her warm, curved body in his arms, he'd been blasted with an emotion too uncontrollable to deny.

Lust, he told himself. *Nothing more.* Most likely, Megan had felt it, too. It was the only explanation for the way she had lingered in his arms.

Why else, when they were enemies?

For an instant, when she'd accepted his comfort so eagerly, Gabriel had felt tall enough to snatch real stars from the sky. Proud enough to kneel at her feet to give them over. But reality had returned when she'd asked him to say again the endearment that had slipped from his lips.

Meg, Meg.

Damnation. Nothing like this had ever happened to him before. Not on a case. Not ever. And he swore now that it never would.

Shaking his head, Gabriel stared across the table at Megan's fingers clenched tightly against the *Citizen.* Doubtless she felt more comfortable behind several inches of newsprint and animosity than she had with only the easily shed clothes and honor that had stood between them last night.

She slanted him a glance across the top of her newspaper. He'd had kinder looks from men in irons being dragged to jail. In no mood for more games, he scowled straight back.

She sniffed and went back to her reading.

Inexplicably, his mood softened toward her. His wariness, on the other hand, remained. If she'd held a knife at that moment, he had little doubt she'd use it—to escape from him, if nothing else. Grimacing, he slid her heavy silver butter knife from her place setting nearer to his. What had possessed him, to spend his time in Tucson with a she-devil like Megan Kearney?

His case, Gabriel remembered, and issued her a level look. If he hoped to enlist her cooperation, he couldn't go on tussling with her.

He forced a stiff-feeling smile to his face. "In any case, sugar, the wait was worthwhile. You look beautiful."

"Humph." She put down her newspaper in preparation for further battle and then tossed her head, making the doodads on her hat wobble. "You needn't bother wasting your Irish blarney on me. Your flattery can hardly turn my head, now that I know what you're really about, Agent Winter."

"Gabriel," he reminded her. "And I haven't a speck of blarney in my nature." He smiled at her obvious, open-mouthed skepticism. "It's more than flattery when it's true."

In the midst of reaching for the coffeepot, Megan paused. Only inches away from the gleaming silver handle, her fingers trembled; and beneath her hat's gaudy brim, her brows snapped together. Whether because of flattery, truth, or something else, the lady was not as unaffected as she wanted to seem.

Pressing his advantage, he said, " 'Tis true, Megan. You're a rare sight to behold."

And a handful to reckon with.

No sooner had he made the observation than she whisked her hands beneath the white linen tablecloth and folded them in her lap.

"Stop. Just stop!" Megan raised her pleading gaze to his. "Save your sweet talk for someone more gullible than me. I'll not believe a word of it."

To his shock, he saw that tears shimmered unshed in her eyes. They captured the light from the dining room's crystal chandelier, splintering it with pain. In the moment before Megan looked down again, a kind of defiant hurt hardened her expression.

Dumbfounded, unable to see her face clearly while she kept it downturned, Gabriel stared instead at the silk flowers and bows at the crown of her hat. He could have sooner named all the geegaws spread before him than he could have made sense of her reaction.

How could it be that their sparring troubled her less than his compliments did?

Her response confounded him. It was, like her, contrary above all and nigh impossible to deal with.

He'd wounded her somehow. He didn't know how, or why, but all at once Gabriel wanted to steal the sadness from her soul. He yearned to replace it with something real and lasting and glad.

The notion that he wanted nothing so much as to make Megan happy astonished him. It had to be some trick of their closeness yesterday—and all through the night, thanks to their shared handcuff bonds. It had to be some form of madness, specially spun by a woman set on deceiving her way past the Pinkertons and Gabriel alike.

It felt like madness and more. But the tears in her eyes were real, and so was the unaccountable impulse he felt to wipe them away.

Gabriel touched her chin, urging her face to turn toward his. "Why can't you believe it? The evidence is here in my hands. I'd rather see your face frowning at me"—she wrinkled her nose with irritation—"than any other face lit up with joy."

It was true, he realized. God help him. He wanted Megan Kearney, and no other woman would do. Though she hadn't seemed precisely beautiful to him at first, now Gabriel couldn't begin to remember why.

Her eyes widened. He felt the renewed tremor in her fingers as she raised them to his wrist. Belatedly, he realized she was trying to wrest away his hand.

He didn't want to let her go.

After a moment, she jerked her chin away. Blinking rapidly, she delivered the rebuke he should have expected . . . but hadn't.

"A lie for every occasion." She smiled thinly. "How resourceful of you."

Remembrance struck him. Compared with her poisonous tongue, the kick in the shin she'd given him when they'd met had been nothing at all. She had more defenses than an army's fort, and better weaponry than all the Pinkerton operatives combined.

Too bad she hadn't mustered those defenses for the sake of something—or someone—worthwhile. Admirable as it was, Megan's continued support of her father was misguided as hell. She'd be better off to recognize it.

And Gabriel would be better off to remember it.

"Do you think I'd be a spinster," she went on, "if I were really as attractive—"

"—beautiful."

"—as you say? Everyone knows a man wants beauty and obedience in a wife, Agent Winter, and I can muster neither. Not that I should care to," she added quickly.

Her moods changed with the swiftness of odds at a gambling table, and with just as little predictability. Typical of a woman . . . but maddening as hell. If he emerged from this case with his wits intact, Gabriel figured it would be a miracle. Still, he was willing to go along with her apparent lightheartedness, especially since she'd stopped crying, and to go on arguing in her favor.

"Beauty and obedience? You possess at least one of those qualities in abundance." Grinning, awash in a sense of relief he refused to consider more deeply, he filled her cup with coffee and replaced the silver pot in its place. "The other can be obtained easily enough."

"Conveniently said, for a man with shackles in his pocket." Megan frowned into her cup, as though imagining it filled to brimming with arsenic along with the steaming Arbuckle's he'd poured. She spooned in some sugar, then shrugged as she stirred. "With accoutrements like that, your success is assured."

"I plan for it to be. In all things."

"Not if I can help it." She removed her spoon, then sipped her coffee and smiled. "Mmmm. That's better, thank you. I never feel quite right until I've had my morning cup."

"Obviously."

She pulled a face at him over the rim, but with her next sip Megan's expression turned downright pleasure-filled. The golden brown hue of her eyes mirrored her appreciation, as did the subtle blush warming her cheeks. Fascinated, Gabriel propped his elbow on the table's edge, put his hand in his palm, and watched her.

With tantalizing slowness, she licked her lips. "As for the other marriageable quality," she went on, waving her fingers airily, "that can be managed, too. Quite successfully. In fact, I believe it's worked its deception on you already."

"It has?"

"Yes." Looking self-satisfied, Megan settled into her chair and regarded him with a smirk. "Otherwise, you would never imagine me beautiful."

"I think I would."

She shook her head. "It's only my skill that makes you believe such a thing."

"Your skill?" This ought to prove enlightening.

"Yes. My skill at dressmaking. It's the only possible explanation." Her smirk widened into a prideful smile as she replaced her coffee cup in its saucer and then spread her arms high to the side, baring the lace-bedecked, high-buttoned bodice of her gown to his view. "I made this very gown, in fact, and altered my parasol to match."

"And your hat, as well?" Gabriel guessed.

She nodded and touched her hat's brim. "Yes, that too. I enjoy a bit of millinery now and again, but only as a sideline. For some reason, there's not the same demand for my hats as there is for my dresses."

As though wondering over the reason, Megan frowned briefly. Gabriel decided he'd be better served *not* to point out that her hats would make fine playthings for parakeets, or for old ladies' house cats. Instead, he kept his mouth shut.

In truth, he was becoming almost fond of her ridiculous headgear, except for the fact that it hid her hair—and oftentimes her face—from his view.

He wondered what she'd look like with her dark hair unbound and free. Last night she'd refused to loosen her hair beyond the long plait she'd uncoiled one-handed from the back of her head, too filled with fury at his handcuffs to indulge Gabriel's offer to unbraid it for her.

Now, he looked at the knot of freshly bundled hair at her nape, and wondered what it would feel like to sift his hands through its glossy length. He imagined it would be soft and thick, long enough to spill across a man's pillow or caress his arms and chest while he held her close.

Not that he'd fall prey again to such a dangerous, addle-headed move himself. Their nearness last night could never be repeated—especially while Megan was awake to recall it.

"You sell your creations, then?" he asked, hoping to turn his thoughts in a new, less temptation-laden direction.

To his surprise, she nodded. This dressmaking venture of hers was something Gabriel hadn't learned of during his preliminary investigations. It would explain much about her headstrong nature, though, if she really were engaged in business for herself, unlikely as the notion seemed.

"Yes, I do." Her eyes gleamed with enthusiasm. "I have for some time now, although orders are a bit hard to come by when I spend all my days at the station. Ladies are a bit scarce there, as you recall."

He thought of the giant, taciturn station hand Mose, and all the men working in the yard behind him. "That's true." He poured more coffee, and sipped. "But you're a grown woman, as you said. You should leave, and set up shop in town, where business is plentiful."

Her lips turned downward as she idly twisted her coffee cup in her hand. To all appearances, she was piqued at being offered advice.

"I intend to," she informed him archly.

"You do?" With interest, Gabriel leaned forward.

"Certainly. Just as soon as I've"—she paused, biting her lip in thought, then glanced up at him brightly—"that is, once I've gathered the necessary funds."

"Funds?"

"Yes. It takes money to open a shop, Agent Winter. Surely someone so worldly as you knows that."

Abruptly, she fell silent, seemingly consumed with spooning exactly the correct quantity of sugar into the new cup of coffee she'd poured. Curiously, Gabriel watched her.

Megan was hiding something. Something new, that he

hadn't been aware of before. Suddenly, Gabriel felt sure of it, and he wanted to kick himself for not questioning her more closely until now. Was it the location of the missing shipment of payroll? Her father's whereabouts?

Her own guilt?

He didn't want to believe it. Could not believe it. But the fact remained that, by her own admission, Megan Kearney spent her days at the stage station. Could she really be as uninvolved as he'd assumed with the station's business?

Unanswered questions filled his thoughts. The approach of a uniformed hotel employee cut short Gabriel's opportunity to have them said. With the burgeoning conversation between him and Megan waylaid, he could only watch as the white-aproned serving girl presented three plates laden with the griddle cakes and maple syrup, breakfast buns, and toasted bread with strawberry jam he'd ordered. Then, with a curtsy, the girl left them to their meal.

Smiling, Megan gazed down at her plate. "I see you have a bit of a sweet tooth. Do you suppose there's any sugar left in the kitchens, after this?"

"I hope so." Gabriel grinned back at her. Despite his new misgivings, the teasing, almost affectionate expression she wore loosened something inside him that until now he'd kept tightly held. "I'll probably want more later."

"You will?"

He nodded. Shaking her head with mock disbelief, she speared a bite of griddle cake and tucked the buttery, syrup-drenched morsel between her lips. Her tiny moan of delight increased his appreciation of maple trees and griddles tenfold.

"A man's appetite is a curious thing, sugar," Gabriel acknowledged, watching her close her eyes in apparent bliss as she chewed and swallowed. "Sometimes it won't be satisfied with less than the sweetest thing within reach."

Not even if that sweetness could cost him dearly. Deeply aware that what he'd learned this morning placed her squarely among his likeliest suspects, he kept his words teasing . . . but they were nonetheless true. He did want her, in spite of the ever-mounting reasons not to trust her.

Laughing, Megan eyed his overflowing plate. "I do believe you're more insatiable than most."

"Perhaps." He let his gaze slip to her breasts. *Definitely.* How she could hide such sweetness as that behind those stiff-starched, prissy dresses of hers was beyond his understanding.

He'd have dressed her in something softer and paler, something more befitting the woman he glimpsed underneath her defenses.

Something like bare skin, and little else.

Oblivious to his thoughts, Megan munched on a triangle of toast and smiled at him from across the table. Apparently, she had a fondness for sweetness, too. He could hardly believe she hadn't ordered fried eggs and bacon, just to be contrary.

Needing time to think about all that she'd said, Gabriel turned his attention to his meal. A thought nagged at him, all through his first cinnamon bun and partway through his first slice of toast. It wasn't until he reached for the dish of extra jam the serving girl had left, and glimpsed the third filled plate at the place setting to his side, that he realized what it was.

He put down his fork and gazed pointedly at Megan. "So," he asked, folding his hands, "what have you done with McMarlin this time?"

Twelve

The bite of toast in Megan's mouth turned to sawdust at Gabriel's question.

What have you done with McMarlin this time?

Dismay stopped her mouth in midchew. Forcing herself to go on munching as cheerily as she could, lest Gabriel guess how well he'd unbalanced her already this morning, Megan pondered his question.

Doubtless, Agent Winter believed she'd done something terrible. Especially after last night. She still found it hard to believe that she'd taken on a Pinkerton man in the midst of a dark alley, even while scared out of her wits, and won.

She hoped last night's success boded well for her efforts with Gabriel. Realistically, though, she realized those hopes might be a trifle optimistic. The man seated across from her seemed far stronger and faster—and measurably more daunting—than his cigar-smoking cohort.

Even Mose hadn't been foolhardy enough to challenge Gabriel Winter directly.

Slowing her chewing to buy time to think, Megan tried to summon up a bit of the iron-shackled ire she'd come downstairs to the dining room with. Being handcuffed to Agent Winter—being forced to *sleep* with him—should have been the ultimate humiliation.

Instead, it had proved not half so arduous as she'd feared. In truth, parts of her overnight confinement had been surprisingly pleasurable . . . like waking up suffused with the kind of warmth no rising sun alone could kindle, and finding herself held close in Gabriel's strong, hard-muscled arms.

Her body fairly tingled at the memory . . . not that she meant to reveal as much to him. The scoundrel deserved whatever regrets she'd heaped upon him when she'd arrived at breakfast, Megan assured herself. In fact, he deserved worse, just for daring to serve up such an audacious smile to her when he'd first spied her in the dining-room doorway.

To be the recipient of such obvious masculine favor, especially from a man like Gabriel, had thrilled her to the tips of her poor spinster's toes. And beyond.

At least it had until she'd come to her senses, and realized what a sham he must be trying to play on her again.

Clearly, he meant to use every weapon at his disposal to persuade her to give away her father's whereabouts. That potent charm of his was just another of those weapons, not the genuine fondness Megan sometimes found herself foolishly hoping for. If only she could make herself remember it!

In all, though, for a man who would put an innocent woman in chains, Gabriel had proved remarkably tender as a sleeping companion. Despite the fact that his tall, lean body had felt large enough to sprawl over the entire four-poster bed they'd shared, he had gallantly made room for her on one side. He'd fluffed up her pillow, offered to find extra quilts if she was cold beneath the coverlet, brought her a glass of cool water from the *olla* in the corner.

Of course, she'd had to shuffle along behind him while he did it, thanks to their shared handcuffs. But his intentions had been kindhearted, at least.

In short, Gabriel had cared for her.

To assuage his guilty conscience, Megan reminded herself. After all, she wasn't his suspect. Her father was! Perhaps he'd realized the questionable ethics of all but kidnapping a suspect's daughter, and meant to make amends with her today.

If so, he was off to a mighty slow start.

"Well?" he prompted, drawing his eyebrows together.

She frowned at his demanding tone. He was most certainly off to a slow start, if this was his way of mending fences with a person.

Since time had done nothing to prepare her for answering his question, Megan surrendered to the inevitable. She swallowed her toast and gave him her bravest look.

"I believe Agent McMarlin has left the hotel," she said coolly. With interest, she noted the flush creeping into Gabriel's lean cheeks. Yes, this ought to take his mind off questioning her quite nicely, she figured. "Something really ought to be done about him, don't you think so? The man is far too lax in his duties."

"*Lax?*"

"Yes." Calmly cutting herself another bite of the hotel kitchen's delicious pancakes, with hopes of reawakening her rapidly failing appetite, Megan spared him a quick glance. She hoped he hadn't noticed how her hands were trembling. "You must agree, especially after this latest escapade of his."

Spoken through clenched teeth, his reply was menacing. "Megan, I swear, if you've—"

"If I've what?" she interrupted quickly, not at all sure she wanted to know the nature of his threat or of his suspicions of her.

He scowled. She shrugged. As a woman who routinely felled great Pinkerton detectives, she guessed she oughtn't to be surprised he'd grown wary of her. The notion gave her an exciting, if short-lived, sense of power.

"If you've done something with McMarlin, there'll be hell to pay this time," Gabriel said. "Damnation," he muttered. "I never should have left the two of you alone together."

Perhaps a further bit of diversion was in order, Megan decided.

"Jealous, Agent Winter?" she asked.

Disbelief shadowed his expression. "Jealous? Of what?"

"Of Agent McMarlin, of course." She sipped her coffee. "I'll admit, he does receive a great deal of my attention . . . at least in between escapes, he does."

His level, all-too-comprehending look could have nailed her to her chair. "You ditched him again."

"Ditched him? Hmmm." Pretending to think about that, she bit into her cinnamon bun and savored its spicy sweetness. "Well, I will admit that Agent McMarlin may have mistaken the knotted bedsheets I dangled from the balcony for an escape route." She shrugged. "Who can say if he followed it or not?"

An unintelligible sound of frustration issued from her dining companion.

"Agent Winter, are you all right?" With a great show of observation, she leaned forward. Gabriel's freshly shaven jaw, clean scented dark hair, and handsome suit were all just as she'd expected. The fearsome set to his expression was not.

Trying not to lose her nerve in the face of it, she nonchalantly raised her pancake-laden fork and said, "I didn't know a man's eyes could bug out quite so fiercely as that. You're quite remarkable."

His fingers tightened around the knife he'd been using to spread glistening strawberry jam on a slice of toast. Gabriel glanced from his knife to her throat, undoubtedly entertaining visions of quieting her for good, the scoundrel. Then, to Megan's astonishment, he laughed.

Great guffaws of amusement burst from his lips. Louder even than the scrape of cutlery against china and the rattling of the serving carts surrounding them, the sound of Gabriel's laughter drew the attention of every dining-room patron.

Nonplussed, Megan stared. What in heaven's name did he find so funny? Perhaps he'd finally gone 'round the bend, driven to lunacy by the demands of tracking criminals who weren't—like her father—and needling their daughters—like her.

Retaining her composure in the face of his hilarity wasn't easy. Her mention of the way she'd sidestepped Agent McMarlin had been meant to distract Gabriel from asking any more questions about the money she intended to use for her dressmaker's shop, not to position her as the subject of his joke. She couldn't have him delving too deeply into her missing nest-egg money—or her reasons for believing her father might have taken it. To be sure, Gabriel Winter would suspect her father still further if he knew about Joseph's gambling habits.

But she hadn't intended to amuse him so much as this! Crossing her arms, Megan watched the play of laughter on his face. In an instant, the harsh lines of his face eased, and his demeanor took on a lightheartedness she'd never glimpsed in Gabriel before. His body shook with wholehearted mirth.

At the sight, something inside her softened. Like this, Gabriel seemed younger, less cynical . . . as though there were infinitely more to him than the relentless Pinkerton man he'd allowed her to see.

His laughter subsided quickly, like a summer storm spent in moments. She should have known, Megan reminded herself staunchly, that any carefree behavior from Gabriel Winter would be short-lived.

The man was as determined and single-minded as the Arizona Territory sky was blue.

Just like her.

Something in common, the rebellious, lonesome part of her whispered. Deliberately, she pushed back the thought and focused on Gabriel's newly serious expression.

He caught sight of her undoubtedly curious regard . . . and actually chuckled anew.

She reached for his coffee cup, tilted it toward her, and sniffed its contents suspiciously. "Have you been imbibing already? I didn't notice any liquor on your breath, but perhaps the coffee disguised it."

"I don't need liquor to recognize when I've met my match," he said, retrieving his cup from her grasp. "Or to know that leaving you out of my sight, even for the length of time it takes a lady to get gussied up, was a mistake. A mistake I don't mean to repeat."

Affronted by his insinuation that she needed a *length* of time to beautify herself for the day, Megan lifted her chin. "Fine. Release me, and we needn't concern ourselves with each other any longer."

"No." He finished slathering jam on his toast and crunched off at least half of his triangular-shaped slice with one bite.

My, the man was large. Large mouth, wide shoulders . . . big hands. Her gaze lowered to his strong, capable fingers as they cradled his toast. The deft, delicate way he handled that slice of bread as he prepared it for consumption reminded her of the way he'd cupped her jaw in his hand yesterday . . . in preparation for his kiss.

Remembering that kiss, she felt anew the prick of the adobe wall at her back when he'd pressed hard against her, holding her in place with the shocking tilt of his hips on hers. She tasted again the heated textures of his lips and tongue, felt the seductive slide of his hand moving down her neck to hold her still. Gabriel had known exactly what he'd wanted from her. She'd been all too happy to give it, believing herself fully in control of all that happened.

Believing herself well protected against caring whether he wanted her at all.

Now Megan knew no such certainty. The realization scared her—almost as much as the sudden stillness of his hands.

She looked up. Belatedly, she realized he'd been speaking to her . . . and she'd heard not a word, thanks to her unlikely girlish daydreams. What was the matter with her?

Clearing her throat, Megan took a moment to gather what poise she could. "I'm sorry," she said, taking up her fork again. "I was speculating how far afield Agent McMarlin might have gone by now. What did you say?"

His eyes, dark as her chances seemed of finding her father in time, gleamed at her from across the table. Her heart sank. Gabriel believed himself to have the upper hand.

He was probably right.

Drat the man and his nimble, seductive fingers!

"I said, I'm surprised you didn't clobber him on his way down the bedsheets."

"I couldn't." Neither could she conceal the mischievous smile that crept to her lips. "I was hiding beneath the bed."

His mouth quirked upward in an answering grin. "I'm beginning to think you're not as ferocious as you pretend, sugar."

"Ferocious?" Even knowing he had to be teasing her, she shuddered. If the gossips in town caught wind of such an accusation, she'd never hear the end of it. The marriageable males for miles would scatter to the corners of the Territory, scared away by the latest tale of the spinster Kearney.

Why that notion should pain her now more than ever, she couldn't begin to guess.

"Not hardly," she went on with an arch of her brow. "I did wash and bandage the lump on poor Agent McMarlin's head last night, remember?"

"As the man on the other end of the handcuffs, I could hardly fail to notice."

"See? For my part, Agent Winter—"

"Gabriel."

He sounded fit to be tied at her refusal to use his given name. Naturally, that only compelled her to refuse still further.

"—I'm beginning to think you're not as relentless as *you* pretend."

"Don't lay bets on that." His mouth drew taut. "You're living proof that women's intuition is less reliable than facts. Hasn't anyone told you assumptions are dangerous?"

"Hasn't anyone told you actions speak louder than words?"

Unbidden, an image of Gabriel's face, relaxed as it had been in laughter, pushed its way into Megan's mind. She pushed it straight back.

"Take your actions, for instance," she went on pointedly. "You're still sitting here, calmly having breakfast with me. Why haven't you already gone to retrieve poor misguided Agent McMarlin?"

Meet the master of *Alexandra's Dream!*

A ten-year veteran of the Greek navy, Captain Nikolas Pappas is one of the youngest captains in the cruise industry today. Growing up in a Greek fishing village, Captain Pappas always knew that he wanted to spend his life "on the high seas." Through hard work and discipline, he rose to his current position as master and is proud to wear the epaulet with the commodore's bar and braided stripes that is unique to his office.

Curious about what the master of a cruise ship actually does? Be sure to attend the captain's cocktail party later today in the Garden Terrace on the Helios deck. There you'll be able to speak with Captain Pappas in person. Be prepared: most passengers are awed by the scope of the captain's responsibilities!

Until then, relax, and enjoy all that Liberty Line's premier ship has to offer. Sail through the Mediterranean knowing you have nothing to worry about but having a good time, day and night. Master Nikolas Pappas feels honored and privileged to serve as your captain. He and his team of professionals will do everything they can to ensure your time on their ship is memorable.

KAREN KENDALL

is the author of many disasters and sixteen books. She was first published in 2001, and since then her books have garnered top reviews and several awards, including the Book Buyer's Best, Write Touch, Maggie and *Romantic Times BOOKreviews* magazine's Top Pick and Reviewer's Choice.

Karen grew up in Texas, graduated from Smith College and now writes full-time. She lives in south Florida with her husband Don, rescue greyhounds Lilah and Merry and attack-cat Boo, who turns up her nose at chicken and fish but adores asparagus and mint-chocolate-chip ice cream.

For more information, visit her at www.KarenKendall.com.

Mediterranean
NIGHTS™

Karen Kendall

AN AFFAIR TO
REMEMBER

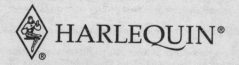

HARLEQUIN®

TORONTO • NEW YORK • LONDON
AMSTERDAM • PARIS • SYDNEY • HAMBURG
STOCKHOLM • ATHENS • TOKYO • MILAN • MADRID
PRAGUE • WARSAW • BUDAPEST • AUCKLAND

ISBN-13: 978-0-373-38964-3
ISBN-10:   0-373-38964-7

AN AFFAIR TO REMEMBER

www.eHarlequin.com

Printed in U.S.A.

Dear Reader,

I love a reunion story, especially one involving two
people who truly deserve their happy ending, like
Nick and Helena, the main characters in this book.
And what setting could be more breathtakingly
seductive than a luxury cruise ship in the azure-blue
Mediterranean?

Writing *An Affair To Remember* was a pleasure
because I got to take a virtual tour of exotic places
like Dubrovnik and Santorini while visiting old
favorites like Venice and Rome.

But the real story behind the story is that I fell
in love with Nick, the hero, myself! (Shhh, don't
tell my husband.) Nick, the captain of cruise
ship *Alexandra's Dream,* is one of those men who
become even more handsome over the years,
seasoned with knowledge, responsibility and…
regret.

No one would ever guess that beneath his
disciplined, emotionless captain's persona beats the
heart of a romantic who's still in love with a woman
he knew fifteen years ago. Nick may command an
entire ship, but he can't control his heart where
Helena's concerned.

I hope you'll enjoy reading *An Affair To Remember* as
much as I enjoyed writing it.

Bon voyage!

Karen Kendall

ACKNOWLEDGMENTS

A huge thanks to the following people,
without whom I couldn't have written this book:

Marcia King-Gamble, for her kindness
in sharing her knowledge of cruise ships
and the cruise industry in general.

Gordon Buck, Vice President, Caribbean Relations
for Carnival Cruise Lines, for answering innumerable
stupid questions about ship captains, protocol and
security (as much as he could tell me
without having to kill me!).

Marianna Jameson for sharing her expertise
on digital security issues.

Linda Conrad for her keen editorial eye
and great advice on character conflict.

And last but not least, Aleka Nakis, for providing me
with Greek words and phrases for the text.

Any mistakes are my own.

Karen Kendall

DON'T MISS THE STORIES OF

Mediterranean
N I G H T S ™

PROLOGUE

THE HOT MEDITERRANEAN SUN poured into a luxuriously appointed office. On a polished mahogany credenza, inside a scale model of the Roman Coliseum, a tiny Christian faced off against a voracious lion in a bloody, unequal battle. The woman standing over it smiled, picked up the hapless man and fed him head-first to the beast.

Kitty's got you now, you arrogant s.o.b.

The telephone rang, interrupting the morning's entertainment, and the woman sighed, turning toward the phone and taking perverse pleasure in leaving the little male figure dangling from the lion's mouth. Soon Elias Stamos, owner of Argosy Cruises, would be in exactly the same position.

At the touch of a button, a distinguished male voice with a Continental accent filled the room.

"The first officer on *Alexandra's Dream* tried to make a buy yesterday," said the Swiss caller.

"He *what?* A black market buy? On his own?"

"Yes."

"What does Tzekas think he's doing? He's endangering everything!"

"My thoughts exactly. I think you should know that

Tzekas is not…stable. I'm hearing reports of a lot of alcohol when he's off duty and a possible gambling problem. Would you like something done about him?" he asked in prosaic tones.

"No. He's the son of the owner's best friend. If anything happened to Giorgio, Elias Stamos would leave no stone unturned in his search for answers. We cannot afford that. Just try to keep him busy."

"Fine. I'll check back in a couple of days."

"Do that." Deeply concerned, the woman cut the connection.

CHAPTER ONE

HELENA STAMOS WAITED in a long security line to board the cruise ship *Alexandra's Dream*. She gripped her oversize leather portfolio in one hand, her purse in the other. She'd truly intended to leave the portfolio behind on this vacation, but at the last moment she'd snatched it up before running out the door to her taxi.

Naples was hot, dry and sunny—a marked contrast to the damp London weather she'd left behind instead of her paintings and sketches. She'd accepted a new contract to design costumes for next fall's production of *Tosca*, and ideas were coming to her with too much force to ignore. She'd have to get them down on paper, even if it meant turning her brief vacation into a working one.

Though she'd finally slept the night before, she was exhausted from the weeks leading up to the dress rehearsal for her last play. Her only brief respite had been two weeks ago, when she'd joined this same ship for a few days to meet her half-brother, Theo, for the first time. Although she had known about Theo's existence for a while, she was still trying to get used to the fact that she had an older brother, one who looked disconcertingly like her father, Elias.

"Ms. Stamos!" exclaimed Gideon Dayan, who oversaw security for the ship. "You don't need to wait in line. I'll send your things through right away."

Several passengers turned to look at her, trying to figure out why she was special, and Helena smiled at them politely. "That's all right, Gideon, really. I'm just another passenger. It will only take a few minutes."

"Suit yourself." He nodded to her. "Welcome aboard. It's good to see you again—I'd stay to chat but I need to get a report to Captain Pappas."

Helena tightened her grip slightly on both handbag and portfolio at the mention of Nikolas Pappas's name. "We'll catch up later, then."

Dayan bypassed the line and vanished into the massive, dark-blue belly of the ship.

"Are you famous?" A little redheaded girl standing in front of Helena looked up at her through inquisitive hazel eyes. "Is that why the man said you don't have to wait in line?"

Helena laughed as the girl's parents turned around, obviously a little embarrassed. "No, sweetheart, I'm not famous. I've just done some work on board the ship, so the staff knows who I am. And that's why I can get on in the middle of a cruise like this." The other passengers were simply reboarding from a shore excursion and had been sailing with *Alexandra's Dream* for a few days already.

She didn't feel the need to announce to everyone that her father owned not only the ship but also the cruise line.

"Oh. Well, even if you're not famous, I like your bracelets." The little girl pointed at them. "They make music."

Helena threw the strap of her purse over her shoulder and extended her left arm to let the girl examine the wide stack of hammered-gold bangles. "Thank you. They were a gift from my mother."

"Pretty. What did you do on the boat?"

"Angela, it's rude to ask personal questions," said her mother in an American Southern accent. "You don't even know this lady's name."

"My name is Helena, Angela, and it's quite all right." The parents introduced themselves as Connie and George Tripp, from Arkansas. This was the family's first cruise.

"We're pleased to make your acquaintance," said the little girl, as if she were reciting the words from an etiquette book. She dimpled, responding to Helena's warm smile.

"It's very nice to meet you, too. And to answer your question, I worked on the interior design, which means that I helped choose furniture and fabrics and paint and lights—that kind of thing."

"Wow. Did you go to school for that?"

"No, I studied art in school, sweetheart. But it helps."

Angela's face lit up. "That's my favorite!"

"Is it?" Helena asked as they moved forward in line. "What do you like to do, draw or paint or make things out of clay?"

"Paint. And I like papier-mâché, even though it feels so goopy and slimy and cold when you put your hands in it."

"Yes, it does," said Helena, chuckling. "So what did you make with papier-mâché?"

"A big mask of a alien!"

"*An* alien," corrected Angela's mother.

"Wow! That sounds exciting," Helena said. "I make masks sometimes, too, for plays and operas and movies."

"Movies?" Clearly, the little girl was awed.

Helena nodded, but she really didn't want to talk about herself or her work. She was more interested in Angela. "So what color was your mask?"

"Purple. And green. With silver thingies—"

Their conversation was cut off when it came time for the family to place their belongings on the conveyor belt to be screened. Angela had to put her *101 Dalmatians* knapsack down and watch it go through.

Helena didn't mention the fact that she thought the costume designer for Glenn Close's Cruella De Vil was brilliant. The little girl might think she approved of people wearing puppy fur, which certainly wasn't the case.

"Bye, Miss Helena!" Angela called as she and her parents got the green light to board. "So can we be friends on the boat?"

"We certainly can. I'll probably see you in the children's center, where my niece works. How's that?"

"Okay! Bye!" And Angela disappeared with her parents into the crowded corridor.

So adorable. Helena put her purse and portfolio on the conveyor belt and tried not to think about the baby she'd lost. Had it been a little girl? And could it possibly have been as long as a year and a half ago that she'd been pregnant?

She fingered her bracelets, turning them on her wrists in a nervous habit she'd been trying to break for years. Then she put the thought out of her mind, slipped the bracelets off and dropped them into a plastic bowl. She walked through the metal detector.

"Welcome to *Alexandra's Dream,* Ms. Stamos," said a female security clerk in a blue uniform as she handed back the jewelry. "Your luggage has been delivered to your suite."

"Thank you." Helena took her passport back, along with the plastic ship card that served as her ID and credit on board. She slid the stack of bracelets back onto her wrists, dividing them this time so that six adorned the left and six the right.

The bracelets jangled like her nerves as she tucked her hair behind her ears. She picked up her things, took a deep breath and moved toward the stairs, bracing herself once again to see Captain Nikolas Pappas—the man who'd broken her heart fifteen years ago.

The excited buzz of the other passengers filled her ears, but her mind traveled hundreds of miles and tiptoed through time zones that no longer existed.

Instead of the plush, carpeted floor beneath her flat ballet slippers, she imagined the steel floor of a Greek freighter, studded with bolts and stamped with an ugly pattern. The still Mediterranean air was replaced by a crisp, bracing wind that whipped her long, dark hair around her face.

Instead of the excited conversations all around her, she heard the rough groaning of a massive industrial engine propelling the vessel into the harbor at Newport, Rhode Island, where the ship was making a delivery stop. Huge crates full of Italian antiques were unloaded with the aid of forklifts, chains and big, strapping Greek men.

Fifteen years ago Helena had joined the freighter in New York, deciding to try a sail across the Atlantic to Spain instead of the confinement of another boring flight. Her father owned the freighter, so even though she was an art student short of cash at the time, she could travel free.

She'd looked like an art student, too—in ragged, paint-stained jeans and a faded black tank top, her fingernails bitten and blackened by the charcoal and oil crayons of her advanced life-drawing class. She'd been bare of any jewelry except a pair of silver earrings shaped like dolphins. One simply didn't wear "bling" to art school. It was far more chic to be desperately poor, spout existential philosophy and say the *F*-word a lot.

So, even though Helena couldn't bring herself to sprinkle her speech with obscenities, she kept her 18-karat gold bangles in the pocket of a ratty ski parka and her hefty diamond studs in a plastic pill box under a cotton ball and some aspirin.

Still caught up in the past, she heard the clatter of giant chain links as the ship's anchor dropped at Newport. Sailing had always been one of her deep loves—she felt an affinity for the water that she couldn't explain. Her mother, Alexandra, had teased Helena that she was a reincarnated naiad, one of the nymphs in mythology who gave life to rivers, streams and lakes.

It was cold on the freighter deck, and goose bumps erupted over her skin as she watched several burly guys grapple with the large metal containers and swing them off the freighter via chains and a massive hook on a crane.

One of the men in particular caught her eye. Deeply

tanned, broad-shouldered and tall, he seemed to work harder than all the rest. When he finally paused on top of one of the containers to take a breather, bending over and leaning his hands on his knees, he turned his dark head and looked right at her. Then he winked and she experienced an odd sense of recognition even though she'd never set eyes on him before.

It was an exciting but unsettling feeling, and she smiled back at him as she shivered.

He stood immediately and untied the army-green jacket around his waist. Before she could register what he was doing, he tossed it to her—and she put out a hand instinctively to catch it.

Under his unwavering gaze, she slipped her arms into it and waved her thanks. He nodded, grinned and gave her a jaunty, two-fingered salute before turning back to work.

That was Helena's first glimpse of Nick Pappas, and as she stood there swimming in the folds of his big jacket, she couldn't help taking another. Perspiration glistened along his bronzed neck and shoulders, high-lighting the bunched muscles and catching the sun. He was truly breathtaking. She stayed there, mesmerized, as she watched him work. She pulled his jacket more tightly around her, hugging it. And when she was sure he wasn't looking, she buried her nose in the rough cotton lapel and inhaled his scent, which was pleas-antly musky and held a hint of Seville oranges from an aftershave.

She stood there for a long time, the sketchbook under her arm ignored, pretending to be fascinated by the play of the dark waves, the salt spray and the golden light reflected off the water. But out of the corner of her eye, she watched him. He was a natural leader, getting everyone to work together for maximum efficiency. His deep, hearty laugh rang out when other workers cursed instead. And when he gulped water from a two-liter bottle, she wondered if he kissed—or made love—so thirstily.

Why didn't they bring *him* into her art classes? Instead, she had to make contour drawings of bony old men and fleshy, overblown female models who didn't look their best under the harsh fluorescent lights.

Helena wanted to know his name, but it looked as though she'd have to wait until he came to reclaim his jacket….

THE FRONT EDGE of a walker jabbed her in the calf, bringing her back to the present and *Alexandra's Dream.*

"Oh, I beg your pardon, madam!" said an elderly man. "It's a little crowded—I didn't mean to do that."

"No worries," Helena said with a smile. "I was daydreaming, so I may have stepped back."

She needed to stop thinking about Nikolas Pappas, anyway. Why couldn't she forget the past? Probably because she had unwelcome suspicions about why Nick had left her so suddenly, without a word…and why, despite a scandal on his former ship, her father had put him in charge of this one.

They weren't suspicions she wanted to entertain, and whatever the circumstances of their parting, he had always struck her as a man of integrity. She'd once have staked her life on it. But now that he'd risen so high in

Elias's employ, she couldn't help but wonder. Had Nick been paid off to leave his employer's daughter alone?

Helena tried once again to push the ugly thought away. She didn't want to have such doubts about Nick or her father. Pappas was clearly very good at his job, and Elias hired the best.

She was finally able to squeeze into an elevator among the throng of passengers, and she tried to push all thoughts of Nick out of her mind. There was no reason to obsess over the past, and if he had indeed taken some kind of deal from her father, then he wasn't worth the time of day.

They each had very separate lives now, despite their occasional limited encounters on board *Alexandra's Dream*. And they were complete opposites.

Nick was a man in a white uniform; she was a woman in a low-cut scarlet dress. He was formal and she was passionate. He operated with all the discipline of a navy man; she flew by the seat of her creative pants.

A flash of recognition, a polite greeting, a brief smile for the past follies of youth—that was all that would pass between them; nothing more. So why did her palms sweat and her stomach turn over each time she boarded *Alexandra's Dream*?

CHAPTER TWO

"WHAT DO YOU MEAN, Ariana Bennett is missing?" asked Captain Pappas, looking up from a stack of data.

"She never returned from her shore excursion yesterday, sir." Chief Security Officer Gideon Dayan's blondish-brown hair glinted in the hot late-August sun. His deeply tanned face was dotted with droplets of perspiration and his eyes reflected concern.

Nick's whole body went on alert. Ariana Bennett, the ship's librarian, was always prompt and responsible. Nothing could be less like her than to disappear and not return by the time *Alexandra's Dream* was scheduled to depart from Naples. Something was wrong.

Nick tightened his mouth. An uncomfortable sense of déjà vu settled onto his shoulders along with the weight of his command. "Have you asked the other staff? Did anyone accompany her to shore? When was the last time anyone saw her?"

"Other staffers remember seeing her yesterday in Naples, but she seems to have been by herself. How do you want to handle this, sir?"

The déjà vu dug talons into the back of Nick's neck like a large, hungry vulture preparing to snack on his carcass. Two years ago, on his previous ship, a woman had vanished…but for good reason and with his help.

But the cloud of unease took a backseat to his need to know that Ariana was safe. She was a lovely young woman, if a little serious and intense. He hated to think of her alone and vulnerable in a city like Naples. Tension coiled in his gut. *Where is she?*

Passengers did miss the ship occasionally. But staff? Never. He frowned and looked at his watch.

"If she's not back by the time we sail, alert the police, Gideon. Go ahead and write up a missing persons report now, in case we need to file one. This isn't sitting right with me."

"Yes, sir."

Strange things had been happening on board *Alexandra's Dream* ever since a stash of stolen antiquities had turned up on their first cruise. The more Nick thought about it, the more the hair on the back of his neck rose.

The stolen art, a little boy in danger from the Russian mob and now Ariana missing. *What is going on aboard my ship?*

Nick didn't like it, and he knew Elias Stamos, owner of Liberty Line and its parent company, Argosy Cruises, wasn't going to like it, either. Elias had seen fit to give Nick command of a $425 million luxury liner named after his late wife, Alexandra. Stamos wouldn't want even a breath of scandal attached to her name, and who could blame him?

Alexandra's Dream wasn't only Elias's dream, but also her captain's. She was not the largest cruise ship on the water, but she was one of the most elegant. Nick

loved every inch of her, from her massive, deep-blue
hull to her polished decks; from her bow to her stern.
She rose twelve sumptuous decks high and stretched as
long as a city block. She was a beautiful, majestic lady,
and wore her necklace of silver and gold stars—the
logo of Liberty Line—with pride.

Alexandra's Dream had started life as a small and un-
remarkable American ship, one of three belonging to
Liberty. Elias Stamos had purchased all three, renamed
them and spared no expense in refurbishing them. He'd
done it as a tribute to his late wife and her vision of
bringing glamour and sophistication back to cruising.

This ship did her proud—it was a champagne-and-
caviar setting, a true diamond of the first water, thanks
in part to the vision of Elias and Alexandra's younger
daughter, Helena.

But Nick didn't allow himself to think of Helena. The
girl he'd known a lifetime ago was married to someone
else, some plumbing heir, of all things. He'd seen the
wedding photos in the press a couple of years ago, the
ones in which she wore a white gown, fabulous jewels
and a hint of sadness in her smile. He'd never thrown
away a newspaper so fast.

As captain of *Alexandra's Dream,* Nick was responsible for the health and well-being of 570 crew and
1000 passengers, and every last one of them mattered.
He checked his watch again as Gideon left the bridge,
all too conscious that the ship was due to depart in less
than one hour. Any staff who'd gone ashore should have
been back an hour before the passengers.

The voices of reporters echoed in his head. Had it

really been two years since he'd had to resign from his position at Blue Aegean Cruises?

Captain Pappas, why did you leave port after a passenger was reported missing under suspicious circumstances?

Rumor has it that she drowned. Is there a cover-up going on, Captain?

What happened to her, Pappas? Was she murdered? Did you have something to do with it? Did one of your crew?

Nick, do you have anything to say to the distraught husband? Don't you owe him an explanation or apology?

Nick would have loved to deck the guy who'd shouted the last question. If the reporter had been better at his job, he might have stumbled across the truth. But the truth didn't make such intriguing headlines. The truth was sad, ugly and all too common.

Nick stared out to sea, at the horizon where water met sky and no land interrupted their broad, endless kiss. He'd done the right thing, even if it had cost him his ship and his reputation.

He'd protected a woman from harm, from the man who was supposed to cherish her. He'd helped her escape from her own husband. When he'd resigned, he might have lost his position, but he'd kept his integrity, his honor and his conscience intact.

Those qualities were far more important than anything that could be embroidered on his shoulders.

Nick's thoughts returned to Ariana Bennett. The port of Naples stretched before him, a city with a population of over a million. Birthplace of such luminaries as the sculptor Bernini, the opera singer Caruso and the parents of Al Capone, the city had quite a history and was built over a series of catacombs. It was no place for a woman alone to get lost.

ARIANA DIDN'T return.

Surrounded by key staffers, Nick reluctantly followed all protocol for departure to Palermo without her. He ordered Gideon to file the police report and compartmentalized his own concerns for her safety.

Though they no longer sounded the ship's horn because of noise regulations, hundreds of passengers gathered along the starboard rail on the Helios deck, waving goodbye to Naples and sipping early cocktails.

For them, the cruise was a wonderful vacation. For Nick, it brought the usual maritime headaches of paperwork, immigration procedures at each port and management issues, though he had help and was lucky in his staff for the most part.

He had a talented executive chef, Dominique Charest, and an excellent hotel manager, Thanasi Kaldis, with whom he shared a bright and competent assistant, Petra Jones. Patti Kennedy, the cruise director, juggled her responsibilities admirably.

The only staffer that Nick would happily replace was his first officer, Giorgio Tzekas, whose duties mainly revolved around ship safety. Nick constantly had to check up on him, because the man couldn't be trusted, which was disconcerting with so many passengers' lives dependent on Giorgio doing his job. Nick disliked micromanaging people, but in this case he didn't have a choice.

Nick would have despised Tzekas even if the first officer hadn't liked booze too much. He was the sort of rich, pampered malcontent that Pappas couldn't abide, and he already had too much experience with the man, since Tzekas had held a position on Nick's last ship, too. It would be no loss if the *malaka* fell overboard. But Elias had saddled Nick with Giorgio, and wouldn't hear a word against him.

Tzekas was the exception to Elias's usually excellent judgment, but old man Tzekas and Elias went way back, so Giorgio was here to stay despite Nick's dislike for him.

He stood on the bridge now with Nick and several other officers, looking bored and subtly checking out female passengers on the Helios deck below them. The broad planes of his handsome face were a little fleshy, his eyes bloodshot. He was beginning to look dissolute.

"Captain," he asked, with an all too innocent expression, "do you think we should be leaving port with the ship's librarian missing?"

Tzekas knew all about the feeling of déjà vu Nick was experiencing, since Giorgio had been under his command during the scandal. Not having actually seen the abused wife's bruises and injuries, Tzekas had sided with the husband—and allowed himself to be quoted by the press on the subject.

If Nick hadn't resigned, he would have fired the guy for gross insubordination. Giorgio had been stepping more carefully around Nick on *Alexandra's Dream*, but he had now crossed the line. The captain couldn't have him questioning his authority, and especially not in front of other staff.

"Officer Tzekas," he said icily. "I will remind you that I am the captain of this ship and it is not a democracy. Not only am I responsible to Liberty Line and the scheduled itinerary, but I am responsible for a thousand passengers. I cannot delay them because one individual has not managed to get herself back aboard. Do I make myself clear?"

Tzekas was unwise enough to push back. "What if Ariana is in trouble, Captain?"

Nick had spent ten years in the Greek navy, which had taught him military discipline. He gave no sign that he, too, was worried about the librarian. It wasn't appropriate, and there was still a good chance she would contact them with an explanation for her absence.

"While I sincerely hope that Ms. Bennett is not at risk, Officer Tzekas, this topic is now closed for discussion," Nick snapped. "My decisions are not yours to question. Do I make myself clear?"

"Yes, sir."

"Then you are dismissed from the bridge."

"Sir?"

"You heard me."

Resentment written all over his face, Tzekas stiffly made his way to the exit.

"Please make sure that all sports equipment of any kind on board is checked and rechecked. And I'd like your report on the lifeboat drill conducted this morning, Officer. I assume all went smoothly?"

"Yes, Captain." Giorgio used his key card to exit the bridge, smoothing back his hair with his free hand. He stopped to chat with an attractive brunette at the end of the hallway, smiling flirtatiously at her as Nick's mouth tightened.

She was a staffer, but Nick suspected that Tzekas had more than once violated the iron-clad policy on fraternization with passengers. And if Nick caught him at it, the first officer was gone.

NICK SNATCHED a few hours' sleep in his stateroom before heading back to the bridge to read the satellite communications report and tackle a massive amount of paperwork.

He took the elevator from his deck to the bridge, looking at his watch as the elevator stopped on the Helios deck, one level short of where he needed to be. The doors slid open smoothly and Helena Stamos stood there, a startled expression on her lovely face.

He'd seen her before now, of course, in passing during the outfitting of the ship and then briefly at the launch party and on *Alexandra's Dream*'s third voyage. But she'd always stared coolly at him and kept her distance. He'd done the same, even though the sight of her caused a visceral reaction in him. He would never let her know that. He didn't like deception, and she'd betrayed what they once had by practicing it. Helena had never told him that she was related to Elias Stamos.

Nick stared now at Stamos's younger daughter, unable to turn aside. It was as if the years had dropped away: slight body; shock of dark hair hanging in wisps around her face; slightly Roman nose; full, sensual lips. But it was her fascinating, dramatic, confrontational dark eyes that held him. They turned slightly downward at the outside corners, reaching to greet her quick smile.

Gemma, her niece, interned in the ship's children's center. Nick had remarked silently on how much her demeanor reminded him of Helena, and he'd stayed as far away as possible from the girl.

A second flash of déjà vu hit him. All he could do was stand there like an oaf, staring at the woman he'd reluctantly walked away from at age twenty-one. He'd been warned off—she was the boss's barely legal daughter, and he was a lowly deckhand on a freighter.

She was a woman, now, of course. The sun and the years had framed her down-tilted eyes with faint laugh lines, just as they'd gently bracketed her mouth. But she radiated the same beauty—a more potent, more mature loveliness that tightened his throat. Desire punched him in the solar plexus. Hard.

He'd always remember her wearing his jacket on the deck of a freighter ship. Today she wore a full, plum-cotton gypsy skirt and an olive camisole. Her hands were on her hips and a dozen gold bracelets jangled on her slim, tanned wrists. Her small feet were encased in flat, black leather ballet slippers.

She held her chin in the air, but a pulse beat wildly at her throat and she vibrated with nervous tension.

Nick kept his expression impassive. "Hello, Helena. I didn't realize you were joining us. Will you be cruising with us for the second part of the Roman Empire tour?"

She nodded.

"Ah, well. So far it's one of our most popular. Our first stop after Palermo is Venice, then Dubrovnik, its former rival..." His voice trailed off as he realized that he sounded like a travel agent doing a hard sell. He cleared his throat. "How are you? You look—beautiful."

"How am I?" She expelled a breath, her expression turning ironic. "Oh, I'm just fine, Nick. And you?"

"Great," he said inanely, still leaning on the Door Open button.

"Good." The space between them resonated with all the words neither of them spoke out loud. Finally he got out of the elevator—he would walk up to the bridge— but she didn't enter it herself.

"I saw you only briefly at the launch party," he said, trying to break the awkward silence.

"Yes. I wasn't in a very festive mood, then. I had a lot on my mind. My father was very vocal in his disapproval of my recent divorce."

Divorced from that stodgy Greek plumbing heir? Nick's heart tried to leap into his captain's hat. Stupid, stupid, stupid. What had changed, really? He was no longer a deckhand, but she was still Elias Stamos's daughter, heiress to millions and completely untouchable—not to mention the fact that she must hate him for disappearing fifteen years ago.

"I'm sorry to hear of your divorce," Nick forced himself to say.

"I'm sorry to speak of it. Ari is a nice man. He didn't deserve to be abandoned."

The subtext in her words screamed at him. *I didn't deserve to be abandoned, either, Nick.*

Helena tucked a strand of hair behind her ear. "But I'm not good wife material. Too much Gypsy spirit in me. I never should have let them pressure me—" She broke off, looking miserable and guilty. Then she caught herself and schooled her face into a polite mask once again.

Them? She must mean that her father had played a role in her marriage, which didn't surprise Nick. Elias was a traditional man, an overprotective father. He'd have wanted to see both of his daughters settled and taken care of.

Though he could barely restrain his curiosity, this was none of his business and he did his best to relieve another awkward moment between them. "Do you still sew, Helena? I'll never forget the Dracula costume." He laughed, remembering a costume party they'd attended together. She'd effortlessly transformed him into a Transylvanian count instead of the son of an impoverished Greek fisherman.

Her face lit from within and the bitterness playing around her mouth vanished. "I do—you know I'm a professional now, Nick. I design costumes for theater and ballet productions in London. Sometimes film and opera, too."

"Yes, I'd heard that." He became fascinated as always by the way joy reached for the corners of her eyes. He smiled back at her. "I'm not surprised at all. That costume was a masterpiece. Remember when we won first place in the competition on Mykonos?"

She nodded. "My first glowing review." Her gaze swept his face. "And you've come a long way, too, Captain Pappas."

He lifted a shoulder. "I suppose I have."

"You had some bad press a while back."

He nodded, not sharing details. Not defending himself.

She fidgeted. "Was any of it true?"

"It was in all the papers. On every TV station. So it must be true, eh?"

She shot an evaluative glance at him. "I may not always see eye-to-eye with my father, but he generally doesn't hire incompetents, cowards or liars."

Her words were like a balm. Why didn't she think the worst of him? "You seem very sure of that."

"I am."

"To tell you the truth, Helena, I was just as surprised as anyone else when Elias offered me the job. I figured I'd be steering a fishing charter or a banana boat for the rest of my life—that or maybe a third-class freighter."

Was it his imagination or had skepticism just crossed her face? But all she said was, "My father's an excellent judge of character."

"And what about you?"

Helena folded her arms across her chest and turned the toes of one foot inward. "I thought I was, once."

Fifteen years ago?

Unexpectedly, tears filled her eyes. "But now I don't know," she said. "I don't know."

His heart contracted. He wanted to reach out, touch her shoulder. Take her into his arms. Tell her he was sorry for ever hurting her. But he couldn't touch her. It wasn't fair to either of them. *The past is the past, and there is no future. Keep your hands to yourself, Nick.*

"I have to go," she said, blinking rapidly and turning on her heel. She pushed the button for the elevator to return.

He took a step toward her, then another. She whirled

and they stood chin-to-chest for a moment. He could smell her hair, a citrusy floral shampoo, and it made something inside him contract and ache.

Then Nick sidestepped and buttoned formality around himself like a coat. "I'm...glad we had a chance to say hello. Enjoy your cruise."

She swallowed. "I really just came to check on Gemma for my sister, Katherine. Make sure she's okay and staying out of trouble. That's all."

He nodded, though he had his doubts. Had Elias sent his daughter to check up on Nick, after the odd incidents that had happened on board? That seemed unlikely, but he couldn't help feeling suspicious. "Good of you. Then you've settled into one of the penthouse suites? Is everything satisfactory?"

"Yes, thank you. It's all perfect."

"Let me know if you need anything, Helena."

The elevator doors opened and she stepped inside, then turned back to look at him. "Of course, Nick."

He was aware, once again, of the volumes of unspoken words that stood between them, but for now they'd leave those volumes unopened.

CHAPTER THREE

HELENA SANK onto the bed in her penthouse suite, weak after her encounter with Nick Pappas. His scent remained with her—the clean starch of his white uniform; the Seville orange and musk of his aftershave and the potent, masculine essence of his warm skin.

After all this time, he still made her blood sing. She felt it rushing through her veins, quickening her pulse and infusing her with an energy she didn't want to embrace.

She'd felt lethargic and detached for so long, ever since the miscarriage. And especially since she'd left poor, sweet, uncomprehending Ari. The divorce had come through three months ago. Though her outward appearance was the same, she'd been robed in guilt and depression.

Helena had brightened her lipstick two shades and hung ever more exotic earrings through her lobes. That worked to fool everyone except for those who knew her best, her sister, Katherine, and her father, whom she'd tried to avoid lately.

Elias had a tough, unyielding nature that had served him well in business, but didn't always translate well into family life. His own marriage had been so happy

that he couldn't see how hers could have been otherwise. *Lovely for you, Baba, that the state of your union
brought you so much joy. Mine didn't.*

Helena saw his craggy features in her mind, saw him
as he said words to her that she'd railed against.

*You don't just walk out of a marriage, my daughter.
It's a commitment before God and you must honor it....*

Not if it's a commitment I should never have made!

*Nevertheless, you did make it. A Stamos does not
break her word. A Stamos does not drag her family
name through the newspapers.*

*I see. So a Stamos lives in misery for the rest of her
life because she allowed her father to push her into a
marriage that was a mistake?*

*Oh, it's my fault that you dishonored yourself and
became pregnant!*

*Why is that any different from your not marrying
Theo's mother?*

Her father's face had mottled with temper. *I'm a
man. These things are different for men.*

Helena had just looked at him and laughed, long and
bitterly. *Yes, they are.* She'd tried to please her father by
agreeing to date Ari, tried to go against her own wild,
impetuous nature and settle down when she'd become
pregnant—marry and become a proper Greek wife. But
then when she'd lost the baby...

She dragged her hands over her face. *A shower
will make me feel better. A shower and a glass of
wine, maybe two.*

She slid off the bed and turned on the water in the
bathroom, running her fingers over the gold Venetian

tiles inside the glass door of the shower stall. She allowed herself a little pride in the loveliness of the suite's decor.

A fluffy, French terry robe on a mahogany hanger awaited her. Her suitcases had been unpacked for her, the clothes neatly hung and placed in the drawers of a solid birch dresser.

Elias had spared no expense in the design and construction of *Alexandra's Dream*. Her mother would have loved the olive-toned walls, the light woods, the white curtains and coverlet in this suite. Helena and the design team had even covered the accent pillows in Alexandra's favorite soft green.

The ship was an ode to Elias's wife; a declaration of love; a visual reminder of her. Helena wondered just what it felt like to inspire that kind of devotion. Very few women did—certainly not her. Nick had left her without a word. Other boyfriends over the years had amused her but not inspired passion. Ari, poor man, was sweet but tepid. Bland. A man forever in beige…

Had Alexandra ever met him, she would have liked him but not adored him. Just as there was nothing to dislike—Ari had nice manners, could carry a conversation and dressed appropriately—nothing about him inspired strong feelings, either.

Helena fought a rising tide of childhood memories: Alexandra snipping rosemary sprigs for a lamb dish, wearing a large straw beach hat with silly plastic cherries on it, laughing merrily over a glass of Pinot Grigio and a dish of olives.

Her death hurt still. And Helena missed her gentle,

loving support. Though her mother would very probably have sided with Elias in public; Alexandra would have soothed Helena, taken her hands in her warm ones and talked with her. She would have comprehended, perhaps even taken Helena's issues to Elias in private and forced him to understand.

With a sigh, Helena uncorked a bottle of Sauvignon Blanc—there was no Pinot Grigio, her favorite—and poured herself a hefty glass. She turned off the shower and filled the big whirlpool tub instead, adding Parisian bath salts.

She padded over to the stereo system and put on the Tosca CD she'd brought with her. Then she peeled off her clothes and sat nude on the edge of the tub with her wine, her feet soaking in the water until the level rose higher. She drank the first glass too quickly and poured another before settling into the luxurious tub. She hoped her conflicting emotions would come to the surface and simply pop harmlessly like the bubbles in the water.

GEMMA SLATER went over all of her predeparture checklists of materials, supplies and snacks for the children's center. As the summer-long intern on board, this kind of thing fell to her while the director took care of dotting the i's and crossing the t's on the registration paperwork.

Check: the three computers for the older children were in fine working order, and all the software and manuals in the appropriate boxes on a nearby shelf. The board games and cards and PG movies were neatly in place.

For the younger kids, Gemma had crayons, coloring

books, felt, glue, blunt scissors, tape, construction paper. Check: she had diapers, pull-ups, wipes and baby powder for the few toddlers…. She grimaced. Technically, the children who came to the center were supposed to be two years of age, but she knew now from experience that some of them were not.

Sodas, juice boxes, milk, chips, crackers, apples, bananas… Her list went on and on. But she was distracted by two things. One, the way her aunt Helena's face had gone all sad when Gemma had happened to mention the captain's name—how weird was that?

And two, Gemma had finally met a boy taller than she was. Correction: a *good-looking* boy taller than she was. At five foot eleven in bare feet, Gemma was vertically challenged when it came to men. Which was better than being *horizontally* challenged, but not much. There was something so unromantic about towering over one's date and having feet bigger than his, too.

But this boy she'd just met almost dwarfed her—and had even more skill with a soccer ball than she did. She'd first seen him kicking one around on deck a couple of evenings ago. Tonight, in half an hour, she had agreed to meet him at Just Gelato, the ice-cream place, so she hurried to finish up her tasks.

She inventoried and wiped down everything in the toy chests with disinfectant, which took forever, but finally she was done. She did a final visual check of the room and then, satisfied that she'd covered everything, she locked up and left.

When she got to Just Gelato, he was waiting for her. His name was Chris and he was American. He was part of the maintenance crew and he called other men "dude." He called her "babe."

"C'mere, babe," he said after they'd eaten their ice cream—chocolate for him, raspberry for her—and shared an illicit, off-duty daiquiri that neither of them was supposed to have. She knew they could get fired for it, but it seemed daring and exciting to break the rules. Besides, nobody could see them in the deckside nook they occupied.

He flashed his lazy grin. And he pulled her right up against him, turned those unfairly blue eyes upon her and kissed her like nobody had ever kissed her before.

His lips were firm and a little demanding. He sucked on her tongue and curved his big hands around her rib cage, letting his thumbs move right up under her breasts.

Her heart pounding, Gemma kissed him right back and ran her hands through his blond hair. Gingerly, she tried sucking on *his* tongue but found the sensation very odd.

She was too busy analyzing the whole situation to truly enjoy it.

A lifetime of private girls' schools and heavily chaperoned parties, not to mention bodyguards when her grandfather Elias was feeling paranoid, had seriously curtailed her dating activities. She was probably the only seventeen-year-old virgin for miles around.

Chris chuckled and broke the kiss, sliding his hands down her torso and letting them rest casually at the top of her buttocks. Slowly, the warmth and the weight of them slid down, until he was cupping her whole bottom.

Wow. It felt good, but should she really be letting this

boy touch her like that? She'd only just met him two nights ago.

You're seventeen. You're on your own for the first time ever. No parent is going to pop out of the bushes and tap his watch, calling, "Curfew!"

But still, Gemma hesitated. She was on the verge of pulling back when Chris tugged her toward him, right up against his obvious, er, interest.

She froze, temptation warring with caution.

He moved his hips ever so slightly.

"I, um…" she began.

"You, um?"

"I have to go."

His lazy smile widened and his blue eyes twinkled down at her in the moonlight. "No, you don't."

She nodded. "Really. I do."

"Chicken," he said softly. He bent to kiss her again and she let him, because it felt so good. And he smelled so wonderful, like coconut and banana and rum.

"I have to work in the morning."

"So do I." He slid his hands up to her breasts and she gasped at the contact, even through her bra and cotton shirt.

Chris chuckled again as she ducked under his arms and backed away. "See you tomorrow, then," he said. "I'll come by the day-care center and say hello."

She nodded. Then, before she could change her mind, she darted away.

ARIANA BENNETT OPENED her eyes, surprised that she could still perform the simple task.

I'm not dead….

I'm not dead?

She had been sure that the needle stabbing into her arm had contained a lethal drug.

She felt momentarily euphoric and then petrified again because she didn't know where she was, and two men had just tried to murder her.

Ariana almost wished she were still a quiet librarian who followed all the rules. But she hadn't been that girl in months. Instead she'd begun taking risks in order to clear her father's name. Derek Bennett had been charged with dealing in illegal antiquities but had died before his trial began. Ariana had taken the job on the ship, which was listed in her father's notebook, to check out his contacts in the Mediterranean. She had to discover the truth.

She had become the kind of woman driven to go to a mob-run archaeological site and ask questions. Questions that were evidently unwelcome.

A dark, scarred man named Nico had kidnapped her at a dig site near Paestum. He'd clapped an iron hand over her mouth, twisted her arms behind her back and tied her wrists. He'd threatened to break her neck if she made a sound. And when she couldn't stop whimpering in fear, he'd stuffed a dirty rag into her mouth. Another man, larger and cleaner but somehow more frightening, had stood there and watched, not making any effort to help her.

"We need to find out what she knows." Nico had spat the words in Italian. And he'd shoved her toward the other man. "Then dispose of her."

That was the moment in which Ariana had discovered that maybe knowledge wasn't all-important, even to a librarian. Breathing was.

She hadn't had a lot of time to philosophize about it, however, because the two men had taken her to a dank underground room with a dirt floor and begun to interrogate her. When she hadn't given them the answers they'd seemed to want, Nico slid a long, wicked-looking knife from his pants and would have slit her throat if the big, silent man hadn't stopped him, worried about leaving too much messy evidence.

He'd offered to just put her to sleep, like a dog, instead. Fear paralyzed her; she didn't want to die! And especially not without finding some answers to the riddle of her father's criminal charges and death. But though the big man spoke to her in soothing tones, he was still bastard enough to stab a needle into her arm, and within seconds, everything had gone black.

Ariana swallowed, which was difficult since her mouth was so dry. Where was she now? She registered the pain in her head first, then looked around at the dirty white walls. This place wasn't much better than the first, though someone had bothered to cover her with a thin blanket. She was lying on a bare mattress that smelled of mold and urine.

She pulled the blanket higher over her shoulders, which alerted her to the fact that her hands were free.

Ariana turned her head, which was a mistake. For one thing, pain assailed her; for another, her almost-murderer sat next to her. She instinctively recoiled, which sent fresh shock waves of pain through her head.

"Calm yourself, *signorina*," the big, silent man

ordered, an unreadable expression on his unshaven face. A tangle of dark hair added to his air of menace, and he wore a snug black T-shirt with dust-streaked black jeans and black boots. Last time she'd checked, black was *not* the color of the good guys.

She swallowed hard.

His obsidian gaze raked her body and she felt as if he could see straight through the thin blanket. Oh God. Was he going to rape her? She shivered again.

He stood, pushing back the chair he'd sat on. He went to a rucksack, opened it and yanked out another blanket. Then he unfolded it and draped it over her.

"Thank you," she managed to say.

He turned his dark gaze back on her. "I'll ask you once again. Who are you?"

"I t-told you before. My n-name is Ariana Bennett. I'm a librarian doing research…." Her voice trailed off at his fierce expression.

"Don't lie to me," he said.

"I-I'm not!"

The bearded hulk eyed her cryptically.

"Are you going to kill me?" she blurted.

"No, I am not going to kill you."

Gratitude washed over her, then suspicion. "W-why not?"

"Because I don't have all the information I need from you."

Ariana drew her knees up to her chin. "I don't *have* any more information."

"No? That remains to be seen."

"You can't just keep me prisoner here!"

"I see. You would prefer to stay with my companion? The one who likes knives?"

Ariana shuddered. No, she'd take her chances with this man instead. In spite of her fear, intuition told her that he didn't really intend to hurt her. He just wanted information—or something else. Maybe money?

Ariana's stomach growled loudly.

Was it her imagination or did the corner of his mouth flex? "You are hungry, eh? Tonight's menu is warm Pinot Noir, hard cheese, stale bread and olives. Dessert is more stale bread. Interested?"

He moved toward his rucksack again and dug around in it. He pulled out a bottle of wine and extended it to her.

She inspected the sealed neck. "Do you have a corkscrew?"

He came over to take the wine from her, pulling a pocketknife out of his jeans. He opened the seal and plunged the blade into the cork in a clean, utilitarian movement. Then he extracted the cork from the bottle expertly. He handed it back to her. "Drink."

She was too excited at the prospect of wetting her dry mouth to worry about a glass, and the warm wine tasted like nectar of the gods. She took a hefty swallow of it. "Please, you have to let me go."

"Impossibile."

"The captain and the crew will be worried about me. They'll report me missing. You don't look like the kind of guy who wants to have a chat with the Naples police."

He said nothing, just tilted back his head and drained a good quarter of the bottle. She watched as the muscles of his powerful throat contracted to swallow the liquid. There was something almost sensual in his thirst.

He set the bottle down, reached into his pack again and tossed her a hunk of bread. Then he pulled a knife from a cargo pocket and used it to slice a hard yellow cheese wrapped in butcher's paper. *"Signorina?"* He extended a couple of pieces to her.

"Thank you." She wolfed one of them down and took another swig of the wine, starting to feel marginally better. Her courage revived a little, too. "I don't suppose you have aspirin in there?" She pointed to the backpack.

"Perhaps you will make a trade. Information for painkillers."

"I've given you all the information I have!"

He snorted, but reached into the depths of the pack and pulled out a small plastic bottle. He tossed it to her.

She popped the lid and shook a couple of tablets into her hand, inspecting them to make sure they were really aspirin and not some sort of hallucinogenic drug.

He noted that. "Very wise."

When she'd swallowed them she threw the bottle back at him. He caught it easily, even though his attention was distracted by a noise above them. How had he done it? He must have great peripheral vision.

"What is your name?" she asked him. "And where *are* we?"

He turned his grim gaze upon her again, apparently deciding that the noise was nothing to worry about.

"You will not concern yourself with such things. Eat. It is better that you do not know where we are."

CHAPTER FOUR

AFTER PALERMO, *Alexandra's Dream* had stopped in Venice, one of Helena's favorite cities. Now, a couple of days into the Roman Empire Cruise, she curled up with her sketchbook on a chaise on the Helios deck, gazing out at the beautiful port of Dubrovnik. She'd been there many times, so she felt no urgent need to go ashore, but she regretted the fact that Gemma couldn't get away. She'd have loved to show her niece the city itself, as well as the island of Lokrum in the bay, where Richard the Lionheart had been cast ashore in 1192. The densely wooded island carried a legendary curse dating from the last Benedictine monks to reside there.

Helena's mouth twisted as she thought of another curse, this one attached to the nearby bay of Sunj, and having to do with the tragic story of two star-crossed lovers. *How fitting that Nick and I should be here together.*

Dubrovnik was a popular tourist resort town of about 45,000 residents. The Irish playwright George Bernard Shaw had written in 1929, "If you want to see heaven on earth, come to Dubrovnik," and to Helena's mind, he was right.

High, gray stone fortress walls surrounded the city,

protecting it from both the sea and from invaders. The buildings were constructed of the same stone and topped by red-tile roofs.

Helena sat and sketched her view of the walled city, her pencil almost on autopilot, while her subconscious and the wind, water and waves took her back again fifteen years ago to the freighter.

She'd been sketching then, too, as the workers finished unloading, and the handsome owner of the jacket wiped his perspiring face on his shirt. She should have been disgusted, but she hadn't been. He'd looked over at her with a quick grin and a shrug, and she'd smiled back.

Then he'd walked over to her with long, sure strides as his companions nudged each other and watched.

She quickly flipped her sketch pad closed.

"Hello," he said in slightly accented English. "I'm Nikolas." He had a tousle of dark hair, cut short, and wide, intelligent gray eyes that didn't miss a thing. They took her in like a caress.

Nikolas wiped his hand on his pants before extending it to her.

She looked down ruefully at her own charcoal-smeared fingers. Then she wiped them on the inside cover of her sketch pad and took his hand. He laughed and they shook.

"I haven't gotten any smudges on your jacket—I promise," she said with a laugh of her own. "I'm Helena, and I thank you very much for letting me borrow it."

"Helena," he repeated. "After Helen of Troy?"

She felt heat climb her cheeks. But she nodded. "My parents had some romantic notions."

"The face that launched a thousand ships," he murmured, her hand still captured in his.

Actually, it's my father's face that launches them. And his checkbook. But she didn't say anything out loud about Elias Stamos or his maritime empire.

"What are you sketching, Helena?"

"Nothing much."

She kept the pad snug under one arm and tugged her hand out of Nikolas's big, warm one, though he was clearly reluctant to let it go.

"Nothing much? You don't want to show off your work?"

Definitely not! Not when she'd been drawing him all afternoon.

She shook her head. "Just silly gesture drawings and contour drawings, for warm-up. What we do in class for the first half hour."

"You're an art student?"

"Yes. I'm at Parsons School of Design in New York."

He lifted his brows. "Very impressive."

She felt suddenly shy. Impressive? No, she just liked to doodle and smear paint around on canvas. It beat writing dull research papers.

"As you can see, at the moment I'm at the Freighter Institute of Higher Learning, specializing in physical labor," Nikolas said, his eyes dancing. "But I'll be entering the navy in a couple of months. One day I'll command my own ship."

He'd look so handsome in uniform. "That's great. I'm sure you will." She didn't doubt it for an instant, after seeing the way he worked.

They stood without speaking for a moment. She felt oddly tongue-tied, which was unlike her. But his physical presence almost overwhelmed her. He was big and perfectly proportioned, and he had the sexiest neck she'd ever seen. As an art student, she probably noticed things that other people didn't. Her sister, Katherine, would think she was daft for fixating on the nape of a man's neck, but Helena was fascinated by the sheer strength of it, the way his head sat proudly on it and how those powerful shoulders flowed from it. The musculature of the man got to her.

I'm a crazy art student. Why don't I look at his butt, like any other girl? She flushed as she clearly recalled doing that, too.

"I should give back your jacket," she said, starting to shrug out of it. But he caught the lapels and held her lightly by them, smiling down at her.

My God, his eyes. They were thick-lashed, beautiful and as dependable as regular rain in a New York spring. This was a man who was trustworthy; she'd swear it.

"Keep it for the moment. You're cold, and I'm over-heated. You can give it to me later. Meet me on deck at the stern of the ship this evening, when I go off duty." His gaze held integrity, honesty and something intense that she couldn't define. She was fascinated by the clean and commanding line of his jaw. And then there was his mouth, the curve of his lips. She knew an urge to feel them against hers, fit the two of them together like living, breathing puzzle pieces.

Without even thinking, Helena nodded. "All right. I'll meet you later."

"You have my word that I'll smell better," he said, the corners of his eyes crinkling.

"I didn't notice," she said honestly. The only scents she'd caught were those of the salt air and the ship's diesel fumes.

"Nick!" shouted one of the other workers. The man gestured that he was needed.

"I have to go," he said. "But I'll see you this evening. Seven o'clock?" He touched his fingers to hers, not greedily but reassuringly.

She nodded. "All right. Don't work too hard."

He gave her a supremely masculine shrug and a wry smile. "Who says this is work? I'm enjoying myself—because you're here."

She watched him walk away, her eyes once again on his powerful shoulders. She had a feeling she'd just met someone quite remarkable, someone she wouldn't easily forget.

THE HARSH CRY of a gull brought Helena back to the present, and she shook herself out of her reverie, glancing at her slim gold watch. Almost time to meet Gemma.

She went back inside the suite and closed the veranda door. She got dressed, pulling on black slacks and a cobalt-blue tank. She rummaged in a quilted bag full of costume jewelry and excavated a pair of dangly earrings that looked like peacock feathers. And she applied a crimson lipstick and some bronzer to her pale, drawn face. She thought about dispensing with eye makeup, but she didn't want to scare Gemma, after all. By the time Helena left to walk down to the day-care center to see her niece, she resembled a chic department-store mannequin, albeit a short one.

If Gemma didn't have plans after her shift, she could come to dinner with her aunt at the American Grille, one of the ship's more casual restaurants. Helena didn't feel up to making small talk with six to eight strangers at a formal dinner this evening.

She walked past the hot tubs, tennis courts, fitness center and the Starlight Theater of the open Helios deck, and decided to take the scenic route through the Court of Dreams, since a check of her watch told her she had fifteen minutes or so until Gemma's shift ended.

On the Artemis deck, the Court of Dreams dazzled everyone who saw it. It was the ship's main lounge, with monumental Doric columns that spanned three stories.

Over the vast open space hung a fiber-optic chandelier, which made it appear that stars twinkled in the mezzanine ceiling. Among the stars playful cherubs cavorted between clouds and greenery, bringing the Renaissance to the passengers of *Alexandra's Dream*.

A sweeping divided staircase featuring ornate gold railings took her down to groupings of white-and-gold upholstered chairs and sofas, the satellites to a large, black grand piano.

Multitudes of roses and other blooms greeted her from extravagant floral masterpieces, and over all of it presided statues of Aphrodite, Artemis, Athena and Poseidon.

Helena passed the indoor pool called the Mermaid Lagoon before descending another level to the Bacchus deck, where she made her way to the Rose Petal Tearoom, the room she'd designed in honor of her mother. A portrait of Alexandra Rhys-Williams Stamos hung on one wall.

Hi, Mama. Alexandra wore a gentle, refined smile and a diamond pendant on a fine gold chain. She gazed out of her gilt frame at a virtual English garden furnished in Wedgwood pastels, chintz and dark wood. A gold harp stood in one corner, complemented by gold-tiered serving stands and touches of gold in the large Chinese vases that held plants.

The tearoom seemed to reflect everything about Alexandra, the English rose Elias had spirited away to the Greek isles. She had traveled far from her original home, but kept many of her English traditions.

Alexandra had always served afternoon tea to the children and Elias, though in truth he preferred a good single-malt Scotch or grappa. She'd often made tiny tea sandwiches for them herself, and served lovely English biscuits with clotted cream. Helena smiled at the memory.

Why couldn't she be more like her mother? What drew her to modern art instead of refined antiques, brash, saturated color instead of dignified pastels? She didn't know.

Her sister, Katherine, was more like Alexandra, yet Gemma seemed to take after her aunt.

Helena left the Rose Petal and finally headed back to the Helios deck, where the children's center was located. There she found Gemma surrounded by young children and a few toddlers and looking a little frayed. She didn't appear to have much help, since the other intern was working with the older kids.

"Hi, Gem," Helena said as one of the toddlers gleefully tore off the pull-ups her niece had just attached to his bottom, and waved the disposable pants in the air.

"Aunt Helena!" Gemma's face lit up and she rushed over for a hug and a kiss. Then she turned away again. "No, sweetheart, you have to keep those on."

Ignoring her, he dropped the pull-ups and pointed at a plastic vehicle another little boy had in the sandbox area. "Twuck! Twuck!"

"Very *good*," said Gemma. "Yes, that *is* a truck."

"Want twuck!" he howled, while a pair of little girls began to wrestle over a coloring book and another child bashed his companion over the head with an Elmo toy.

The toddler wriggled into the sandbox naked and pulled the truck away from the older boy, who yelled, "Mine!" and knocked the little one over.

The little one spat sand out of his mouth and then launched into a meltdown of epic proportions.

"Dear God!" said Helena, horrified.

Gemma took it all in stride. "Adam, we do not hit other children. If you do that again, I will put Elmo away. Tomas! You know better than that. We never, ever, push anybody down. That's not nice. And he's smaller than you."

"But it's *mine!*"

"It's not yours. We share toys here. But Alexei should have asked you if he could play with you. Right, Alexei?"

"Whaaaaaaaah," the little boy blubbered.

"You're all right, sweetheart. It's just a little sand in your mouth. Come here...."

The squabble between the little girls over the coloring book escalated and Helena jumped in to help where she could. Thankfully, the children wore name tags.

"Thalia, if you two put the book flat on the art table and open it up, you can each have a drawing to color. Like this, sweetie. See how that works? Giannina, you sit here. Now, just be careful not to bump Thalia's arm while you're coloring, okay? Perfect."

"Thank you, Auntie H!" called Gemma, busy with the naked toddler's pull-ups.

"You're welcome. I came down to see if you'd like to have dinner after your shift."

"Love to! Just let me survive the next—" she looked at her watch "—seven and a half minutes."

Helena chuckled.

They were on their way to the American Grille twenty minutes later, after Gemma had a chance to take a quick shower and jump into a simple dress.

Gemma wiped her brow in a classic gesture and laughed. "Whew! What a circus."

Helena had to agree. "So have you talked with your mother lately?" she asked.

Katherine handled public relations for the Liberty Line cruise ships, and sometimes Helena wondered how she could take the stress.

Gemma nodded. "Grandpa is pushing her and my dad to take a romantic vacation together, but they're both so busy. Neither of them has the time."

Good old Elias—meddling in his other daughter's life, too. Helena wasn't surprised.

Gemma echoed her thoughts without realizing it. "I know he loves us all, but sometimes Grandpa tries to run the family like he runs his business."

Helena chuckled. "You're very observant."

They had almost reached the door of the American Grille when a hearty male voice boomed, "Helena Stamos! How are you, beautiful?"

Ugh. She knew that voice. Helena and Gemma turned as one to find Giorgio Tzekas behind them. "Hello, Giorgio." She unwillingly kissed him on both cheeks. "You remember my niece, Gemma?"

"Of course I do," he exclaimed, bringing his lips to her hand. "There was a time when I might have been your father."

Gemma's social smile became fixed and Helena almost snorted. Katherine had barely given him the time of day.

To be polite, she asked about his parents and siblings, but kept edging toward the American Grille.

"So you're having a nice casual dinner tonight?" Giorgio asked, and they nodded. Helena felt forced by good manners to ask if he'd like to join them. After all, his father was a good friend of her father's, and they'd been in and out of each other's homes when they were younger.

"I wish I could, but I'm on duty starting in just a few minutes."

Thank God for small mercies.

He let his eyes rove over her body in an ungentlemanly way.

She flushed.

Then he did the same thing to Gemma, looking as if he liked what he saw there, too.

She's seventeen, you lecher. Helena took Gemma by the arm. "The poor girl is starving after working all day with the children, Giorgio. I must get her fed or I'll have to answer to my sister." She flashed a cool smile at him.

"Of course, of course. Wonderful to see you." And Tzekas departed, to her relief.

"I don't like him," said Gemma baldly.

Helena squeezed her shoulders. "You have excellent instincts, my dear. I don't, either."

THE MAN TRAVELING under an alias watched the little rich bitch flirt with the first officer. Yesterday she'd been making eyes at the captain. What a whore.

He held his espresso cup to his lips and flicked his tongue back and forth along the rim in a habitual gesture. It helped him think, calmed him.

Women—they were all the same. Rich, poor, big, small, smart or dumb: good for one thing, and one thing only. He liked screwing them, but he liked even better to show them who was boss. Humiliate them a little, put them in their places. Just thinking about it got his blood going.

Helena Stamos was only marginally attractive—he liked them blond and tall with more generous assets. She didn't fit the bill, but while he had zero interest in Ms. Stamos physically, he'd watch her. Because she might be useful, judging by the way the captain looked at her when he thought nobody noticed.

Yes, she might be useful, the man mused. He didn't know how yet, but he'd sleep on it.

He held the small cup to his lips again and after sucking in some of the hot, bitter black liquid, he fastened his teeth around the rim and continued to rub his tongue on the edge, harder this time.

For too long his quarry had eluded him. But no longer. He would get a location out of Pappas even if he had to blow off every one of the man's extremities to encourage him to talk.

But it would be tricky getting Pappas alone, somewhere they wouldn't be interrupted. Somewhere relatively soundproof.

The man narrowed his eyes again on Helena Stamos. Yes, she could be quite useful in executing his plan. And if anything were to happen to Helena while the ship was under the command of Nikolas Pappas, Elias Stamos would be most displeased.

The disgrace Pappas had faced at Blue Aegean? That was nothing. He would be shamed beyond recovery this time. And dead, to boot. Corpses couldn't defend their reputations.

The man smiled grimly and drained his espresso, amused when Helena turned and looked into the crowd of diners as if she could feel someone's eyes upon her.

Enjoy the sensation, bitch. Because I certainly do.

CHAPTER FIVE

ALEXANDRA'S DREAM was docked in Corfu. Nick gazed out at the island from the Helios deck while passengers disembarked by the hundreds. He loved the myths of Corfu more than the island itself, which tended to be overrun by wild partiers participating in all kinds of illicit activities. He'd much rather think of the Corfu in Homer's *Odyssey* and in the ten labors of Hercules.

Legend had it that Corfu was put on the map when Poseidon fell in love with a nymph, Korkyra, the daughter of the river Asopos. Not one to take no for an answer, Poseidon abducted her and brought her to an unnamed island, which he named after her. Corfu, or Kerkyra, became her new home.

Corfu's history was just as complicated as Dubrovnik's, full of battles and conquests and drama. Today the island was still enclosed by two castles and dubbed an official Kastropolis, or Castle City, by the Greek government.

Nick was standing in his shirtsleeves, lost in thought at the rail, when Helena unexpectedly appeared in enormous Jackie O sunglasses and a black bikini printed with jasmine blossoms. A matching silk kimono hung over her arm and she carried a straw bag full of suntan lotions, a book and a sketch pad.

She looked as if she'd just stepped out of a magazine, and he struggled to reconcile her with the girl he remembered in paint-stained cargo pants, hair streaming down her back in a dark, exotic river.

She hesitated when she saw him then put her things down on a chaise and came over to join him. They'd parted so awkwardly the day before that he didn't know quite what to say to her. *Are you here to spy on me?* No, that didn't seem like a winning opener.

"Enjoying the cruise?" he said, feeling that this greeting, too, was entirely inadequate.

She cast him a glance that told him she'd play along. "Yes, Captain, I certainly am. And how are you today?"

"Very well, thank you."

They stood there woodenly, looking out at Corfu and Pontikonisi Island. Nick could smell her perfume, a light floral scent, and perhaps it was addling his brain. He felt like a supreme jackass. *Think, Nick. Think of something interesting to say.*

"Your father is very proud of what you've done with the ship's interior." There, that was a start.

She blinked.

"So am I," he added. Not that he had a right to be proud of her. "I mean…it's a pleasure and an honor to command a ship this beautiful."

"Thank you. I wish I could take credit, but all I did was transfer my mother's tastes."

"That's a bit modest, don't you think? You did a tremendous amount of work and communicated her vision artistically—I saw the design boards, you know. Each with a tiny, scrawled *H.S.* in the corner. They were lovely. Little paintings and collages."

He didn't mention that one hung in his stateroom, and that he'd matted and framed it himself. He also didn't mention that he had another "painting" of hers framed, at his rarely used apartment in Athens. A bit of silliness, really. He'd cut the cover off a London theater program that featured a costume rendering of hers.

"Thank you." Helena looked a bit uncomfortable, focusing on spinning the gold bangles on her thin wrists round and round. She noticed him watching her and stopped.

Again silence descended upon them.

Nick, for pity's sake. You spend your life making small talk....

"You know about the legend of Corfu?" he asked.

"Poseidon and the nymph," she said lightly, looking far too much like a nymph herself. "Yes, of course. He decided he had to have her, and stole her away for his pleasure."

Her hair blew back from her cheeks and her soft lips curved. She looked mysterious, alluring and sensual, her skin glowing bronze under the sun. *Poseidon may have had the right idea.* Nick couldn't help but think of stealing Helena away for his pleasure...and hers, too.

Get your head together, you idiot.

"Which castle do you like the best?" he asked, making a sweeping gesture toward both. "The Old Citadel—the Palaio Frourio—or the Palaia Anaktora with her lush gardens?"

"I like them both," she said, "for different reasons. The Frourio is stark and crude but also dramatic and melancholy. The Anaktora is magnificent, so civilized and beautiful. They are rather like male and female, don't you think?"

Does that mean you think I'm stark and crude? But Nick didn't say it out loud. A very different question burned within him. One that he'd wondered about for years.

Instead he asked, "Aren't you going ashore?"

"Are you offering to escort me, Nikolas?" She tilted her head at him, but he couldn't tell anything about her expression behind the huge dark glasses.

"I wish I could," he said, surprised to discover that it was true and not just a formality. *Stay away from her, Nick. What has really changed over fifteen years? So you're captain of a floating hotel—she'll own a fleet of them one day. In the scheme of her world, you are insignificant....*

Her chin went up a notch; her lips flattened ever so slightly. But that was the only indication she gave to him that she cared about having his company.

"I have a mountain of work waiting for me," he said by way of apology.

"Of course. Well, perhaps I'll join one of the shore excursions and have a ramble by myself. Care for a T-shirt, a mug or a snow globe?"

"I'm trying to cut down," he said wryly. "But thanks."

"Well, I'm off to lie in the sun for a bit. Have a nice day, Nikolas."

He had to ask her now or he never would. He touched her arm. "Helena…"

She stopped immediately at the physical contact. "Yes?"

Damn it, he wished she would take those sunglasses off so he could see her face properly. "Why did you never respond to my letters?"

Her mouth parted slightly and she stared at him. "What letters?"

"I wrote to you twice after I left that morning."

"You wrote to me?" She put a hand up to her glasses and finally took them off. Her eyes reflected genuine puzzlement. "Where did you send the letters?"

"To your home."

She knit her brows. "My father's house?"

"Yes."

Her mouth twisted. "Nick, I never got any letters. I had no idea you'd ever tried to get in touch with me again." She looked troubled. "I'm sorry. I just assumed…"

"That I was an uncaring bastard."

She looked miserable and stayed silent.

"Well, perhaps I got the address wrong," Nick said lightly, but he knew damn well that he hadn't. "Enjoy the sun. Won't you join me at the captain's table for the second seating of dinner this evening?"

Judging from the way her lips parted, she was a bit taken aback. But after a small pause she said, "Why not? Thank you. I'd like that."

He nodded. "Good. Then I'll look forward to seeing you." How troubling that again his words weren't simply a formality.

Nick watched Helena glide away in the bikini, which showcased a lithe body that hadn't changed at all, as far as he could see. The rest of her had been gilded and polished to a sheen, making her seem untouchable.

Don't ogle her, man. It's unseemly and inappropriate. Nick's eyes went to the bridge, a reminder of a desk groaning under the weight of all he had to do. He started for the elevator, forcing himself not to look back at her.

GIORGIO TZEKAS NEEDED TO TALK to Mike O'Connor and he needed to talk to him now. He found him ensconced in the library as usual, finishing up one of his pseudo-erudite lectures on Greek antiquities as the charming Father Patrick Connelly.

"Now, as I said, the end of the second millennium B.C. saw the last of the Bronze Age. During this time more and more Greek-speaking tribes appeared in what we now know as the Greek isles. Thus the *sub-mycenaean* style gave way to the *protogeometric*, which you can see on this terra-cotta figurine of a centaur from Lefkandi."

Mike O'Connor, a man with a shadowy past and superb acting abilities, had a pleasantly weathered face and so much natural charm that people trusted him on sight—fools that they were. No one would ever have guessed that he'd lived in a hippie commune in Oregon, possessed a Screen Actors Guild card and loved women more than whiskey.

Today, those bright blue eyes above the snowy-white collar at his neck expressed nothing but earnest scholarship.

Giorgio had difficulty restraining a snort, since he knew that the "good father" had been downloading information from the Internet and then memorizing it, complete with dramatic pauses and facial expressions.

"You will note more sophistication of technique in terms of representation," the charlatan continued, using a pointer as if he'd been born with it in his hand, "as well as more elegant and difficult contours in the vases and pots themselves. The old nature-based decorative motifs give way to abstract ones."

Tzekas tried to stop his eyes from rolling back in his skull. He didn't give a damn about all this crap, and neither did Mike—er, Father Connelly. All they cared about was the amount of cash these dusty pieces of history would bring on the black market.

"You see triangles, rectangles, cross-hatching and concentric circles. All of these emphasize the rigidly defined contours that are characteristic of Greek ceramics."

Giorgio looked at his watch.

"Have any of you ladies and gentlemen ever tried to throw a pot on the wheel? It's very difficult."

"I threw a pot at my ex-husband once, Father," quipped an elderly lady, grinning like a monkey. "I thought it was pretty easy."

Several people in the group laughed.

Mike touched his priest's collar and cleared his throat, but his eyes twinkled. "Yes, well. We all know the blessed state of matrimony can be challenging at times." As a teenage girl stared at him in curiosity, he added, "From what I hear." He smiled broadly.

Yes, better not to mention your two ex-wives, Father. Giorgio waited impatiently while O'Connor nodded indulgently at the passengers' silly questions.

He seemed to be encouraging them, when he knew damned well that Giorgio needed to speak with him.

Finally all of the idiots left the ship's library and they were alone.

"Shall I forgive you?" Mike asked, the sacrilegious bastard. "For there is no doubt that you have sinned."

"I've sinned? Are you crazy? It's *you* that people are gossiping about!"

"Me? I'm a holy man. Why would anyone talk about a priest?"

"Oh, I don't know," said Tzekas with heavy sarcasm. "Perhaps if the priest were seen *without his collar* in a *bar* on shore, tipping back a healthy amount of whiskey."

Mike lost some of his mocking assurance, but quickly recovered. "Clearly, they were mistaken. Father Connelly would never go to a bar or drink whiskey. It was dark. Whoever saw him was probably under the influence."

"Oh, yes? And how does Father Connelly explain why he's been flirting in a very unpriestly way with that California widow on board?"

Mike reddened. "Ah. Well. Let us keep in mind that the good Father would never act upon any…base urges…he might have in that direction."

Giorgio folded his arms. "He'd better not, or he'll endanger the whole smuggling operation."

"Keep your voice down! And speaking of our entre-preneurial forays, you've been busy, Officer Tzekas. Busy doing things that you shouldn't. Did you think I wouldn't hear of it?"

"What are you talking about?" Giorgio avoided Mike's gaze. He couldn't possibly know!

"The amphora you tried to purchase? From the dig in Naples?"

Giorgio leaned his head back and cracked his neck to alleviate tension. "So? What of it?"

"The boss gave us very clear roles, Tzekas. *I* make the buys. *You* ensure they are properly hidden on board the ship."

"Yes, and you're doing such a good job helping with that, *Father,* bringing them into plain sight in the library and mixing them with the reproductions! You must be crazy."

"And you did better, did you? The captain was mighty pleased when they discovered those stolen antiquities in the potted plants on our very first cruise. Brilliant hiding place. You almost cost us the whole scheme."

Giorgio clenched his fists. "The captain." He spat. "I hate that man. He's such a tight-ass, so morally superior. As if he's better than we are." He snorted. "I'd like to see him turn down this kind of money."

"He would, you know. But you'll just have to keep your mouth shut and deal with him, because he's not going anywhere, and he *is* your boss."

"I don't answer to that piece of sh—"

Mike clamped a hand around his forearm. "You *do* answer to him, Tzekas. So you'd better watch your step. Keep your pride in your pocket and your drinking under control. And don't try to make any more buys on your own, you stupid bugger. Do you hear me?"

Tzekas glared at him. "I don't answer to you, either, O'Connor. And instead of lecturing me, you'd best keep your *pecker* in your pocket and your ass out of bars."

CHAPTER SIX

DINNER WAS A FORMAL affair on *Alexandra's Dream*, an opportunity for the ladies to shine. And they did—but to Nick's eyes Helena Stamos outshone them all. She was, quite simply, dazzling.

She put even the elegance of the Empire Room to shame, difficult to do with its silk wall-hangings, fine china and glittering crystal.

The low-cut, green-silk gown she wore clung to every curve of her body. The color set off her dark hair and her tanned skin glowed in the low, romantic lighting. Emerald drop earrings dangled from her lobes, bronze sandals lent her stature and she looked like some kind of woodland goddess. She was beyond beautiful.

But since the gentleman on her right held her attention, Nick was forced to make polite conversation with the lady to his left, the wife of a former U.S. ambassador who enjoyed dropping the name of every important person whose hand she'd ever shaken.

"I had the pleasure of meeting Camilla Parker Bowles before she and Prince Charles tied the knot, *Capitano*. I thought she was just lovely, couldn't have been nicer. Rather a pity that we'll never see a Queen Camilla…."

Nick smiled and nodded while consuming his lamb. He had an endless supply of stories and amusing anecdotes at his disposal, but this woman rendered them moot.

"And when I was in Italy years ago, do you know whom I ran into at a cocktail party? Gianni Agnelli himself. Now wasn't he the dapper don? Such a loss when he died. He had some fascinating stories to tell!" She launched into one of them with gusto while Nick tried to pay attention, but he couldn't help being distracted by Helena.

He remembered in unfortunate detail the first "date" they'd ever shared, standing at the stern of the Greek freighter he worked on. A freighter owned by Elias Stamos, coincidentally. Nick had brought her a bottle of Pelegrino and a smile, not knowing that Helena's other boyfriends probably supplied champagne, four-star menus and impossibly expensive jet-fueled junkets.

HE HAD ARRIVED first at the meeting point, but she was prompt, looking a little sleepy and carrying his jacket over one arm. "Hi," she said.

Nick *was* on a high—just by looking at her. "Hello. May I interest you in some warm Pellegrino from my pocket?"

She'd looked up at him and laughed, the curves of her beautiful mouth reaching for her eyes and lighting them. "Best offer I've had all day—except, of course, for your jacket." She handed it to him, but as he took it, she shivered.

Over her protests, he wrapped her up in it once more,

shaking his head sadly. "I'm never going to get it back, am I? This is all a feminine plot to rob me of my clothing."

When he thought of it now, he cringed. As if the daughter of a billionaire would want to snake his crummy canvas coat. But she'd never let on, the girl with the silver dolphins in her ears. Not once.

"You're on to me." She nodded, her lips quirking saucily. "I just thought your jacket would look divine with a pair of stolen midshipman's pants I have."

Nick raised his eyebrows. "I don't think I want to hear the story of how you got those. I might become jealous."

She'd blushed. "I was kidding. Besides, you can't be jealous over someone you've only just met."

"If it's you, I can." Nick restrained his urge to smooth her hair out of her face and shoved his hands into his pockets instead. "I don't let just anyone wear my coat."

HELENA'S LAUGH RANG OUT as the old gentleman on her other side said something amusing, and Nick did feel jealous, which was silly. But he couldn't help wondering if she'd ever laugh like that again for him.

Ridiculous. He needed to banish such notions. He'd given up any claim to Helena Stamos fifteen years ago, and nothing had changed.

But as he chatted and chuckled and charmed the rest of the table, he continued to be acutely aware of her, drinking in her smallest gesture.

At the end of the meal, strains of traditional Greek music began in the Polaris Lounge above them on the Bacchus deck, and Nick took that as a welcome cue to perform a last social duty or two before departing for the peace of his stateroom. He touched his mouth with his napkin and then laid it on the table before turning to the lady and gentleman on Helena's right.

"Sir," Nick asked, "may I steal your lovely wife away for a dance?" If he danced with a couple of other women first, he could fit it into protocol to lead Helena onto the floor—assuming she'd allow it.

The gentleman rubbed his beard thoughtfully, while his wife blushed like a girl. "I don't know, Captain. What are your intentions?" His eyes twinkled and his wife smacked him lightly on the arm.

Nick's lips twitched. "Strictly honorable, sir, I promise."

"Well, now, isn't that a bore. I won't be able to challenge you to a duel?" His wife gasped and broke into laughter and he waved his hand at Nick. "I think you'd best have someone else's wife to dance with, Captain. Or even a single lady," he added slyly, looking straight at Helena. "What do you think?"

Had the older man noticed Nick watching her during dinner? He'd thought he'd been discreet.

"Oh, I'm not much of a dancer," Helena said quickly, her color rising.

Nick decided to accept the old man's help, unexpected though it was. "I'd be so very honored," Nick told Helena, "if you would join me."

Faced with no graceful way out, she allowed him to draw out her chair and take her hand, which quivered slightly in his. Interesting.

"Thank you all very much for joining me this evening," Nick said to the table at large. "The pleasure has been all mine." There was a chorus of similar responses, and he smiled easily and wished them good-night.

Then he drew Helena toward him, took one glance at her skyscraper heels and led her from the dining room to the elevator. He finally had her to himself, though she remained expressionless and politely aloof as they walked out of the elevator and onto the Bacchus deck.

Her elbow felt so delicate in his big palm. Nick slowed to allow her to keep pace with him, and caught a whiff of her exotic perfume—a floral that wasn't over-poweringly sweet. Gardenias? Jasmine? Honeysuckle. It reminded him of honeysuckle.

This was a different perfume from the one she'd worn at eighteen. Then she'd smelled of a soft soap and…the name escaped him. It flashed into his subconscious. "Chanel No. 19," he said out loud.

She stopped, looked up at him, her expression arrested.

"The scent you wore when we met." He smiled.

"Yes. I can't believe you'd remember that."

"I remember everything about you."

"Surely not everything," she said with a skeptical laugh.

"No? Your favorite music, opera. Specifically, *The Magic Flute* and *Aida*. Your favorite book, *The Odyssey*. Favorite food, French profiteroles. Favorite wine, a chilled Pinot Grigio. Favorite place to relax, Santorini."

"Be still my heart," Helena said lightly after a small, stunned pause.

They had reached the Polaris Lounge, and Nick slid his right arm around her waist and took her hand in his. He looked down into her upturned face, fell into those dark eyes of hers and got lost.

She was lithe and graceful; always had been. They moved together in perfect fluidity, and Nick began to enjoy dancing with her far too much.

"You look beautiful tonight," he said formally.

"And you look handsome."

The compliments were clunkers, spoken on automatic pilot. Awkwardness and tension built between them. Helena's expression, underneath the social smile, was miserable. Did she hate him that much?

Regret sliced into him. Once, he could have sworn she'd loved him. Once, she'd been his and the future had looked golden, stretching ahead of them like one long holiday. Until the afternoon on Santorini when he'd gone back to the freighter to help with the provisioning. He'd been scheduled to rejoin the ship in the morning.

His superior officer had asked if he'd had a nice vacation. In an odd tone.

Oblivious, Nick spread his arms wide and grinned. "Of course. How could I have a bad one? We're on Santorini and I'm in love!"

His boss had taken Nick aside. He could still see the man clearly as he stood in his office on board. Franco was a small, portly man with sparse, graying hair, a nose like a button and a thick, coarse, silvery mustache that resembled a scrub brush.

"Sit down, Pappas."

Nick sat. "Is something wrong, sir?"

"That all depends upon how you look at it."

"Sir?"

"Pappas, what do you know about the girl you've been romancing?"

Nick stiffened. "I don't see how that's—"

"You're right." Franco overrode him. "It wouldn't normally be my business. However, she's Elias Stamos's daughter."

Nick stared at him. "The shipping magnate?"

Franco nodded. "The man who signs your paycheck. And mine. Very protective of his girls. Do you understand?"

But Nick barely heard his words. His thoughts flew back to the night when he'd asked Helena, half kidding, if she were related to Elias. They'd been on the beach at Mykonos that evening, drinking wine and kissing in the moonlight.

She'd laughed easily. *Stamos is a very common name, Nikolas....* And she'd headed for the water, looking like temptation itself. He'd followed, and that had been the very first night they'd made love, in the tiny little room they'd rented, with blue and white furniture.

Nick blinked at his boss. If that had been heaven, then this had to be the gateway to hell. He had a ring in his pocket for her, had planned to propose that very night. *And she'd lied to him about her identity.*

"Pappas, do you hear what I'm saying? If you're smart, you'll end this affair. Now."

"Sir, with all due respect, this is my personal life," Nick said evenly.

"In this case, it's also your professional one. And mine. If you're smart, you won't mix the two."

"Thank you for your concern, sir," Nick said between gritted teeth. His thoughts went haywire. How could Helena have lied to him? Had she just been having a fling at his expense? The shipping princess, slumming it with the deckhand?

Franco sighed. "Pappas. I know this isn't easy to hear. It's not easy for me to say. I don't enjoy it. But you're a fine young man, and I'd hate to see your future ruined. Take my advice. Forget about this girl. Work hard in the navy. Study. And learn to take orders a little better, eh? You like to do things your own way, I see that. But let that come later. Learn the rules before you break them. All right?"

Nick stared at him stonily. "Am I dismissed, sir?"

His boss nodded, his eyes full of understanding that Nick could do nothing but resent. "Dismissed."

NOW HE STOOD in the moonlight again with the boss's daughter. He was a captain now, not a deckhand, but it made no difference. All of the shiny buttons on his dress uniform were nothing but brass.

They didn't hold a candle to the flawless emeralds in her ears or anything else in her jewelry box. Top brass had nothing on royalty, and to Nick, Helena was royalty.

He'd never confronted her about what he'd learned, which was unlike him. He'd simply been too stunned. He'd made love to her one last time in the little bed, pretending that everything was fine.

"Is something bothering you, Nikolas?" she had asked.

"No, *agape mou*," he'd lied. Because he still hadn't made up his mind to walk away. He hadn't bought an engagement ring lightly.

But in the small hours of the morning, as he'd

watched her sleep, he'd at last come reluctantly to a decision. Even if she wasn't playing him, slumming for fun, he couldn't marry someone who'd deliberately hidden her identity from him. And the daughter of Elias Stamos, a billionaire, wouldn't have him, anyway. It was out of the question.

He could have woken her. Could have gotten some kind of explanation. Could have said goodbye. But instead he'd moved silently around the tiny room, gathering his things into his ancient duffel bag. She hadn't stirred once.

He'd stood gazing at her; almost changed his mind. Then he'd bent and kissed her lightly on the lips before leaving for good.

SO WHAT WAS HE DOING with her in his arms tonight? Torturing himself? Trying to relive the past? All he knew was that he didn't want her to hate him, as she seemed to.

"Tell me about your work, Helena," he prompted. "What's it like? How do you even begin to design costumes for every last actor in a production?"

She shrugged slightly. "I talk with the director first, to make sure we're on the same page. I find out what his or her vision is. And then I begin to think of designs, fabrics and details that will distinguish each character but still contribute to an overall 'feel' for the project. I make sketches and then complete illustrations of how I see the character. I meet with the director again and incorporate any suggestions or changes. Then I start choosing fabrics and making patterns."

"You do it all yourself?"

"I create the patterns myself. I have help with the cutting and sewing."

"You love what you do—I can tell from your voice."

She nodded. "I do love it. There are challenges, as with every job. Sometimes a design may be utterly unsuited to a particular actor or he may interpret his role very differently from the way I do. In that case, we have to fall back and regroup. Then there are always adjustments and issues, right up until opening night. After that, I can relax and let assistants handle anything that comes up during the stage run—unless it's a film. Then I have to be on set almost constantly."

"I admire you," Nick said. "I don't have a creative bone in my body."

She looked up at him with a small smile. "You might be surprised. Creativity is mostly problem solving. The rest is just skill and practice. I would assume that you problem-solve every day."

He nodded slowly. "I can't even draw a stick man, though."

"You could if you studied it. I promise. It's just a different way of seeing."

They fell silent for a few beats, and Nick enjoyed the feel of her in his arms.

Then she asked, "So what do you like the most about your job?"

"Being on the water and in constant motion," Nick said. "I'm a Gypsy at heart, just like you. And I like meeting all sorts of different people. The paperwork—that I could do without." He chuckled.

Helena had begun to relax slightly but now he felt

tension work its way back into her shoulders and her posture. He wondered why.

Her mouth quivered and her next question came after what was clearly a great internal struggle. "Nick…what did you do to earn your captain's hat?"

He misunderstood. "I spent ten years in the navy, piloting every kind of vessel. I worked damn hard and studied for hours every night. I learned proper etiquette in my nonexistent spare time. And I never doubted that one day I'd have my own ship."

"I know…you told me you would, the first time we met." Her dark eyes held some emotion he couldn't quite read. Regret? Suspicion? Condemnation?

He studied her, trying to comprehend it. And then he realized that he'd answered her question literally, when she'd asked it with a double meaning. Suddenly he understood why she'd struggled.

She was asking if it was coincidence that they'd met aboard her father's freighter, that he'd suddenly put an end to their relationship and disappeared, and now fifteen years later he was in command of one of Elias's ships….

His jaw tightened and he almost left her on the dance floor.

"I did *not* earn it by walking away from the daughter of Elias Stamos," he said icily.

She searched his eyes, her own full of old hurt and suspicion. "Nick, I'm so sorry, but I had to ask. I love my father, but I do know what he's capable of. He doesn't mean to do harm, but…"

Nick glared back at her. "Did you really think so little of *me?*"

Her lips trembled. "I didn't know what to think of you, Nikolas. You left without a word. I woke up and you were gone. I imagined all sorts of things, every possible scenario."

"You shouldn't have imagined that one." His tone was harsher than he meant it to be, but even now, after so long, he was hurt.

She looked away. "Then truly, I'm sorry. But I still don't know what to think of you, Nikolas. You're an enigma."

"And you're a riddle." He tossed the comment back at her.

"Meaning we both need answers?"

He paused for a moment. "Something like that."

The music continued and other couples whirled by, but the two of them were silent. At last the song ended and Helena pulled away. "I'm going to go back to my room. I just don't feel comfortable here with you."

She looked vulnerable, lost, confused.

In spite of her expert makeup, the exquisite jewels, the couture gown, she suddenly seemed much more like the girl he'd left sleeping one morning all those years ago. The careful social mask had dropped.

Though he was still insulted, he felt regret that the evening was ending this way. "Then you have my apologies."

"Do I?" Helena asked. "I've waited fifteen years for them. That's a long time."

He could feel his jaw bunching as he looked at her. She owed *him* an apology. He said nothing at all.

Her chin came up. Banked hurt and pride glittered in

her dark eyes. "Thank you for the dance, Nikolas. Take care." She turned on one elegant heel and walked away.

He caught up in three smooth strides and rested his fingers lightly at the small of her back, trying not to touch her any more than necessary. "I'll see you back to your room."

"That's not necessary," she said coldly.

"To me it is. If a woman is in my care, I see to it that she gets home safely."

She raised her eyebrows, but didn't debate him verbally. Yet in that simple dubious expression she reminded him that he hadn't seen her home safely on that last morning so many years ago. He'd disappeared without a note or an explanation, leaving her to wake up to an empty bed.

But she had lied to him. She'd been a princess toying with a deckhand, slumming it on a freighter for fun and a change of scene. She'd never been serious about him—he wasn't the kind of boy she could take home to meet her family.

Yes, he could picture that scene.

Daddy, this is my boyfriend, Nick, who grew up in a three-room cottage. His father is a fisherman. He owns three shirts, two pairs of pants and a 1964 Fiat that only runs a third of the time. He's never been to the opera, didn't finish school and probably thinks that the Nike of Samothrace is a gym shoe....

Anger suffused Nick as he politely escorted Helena back to her penthouse suite and opened the door for her. When had she planned to tell him? Clearly, not until after she'd had her fill of how the other half lived.

She paused in the doorway, hesitated as if she were about to say something. Then she shook her head. "Thank you, Nikolas," she said in formal tones.

He nodded stiffly. "Sleep well."

CHAPTER SEVEN

HELENA DIDN'T SLEEP well at all, in violation of the captain's orders. She was too conflicted about the conversation she'd had with Nick. On the one hand, she was relieved that he did have integrity. Her father hadn't purchased his life and behavior like a bag of nuts at a bodega.

On the other hand, she was saddened even more that Nick must have tired of her after a brief but intense romance. She didn't know what she'd done wrong.

They'd had so much fun together when they'd arranged to meet again after her freighter trip. A half summer of love. They'd gone sailing on a catamaran during the daytime, skinny-dipped in the ocean at night, shared picnics on the beach and restaurant meals on Santorini. She'd pulled him into art galleries, where he was clearly out of his element but intrigued by many pieces.

She'd sketched him while he lay on his stomach, reading an action-adventure novel. If she were honest with herself, she'd acknowledge that she still knew exactly where that sketch was, in her old college art portfolio. She'd never taken it out again to look at it, but she hadn't ripped it up, either.

There in the dark, surrounded by nothing but time

and thought, Helena began to weep silently, something she hadn't done since she'd lost the baby. Her tears weren't for the hurt she felt, but for what might have been if only Nick had given them a chance.

But he'd been a typical twenty-one-year-old male, ready to sample as many women as the world would offer up to him on a platter. He had probably moved on to someone he found more intriguing, or sexier, or just different.

She reminded herself that she'd moved on, too. Within weeks she was dating another student back at Parsons, a guy with a ponytail, a ring through his nose and a black-leather attitude. She couldn't even remember his name now.

Since then, she'd gone out with bankers and lawyers and doctors. She'd even had a somewhat passionate affair with an Austrian chef—forced to leave him when she admitted to herself that it was mostly for the food.

And finally, Ari had come along. Or rather, he'd been pushed at her by her father.

Helena dried her eyes on a corner of the sheet and rolled over, stuffing her head under the goose-down pillow. Of all the mistakes she'd made, marrying Ari was the worst.

He was so *nice*. A gentleman, if not a scholar. Placid instead of volatile, like the chef. He'd treated her with deference and respect even though he was clearly eager to take things to a more intimate level.

Helena cringed. After six weeks of outings and dinners and charity events, he'd started undressing her one night.

And though she felt mostly indifferent about him, somehow she didn't want to hurt him. He was just so *nice*.

And so she'd given herself to him and made him happy beyond belief.

How could she have done it? When she thought about it now, it hadn't been kind. The kindest thing she could have done was to tell him after that first dinner that it would never work out between them.

Hindsight is twenty/twenty. Two weeks after she'd slept with Ari, she'd been horrified when she didn't get her period. And though she knew many people who'd terminated pregnancies, it didn't once cross her mind.

She was thrilled as the baby grew inside of her. And then Elias became involved. Her child needed a father, and wasn't it selfish of her to deny it that, merely because her would-be husband didn't excite her?

Katherine had remained neutral on the subject, telling Helena to follow her heart. But what was the correct answer?

She'd finally done the "right" thing…then lost the baby in an unexpected, heartbreaking turn of events, and ended by hurting Ari terribly. Three months after the divorce decree, she still felt like a lower life form.

Her thoughts turned back to Nick, the man she'd been so sure she'd have children with one day. How could she have misread him so completely? Did he look at every woman the way he'd looked at her? As if she were the only one in the world?

Get over it, you silly twit. Still mooning after your first lover—ridiculous. And why? Because he took your not-so-prized virginity?

She gave up on sleep, at least for the next few hours. At last Helena fumbled for the bedside light, switched it on and went to her portfolio. She pulled out a sketch pad, a Conté crayon and a box of oil pastels. She'd brainstorm for the *Tosca* production, flood her mind with line and color and draping and pattern. Because otherwise, she'd drive herself crazy thinking about the past.

The ideas came, thank God. They rushed into her mind so fast that she could barely get them down on paper before they disappeared. She worked like a madwoman through the dawn, then through noon. She ordered coffee and a light lunch from room service and continued to work until sunset, telling her niece what she was up to.

Two-thirds of the sketch pad was full, and she'd explored three possible color schemes.

Finally, her neck and shoulders screaming from being hunched over for so long, she put everything aside and went to scrub her hands, which were covered in streaks and smears. The mirror over the sink let her know that she had smears on her nose and cheek, too.

It was time for a long, hot bath and a nice glass of wine. Maybe even two—she'd worked hard and deserved to relax now.

NICK STOPPED outside Helena's penthouse suite door and took a deep breath before knocking. *I just want to clear the air between us, once and for all. There's no need for hostility after so many years.*

He knocked, hearing the strains of *Tosca* from within the suite. She'd loved opera even at the age of eighteen, when most girls had listened to INXS or Tears for Fears or Squeeze.

A moment went by, then two. Perhaps she hadn't heard him over the music? Nick raised his hand to knock again and the door opened to reveal Helena.

His mouth went dry. She stood before him without makeup, tendrils of her hair damp and curling around her flushed face. She wore nothing but a white terry bathrobe and he tried heroically not to remember what lay beneath it. She held a glass of white wine in her right hand and her eyes were a little too bright.

"Nikolas," she said. "What a surprise. Did you come to place a mint on my pillow?"

"I—" He broke off. How could this one woman reduce him to strangled syllables? "I haven't seen you all day." Great—that sounded as if he'd been looking for her. "So I came to check on you and to ask if there's anything you need," he said, trying to recover. "We…parted awkwardly last night and I regret that."

"Why, thank you. How gentlemanly. *Entrez-vous,* Nick. Care for a drink?"

"No, thank you." He stood stiffly outside the door, feeling that it was inappropriate for him to enter, given her state of undress.

"Come in. If you need an excuse, the door to the veranda is giving me trouble." Something dark and reckless shone in her eyes, and it made him wary. However, he stepped into her room.

The plum cotton gypsy skirt lay tossed over a chair and the olive camisole hung from one of the drawer pulls on the dresser. Her gold bangles winked from the desktop. Just what he needed. An unbidden image of Helena walking around the room in only her panties.

Seeing her in the robe was torture enough. The broad shawl collar sat low on her shoulders, exposing too much soft, delicate skin, showcasing those collarbones he'd liked to trace with his fingers when she was eighteen and he was twenty-one.

Nick averted his gaze and went straight to the veranda door, examining the lock. It was indeed stiff, but then so was he, which was humiliating. As if he were a pubescent boy with no self-control. He pretended to fiddle with the lock and looked instead at the vast expanse of blue water, willing his problem to go away.

She stood right behind him, though, and when she turned off the music he could hear her soft breathing. "Why, Nick?"

Slowly he turned to face her. She'd drained most of the wine in her glass and the reckless quality he'd noticed had deepened. It appeared in the curve of her lips and in the tilt of her head.

"Why?" she repeated. "Why did you leave me like that, fifteen years ago?"

He said nothing.

"You came by to see if I needed anything?"

Nick nodded.

"Well, what I need is to know. Right now. What did I do wrong that you couldn't even give me a kiss goodbye?"

"I did kiss you," he said quietly. He had, as she lay there sleeping, her hair spread in a dark tangle across the stark white pillow. He'd kissed those soft lips, the side of her jaw, both eyelids and even her forehead. Then he'd kissed her lips again, clenching the gold ring in his pocket. The one set with the tiniest, most pathetic diamond that a woman like Helena Stamos would ever see.

And he'd picked up his miserable, patched canvas duffel and left the room quickly, before he broke down and cried like a child.

Nick didn't really care to remember the scene, and he didn't want to explain it to her. But Helena stood there in front of him, poking around in the past.

"Oh, you *did* kiss me. I don't remember. Was it good for you? Because it didn't have much of an impact on me."

"You were asleep," he told her.

She came closer to him, too close. "Yes. And you crept out like the proverbial thief in the night. Did you ever think about me again, Nick?" She tilted her head back, gazing intently into his face, and the movement shifted the robe so that it slipped off one of her shoulders. *Lord Almighty.*

"Yes. I did think of you." *You have no idea how much.* But his words came out sounding wooden.

"As a plaything from your past?" She moved within inches of him, her breasts almost touching the white fabric of his uniform. Nick could smell her, look into her dusky, inviting cleavage. *God help me.* His little problem returned, and this time she noticed.

Nowhere to hide, nowhere to run. She was a woman and he was a man. He closed his eyes. "I never thought of you as a plaything," he said hoarsely.

The corners of her mouth quirked up in a peculiarly female smile. "Did you miss me, Nick?"

He nodded.

"Did you miss…this?"

His eyes flew open. She'd untied her robe and dropped it to the floor. *Dear God in heaven.*

He stared helplessly at the body he'd seen so often in his dreams over the years. She had soft, supple breasts with rosy-pink nipples, a trim waist, curvaceous hips and…if she didn't put her robe back on *immediately,* he was going to get reacquainted with every inch of her.

Nick forced air back into his lungs and reached for her robe. "Put it back on," he said, his tone harsh.

She ignored him and cupped her own breasts, raising them in an offering to him. "Touch them, Nick. You used to love them—"

"Helena, you're drunk." He threw the robe around her shoulders, holding it closed. Instead of seductive, she now looked forlorn, lost. Damaged.

She pulled away from him and threw the robe to the floor again. "Tell me you don't like what you see."

"Put. It. On," he said through clenched teeth.

"I'll put it on when you tell me how you could have been such a goddamned coward!" she said passionately. "To leave without a word. I was in love with you, Nick! *In love!*"

His temper started to rise.

"Did you have a girl on the side? Two? Or did you just tire of me?"

Fine. She wanted to know the truth? He'd spell it out for her. "I had a diamond ring in my pocket when I left you." He practically ground the words out. "I was going to propose that very night."

Her face drained of color and she stumbled backward to a chair, her eyes wide.

Nick picked up the robe again and threw it at her. "But you lied to me, Helena."

"*What?* When?"

He strode over to where she sat and placed his hands flat on the table next to her chair. He leaned across it until he was inches from her face. "I asked you point blank whether you were related to Elias Stamos. You laughed it off. You dodged the question. 'Stamos is a common name,' you said. Remember?"

She looked away. A guilty flush climbed her cheeks.

"Yes, you remember," he said flatly. He straightened and walked to the veranda door, turning his back on her. "How do you think it felt," he said conversationally, "when I discovered that I, a deckhand on a freighter, was about to propose to the daughter of a billionaire? With a diamond no larger than the head of a pin?"

Silence greeted his words. A terrible, yawning, painful silence.

"How do you think it felt, Helena?" he repeated. Nick swung around with a savage energy.

Tears poured silently down her stricken face and he couldn't bear the sight. He rushed to her, intending to take her into his arms, when she finally opened her mouth.

"I didn't lie," she said.

And those three words made him angrier than anything else. "You lied."

She took a deep, shuddering breath. "I avoided the question." She wiped her streaming eyes on the robe, which she clutched to her nakedness.

He looked at her scathingly while a war escalated inside him. He wanted to comfort her, stop the tears, but he also wanted to shake her. "Semantics, Helena."

"I wanted to know that you loved me for myself, and not for my money or my connections."

She may as well have slapped him. She'd already questioned his integrity and his honor once. But twice? The professional calm of years threatened to completely abandon him, but Nick had learned to be disciplined. "Well, now you know."

Helena sent him a single anguished glance. Her mouth trembled with emotion and probably too much wine. Then she collapsed, quietly weeping, onto the table.

Again, he found himself wanting to comfort her, and this time that instinct won out. He strode to the chair and picked her up bodily, cradling her in his arms. "Shh, *agape mou*. Shh, my love. It's all right. It's all right. Shh."

He sat on the edge of the bed with her and kissed her forehead. He stroked her hair and murmured endearments to her until she quieted. He shifted her onto the coverlet and went into the bathroom for a washcloth, which he wet with cold water.

Nick sat with Helena on the bed again and tilted up her chin with his finger. He gently wiped the tears from her cheeks while she sniffled and her eyes welled up again.

"I did lie," she whispered.

That was all it took. "Yes, you did." He forgave her instantly. He wasn't sure how he felt about that.

"I'm so sorry, Nick."

"Shh. It's okay."

"It's not," she insisted. "But I loved you so much that I couldn't bear it if it wasn't real. I felt I had to hide my identity, protect what we had at all costs...."

And in doing so, she'd destroyed it.

CHAPTER EIGHT

As Nick held her and rocked her and wiped away her tears, Helena wished all the layers of fabric between them would simply disappear. How ironic that all of the material was white: white terry robe, white captain's uniform, white coverlet on the bed. The color of innocence, virgins and weddings. A sardonic chuckle escaped her—white was certainly not her color.

Scarlet's my color. And rich purple. Dramatic, emerald-green. Blazing orange. Not white.

She eventually lost herself in her scattered thoughts and fell asleep cradled in Nick's arms, her head on his chest. At some point he must have fallen asleep, too, but when she woke three hours later he was watching her, his gray eyes clouded like a London sky.

She looked into his face, marveling at how the years had changed him, and yet how familiar he still looked. The slight crinkles at the outside corners of his eyes only made him more handsome. Sun and time had etched deep grooves along the edges of his mouth, and his skin told the story of a life spent aboard ship.

But he was still the Nick she'd known and loved once; still the Nick who'd changed her from a girl to a woman.

She wanted to reach up and run her fingers along his strong jaw, but it was such a bad idea. Just as it was a bad idea for her to lie in his arms for hours. She was still stunned at his revelation—and now that the effects of the wine had worn off, embarrassed at her own behavior.

Another man might have taken her up on her offer, but Nick hadn't taken advantage of her intoxication— even though he'd clearly been aroused. "An officer *and* a gentleman," she whispered.

He laid a finger across her lips, then shifted so that she lay on her side and he could prop himself on his elbow. He continued to look into her eyes as if he sought the answers to some immutable truth.

"God help me," he said huskily. And then he bent his head and kissed her.

A welcome shock; sudden electricity in her veins; a deep, wrenching desire—Helena felt all of these as she opened to him, welcomed him as he made love to her mouth.

He cupped her chin, traced her collarbone, trailed an index finger down from the hollow of her throat to the hollow between her breasts. This time it was Nick who parted her robe, and he did it not with recklessness, as she had, but with an exquisite sweetness, as if he were unwrapping a long-awaited gift.

She quivered under his hands, unsure of how far she should let this go, yet knowing that if she stopped him she might never forgive herself.

Then Nick did something unexpected. He pressed his cheek against her abdomen and simply looked up at her. "What do you want, *agape mou?*" His voice was still husky, not smooth and rich as it normally was.

"I want…" Her voice trembled. "I don't want you to stop."

"Are you certain?"

"Yes, Nikolas. But this time it's different. We're adults, not starry-eyed kids. No promises are necessary, no words at all."

Nick listened to her heartbeat and the tiny noises of her stomach and hesitated. He inhaled the scent of her and tried to think clearly, pushing aside the fog of desire and some primal, masculine urge to make her his, and his alone. It was sheer lunacy for them to do this, and for what? Some memories of the past? Unresolved feelings and a need for closure? For God's sake, they lived in different countries and different social circles, separate worlds, really.

He also wasn't sure he liked her terms—or non-terms. No promises…meaning no complications. Nothing meaningful or substantial. No pot of gold at the end of the rainbow. His mouth twisted.

Yet was there any other way for him and Helena Stamos to be together? A woman like her wasn't going to marry the son of a fisherman. And it still troubled him that she'd deceived him, even if he understood it more now.

Do you want her? That's the question. Now, in this moment?

Hell, yes.

Then admit it, Pappas. Your hands are tied.

"Nick? Really, this doesn't have to be difficult. No promises. You don't want any, and I'm too damaged to make them at the moment."

Her words told him more than she intended to. They told him that the urge was there—she had feelings for him. Part of him was elated, part of him sad. He didn't think he'd ever get married again. He'd hated the feeling of letting his wife down, watching the light dim in her eyes over the months and then simply turn off. They'd been wrong for each other, just as Helena and Ari had been. But what guaranteed that Helena and he would mesh any better? They'd spent half a summer together long ago.

"Nick?"

He looked down at her upturned face and slid his hand from the small of her back. He put a finger under her pixie chin and surprised himself by saying, "I never had difficulty making promises to you."

"I don't want them," she said, her voice catching. "I'm done with unkept promises."

His back went rigid. "I never made you a promise that I didn't keep."

"Relax, Nikolas. I'm not talking about you—I'm talking about me. I walked away from my wedding vows."

"And I walked away from mine," he said after a moment. "Do you think I'm proud of that?"

"I didn't know you had married," she said in a small voice. "But of course…"

"Yes. I was married for five years before she asked me for a divorce."

"Why?"

He sighed and shrugged.

"Children?" she whispered.

He shook his head. Nick gently smoothed a few strands of hair from her face.

"Were you devastated? Still deeply in love with her?" Helena asked as if she wasn't sure she wanted to know the answer.

Again, he shook his head. "I didn't love her the way...that I once loved you."

Helena's eyes widened. "I-I'm sorry."

"Don't be."

"Did that break her heart?"

"Such a romantic you are. No, the truth is that she was much more interested in the big house that I bought her, on dry land, than she was in her dashing sea captain husband."

He smoothed his hand over her skin, avoiding the apex of her thighs and her nipples, noting how the small buds tightened and hardened anyway.

"I wasn't quite so dashing when forced to look after a house and walk a bad-tempered Yorkshire terrier." He smiled a little sadly. "The truth? I'm not cut out to live on land. I'm happiest at sea or traveling. And Linnea—she couldn't live aboard ship. Loathed it—the small rooms, the hotel feel of it. We didn't have a happy marriage."

"So...it's better now. She's happier? You're happier?"

He nodded. "It's better."

"My father doesn't believe in divorce." Helena shivered in the cool air of the suite.

Nick ran his hands up and down her arms, trying to erase the goose bumps. "I didn't think I believed in divorce, either. I don't, in principle. I wouldn't have been the one to end our marriage. But what was I to say when she asked for her freedom?"

"You would have stayed married and miserable?"

He shrugged. "Yes."

"And what if you'd met someone else?"

He lifted an eyebrow, and grimaced. "I wouldn't have. I was a married man."

"You have honor, Nick," she said in a small voice. "I should never have doubted that."

He said nothing, just caressed her jaw with the backs of his fingers.

"But if that's true," she said with a self-deprecating laugh, "then I have none."

"Don't be ridiculous, Helena."

"I left Ari. I made promises to him that I couldn't keep."

"You're divorced now, right?"

She nodded.

"Then it's done. You have to stop feeling guilty."

"I can't."

"You can."

"No. I keep seeing Ari's hurt expression, the puppy-dog eyes. I keep hearing my father's voice. 'You don't walk away from a marriage, my daughter.'" She deepened her tones and did a credible imitation of Elias.

"Guilt is a useless emotion. Truly."

"But it's inescapable. It's real…."

Nick leaned over her and cupped her face in his hands. "No, Helena. *This* is real." And he touched his lips to hers again.

SHE'D NEVER BEEN ABLE to resist Nick's kiss. He made her body come alive, her nerves sing, her mind soar. She'd had sex with a few other men—but with Nikolas it had always been making love. He initiated a glow deep in her subconscious, one that spread like warm honey throughout her whole body.

Helena curved her mouth to his and opened to him, thinking as she did so that she was crazy, but not caring. The chemistry between her and Nick was real and explosive enough to shove her hurt feelings aside for the moment.

He pulled her up to a sitting position and cradled her head in his big hands, deepening the kiss and stroking his fingers through her hair. He caressed her scalp, caught her earlobes between his thumbs and forefingers and gently rubbed them. It was sheer bliss, the way he had of making love to every inch of her.

He kissed her neck and shoulders, nibbled at the hollow of her throat and finally lifted her breasts in his warm palms.

"Beautiful," he murmured, and grazed his lips over one. "They're fuller."

True. They were larger since her brief pregnancy. She said nothing, just gasped as he took one into his mouth and gave her exquisite pleasure. He shifted their positions so that she sat astride him, and he transferred his attentions to her other breast.

She closed her eyes, blocking out everything but the sensations that his mouth and hands created. It was only when he stopped that she became aware of the fact that he was fully clothed and she was nude, her bare thighs pressed to the white cotton of his uniform.

She looked down at him and, a little shyly, unbuttoned his shirt. Underneath it was a white undershirt, and she helped peel off both of them. Helena traced those shoulders she'd once sketched, shoulders that were still just as taut and lean and muscled as they'd been the first day she'd seen him. So was his abdomen.

He wasn't as bronzed and his chest hair held a sprinkling of gray, but she loved it. Somehow it made him sexier.

He smiled as her hands went to his fly and they made quick work of shucking his pants. Finally he was gloriously naked and he pulled her back on top of him. She lay with her full length pressed to his warm skin, feeling his heart beat solidly against her own pulse.

He stroked her shoulders and back, slipping his hands down each notch of her spine and then spreading them over her bottom. She shivered because it felt so good. Then his fingers dipped lower still and the breath caught in her throat.

Gently, Nick turned her so that she lay with her back to his chest, nudging her bottom with his arousal. He caught her breasts in his hands again and toyed with them, making her ache with want. When she tossed her head restlessly, he nibbled at her ear and continued to tease her nipples.

Then he smoothed his hands down her stomach to tickle the light hair at the apex of her thighs. He found the center of her expertly and stroked while she went rigid against him, then arched her back and disintegrated into sudden, surprising pleasure. "Nikolas…"

His chest rumbled with contentment under her; his arms wrapped around her and held her tight. She felt his warm breath in her hair.

She expected him to move, to roll her body under his, to take her. But he didn't. She stirred against him. He was rigid against her backside, so she knew that he wanted her.

"Nikolas?"

"Mmm?"

"Don't you—" She bit her lip. "What about you?" She wanted him inside her, wanted the fullness and the intimacy and the memories. She wanted to feel him lose control as she just had, without warning.

"I don't have a condom, sweetheart."

"It's all right. I'm back on birth control."

"Back on it?"

She hadn't meant to say that. "I was, well, off it for a while."

He gently rolled her over. "You and Ari were trying to have a baby?"

Baby. That sweet four-letter word that got to her every time she heard it. Helena swallowed and shook her head. She really didn't want to talk about this. "No, no. My doctor took me off the pill for, ah, medical reasons."

He looked at her as if he knew she was omitting something, but said nothing. "Helena, do you want me to make love to you?"

"Yes," she whispered.

He hesitated. "It's better if we use a condom," he reiterated. "It's been a long time since we...knew each other."

Did he suspect that she'd been promiscuous? Had a disease? Or was he cryptically dancing around his own sexual past? She had no way of knowing.

"I don't have a condom, either," she said after a long moment.

"I can go and buy some tomorrow." Nick sat up and ran a hand through his hair. "If you'd like."

She nodded, reaching for her robe and feeling awkward. She averted her eyes from his healthy erection, feeling as if she'd somehow let him down, even though he was the one calling a halt to things.

He'd given her pleasure; she hadn't returned the favor. "Would you like me to—" She broke off, unable to say it.

"No, no," he said quickly and a little too reassuringly. But he was right; it would be uncomfortable at this point.

Helena slipped off the bed, wrapped herself in the robe and took a moment in the bathroom to pull herself together.

When she came out, Nick was almost fully dressed, just tucking his shirt into his trousers. She remained silent as he put on his socks and shoes, then checked his hair in the mirror.

"Do you want to shower?" she asked.

"I'll do that in my stateroom, where I have a change of clothes. But thank you."

So polite. So formal. So lacking in emotion. No, no, she thought ironically. Thank you for the nice little orgasm. Of course she didn't say anything of the sort out loud.

He hesitated for a split second, then of all things, kissed her cheek! As if they hadn't recently been intimate, although not as intimate as she would have liked.

"I'll…call you," he said.

She stared at him. "All right."

And then he opened her door and stepped out, nodding to a white-mustached old gentleman shuffling his way down the corridor with the aid of a walker.

CHAPTER NINE

NICK WENT ASHORE at Santorini for a while, alone with his thoughts. Santorini, their old stomping grounds—his and Helena's. It was a magical place, a group of gorgeous little volcanic islands. Santorini's towns all clustered along the top of cliffs that sloped down toward a central lagoon, where *Alexandra's Dream* and other ships had docked.

He wandered, bought some local wine and wandered some more, happy to be away from the ship for a little while. He still couldn't quite believe that he had been naked in bed with Helena, and that it had felt utterly right until he'd come to his senses.

Had they cleared the air, as he'd intended? Well, somewhat. But they'd managed to muck it up again, too.

It was so easy when he was with her to just forget everything but the past and his desire for her. But the realities of their situation were complicated. For one thing, as the captain of the ship and an enforcer of rules and protocol, he had no business fraternizing with a passenger. Especially not one as high-profile as Helena Stamos!

He could hardly say anything to Giorgio Tzekas or any other crew member who stepped over the line when,

as captain, he had done a hell of a lot more than frater-
nize. He'd come within seconds of making love to her—

Nick sighed. Oh, come on. He was splitting hairs. He
had made love to her. He was in direct violation of the
rules of his own damn ship—and with the owner's
daughter, no less. How could he have let this happen?

And added to that was his suspicion that Helena
wasn't on board for a simple vacation or to check on her
niece. He couldn't get rid of the notion that she was
there as a representative for Elias, checking to make sure
things were going well on the ship under his command.

Though he hated the idea, he wondered if he might do
the same thing in Elias's shoes—send someone trustworthy to check out the situation and report back. Could
he blame the man? Not entirely. Nick's reputation had
taken a beating after his resignation from his previous job.

Could he blame Helena? Oh, hell. That was where
things got complicated. Now that they'd been so
intimate, was it fair of him to expect her loyalties to
change? Expect that she'd come clean with him and tell
him why she was really here?

Nick walked along the main thoroughfare of Oia and
thought about it. If she did come clean, then he'd know
that she was trustworthy, and that she didn't make a habit
of lying. If she didn't, then he'd know that it was time to
get over any vestiges of feeling he had left for her.

The heat beat down upon him and a trickle of perspiration slid down his spine. He ducked into a little shop and
grimly purchased some condoms, wondering if he'd lost
his mind. But he sure as hell couldn't buy them on board
and have everyone wondering who the captain was balling.

A little devil on his left shoulder said, "C'mon, buy two or three boxes! You've already violated that no-fraternization policy. May as well make the most of it, eh?"

A little devil on his right shoulder smirked and added, "Besides, in order to get to the bottom of why Helena's on board, you have to spend more time with her. And you will inevitably end up in bed."

Nick shoved his change and the condoms deep into his trouser pocket, thankful for the anonymity of his simple collared shirt. To all appearances, he was just another tourist.

He stopped in a shop specializing in original prints and maps and bought a small, eighteenth-century Italian maritime chart for his growing collection. He loved old maps and what they told of history.

Finally he had some lunch in a little café and then headed back to the ship and his office. Nick went up the separate crew gangway and put his new map, rolled into a tube, through security. He thanked God that the condoms could remain in his pocket and not be X-rayed by curious ship personnel.

He stowed his things in his stateroom and changed back into uniform before making his way to his office. Curiously, Petra, the secretary he shared with the hotel manager, wasn't there. And odder still, his door was open.

Nick frowned and looked around. Nothing seemed out of place, but the papers on his desk had been disturbed.

A filing cabinet drawer wasn't shut properly, and he pulled it out, checking inside. If someone had opened it, what had they been looking for?

This was the drawer that held personnel files and incident reports. Normally it was locked, but a set of keys dangled from the keyhole at the top. Keys that were normally kept inside his assistant's desk.

Where was Petra?

Nick tried to shrug off a feeling of unease. She'd probably needed something out of the drawer, and had then gone for a late lunch—forgetting that she'd left the keys there. But she was very detail oriented and conscientious, and to do such a thing was unlike her.

He'd just gotten down to reading the satellite communications report when she bustled back to her desk, a slight frown on her face.

"Well, that was a wild-goose chase," she said.

"Pardon?" asked Nick.

She shook her head. "I was summoned to the purser's office because they supposedly had an envelope there for me. But when I went down there, they didn't know what I was talking about. They sent me over to the Tourist Information desk, which sent me to Communications. No envelope anywhere with my name on it." She rolled her eyes.

"Sounds like it took a while," said Nick, his tone sympathetic.

"Half an hour of my time! Wasted."

"Frustrating. Oh, by the way, did you need something out of the personnel file?"

She looked puzzled. "No. Why do you ask?"

Nick gestured behind him, toward his office. "It was open and the keys are dangling from it."

"*What?*"

"My office door was open and unlocked, too."

"Oh dear—I don't know who or why…" Distress spread across her plump, good-natured face. She opened the top drawer of her desk. "My keys are gone. Whoever was in your office must have taken them out."

"It may have been Thanasi," Nick said, half to reassure her, half to reassure himself. "He may have had to check on a staff member's file for some reason."

But the hotel manager didn't know what he was talking about when Nick called him. Pappas thanked him and hung up.

"Petra, have you seen anyone suspicious nearby?"

"No."

"Has Giorgio Tzekas been in here for any reason?" For reasons of tact, Nick hastened to add, "He might have needed a report while I was ashore."

She shook her head.

"Helena Stamos, perhaps? She may have needed to check a design file."

"No, sir. Nobody has been here, to my knowledge."

They both stared through Nick's open office door at the keys dangling from the file drawer. *Oh, yes. Somebody has. The question is, who? And why?*

The intruder had been smart enough to get Petra out of the way for a while; smart enough not to let himself— or herself—be seen.

Nick was not happy, but he didn't show his displeasure to Petra. "If you're called away for any reason during your shift, make sure everything is locked up and sealed tight, all right?"

"Yes, sir. I'm sorry, sir."

Nick locked the drawer and handed her the keys. "And keep those secure." He sat at his desk and went through the motions of some work, but his brain whirled. Tzekas? Looking for any possible dirt to make Nick look bad? Or Helena, checking through his files for her father? Someone had undoubtedly been here, and was up to no good.

UNLIKE THE GORGEOUS weather, Helena's mood today was cloudy with a chance of rain. She turned her focus to the canopy of her veranda, trying to find calm in the simple green-and-white stripes, the blue of the ocean and the pinky-orange glow filling the sky. She always found her center in color and design.

At the moment she wasn't even sure she had a center, though.

Nick's behavior, past and present, puzzled her. He had had a ring in his pocket. *A ring.* Nick had been prepared to propose—so why hadn't he just talked to her that night? Confronted her with his feelings...both positive and negative? Why had he pretended that nothing was wrong, then just left her without a word?

Nick was, plain and simple, emotionally repressed. Emotionally unavailable. She thought ruefully of her outburst the night before—she was the opposite.

But if he'd just talked to her—they could have been married all of these years. She might have been the mother of a teenager by now. The thought stunned her— she put a hand over her belly.

Then she realized that though she would have said yes to Nick's proposal, Elias would have roared a resounding no. He would never have allowed his daughter to marry a deckhand on a freighter ship. And at age eighteen… Helena's mouth twisted. She'd allowed herself to be manipulated by her father even recently, in her thirties.

Elias wasn't physically a big man, but the force of his personality more than made up for what he lacked in stature.

Helena rose and walked to the railing, where the breeze blew back the loosely belted robe. She didn't care. Nobody on Santorini was close enough to see one nude woman on a private deck.

And besides, she was through with convention—it didn't suit her. She was also through with pretension. What good came of valuing one's family name over one's very soul?

And so, having bared her body to Nick, she bared it to Poseidon, Zeus, the gulls and the sea creatures. To the last rays of Apollo. She asked for guidance from Wind, Sea and Fire because Earth had failed her.

And they sent her not answers but more questions. Would she have been happy even married to Nick? Was romantic love enough to hold her and ground her? She loved her independence. She loved to travel. She loved her work, all aspects of it.

If she'd had a baby on her hip and a husband demanding meals, could she have made it in costume design? It was not impossible, but it was doubtful.

The throaty, sensual and defiant words of Edith Piaf played in Helena's mind: *"Non, je ne regrette rien…"*

Do I have regrets? she asked herself honestly.

She did. But, like heartbreak, they were part of the fabric of her life; part of what made her who she was. Given the opportunity, would she turn back the clock? Erase the omissions and lies and abandonment and walk down the aisle with Nick?

She wanted to say yes. But to her surprise, she couldn't. And that realization brought not only a measure of peace but a peculiar freedom.

Should I have kept my identity from Nick? No. That was neither right nor fair. But the past was the past, and now she had the closure she'd sought for so long. More troubling was the way her body still responded to Nick.

And most troubling of all was the way he'd avoided making love with her, even after her statement about being on the pill. She felt odd about losing sexual control in front of a man who, well, didn't.

The kiss on the cheek and the promise to call her had been almost patronizing. They'd been the actions of a man who wanted to get to the door. She was tired of the mixed signals he sent her. When she withdrew, he pursued. When she gave a green light, he stopped. When she'd said there were no strings attached to a sexual relationship this time around, he'd seemed offended.

It all made her want to throw something. She decided instead to visit Gemma again in the children's center, where things might be chaotic, but they were also straightforward.

CHAPTER TEN

HELENA WAS DELIGHTED to see Angela, the little girl she'd met while boarding, in the children's center.

"Hi, Miss Helena! Are you having fun on this big boat ride? I am!"

Was she having fun? Not...exactly. The situation with Nick was too disturbing. "Yes, I am," she fibbed. "It's good to see you again, Angela."

"I wanted to call your room yesterday, but Mommy said we couldn't bother you," she confided.

Helena was touched and taken aback. "Well, sweetheart, here I am today. So what are you up to?"

"Miss Gemma taught us how to make beads out of colored clay. It's called Fimo. She's going to see if they'll bake the beads for us in the galley—did you know that's what they call a ship kitchen? Do you want to see my beads?"

"Yes, I do!" Helena caught Gemma's eye across the room and waved to her. She was reading stories to a circle of rapt children and looked less frazzled today, since she was working with an older age group. Another intern was handling the toddlers.

Since it looked as though she'd have to wait a while

to interact with Gemma—at least until Horton heard the Who—Helena sat with Angela and admired her beads.

"These are special princess beads," the girl told her.

"They're lovely," Helena said. "I like the way you swirled the pink and yellow and purple together."

"D'you know how I did that? Gemma taught us to roll long, snakey things and then braid them! Then we rolled them into one *big,* long snake, and we cut it up. Isn't that way cool?" Angela's face shone with excitement.

"It certainly is 'way cool,' sweetheart."

"But now I need a princess costume. You said you make costumes for movies and stuff. Can you help me make a princess dress?"

"Sure, why not?" Helena ruffled the girl's hair and pursed her lips, looking around the room at the available supplies. They were limited to construction paper, paint and…her eyes lit on a box of white trash bags on the counter next to the sink. "Brilliant! We'll start with one of those." She went and got one.

Angela frowned. "Princesses don't wear garbage bags."

"Ah, but this is no ordinary garbage bag."

"It's not?"

"No, indeed. Shh, don't tell anyone, but that box of bags is really a whole trunkful of princess dresses. A wicked witch has cast a spell upon the trunk, though. And it's our job to reverse the spell and transform them back into beautiful frocks."

Now Angela looked intrigued. "Really?"

Helena nodded solemnly. "But first, in order to reverse the spell, I need to know what kind of princess she is. A city princess? A mermaid princess? Or a woodland fairy princess?"

"Mermaid! No, woodland fairy. Can she have a wand?"

"Of course. Every woodland fairy princess has a beautiful wand."

Helena fetched construction paper in three shades of green, a brown and, just for fun, a pink and purple. Then she set to work creating leaf and flower patterns. "See, you can help me cut these out," she told the little girl.

"Can I help?" Another little girl had wandered over.

"Sure!" Soon Helena had five girls cutting out big leaves with blunt-nosed scissors. She drew three flower patterns next, and they all cut busily for a while.

Gemma looked over at her and shook her head, grinning. Helena shrugged wryly, but she was having fun.

The next step in the project was to tape the leaves in colored tiers to the trash bag after cutting out neck- and armholes. This took a little more direction on Helena's part, but after they got the hang of it, the girls had a ball.

The only problem was that they *each* wanted a princess dress, so Helena had to promise that she'd come back tomorrow afternoon if they'd cut out all the leaves necessary.

For now, though, the girls stared in awe at Angela, who really did look beautiful and whimsical in the costume. The multicolored leaves cascaded down the "bodice" and "skirt" of the garment, which Helena had nipped in at the waist with a double belt of long, skinny strips of construction paper and staples.

She made the wand out of a cardboard tube from the inside of a roll of paper towels: she slit it, formed two tighter rolls and taped them together to make a longer, skinnier tube. Then she painted the wand and covered it with a few more leaves.

A circle of leaves stapled together formed Angela's crown, and the vision was complete. "*Voilà!* You're a woodland fairy princess," Helena exclaimed.

Angela ran to a large plate glass window to check her reflection and twirled around. "I'm gorgeous!"

Helena turned to watch her and laughed. "Yes, you are, sweetheart." Then she sobered, because on the other side of the plate glass window stood Nick. He smiled at Angela and nodded at Helena.

"May I speak to you for a moment?" he mouthed.

Stiffly, she got up from the small chair she occupied and excused herself. So much for talking with Gemma....

"Thank you, thank you, Helena!" said Angela.

"You're welcome, honey. And I promise I'll come back tomorrow and help you girls with your costumes, okay? If you want to, you can get started by cutting out leaves, the way I showed you."

Amidst a chorus of "Okay" and "Bye!" Helena waved at Gemma and then headed for the door. Nick waited for her right outside, as if he were afraid that she'd slip away and avoid him.

He seemed a bit tense and his eyes had deepened to a slate-gray.

"Hello, Nikolas," she said.

"You seem to be wonderful with the kids."

"You sound surprised."

"Not at all—I just haven't ever seen you with children before."

"It's all right. I'm a little surprised myself, to tell the truth." She played with her bangles, turning them in her old nervous habit. *Would I have been a good mother?*

He seemed to be searching her face for something, and not in the tender manner of a lover. She found it puzzling and off-putting.

She decided to keep things light. "Has a fly landed on my nose, Nick?"

He blinked, collecting himself, then gave a strained smile. "No, no."

"Then what is it? You wanted to speak with me?"

"I thought you might have been looking for me while I was on shore in Santorini."

She shook her head. "After the way we parted last night, I figured you might need some space."

"So you weren't in my office?" he asked, as if the fate of the free world hung in the balance.

"No, Nikolas, I wasn't in your office. Why?"

He shook his head. "No reason."

Helena folded her arms across her chest. "There's obviously a reason. What's bothering you and why would you think I'd been there?"

Nick looked uncomfortable and then checked his watch. "Have dinner with me tonight? In my private dining room? We can talk about it then. I've got to return to the bridge right now."

He's back to being an enigma. She hesitated. Was she up for more of the awkward, tentative tenderness and then sudden physical and emotional withdrawal that he was sure to dish out?

"Please," Nick said, his gray eyes serious.

She nodded. "All right, then. What time?"

"Seven." He bent his head slightly as if to kiss her, then stopped himself. "Until then," he said stiffly.

"Until then."

KEEP YOUR FRIENDS CLOSE and your enemies closer. Nick moved restlessly around his private dining room and wondered for the umpteenth time just what the hell he thought he was doing. Was Helena a friend or an enemy—or, as a long-ago lover, a little of both?

He didn't like not knowing. He was a man who dealt in certainties and disciplined decisions. Black and white, not shades of gray. He had little patience for confusion...but he was confused. His body craved Helena—it had half killed him the other day not to make love to her. His excuse about the condom may have offended her, but he'd had to stop himself. Because Nick had a feeling that once he entered her body again, he'd never want to leave it.

He believed in a man knowing what his weaknesses were. The trick was to acknowledge them and then battle them; never allow them to gain the upper hand.

And Helena Stamos, quite simply, was one of his biggest weaknesses.

But was she spying on him? Nick smiled grimly. What better place to spy on the captain than in his own private dining room?

Her knock interrupted his thoughts, and he quickly lit the two candles on his dining table. Then he opened the door to her.

Tonight she was stunning in a strapless, sapphire silk

dress that ended just above her knees. She wore silver sandals and a sapphire necklace, the large stone nestling at the top of her breasts.

It was lovely, but only served as a reminder to Nick that even on his captain's salary, he couldn't afford to buy her jewelry of that caliber.

"Come in, Helena," he said while his mind warned, *Don't trust her.*

He took her hand and led her to the sofa. "Drink?"

"Yes, please. A martini?"

"Of course. Vodka or gin?" Nick went to the bar in the corner and put some ice into a shaker.

"Vodka." She crossed her legs and he tried to ignore the way her dress rode up, exposing a bit of her thighs. He summoned all his defenses, and yet despite that, he knew he'd make love to her tonight.

He'd do it with his eyes open this time. And he'd do it knowing that there was no future for them. But God help him, he'd do it—if she'd allow him.

He garnished her martini with a twist of lemon and brought it to her without spilling a drop, his fingers brushing hers as she accepted the glass. The cold of the liquid between them was a warning, the heat of their skin pure temptation.

"Thank you," said Helena. "Now, why would you have thought I was in your office?"

She could be a little too direct for his comfort. But then, she was too goddamn sexy for his comfort, too.

"I went ashore today to make a purchase."

"A nice little souvenir of Santorini?"

He could feel his own face heat. "That, and condoms."

She'd taken a sip of her martini and swallowed quickly, then cast him a speculative glance. "Did you? Are you feeling lucky, then, Nikolas?"

The words were teasing but her expression was serious. She was truly a riddle. Hell, no, he wasn't feeling lucky. He had to be the unluckiest s.o.b. alive—at least in love.

He ignored the question. "I returned and went to my office, which I usually keep closed. The door was open." He didn't mention the file drawer.

She set down her drink. "So you immediately jumped to the conclusion that I'd been in there? Doing what?"

"Looking for me," he said diplomatically.

"I see. Nick, you're being so wonderfully tactful."

He just looked at her. Her dark eyes held cynical amusement.

"Is there something you'd like to ask me?"

He sighed. "Helena…"

"Come on, Nick. In the past few days I've insulted your integrity. You should feel free to question mine." That reckless quality was back, that theatrical instinct of hers that liked to push the envelope.

"Fine," he said. "Then tell me what you're really doing here aboard Alexandra's Dream."

"I'm taking a long overdue vacation and I'm keeping an eye on my niece. Why is that so hard to believe?"

"Because from what I understand, you don't take vacations. You hurtle from one project into another."

"Been investigating?" she asked.

"Have you been investigating me?"

"My, haven't we got an ego." She lifted her glass to her lips and drank.

"I didn't mean to imply that it would have been because you were fixated on me."

"Let me do the math then." She set the martini down with a snap. "You believe that I'm actually here to, what, spy on you for Elias?" Her eyes flashed dangerously at him, glittering more than the sapphire at her neck. "Wonderful. Well, I did just invite you to question my integrity, didn't I?"

"Helena, what am I supposed to think?"

"Is there a reason that I should be checking up on you?"

"No."

"All right, then." She must have realized then that she hadn't answered his question. "I'm not."

They stared at each other for a long moment, Nick not knowing whether or not to believe her. She'd lied about her identity once. She could be lying now.

But the truly momentous issue for him was not whether or not she was deceiving him. It was that right here, right now, Nick didn't care. He wanted her whether she was lying or not. What did that say about him? It was deeply disturbing, but the realization didn't matter to his body.

"Dance with me, Helena," he said.

"We're already dancing, don't you think? Around each other."

"Let's dance with each other."

"There's no music."

"Does it matter?" he asked, pulling her to her feet and then hard against him. "Have we ever really needed music?" He led her into an easy samba, noticing that her body molded easily to his with no reservations on her part.

His dress shoes and her sandals tapped together on the wooden floor and the silk of her skirt rustled slightly against his uniform. His breath mingled with her perfume and somehow lit a smile on her face. It started as barely a flicker and then grew.

He wanted to devour it and let it warm him inside. Nick pulled her even more snugly against him and felt her soft breasts and thighs yielding against his body. He buried his nose in her hair, which still smelled the same as it had when she was eighteen.

"I have a feeling that we're not going to eat dinner tonight, are we, Nick?" she whispered.

He shook his head, picked her up and set her on the dining room table. He pushed between her thighs and took her mouth, wanting her so badly that he felt a little insane. The candles flickered wildly behind her and she inhaled sharply as he cupped her breasts. He could take her right here—she'd let him, he knew it.

But this was his Helena. She deserved better than a quickie on a dining room table, and he wanted absolute privacy. There were staff who had master key cards that opened this room.

"Come with me," he said. "We can't do this here."

CHAPTER ELEVEN

HELENA FELT THAT odd sense of being watched again, as they left the captain's private dining room and went to his quarters. She looked around but saw nobody.

"What is it?" Nick asked.

She shook her head. "Nothing."

He had a large room done in masculine shades of navy and green. A businesslike desk occupied one corner; an armchair in green paisley with touches of navy and burgundy took up another. And in the center stretched a massive bed, a bed fit for a captain.

Then she saw it. Behind the desk on the wall was one of the renderings she'd done early on in the design process for the ship. Her initials were in the corner.

Nick had framed the little vignette of the dining room beautifully, adding a two-inch mat around the piece that set it off to perfection. Her heart turned over.

"Nikolas...?" She turned to look at him.

He shrugged as if he were a bit embarrassed. "What can I say? I'm a collector." He took her hand and led her to the big bed, gesturing at it.

"It's a far cry from the single bunk I had on the freighter, isn't it?"

"And that hammock you slept in at your apartment in Athens." She'd visited him there while his roommate was gone for a week, and they'd lived in a sort of Spartan sexual heaven, making love whenever they wanted and eating bread and cheese and olives at odd hours of the night. He lived so differently from most people she knew, with only the bare essentials, but she found it somehow wise. Who needed more? She hadn't missed the expensive clutter, and she'd been charmed by his mismatched plates and silverware. She'd drunk her morning coffee out of a favorite chipped mug, and her wine from a jelly jar.

"The hammock, yes." He chuckled at the memory. "My back would never stand for it these days."

"We had to make love on the couch." She smiled. "Snuggled under that ratty old blanket."

"Hey, that was an heirloom," Nick corrected, somehow keeping a straight face. "My grandmother crocheted that."

"Nikolas, I don't know what your grandmother did to it, but something else—was it rats?—added character to it over the years."

"Character?" He scooped her up into his arms. "Is that what you call those holes, *koukla mou?*"

He'd called her his doll. She flushed with pleasure, even before he laid her down on the bed and caressed every inch of her, murmuring more endearments.

"The rocks on the beach didn't help that poor blanket," she mused. They'd had it on Mykonos, too, when she'd met him there.

That was the end of conversation for a while. Nick's

lips on hers felt so right, awakening passion that had been dormant for years. Passion she had never thought she'd feel again—until the other day. She met his kiss eagerly, welcomed his tongue into her mouth to stroke hers, loved the way he bit her lip gently and then moved to her jaw, her neck and into her hairline.

He kissed her collarbones and the hollow of her throat, then pressed his face between her breasts and groaned. "Helena," he whispered. And then in a single swift movement he tugged down the bodice of her dress and freed them.

He traced the slopes of her breasts with his index finger and then circled the pink nipples while her breathing quickened at the sensation and the look on his face. She thought her heart might stop as his lean, handsome head bent and he captured one nipple in his mouth, stroking it with his tongue.

She cried out, and he transferred his attention to the other one, laving and suckling her while she melted into a puddle of sensual bliss.

She wanted his skin on hers and tore at his jacket. He chuckled and pulled away, helping her. Soon most of his dress uniform lay on the floor, and his glorious male chest was bare.

She ran her hands over it, exploring every inch, brushing his nipples with her thumbs. He didn't give her long to touch him—within moments, he had her on her back again, and this time his hands explored her feet, still in the sandals, smoothed up her calves, and pushed her dress up for access to her thighs.

Her breathing went ragged as Nick pushed his face

between them and kissed her most private place, nibbled at the tender flesh to either side of it.

"Time to dispense with the dress, *glika mou.*" He slid his hands under her, lifted her bodily and set her on her feet. Then he turned her around. She heard the rasp of her zipper and then felt cool air as the dress dropped from her body to puddle on the floor. She stood with her back to him in nothing but her sandals and a black lace thong.

In strangled tones Nick said, "If I die in the next moment, I die a very happy man."

She laughed.

He lifted her hair and kissed the nape of her neck, her naked shoulders. His big hands slid around her to cup her breasts, and she could feel the fierceness of his response to her pressed against the small of her back. But Nick thought of her pleasure, not of his. He turned her to face him, dropped to his knees and pushed her back against the bed. He spread her knees and hooked them over his broad shoulders. And then she nearly blacked out from pleasure at what he did next.

When Nick picked her up she had no idea what had happened to her panties. When he held her against him and slid her, inch by inch, onto him she clutched his neck and whimpered for a long, tense moment. He shook with sexual need, like steel inside her. And then he moved and she climaxed explosively, shuddering and crying out.

He held her naked bottom in his big hands, her legs wrapped around him, and he thrust into her again and again.

How he could find his pleasure while supporting her entire weight, she didn't know, but Nick gave a last, mighty thrust and groaned her name. He stood there with his face buried in her hair, his legs shaking, and they clung to each other for a long moment before falling to the bed in a boneless heap. She never once thought about the condoms he'd bought.

"It's just like it was," Helena murmured against his neck.

"No," he told her. "It's better."

When they'd caught their breath, Nick made love to her again, slowly and sensuously, expertly. It was better. This Nick, Capitano Nick, was a seasoned and patient lover. He was no fumbling, eager boy of twenty-one.

All the awkwardness and suspicion that had accompanied the start of the evening had faded into pure enjoyment of each other. Somehow they'd fallen into uncomplicated nakedness and easy, affectionate banter.

This Nick knew exactly what to do for a woman, and he did it until she begged him, laughing, to stop.

"You've already half killed me," she said severely, sitting up and sliding her legs over the side of his bed.

"I heard no complaints...but if you have some, you're welcome to file them with the captain."

"You think you're funny, don't you?"

"I think *you're* beautiful." He snaked out an arm and tumbled her back onto the bed. "Where are going, mmm?"

She spied his dress hat on the opposite nightstand. Snatching it, she set it on his head, where it looked incongruous against his spectacular nakedness.

Helena saluted him provocatively.

"At ease," he said. "But I prefer that you take your ease nude."

"Yes, *Capitano*," she said faux demurely. "Will there be anything else?"

He nodded. "There will be. But first, would you like some champagne now that I've had my wicked way with you?"

She nodded.

He vaulted off the bed, still wearing his captain's hat, and strode to a small minifridge he'd had installed.

As Nick opened the champagne, a nice Perrier-Jouet, Helena admired his backside. Taut and muscular, it really was quite spectacular. It reminded her of Poseidon's rump in the Court of Dreams, and she repressed a chuckle at the idea of Nick wearing a long beard or a fig leaf accessorized by a trident.

He turned with a flute of golden, bubbly liquid and caught her. "Is there something about me that amuses you, Miss Stamos?"

She nodded.

"Care to share?"

"Not really," she said.

"As your captain, I demand that you do."

She raised a brow. "Oh, fine. Then I was thinking that you have a backside to rival Poseidon's."

He burst out laughing and handed her one of the crystal flutes. Then he became serious. "Don't anger him by comparison with a mortal, Helena. He rules the sea, make no mistake. I'm simply allowed to navigate it."

Interesting. But it made sense, given that Nick had grown up in a seaside village, son of a fisherman who had seen many friends and companions die when the ocean turned aggressive and vengeful.

"You really believe that?" She slipped off the bed and stood near him, splaying her hand against his broad chest. Her fingers looked small and white against his bronzed skin, even though she herself was no stranger to the sun.

"Yes, I do." He brushed a tendril of her hair from her face and kissed the tip of her nose. "Cheers, *agape mou*. To our reunion…in Santorini." He clinked his glass against hers.

"Cheers," she said, trying not to think about the past. She stood on her toes to kiss him. Reunion …what did Nick mean, exactly?

"Did you know that in our home, we used to make offerings to the sea?" He sat on the bed and she followed suit.

"What kinds of offerings?"

He plucked the captain's hat off his head and settled it on hers, smiling in approval. "All kinds of things. My mother did it, mostly. A loaf of bread one day, a little dish of oil the next. Once, during a terrible storm when my father's boat was still out, I saw her take off one of her good earrings—she only had one pair—and she ran outside, down to the shore. She threw it as far as she could into the water. Came back in soaked to the skin, wearing just the one."

Nick's mouth twisted at the memory. "And when my father returned safely, she said a prayer of thanks. She slipped the other earring onto a chain to wear as a necklace. She wears it to this day."

"Did your father ever notice?"

Nick nodded. "He'd given those earrings to her as a wedding present. So of course he noticed when she was missing one. She told him she'd lost it, and he stomped around like an angry bear for a day...until I told him the truth."

Helena listened, charmed.

Nick looped his arms around her and grinned. "That evening my brother and I were sent on a silly errand. Told to walk very slowly to the next town and back."

"I can't imagine why," Helena said dryly.

"I was only ten, but I knew exactly why we were trudging to the next village for something I could have gotten quite easily in our own. Our cottage had only three rooms and the walls were thin."

Helena hadn't grown up in a village or town. She'd lived her childhood in a bougainvillea-draped, cliff-top villa. Just short of a palace, really.... Elias had already been raking in millions and he wanted his English wife to live in Mediterranean luxury.

Elias hadn't made offerings to the sea, though perhaps he should have, since he'd made his living from it just as Nick's father had. Elias had been more likely to make offerings to political candidates and causes.

A three-room cottage... The small yellow playhouse in which she and Katherine had arranged their dolls probably was larger than Nick's whole cottage. The playhouse was still there, complete with planted window boxes, white trim and even a small garage for their two push-pedal cars. Gemma had loved it when she visited *Pappou* and *Yiayia,* Grandpa and Grandma.

Nick lay back against the pillows of his bed and snugged Helena against his chest. "So you've never made a sacrifice to the sea, eh?" He stroked the underside of her breast.

She hesitated and then took a sip of her champagne, letting it roll along her tongue while the bubbles popped inside her mouth. "I dropped my wedding and engagement rings into the ocean."

His fingers stilled. "Did you?"

"Yes."

"Not an offering, then. A repudiation. Why were you so angry, Helena, if he was a nice man, as you said?"

She sighed. "I was throwing the idea of marriage as far away as I possibly could. I was angry at my father. I was angry at myself. I wasn't angry with Ari. He was the one innocent party in all of it—he and the—" she broke off, unable to say it. She would not, *could* not, speak of the baby. Tears sprang to her eyes, but thank God, Nick couldn't see them.

He tightened an arm around her, set his champagne on the nightstand and then hugged her from behind. He kissed her head, her ear. "Shh, it's all right, *glika mou.*"

How does he know? Her tone of voice hadn't changed. He couldn't see her eyes. *How does Nick know there's a lump in my throat the size of a lifeboat?*

"What did your father have to do with your marriage?"

Helena stiffened in Nick's arms, then forced herself to relax. She took in a deep breath. "My father...had everything to do with my marriage."

Nick remained silent, encouraging her to talk but not demanding it.

"'Just go out on a date with Ari,' he said to me. 'The boy is mad for you. What harm will it do?' So I went out on one date. 'Just go with Ari to the regatta,' he said next. Then, 'Just go with him to Santorini. You love it and he wants the company.' And so on. Before I knew it, we were an item. And he was nice enough…I felt affection for him." She stopped. How could she say any more without speaking of the baby?

Nick just threaded his fingers through her hair, twisted it into a loose knot and dropped a kiss on the nape of her neck.

"One thing led to another," she said lamely, "and then he gave me a ring. I wouldn't take it at first, but he put the box into my evening bag and told me to think about it."

"And Elias got wind of it and pressured you?" Nick asked.

Helena sighed. "More or less. I told him that I wasn't in love with Ari, even though I'd tried to be. That I knew he was kind and decent, but he wasn't exciting. But my father pushed and pushed and pushed…until he'd shoved me right down the aisle of the church."

Nick rolled her to face him and put a finger under her chin. "You're leaving out a chapter of this story." His eyes weren't judgmental, they were sympathetic.

How does he know? A sob rose in her throat. *How can he read me so well, even after all this time?*

"I was pregnant," she whispered. "That's why I married him. Elias couldn't stand the idea of my giving birth to a Stamos bastard. My baby had to bear his father's name. Very interesting in light of the fact that Elias didn't give his to Theo."

She knew Nick had met Theo Catomeris and was aware of the story of his birth, which had occurred a couple of years before Elias had married her mother.

Helena tried to suppress her threatening tears. "Poor

Theo—we only just found out about him! He's had sisters all his life. It's so unfair to all of us."

She paused for a moment and he stroked her hair, the side of her cheek. "The truth, Nick, is that I married Ari for the baby, not for Elias."

"What happened, *glika mou?*"

It was no use to fight the sobs. *"I don't know,"* she cried, tears streaming hot from her eyes and down to the pillow between them. "I didn't do anything risky— didn't drink or smoke or skydive, for God's sake. I didn't even exercise. But one day I woke up and…" She could barely get the words out. "There was so much blood. I'd lost the baby, Nick. Lost it…"

He gathered her close and kissed her wet cheeks, her eyes, her mouth. "Oh, Helena. *Agape mou,* I'm so sorry." He continued to stroke her hair and rub her shoulders until she quieted.

They lay in silence for a few moments and then, as if deliberately to distract her, Nick moved his hands from her waist up to her breasts. He lifted them, caressed them, rubbed the nipples with his thumbs, until she let desire wash away the pain and turned her head to meet his kiss.

Then Nick's clever, seeking fingers moved lower, smoothing over her belly and stroking between her thighs. The captain was truly expert at steering a different course.

CHAPTER TWELVE

NICK'S TELEPHONE RANG, waking both him and Helena. She murmured sleepily and rolled over, while he slid across the bed to answer it. "Yes?"

The ship's operator said, "I have a Mrs. Eva Manolis calling for you, sir."

Eva Manolis. Nick felt his heart spasm as if someone had held a cattle prod to it. Eva, the woman he'd saved—his mouth twisted—*in memoriam.* For Carolina, his cousin.

He swung his legs over the side of the bed, found the floor and then groped for his desk chair. He sat, heavily. He'd gotten Eva Manolis's postcard a year ago. Why was she calling him now?

"Shall I put her through, Captain?"

"Yes, thank you."

A soft, shy voice said, "Hello? Captain Pappas?"

"Yes, Mrs. Manolis." He could picture her, a thin, weary blond woman with sagging shoulders and dark circles under her eyes.

"How are you?" He didn't ask the question casually. He asked it because she might not reply that she was fine.

"I'm very well, thank you. And you?"

"Couldn't be better."

She hesitated for a moment and then plunged right in. "I'm so sorry about what happened at Blue Aegean— I knew my husband would make trouble, but I didn't realize that he would focus on *you*—create such a mess that you'd be forced to resign."

Nick exhaled. He'd never met a nastier excuse for a man than Kostas Manolis. Many wife beaters were simply pathetic. He'd been malevolent.

"I know that, Mrs. Manolis. It's a pity that he woke from his drunken stupor before we sailed, but these things happen. I'm just glad that you got away from him." *Some women aren't so lucky.* Thinking about it made his blood feel heavy and thick as failure, guilt and cold anger worked through his veins.

"I—will you please call me Eva? I can't—I can't *bear* his name. I'm living under an assumed one at the moment, but I've also changed back to my maiden name since the divorce was final."

"Where are you, Eva?"

She hesitated. "Canada. I'd rather not say exactly where."

"I understand."

"It's not that I don't trust you, but he has people looking for me."

Nick went rigid. "You're sure?"

"Yes. He'll never give up. That's part of the reason I'm calling, Captain. I'm afraid that he might be out for revenge—against you."

Nick was taken aback. "But surely he got that when I resigned?"

Eva released an audible breath. "Kostas is, as you know, a violent man who does not like to be crossed. He hasn't given up searching for me. And the more frustrated he grows, the more he'll need to pursue another target to vent his rage. I've talked with a psychiatrist about Kostas and his behavioral tendencies. It was the doctor's opinion that I should contact you. Warn you."

Although Nick appreciated Eva's concern, he found it groundless. "Thank you for letting me know, but there's no need for you to worry. I'm at sea for the next few months, hardly ever in one port more than a day. He'd have a devil of a time tracking me, or getting past shipboard security."

"Captain, don't underestimate Kostas. I'm convinced now that he's a…psychopath. He's quite capable of purchasing a cruise just to get to you. As you know, he has the means."

"Duly noted. Again, I appreciate your concern. I'll make sure that Security has his name and description."

"Good. I'm glad to hear you say that. It sets my mind at ease." She sighed. "Again, I'm sorry that I ever got you tangled up in this…."

"You didn't," Nick replied. "You came to the authorities for help. That's all. We gave it to you. You deserved protection. Never, never apologize for seeking help, Eva. All right?"

"But—"

"Eva, you are *not* responsible for your ex-husband's behavior. You never were. No matter what he told you or how he made you feel, you didn't deserve the abuse. Please, please accept that."

"I have," she said in a small voice.

Nick struggled before saying his next words. "I had a cousin who was in a similar situation. Like Kostas, her husband seemed nice enough on the surface. None of us knew what really went on—that he was nasty to her and hurt her behind the scenes. She never told anyone. Never."

"What...happened to her?"

Nick swallowed. He rubbed at his eyes. "She's...she's fine," he lied. He curled his fingers around the empty champagne bottle still on his desk. He gripped the bottle until the tips of his fingers turned white.

"I see," Eva said in a strained voice, as if she knew he wasn't telling her the truth. "Well, she was lucky that her family was there for her."

"Yes." *Goddamn it all, why weren't we there? Why?*

Neither of them spoke for a long moment. Then Nick said, "I think perhaps it makes you understand why I helped you. It was the right thing to do, but I also did it for Carolina."

She fell silent for a few moments. At last she asked, "What happened to Carolina's husband?"

"Vigo is in jail where he belongs," Nick said harshly. *I hope to God he rots there.*

"I wish Kostas were in jail," Eva murmured. "Then I might not wake up screaming at night."

Nick made a sound of pity. He wondered if the woman would ever stop being afraid.

"I have adopted a dog," she told him. "A German shepherd."

"I'm glad to hear that." It was a good sign. Eva

Manolis sounded stable, if not completely healed. That might take years. "Thank you for calling, Mrs. Manolis."

"Please be careful, all right?"

"I will," Nick promised. "Don't worry about me. You take care of yourself."

He hung up the phone and stared into the darkness, then let his face drop into his hands. *Carolina...*

And I gave her away at the wedding. To him.

His uncle had died two years before, so Nick had done the honors. He still saw her laughing face, glowing with happiness that day.

How could I not have known?

He glanced over at the sliding-glass door that led to the balcony. He would find peace outside, in the water and the sky. He wasn't going to find it in his mind.

CHAPTER THIRTEEN

HELENA HADN'T MEANT TO eavesdrop, but lying there in the bed, she couldn't help but overhear Nick's end of the conversation.

When he got up after hanging up the phone, she stretched a hand out to him. "Nick?"

"Sorry that the telephone woke you." He was oddly formal after what they'd shared, and she didn't know what to make of that. Was it because she'd overheard a very private exchange?

"No, it's fine. I should be getting back to my room, anyhow." She slipped from under the covers and located her clothes, pulling on her thong. She hoped that Nick would say something about the conversation he'd just had with the mysterious Eva, but he didn't.

Finally she couldn't help herself. She shouldn't be sleeping with him—it complicated things so—but she'd be a liar if she claimed that she didn't care about him. "Nick—are you in danger?"

He smiled grimly, but it didn't reach his eyes. "No, Helena. We have excellent security on *Alexandra's Dream.* You shouldn't worry."

"You had to resign because you were protecting that woman from her husband?"

He shrugged. "It's more complicated than that. But, essentially, yes." He didn't elaborate.

"So you were the hero of the situation, not the villain the press made you out to be."

"I was no hero. She came to me, the captain, for help and protection. I gave it to her. End of story."

"And my father knows. He must know the real version of events."

"If your father knows anything of it, he didn't hear it from me."

She nodded. "And he'd respect that. But he knows. He'd have made it his business to find out everything about you."

She hesitated. "Nick…what happened to Carolina? She's not fine, is she?"

He shook his head. "Her husband killed her," he said baldly. He didn't go into details. He didn't want to think about them himself—the blue-black marks around her neck, the other bruises on her body, her broken fingernails with her husband's skin under them. Even now, it made him physically ill, and her open eyes haunted him. They always would. "The bastard killed her when she tried to leave him."

"Oh God." Helena put a hand over her mouth. "I'm so sorry." She'd met Carolina once, when Nick's cousin had come to his apartment in Athens. She'd been so young, so full of life, with her future spread before her. Tears filled Helena's eyes. "It's awful," she said inadequately.

He turned away, picked up his pants and put them on. The playful, affectionate Nick she'd made love with and drunk champagne with had vanished, to be replaced with a maritime officer under the weight of unpleasant memories and hundreds of responsibilities.

His silence alarmed her. "Look, I didn't mean to pry. Or to listen. But I couldn't help overhearing."

"I know. It's all right." He reached for his undershirt and pulled it over his head, tucking the hem neatly into his trousers.

"You seem angry," she ventured.

He turned to face her again, and his gray eyes were like steel. "I am angry. But not at you. I'm angry that we didn't see what Vigo was like. That we allowed Carolina to marry him, left her helpless, with no support. I'm angry that we didn't prevent what happened. I'm furious that we didn't just—" He broke off, his mouth grim.

"You can't blame yourself for what happened!"

"Yes, I can. And I do. It was the job of the men in Carolina's family to see to her well-being. I'm one of those men. We let her down. So you see, Helena, you're not the only one who feels you've failed your family."

"Oh, Nick." She went to him and put her arms around him, but he stood unyielding. She may as well have been hugging the stone Poseidon down there in the Court of Dreams. "You didn't fail anyone. How were any of you supposed to know when she didn't confide in you?"

"She must have felt that she couldn't," he said. "That's our fault."

"Or she was too ashamed!"

He shook his head.

"Nick, think about it. How many family members did this poor woman Eva call? None. She finally asked for help from a stranger, because it was probably too painful to face those she knew well. She was humiliated."

Helena finally had his attention. "It wasn't your fault," she repeated. "Women are expert at hiding things."

Suddenly the atmosphere between them shifted. "Yes, they are. You are."

He took a step back from her. Distance and distrust seemed to lie between them now.

Helena retreated. This had all been a mistake—agreeing to have dinner alone with him, coming to his room. They couldn't just roll back the years and take up happily where they'd left off so unhappily.

She picked up her dress, which lay on the floor like some unlucky sapphire. She stepped into it reluctantly—it was far too glamorous and carefree for the way she felt at the moment.

Without being asked, Nick crossed the divide between them, at least physically, and zipped her into it with an air of finality. She felt his warm breath in her hair; it sent a shiver of need down her spine. But she moved away with casual thanks and found her sandals.

She needed to get away from him now, gather her thoughts and try to make sense of them. Helena slid the silver leather straps over her feet and fastened them behind her heels. She wished her sandals were like the winged ones of Perseus and could carry her back to her room in a flash.

But they weren't. So she finger-combed her hair in the mirror, all too aware of Nick's unreadable eyes on her. And then she allowed him to walk her back to her room.

NICK LEFT HELENA at her door with a brief kiss that communicated absolutely nothing. No regrets, but no joy, either. No promises, which she'd said she didn't want. And no reaction to what had occurred between them during the last few hours.

How could it be otherwise? He didn't know what the hell to think. Nothing had changed, yet everything had changed…and he was an idiot of epic proportions.

Did you have to sleep with her, Pappas? Are you crazy?

Clearly, he was. Because he couldn't touch her, kiss her, caress her without becoming emotionally entangled with her.

Helena was not just any woman. He hadn't simply been using her body for pleasure. Nick had thought of her needs and desires first; her gratification had been more important than his.

The recent memory of her lips on his, her hands raking through his hair, her soft, warm skin sliding against his…her muted cries and exclamations. He was afraid that she'd ruined him—again—for any other woman.

He cursed under his breath. What had he been thinking? That they could take a simple trip down memory lane and then be done with it?

He hadn't been thinking, and that was the problem. He'd been under the influence…not of alcohol but of Helena. And she was twice as intoxicating.

But where did it go from here? Where did it stop? Because it had to end. She had a satisfying and successful career in London. His place was at sea.

Nick shook off his thoughts, which only frustrated him, and began his walk to the bridge. He needed to make sure that all paperwork was being filed correctly with immigrations officials for their docking in Katako-lon, where the main tourist attraction was Olympia, the site of the very first Olympic Games.

At least four officers were on the bridge at all times, and right now it was the quartermaster at the helm, First Officer Tzekas at the coffeepot and two junior officers. These last two checked and revised maritime charts for things like shifting sandbars and coral reefs. They also monitored satellite communications for unusual cur-rents and weather information.

All four men were licensed captains in their own right, fully certified to run *Alexandra's Dream* if anything should happen to him. But Nick himself was the "Master," the head captain, and he, for one, wouldn't put Giorgio Tzekas in charge of the head on a shrimp boat.

Nick's eyes narrowed on Tzekas, who was focused not on monitoring safety operations for the ship, as he should be, but on getting just the right amount of cream into his late-night coffee. The man was just too casual about his duties and responsibilities.

Something in his gut told Pappas that the first officer was dirty. He was what Nick called a *roufiano,* or a man without honor. But how dirty was he? Was it Tzekas who had been in his office, digging through his files? And why? To try to get some information he could use against Nick? Suspicion roiled in Nick's gut.

The waters were rough tonight, the wind blowing at about twenty knots in his estimate. If it gusted any more and the waves kicked up higher, they'd have to slow their progress into Katakolon. The ship couldn't operate at full speed in bad weather conditions.

The delay would mean further headaches and scheduling issues with everything from excursions and tendering the passengers ashore to crew exchanges and provisioning. But it was all business as usual, and Nick had been dealing with these same problems for years.

"Tzekas," Nick said in neutral tones, "have you conducted a thorough inspection of the fire alarms and made sure all the extinguishers are operational?"

"A check is scheduled, sir."

"Yes, Officer, it was scheduled for today. Is the inspection complete? Because I don't see a report."

"Er. There's been a delay, sir, because the crew swapout at Santorini didn't go as smoothly as it, er, could have. So I didn't have the manpower…."

"The crew issues were ironed out by 0100 hours yesterday, Tzekas."

"Well, sir, all I can say is—"

"All you can say is that the inspection has not been done, correct?"

Giorgio stared at him resentfully. "No, sir."

Pappas nodded. "I see. Well, I'd like that report on my desk by 0800 hours tomorrow. All right, Tzekas?"

"Yes, sir." His color high, his breathing shallow and irregular, the first officer looked as if he wanted to choke his superior.

"Excellent." As Nick walked away to speak to the quartermaster, he heard Tzekas say something under his breath.

"I beg your pardon, Officer?" Nick demanded.

"I didn't say anything, sir. Just cleared my throat."

Nick held his gaze for several beats before the first officer broke eye contact. "That will be all, then. Dismissed."

CHAPTER FOURTEEN

ARIANA COULDN'T HELP BUT be nervous again as her captor hustled her up the irregular stone stairs of their rough underground refuge. Expecting to see sun, or at least clouds, she was disappointed when the darkness was unrelenting outside. She didn't know what time it was, but guessed that they were moving in the wee hours of the morning. A small sliver of moon hung in the Mediterranean sky like a glinting scimitar, offering little visual aid and no comfort.

"Where are we going?" she asked the hulking man.

"On holiday," he said with irony.

He'd been out of sorts since he'd gone off by himself with his cell phone. He'd stomped around in those black boots of his, and every muscle in his body had been tense.

"*Andiamo!* Hurry," he said, dragging her to a car no bigger than an American hamburger. He wrenched the passenger-side door open. "Get in."

Okay, *maybe* she could fit in there. But him? No way. It would be like the Incredible Hulk driving off in a Matchbox car. With a little help from the push he gave to the small of her back, Ariana wedged herself into the vehicle. He slammed the door on her and rounded the hood to get in on the driver's side.

Go! Her chance was now. She wrenched the door handle and shoved hard for freedom. She hurtled forward blindly and heard him curse behind her.

Three, maybe four footsteps pounded the earth and then suddenly an iron arm caught her around the waist and she went airborne in reverse.

The big man jerked her back against his body and she flinched in terror. *Oh, God, he's going to kill me now.*

"*Da tutti i santi,* do not try my patience at this moment, *ragazza!*"

"*Mi dispiace, mi dispiace,*" she babbled.

"You endanger us both, do you understand?" He said this in gentler tones. "What do you think they will do if they see you alive? They'll be looking for me, too, since I did not return to the site."

"Who?"

"Get into the car, and keep your head down."

Shaking with both adrenaline and fright, she did as he said.

"Do you not understand what kind of men these are? They would have their way with you before killing you, eh? Do you want that?"

"No! No, no."

"Then do what I say and don't cause me any more grief."

She crouched obediently in the passenger seat, her head as low as she could force it, while her captor somehow folded his enormous body into the sardine can and started the engine.

They shot forward onto a dirt road, the car's engine sounding like a lawnmower. Every time he switched gears, he elbowed her and grunted an apology.

In such close quarters she couldn't help but be intensely aware of him physically, even if he hadn't been touching her.

But his muscular arm pressed against hers even when he wasn't shifting gears, and she was aware of his scent—musky, ripe and disturbingly attractive.

He'd floored the gas pedal and they careened around corners on a dark, twisty road. She'd hoped to see the lights of civilization ahead soon, but they didn't appear. He seemed to be taking the scenic route through the back of beyond.

"Where are we going?" Ariana asked, even though she had a feeling he wouldn't enlighten her. He hadn't even told her his name.

"Somewhere safe," he answered.

For a few moments she was too busy getting over the shock of a reply to press for more information. She braced herself against the seat and the now-locked passenger door while they drove, and tried to focus on the mustiness of the carpet and the mild chemical smell of the vinyl seats instead of the scent of her kidnapper.

It didn't work. He smelled overpoweringly male.

"Excuse me," she ventured above the noise of the engine and the gravel that was now clinking against the bottom of the car, "but if you're going to kidnap me *twice,* could you tell me your name?"

He cast a dark glance at her. "I could," he answered.

She waited.

He said nothing else.

"Well, will you?"

"Dante," he finally said.

Dante. Like in Dante's *Inferno?* "Of course your name is Dante," she said. "It had to be. Do you mind telling me which circle of hell we're visiting at the moment?"

He rewarded this question with a flash of white teeth in the darkness. "My own private circle. The one I reserve for…how you say? Smart mouth? Yes. Smart-mouth women."

Okay. So he had a sense of humor. That was welcome news. And he hadn't killed her when he'd had the chance, though that was still a possibility.

Was he after a ransom? Ariana tensed. Since her father's death, money had been an issue. Although his case hadn't gone to trial before he died, they'd already spent a fortune in legal fees.

"If you were going to kill me, you'd have done it back in that cavelike place, right?"

Again, that obsidian gaze flicked over her. "If I were going to kill you, I'd have done it the way the Camorra suggested, *bella.*"

"So you're not going to?"

"No. I told you that."

Had he? If so, he hadn't been a hundred percent re-assuring. Then again, she was quite sure he hadn't been hired for his diplomatic skills. She eyed his muscular build, unable to help herself. "Then why won't you just let me go?"

He shook his head, took a hard left that had her

sprawling against him, and then a hard right that tossed her in the other direction. Water. She saw water—and a ferryboat. He drove right toward it, and her throat tightened. It was one thing to be on a massive ship, where she couldn't feel the waves beneath her. It was quite another to take a small ferryboat. Was he going to throw her overboard?

He noticed her discomfort right away. "I'm not going to toss you overboard," he said as if he could read her thoughts. "We're just leaving Naples."

"Where are we going?"

No answer.

Dante steered the car expertly onto the ferry and her tension grew. What if something happened and the car slid off into the water? She couldn't swim and had an irrational fear of small boats.

He glanced at her sharply. *"Va bene?"*

No. She wasn't all right, and she was beginning to wonder if she'd ever feel all right again.

"Signorina, there is nothing to be afraid of," he said in bracing tones.

Despite her fear, she cast him a sardonic glance.

"Ah," he said. "You are wondering which is worse, me or the water."

She didn't reply, and remained silent throughout the short trip. Soon they were docking at what she guessed to be Capri, judging by distance alone.

She relaxed marginally as Dante drove them off the ferry and onto dry land, where he took a series of twists and turns that she had difficulty remembering. Soon they clattered across a small metal bridge and turned down a drive that led to a nondescript house with a tiny yard. Dante stopped the car in front of it.

Her fear started to rise again, especially as she saw two armed men round the sides of the little house. They were going to shoot her and then bury her. She looked around wildly for any possible escape route.

"Relax, Ariana. I told you that I have no plans to kill you."

"But…" she said, shaking. "Then what *are* you going to do with me?"

He exited the car, rounded it and opened her door as if they were on a date. He extended his hand to her, his dark eyes enigmatic. "An excellent question, *signorina*. An excellent question."

THE MAN TRAVELING under an alias cursed, looking at his watch. Too much time had elapsed—he had to meet the silly old cow he'd been carrying on a shipboard "romance" with, or she'd come looking for him and make a fuss.

He'd have to abort his plans yet again. Who knew the rich bitch would spend so much time at an ancient site she had to have visited before?

He'd hoped to overpower her here in her room, then summon the good captain and start the games. He wanted to disappear long before the ship got back to Rome.

Goddamn women. Out of sheer spite, he pulled the drawings out of her portfolio and ripped up every other piece. It was all melodramatic shit anyway, the pretentious scrawls of a gold-plated whore.

Savagely, he thrust the papers back into the flat case and

zipped it. Then he cursed again and carefully let himself out. Things were getting complicated, harder to organize.

He fingered the revolver in his pants, itching to put a hole right through Nick Pappas's skull. It had taken some doing to get the gun on board. Security on *Alexandra's Dream* was particularly tight with that Israeli in charge. But every system, without exception, had weaknesses to exploit. One simply had to find them, and he had.

The right amount of money and a conveniently amoral contact in food services had made it possible for him to smuggle the piece inside, of all things, a hollowed-out pineapple.

Voilà! One tropical fruit basket, delivered to the room of elderly passenger Mr. Craig Peters. Yes, the poor guy who couldn't get around without the aid of a walker, and was having his last hurrah before he became permanently bedridden. Terribly sweet, he was, always draped in a pale blue cardigan over his plain, white short-sleeved shirts. Shuffling around from one senior activity to another, but mostly playing cards and drinking black coffee.

Craig Peters, the old fart who couldn't wield so much as a flyswatter if he had wanted to.

The man smiled grimly and stroked the master key card he'd also paid dearly for. He was untraceable—too bad the maids and delivery people were not. They'd have some nasty questions to answer later.

CHAPTER FIFTEEN

HELENA WENT BACK toward her room after her shore excursion to Katakolon. She'd walked to her heart's content, sketched some of the ruins at Olympia and eaten a late lunch.

She returned to the ship feeling refreshed and relaxed in body, if not in mind and spirit. It bothered her more than she wanted to admit that Nick had pokered up after making love to her. He'd retreated to some distant emotional place, far away from her.

He had the uncanny ability to read *her* emotions, but unless he was seriously provoked, he tended to keep his to himself.

He could be capable of such warmth and humor, and yet at other times be emotionally repressed. A complicated man.

She got off the elevator and took the corridor to her suite. From the moment she opened the door, she knew something was wrong, and it wasn't just the fruit basket on her dresser.

Her scalp prickled in alarm and the hairs on the nape of her neck rose. There was an energy that didn't belong there; the room oozed menace from every corner.

She almost ran. But there was nobody inside, as far as she could see. She stood in the doorway, gripping the jamb, and caught a scent that made her ill, a sweetish musk overlaid with cigar smoke.

Helena shivered and backed out of the room, clutching her tote bag to her chest. She snatched the key card out of the lock and hurried down the hallway again, emerging into the sunlight with relief. She took several deep breaths of the warm Mediterranean air, preferring the smell of sea salt to that awful sweet, smoky musk.

"Madam? Are you all right?" A passing steward put a hand on her arm.

Helena blinked at him. "Oh. Yes. Yes, I'm fine. But— if you have a moment, would you mind accompanying me to my suite? I—"

He gave her a strange look.

For God's sake, did he think she was propositioning him? "I think someone's been in there," she finished. "I'm afraid."

His expression cleared. "Of course, madam. I'm sure everything is fine, but I'll be happy to check the room for you."

Out here, in the bright, hot sunshine, she felt like a fool. The Helios deck was dotted with passengers lying on lounge chairs, perched at the bars, talking and laughing in groups.

Honestly, Helena. As if the boogeyman boarded Alexandra's Dream *to pop into your suite. You are beyond silly.*

But she walked with the steward back to her door

anyway. He slid his master key card into the lock and they entered.

The smell was still there. The first thing she did was open the veranda doors and all the windows to get rid of it. Then, as the ocean breeze cleansed the atmosphere, she began to look around.

Nothing seemed out of place at first. The fruit basket had been sent compliments of Thanasi Kaldis, the hotel manager, which was very thoughtful of him.

She threw open the closet doors, but everything was as she'd left it. She swallowed and moved to the dresser, opening the top drawer. A quick glance told her that someone had pawed through the contents. *Dear God.* Who would do this?

Helena shoved the drawer shut, since she didn't want yet another stranger, and a male steward at that, seeing her lingerie.

She told herself that the intruder was probably a crew member, hotel staff, and could have been female. It didn't bring much comfort. Then she remembered the musky, smoky smell. Male. Definitely male.

The involuntary shudder that racked her body was tinged with hysteria.

"Madam?" The steward eyed her with concern again.

"Someone's been in here. I'm sure of it. My things have been tampered with."

"I'll call security right away. Is anything missing?"

"I don't think so." She looked around again, wondering what else this creepy stranger had touched. She went into the bathroom and found all of her cosmetics in disarray, though she didn't spot anything missing. She backed out, feeling claustrophobic and violated.

The steward hung up her phone and said, "Officer Dayan will be here directly. He is the head of security for the whole ship."

"Thank you." Her eyes fell on her portfolio, which she'd left leaning against the desk. It was still there, but it, too, had been moved. Helena hurried toward it, her heart in her throat. Of all the things she'd brought with her, her work meant the most to her.

Everything else could be replaced, but her sketches and notes were, to her, priceless.

She reached for the leather case just as the steward cleared his throat. "Madam, I wouldn't touch it just yet." She froze.

"Sorry," he added. "Security may want to take photographs."

"But I have to see…" Had he opened it? Moved things around? Taken something? It was horrifying that the intruder had poked through her toiletries and her underwear. Her clothing. But this possibility was the worst of all.

Her soul was laid bare in that portfolio. Set out for anyone to see in swatches of brilliant color, curved and lyrical lines, sweeps of her brushes, ideas of her heart. Those weren't just costume designs to her. They were living, breathing proof that she was a woman in her own right, not merely the daughter of Elias Stamos, one of the richest men in Greece.

She opened and closed her hands convulsively and tried to swallow, but her mouth was dry.

"Would you care for some water?"

"Yes, please." She sat in one of the chairs in the breakfast area.

The steward got a bottle from the small refrigerator, opened it and poured her a glass, which she accepted gratefully.

Finally a knock sounded on the door. "Miss Stamos? It's Gideon Dayan, head of security."

"Yes, come in." She explained the situation to the pleasant-looking man with the grim gaze. He surveyed the room, and she had the feeling that he missed nothing, not even the placement of so much as a paperclip.

He dismissed the steward and called in another woman to write details of the report. They would immediately change the key code on her door, and if she liked, they could switch her accommodations.

"No, thank you. I'll be fine here as long as the key codes are changed."

"We'll also run a report on which keys have been used to access this room. That will give us a list of suspects, Miss Stamos."

"Thank you. You've been most helpful, Gideon. I very much appreciate it." She sighed. "Since your staff will probably be occupying my quarters for the next few hours, I may just go to the spa, if they can accommodate me."

"I'll make sure that they do, Miss Stamos. And we will alert you as to when you can come back and make yourself comfortable."

"SOMEONE WAS IN Helena Stamos's suite?" On the bridge, Nick stared at Gideon and jumped to his feet. "When? Why? Is she all right? Was anything taken?"

"She's fine. Nothing appears to be missing, but the intruder clearly went through her things." Gideon raised his eyebrows. "Her very personal things."

Nick felt anger heat his cheeks. "You're joking."

"No, sir."

"Ms. Stamos and the steward who accompanied her to her suite both noted that a man's cologne hung in the air."

Nick's gut roiled at the thought of some pervert in Helena's rooms, groping through her belongings. "Have you checked the key codes?"

"Yes. That's the first thing we did after ascertaining that nothing was stolen. My staff is still examining the room—"

Nick cut him off. "Well, who has been in there?"

"Miss Stamos herself and two staff members. Both are being questioned, but one says she only delivered a fruit basket and the other claims that all she did was clean and tidy the rooms."

Nick narrowed his eyes, but Gideon continued before he could voice suspicion.

"I think they're both telling the truth. Neither admitted anyone to the suite—unless someone managed to slip in behind them and hide. The associate who delivered the fruit basket reported that she had an 'odd feeling' about the room but thought her imagination was running away with her. She says nobody was in the suite during her delivery, but she, too, noticed the scent of men's cologne and smoke."

"Where is Miss Stamos?"

"She's in the spa, sir. We gave her complimentary

treatments for the rest of the afternoon because of this incident. And we've apologized profusely."

"I'll need to make apologies in person and check on her. Gideon, I know I don't need to remind you that this is Elias Stamos's daughter. Of all people to fall victim to a security breach…"

"Yes, sir, I realize the gravity of this issue. I will continue to look into every possibility."

"If Ms. Stamos is at risk…"

Gideon nodded. "Captain, as you know, we have excellent security on board *Alexandra's Dream*, but no program is flawless."

"Well, make sure nothing like this recurs. Post a guard outside her door if necessary."

"Will do, sir."

"Go ahead and give me your status report, Gideon, while you're here. Anything else of concern?"

The security officer shook his head. "Just the usual. We had a rowdy drunk in the cigar bar. Had to ask him to leave. An argument between two women, also enhanced by alcohol, that led to actual blows and hair-pulling."

Nick snorted. "Nothing surprises me after this long."

"No, sir."

"Gideon, will you check the passenger list for a man named Kostas Manolis?" Nick frowned. "If he appears, I need to know right away. It's of the utmost importance."

Gideon nodded. "Of course. Anything else, sir?"

"Change the key codes on the doors of both Ms. Stamos and her niece, Ms. Slater."

"Already done."

"Good man. I knew I could count on you." Nick clapped him on the shoulder, and then the man left.

After leaving the staff captain in charge, Nick made his way to the Jasmine Spa. He shouldn't intrude on Helena while she was there, but he needed to see her immediately.

He knew that it would make him, a man, very uncomfortable to know that someone had searched his room and touched his things. But for a woman to realize that a strange man had handled her intimate items had to be terrifying.

And who would wish her harm? Who would want to scare her? Nick gritted his teeth and realized that he was in a cold rage. Had this pervert been in there sniffing her panties? Rubbing himself on her clothing?

Nick didn't want to think about it. His first response was to keep Helena by his side for the rest of the scheduled cruise, to not let her out of his sight. He would book her into his own stateroom so that he could ensure her safety himself.

But that wasn't practical, and neither was the urge to hunt down the culprit and wring the man's neck with his bare hands.

Nick forced himself to stay calm. Helena didn't need to see his worry on top of everything else. He reached the spa, opened the door and addressed the woman at the reception desk. "I know that Miss Stamos is here, Michelle. Is it possible for me to see her at this moment?"

"Let me check, Captain Pappas." She picked up the phone and punched in a couple of numbers.

While she did so, Nick tried not to think of Helena

naked on a massage table, glowing with warm oil. Or nude in a mud bath…or rinsing off suds in a hot, steamy shower.

He shouldn't be thinking about her in those terms at all. He shouldn't have taken her to bed. He'd be wise to stay away from her for the remainder of the cruise….

"Captain?" prompted Michelle. "Miss Stamos will see you now."

CHAPTER SIXTEEN

HELENA TRIED to find comfort in the lovely foot massage she'd had, and in the fluffy white terry robe in which she huddled. They'd even warmed it for her before she disrobed and slipped it on.

The hot tea with lemon and honey should have soothed her, too. But all she could focus on were the torn drawings and paintings security had found in her portfolio. When they'd alerted her, she'd had it sent up to her, and although she'd dreaded what she might see, the reality was worse.

And why? Why, why, why?

It made no sense. She had no enemies on this ship, to her knowledge. The people closest to her on board were Gemma, Giorgio and Nick. None of them, she was sure, could have done this. Certainly not Gemma—there wasn't a mean bone in the girl's body.

Giorgio? She hadn't been entirely warm toward him, but she'd been civil. She'd put up with his outrageous flirting and innuendo. Had he expected her to fall into bed with him? And then resented the fact that she hadn't?

She just couldn't imagine it.

Helena reached for her tea as Michelle called on the intercom. "Miss Stamos? Captain Pappas is here. He wonders if it would be convenient for you to give him a moment of your time?"

The cup rattled in the saucer as Helena set it down. "Of course. Send him back. Thank you."

Her nail technician gathered her things and left. Moments later the captain stood in the room, hat in hand. "Helena, I came as soon as I heard. Are you all right?"

Her hands clenched the wad of paper in her lap. "I'm fine."

His gray eyes drilled into hers. "You're not."

"All right, then," she said carefully. "I'm not. But I will be. Is that a better answer?"

"A more honest one, anyway." He reached for her hand.

She hesitated, then extended her right one, still camouflaging the crumpled paper with her left. He didn't just squeeze her fingers, he raised them to his lips. And then he gently kissed her forehead, which sent a quiver through her whole body.

"I cannot apologize enough that something like this occurred on my ship."

"Nick, it's not your fault."

"As the captain, the ultimate responsibility for everything on board is mine. This happened under my watch, and I'm not happy about it. I don't like to see you distressed."

"I'll admit that I'm not fond of the idea that someone prowled through my suite, but as I said, I'll be fine. Thank you for your concern."

They'd reverted to formality again, despite his quick kiss. But perhaps it was better that way.

She dropped her head back against the spa chaise that

cradled her body, giving in to weariness and confusion. She held the crumpled ball of paper in her hands as if it were made of crystal and could supply the answers she needed.

His eyes went immediately to it. "What is that?"

"It's malice," she said simply. "And I don't know whose. I'm sorry, Nick, but I'm searching for answers just like everyone else."

She let him take it from her lap. He carefully unwadded her watercolor of a costume and spread it out on a side table. "It's beautiful," he said.

"It was."

"It still is. You painted this?"

She nodded.

He followed her eyes to the leather portfolio that she couldn't bear to part with now.

"The prowler," Helena said, hating the quaver in her voice, "destroyed over half the drawings and paintings and notes in there. Why, Nick? Why?"

"Helena, I don't know what to say. I can't think of a reason for it."

"It's so personal, so vengeful and full of hatred. And I don't know why anyone would hate me enough to do this."

He shook his head. "I don't know."

He reached over and covered her hands with his. They sat for a few moments in silence and she focused only on the warmth and steadiness of his hands on hers, and how much she needed that at the moment.

Finally he stood and looked down at her. "We'll get to the bottom of it. I promise you."

"Is it because of my name, Nick?" she wondered. "I suppose half the ship could know who I am."

He nodded. "Maybe it was just someone looking for jewelry to steal. When he didn't find any because of the safe, he got hostile. That's the most likely explanation."

"Mmm." She tried to convince herself of this.

"Enjoy the rest of your afternoon here. What's next?"

"A manicu . A seaweed wrap. And a hot-oil treatment for my   ir. It will be an extremely difficult few hours," she sa   , trying to inject some levity in her voice.

He smiled. "When you return to your room, ask Michelle to call someone to escort you, all right?"

She nodded.

"And in the meantime, we'll take a look at the passenger roster, see if anyone with a record pops up." He walked, hat in hand, to the exit and then looked back at her.

He must have thought she looked forlorn, for he retraced his steps and lifted her chin in one hand. Then he kissed her, thoroughly this time. And while she was still reeling, he left.

NICK WENT BACK to the bridge, checked a few of the sat comm reports and addressed some management issues. But through it all, part of his mind stayed distracted, and not only by Helena.

This was not the first time security had been breached on his ship. A hired assassin had made his way on board during their first cruise, and stolen items had been found stashed in a couple of plants before whoever had put them there could retrieve them. Gideon had increased security measures, but as he had told Nick earlier, there were always those who could find ways around some of the tightest measures, and those who could be bought for the right price. At least Nick had the utmost confidence in the chief of security officer. Gideon Dayan was the best in the industry.

But why would someone enter Helena's room? Had the guy been looking for something specific? He knew the jewelry she wore was valuable, but that was in the safe.

And that didn't explain why her work had been destroyed.

Nick's thoughts returned to Giorgio Tzekas, and his suspicions deepened. Spoiled, irresponsible, a gambler and a drinker. Impressed with his own good looks. A ladies' man... Had he somehow gotten into Helena's room?

He told himself that he was biased against Tzekas after they'd worked together at Blue Agean, and he had warned Elias about the first officer's lack of discipline. But Tzekas's father was a longtime friend of Stamos, and the ship's owner wouldn't budge.

As the captain, Nick had to be fair. He had to struggle with his own prejudices and put them aside in the name of running the ship. Something was off about Tzekas, but he didn't think it had anything to do with Helena.

Nick called Gideon to check on his progress. "Any of the passenger names pop for misdemeanors or felonies?"

"Negative, sir. There's one that cropped up for tax evasion, but apparently it was settled and the charges were dropped."

"Did you find a Kostas Manolis anywhere?"

"Also negative."

That set Nick's mind at ease. He suspected that Eva's nerves had prompted her call, not any real danger to him from her ex.

"I'm at a loss, Captain. All we can do is stay alert and keep watch."

But another idea entered Nick's mind. "We should do a check for Helena's ex-husband. First name is Aristotle. Last name…let me think. Nakis, I believe. Yes, that's it."

"I'm entering it now, sir. Just a moment. No, nothing."

Nick was both relieved and disappointed. "All right. Thank you, Gideon. Keep me apprised if anything comes up."

"Will do, sir." The chief security officer frowned. "Have you thought about the possibility that this is connected to Elias Stamos?"

"How do you mean?"

"Someone wanting revenge because of a business issue or a perceived slight?"

Perhaps that was the key. They couldn't find any links between passengers and Helena, but maybe they should be looking for links to Elias. The man had made enemies over the years. The motive behind this disturbing incident could be to get to Elias through Helena. Make him think someone was stalking her. His daughters were his greatest vulnerability.

Nick nodded thoughtfully. "It's a reasonable theory."

"I'll check into it, sir. And I'll get a security detail on his granddaughter Gemma, too."

"Good. I won't be at ease until this is resolved. If anything happens to either one of them…" He couldn't even think about it. "If we haven't tracked this bastard down by tomorrow, then I think the best thing is probably to get them both safely off the ship at Valletta."

"I agree, sir."

"It will be awkward to explain to Elias, but that can't be helped."

"Yes, sir."

"All right. Keep me posted."

MIKE O'CONNOR POUNDED on the door of Giorgio Tzekas's stateroom. In tones quite unlike the good Father Connelly's, he snarled, "Open the door, you son of a bitch!"

"What do you want?" The first officer opened the door only wide enough to stick his rumpled head out. He wore nothing but a bathrobe.

Mike pushed his way in, only to roll his eyes at the sight of a naked redhead in Giorgio's bed. Her eyes widened when she saw his priest's collar. *"Dios mio!"*

Looking suitably horrified, Mike crossed himself and then averted his gaze.

"Get her out of here," he said.

"We're busy," Giorgio growled. "Say what you have to say. She doesn't speak English."

"Good thing. Priests don't usually swear at their parishioners. But this occasion merits it! Did we not talk about our arrangement?"

"We talked," Tzekas admitted gruffly. "So what of it?"

"You went over to Crete yesterday and picked up another piece for yourself. What in the *hell* do you think you're doing? It's risky enough getting the stuff for the boss."

"I don't know where you get your information, *Father*, but you have no right to keep tabs on me! All I'm trying to do is make a living, just like you."

"Listen to me, you sad sack of shit." Mike said the words in the benevolent tones a priest might use to a confessor. "It's not my problem that you run up gambling debts and buy expensive baubles for your—" he smiled over Giorgio's shoulder at his bedmate "—cheap sluts."

She smiled back at him a little sheepishly, the covers pulled up to her neck. Clearly, she really didn't speak English.

"Don't lecture me, Father. You're always flirting…"

"I'm not endangering the entire scheme—"

"You sure as hell are if people guess you're not really a priest."

"—by lining my pockets to support a criminally stupid habit."

"No? I'm not the only one lining his pockets, my friend. Get out of here before I notify a certain church that their precious triptych is a fake and the original is in the custody of a cruising priest."

Mike shut his mouth. How had Tzekas discovered that?

The man nodded smugly. "I thought so. *Au revoir*, Father. Go and don a hair shirt. You can meditate upon your sins while I get on with mine."

And Giorgio showed him the door.

CHAPTER SEVENTEEN

ALEXANDRA'S DREAM had docked at Kusadasi, a resort town on the Aegean coast of Turkey. The port was named after a rock in the shape of a bird's head on a small island offshore.

Helena had been to the ruins at Epheseus twice before, so she opted not to go ashore. She spent another enjoyable morning with Gemma, teaching a puppet-making class to some of the children who were five and older. It was an opportunity to have fun with her niece, use her creative skills and take her mind off the disturbing intruder.

Helena, who was dedicated to her career, was surprised at how much she loved being around kids. She responded to their simple joy in creating their puppets, and also sympathized with the children who got cranky and frustrated when their less developed motor skills turned out puppets that weren't quite the way they'd imagined. As an artist and designer she understood the gap between vision and end product, and how hard it was to bridge sometimes.

She waved goodbye to the group when the session was over, and kissed Gemma's cheek amidst a chorus of "Bye, Miss H'lena!"

She made her way back to her suite and greeted the cheerful, uniformed young woman who was posted outside her door.

She'd only been inside a few minutes when she jumped at a firm knock. "Who is it?"

"It's Nick."

She let him in immediately, and as soon as the door was closed behind him she stepped into his arms. She didn't think about whether it was unwise. She didn't care that they had no future or that he had left her without a word in the past. She just wanted to feel his strong, solid chest under her cheek and take comfort from the warmth of his presence. .

"Helena, *agape mou*, it's all right. I will keep you safe. I promise." He murmured the words into her hair, holding her tight. He rubbed a big hand in comforting circles on her back, then tipped her head back and kissed her.

She drank him in, as much of him as she could.

"We will find this man, I swear to you."

Helena nodded.

"We're searching the ship manifest, trying to track him down every way we know how. We can't find any connections between other passengers and you. Is there anything else you can tell us?"

"No, nothing."

"Then he may be trying to hurt your father through you."

She breathed in the scent of him and clung to him tightly. "I really don't want to talk about it anymore. There have been so many questions and theories…I just want it to go away."

"I know. I'm sorry, sweetheart." Nick kissed her nose and each of her eyelids, then traced her lips with his index finger.

"Just make it all go away, Nikolas," she said.

"I wish I could."

"You can." She placed her hands flat against his chest and met his eyes. "Make love to me."

He cupped her face in his hands. "Helena…you're reacting emotionally."

"Yes. Is there any other way to react to this?"

He sighed. "There's logic."

"Logic?" she repeated, and laughed. "No. I've had this feeling of being watched, too. And that's not logical—it's pure instinct. None of this is logical. But now all I can think of is that man in my room. Please, push that out of my mind, replace it with something healthy and tender and loving…."

Then Nick's mouth was on hers again and his fingers stroked through her hair and she stopped trying to articulate what she felt because it was no longer necessary.

He understood, just as he always had. He kissed her tears away, and when more fell he gently consumed them, taking them from her and replacing them with his touch so that they condensed into desire.

He undressed for her, dropping his clothes to the floor and never taking his lips from hers. His hands skimmed up under her simple sundress, caressed her thighs, lifted the skirt and tugged it up and over her head. Then he slid her panties down.

Nick picked her up and she wrapped her legs around him. He walked with her to a chair and sat on the edge of it, placing her on his knees, holding her for a few moments against his chest. She could feel that he was aroused, but he made no move to take her.

Restless, she reached her hand down and wrapped it around him, urging him on. Maybe it was shameless but she wanted to ride him into oblivion so that she could block out her panic about the unknown prowler, replace fear with pleasure.

But Nick stopped her, brought her hands up and then placed them on his shoulders. Provocatively, he ran his tongue around her nipples, laving them until she whimpered for more.

He cupped her bottom in his big palms, squeezing and caressing until she squirmed. Then his hands moved along her thighs until his clever fingers crept inward and began to play. He rubbed, he stroked, he slipped inside and out until she felt she was flying, supported by nothing but his hands and the sensations he created at her core.

She arched her back, heard herself cry out—and color exploded behind her closed eyes. Then Nick entered her, stroking inside her, and she convulsed around him, aware only of his own shudder as he climaxed in her arms.

NICK TWINED HIS FINGERS through Helena's silky hair as she lay sleepily beside him among her rumpled covers. "I have to go, sweetheart," he said. "I'm sorry. I wish I didn't have a ship to run."

She stretched a hand out and splayed her fingers over his bare chest. Her touch made him ache for her all over again. "It runs without you, Nikolas. It's not as if you have to keep your hands on the wheel."

He smiled and shook his head. "No, but it's complicated, as you know."

"When I was a little girl, I thought the captain of a ship just stood at the helm in a dashing skipper's hat, occasionally peering through a spyglass and shouting, 'Land ho!'"

He laughed. "You know now that it's closer to running a floating company."

She sat up and pulled the sheet over her naked body, her smile dimming. "Yes. You and Elias."

Nick raised his eyebrows. "What does that mean?"

Helena shrugged. "Always busy. Running from one meeting to another…managing problems. I'm sorry I've created yet another problem for you."

"You haven't created anything," Nick said, hauling her against him. "But speaking of Elias, I'm going to have to call him and tell him what's going on."

She stiffened. "No."

He stroked her cheek. "*Agape mou,* I mean you no disrespect, but I wasn't asking your permission. I will call your father. He needs to be informed."

"Please, leave Elias out of this!" Her voice shook with suppressed emotion. Not anger, exactly. He couldn't put his finger on it. "I am not a child, Nick. I don't need Baba to swoop down and 'make it all better.'"

"It's not a question of that, Helena. The fact is that he's my boss, and he will want to be apprised of security problems on one of his ships, especially if there is a personal angle to them."

"Very diplomatically stated, Nikolas." But her tone was bitter. "However, I am asking you as my friend—and as my lover—not to call him."

Nick was silent.

"He will jet over here and board at the next port. Look, Nick, I love him dearly, but I don't want him here right now. Promise me that you will not call him."

Nick sighed. Elias was his employer. "I *can't* promise that. Don't ask me."

"He'll want to know everything that's being done and he'll demand to see every piece of evidence. Do you think I want my father involved in all this? He's already overprotective.

"As a costume designer, I associate with 'strange people.' According to my father they're flea-bitten artists, crass creatives, nihilistic novelists. Hooligans and homosexuals! I expose myself to the wrong elements, you see. Elias doesn't find my crowd appealing. He would like to rewrite my life for me."

"Helena, he is your father and the owner of this ship. We should tell him what's going on."

She shook her head.

Nick sighed.

She leaped out of the bed and faced him with her hands on her hips, gorgeous even in disarray. "I do love my father, Nick, but he can be overpowering. Did you ever think that maybe I might have had other reasons not to claim Elias as my father when I was eighteen? Reasons that had nothing to do with hiding my financial status?"

He stared at her. "No. I never considered that."

"I just wanted to be *me*. Pretend I was free and happy and not a hostage to his position as the shipping king of Greece." Her mouth trembled and she crossed her arms over her naked breasts.

"You were always free and happy with me." Nick touched her arm.

"Exactly. And I treasured that. I never wanted it to change."

"Everything changes," he told her. "It's the nature of things."

She nodded miserably. "Just please don't call Elias, Nick. Promise me."

He swore. "If I agree not to call him, and we have not found this intruder by the end of today, then I want you to promise me that you and Gemma will disembark at Valletta and fly home. I am worried for your safety."

"Gemma has nothing to do with this situation!" she cried. "Why should she leave? You'll ruin her internship for nothing."

"This may not have to do with you, but with Elias himself. The culprit may wish to get at him through you and Gemma. Upset you or hurt you or both. If we can't track him down, then I want you gone and safe."

Helena locked gazes with Nick. "No. I'm not running from him. This is my vacation. He's not going to scare me off the ship."

"*Agape mou,* I will remind you that I don't need to ask your permission. If I order you to leave the ship, you will go. Do you understand me?"

"Pulling rank, *Capitano?*" she said lightly, but her chin came up.

"No, I'm being sensible," he returned.

"This man is a coward. He lurks and spies. He sneaks in and rifles through panties. He is not confrontational. I don't think I have anything to fear."

"He very well may be a coward," Nick told her. "But there is also the chance that he is not. So if he comes near you, there are two possible outcomes. One of them is entirely unacceptable and I will not risk it."

"Fine, then post a daisy chain of armed guards and call Elias, if your loyalty lies with him. But I will *not* get off this ship."

"You will if I order it." They stood toe-to-toe and she refused to back down.

"Go ahead and order it, Captain. But you'll have to carry me off kicking and screaming. I won't go quietly."

CHAPTER EIGHTEEN

HELENA SAT on a lounge chair on the Helios deck, knees drawn up to support her sketch pad. Her emotions flowed almost madly through her fingertips to the broken nubs of the silky, almost oily Cray-Pas she was using this afternoon.

She sensed rather than saw fellow passengers stop to scrutinize her picture, but her huge dark glasses and hunched posture communicated that she wished to be left alone. Her work today was abstract, and people seemed to lose interest anyway when they couldn't identify a representational object in her drawing.

Dark slashes of black, shades of gray and mottled purples settled over the top half of the canvas, their visual weight suffocating the radiant yellows, cheery cantaloupe-peach and hopeful spring-green wavering below. A lovely, glowing ruby-red had all but disappeared from the bottom right-hand corner, and a jagged edge of midnight-blue splintered a blissful swath of orange that had dared to rise from the bottom center.

Her hands were shaking a bit, but it didn't matter for her purposes. Helena reached the end of both the black and gray Cray-Pas with a gloomy smear across the page and felt some measure of relief. Only more cheerful shades remained. But she didn't pick them up; she simply rubbed her ashy, smoky-looking thumb against the other colorful smears on her fingers.

"Wow," said Gemma from behind her. "The dark colors look like they're eating the bright ones. Are you in a bad mood, Aunt Helena?" Her niece handed her a cocktail glass brimming with fruit juice and sat next to her.

"No, no," Helena said absently. "How are you? How are the multitudes of little monsters in the children's center today?"

Gemma grinned. "They're not monsters. I like them."

"Just a figure of speech. I like them, too. But I have no idea how you control the little ones, Gem."

"Guidelines, activities and a lot of patience." Her niece glanced again at the sketch pad on Helena's lap. "What's bothering you?"

"Nothing. Why?"

"Please don't lie to me. I'm not a kid any longer, okay? There's a guard outside of my room and nobody will tell me why, except that for some reason security is on high alert—for me." Gemma took a sip of her own drink and slid onto the neighboring chaise longue, swinging up her long, tanned legs in their casual slides. "As if I couldn't have figured that out for myself."

Helena remained silent.

"What is going on?"

"Sweetheart, a man has been in my room. It's very possible that someone has targeted me as a way to get to Pappou, all right? And we simply can't take the chance that he might know who you are, too. So yes, security is looking out for us. And the captain has even urged that we consider leaving the ship."

"What?" Gemma's lips set mulishly. "No! I have a job here. I'm not walking away from it because of some vague threat that might not even *be* a threat. Maybe the person was in your room to steal something."

Helena looked over at her. "That's almost exactly what *I* told Nick. Er, Captain Pappas." She smiled.

"He's not going to call Pappou, is he?" Gemma looked concerned. "I love my grandfather, but I don't want him in the middle of my first job. He's already paranoid that I'll be kidnapped on dry land and held for ransom. *Please* tell me the captain won't call him." She frowned. "Hey, since when do you call Captain Pappas *Nick?*"

Helena opened her mouth and then closed it again. Finally she said, "I knew him when I was younger." She could feel a telltale blush spreading across her cheeks.

"Aunt H! You have a thing for him, don't you?"

"I do not have a 'thing' for him." *Liar.* Helena busied herself by closing the sketch pad and wiping her fingers on the cocktail napkin Gemma had brought with her drink.

"You sure didn't look like you minded dancing with him the other night," her niece said frankly. "I saw you."

Helena pushed her dark glasses firmly up on her nose, glad that they were wraparound and completely obscured her eyes from Gemma. "Captain Pappas is an excellent…dancer."

"I'll just bet he is." But Gemma knew better than to pry. Seconds later, Helena wished she had.

"Aunt Helena, let's say that I, um, wanted to *dance* with someone. How do you know when it's the right guy?"

Alarmed, Helena laid the sketch pad aside and took off her glasses, turning her full attention toward her niece. Was Gemma asking what she was afraid she was asking? And how on earth did she answer that question? Couldn't Gem ask her mother?

Helena tried desperately to think of what Katherine would say to her daughter. For her sister's sake, and for Gemma's sake, she couldn't screw this up.

"Well, it's normal to consider…dancing…with an attractive man. But I'd err on the side of caution and get to know him very well first. And I'd think about what your expectations are, regarding that first, uh, dance. I'd also make *very* sure that you know all the steps."

Gemma gazed directly at her. "By 'steps,' do you mean birth control?"

Helena almost choked. "Something like that."

"I have that covered."

"Oh." Helena swirled the ice in her drink.

"You have to realize that I'm probably the only girl in my school who hasn't done this yet."

Helena chose to ignore the fact that she'd only been a year older than Gemma when she'd fallen in love with Nick. "Your grandfather would want me to give you the 'save yourself for marriage' speech here. Possibly your mother and father would, too."

"Don't bother. It's my decision, not theirs."

"That's true," Helena said carefully. "It's your body. But I'd urge you not to do anything just because of peer pressure or a feeling of not belonging to some 'club.' All right? And try to wait until it's someone you truly love." *As I loved Nick.*

Gemma nodded. "You sound so conservative, Aunt H. I thought you were supposed to be the wild one in the family."

Helena sighed and took her niece's hand. "The truth is that I'm really not so wild. Your grandfather has never liked my clothes or my job or my friends. He thinks they all indicate an irresponsible lifestyle. Even your parents tease me about being 'bohemian.'"

"They have it all wrong?"

Helena nodded. Then she added with a smile, "But don't tell them, all right? I'd hate to disappoint them."

Gemma grinned. "Okay. It'll be our secret."

When they parted, Helena went back to her room, her sketch pad under her arm, thinking about Nick and their first time. He'd been so sweet, so tender, so afraid he would hurt her.

And when he'd left her later, she'd wondered if the old cow-and-free-milk adage had been true. She'd wondered a lot of things, but never once had she considered that he might have been about to propose to her. What had he done with the ring when he'd left, angry and disappointed?

Could she get up the nerve to ask him? Would he tell her? She shook her head. Best that she not bring up the subject. She didn't know what they were doing with each other right now, anyway. She was fooling herself if she thought they had a chance at happily-ever-after. They had a blazing physical attraction that was based on hormones, the past and the forbidden, that was all.

He belonged to the sea and she belonged in a city of concrete. London was the heart of theater and film in the U.K. How could she go anywhere else? But tears blurred her vision as she reached her new door and dug into her pocket for her key card. It had been a very bad idea to have another fling with Nick.

She slid the card into the lock and entered her room, looking around quickly. Nothing was out of place. No sickly sweet, smoky male scent. No reason for alarm.

She sighed in relief and tossed her sketch pad on the bed. A light on the telephone flashed red at her and she picked up the receiver for the message, toeing off her sandals as she listened. It was from Katherine, who was calling to say hello and to ask how Gemma was doing.

Helena felt a little guilty at not apprising Katherine of the security situation, but she didn't want to worry her, and there had been no threat to Gemma. If that changed, Helena would alert her sister.

HELENA WAS QUIET as Nick stood stiffly inside the door of her cabin. He was so formal that he made formal look casual, and she knew what he was going to say before he came into the room with her and said it.

"You have to pack your things and leave the ship at Valletta."

"No."

"I am concerned for your safety. We still cannot locate this man. He may be dangerous. So this is not a request, Helena, it's an order." He gazed down sternly at her from his superior height.

"Nick, I'm sorry and I mean you no disrespect, but I won't take orders from you. I've had enough of being pressured by other people to do things that I don't want to do."

He set his jaw and simply walked to her closet, which

he opened. He pulled out her empty luggage and tossed it onto the bed. Then he opened a drawer and began placing her things neatly inside one of the suitcases.

"Stop it, Nikolas," she warned. "I won't have you making my decisions for me. Elias has done enough of that."

"Let's keep your father out of this, all right? By your own request. I run this ship, Helena, and despite the relationship between us, you are a passenger on it. Even though you're essentially royalty on this cruise line, you will follow my orders while you're aboard. Is that clear?" He was Nick in his most buttoned-up state: a military commander, not her sweet and tender lover. He seemed cool and emotionless.

Where was the real Nick? This man in the sterile white uniform barking orders at her was not her first love.

An unwelcome thought formed in her mind. While she was sure that he did, in fact, have her safety in mind, was this also a convenient opportunity for him to say a hurried goodbye?

He couldn't possibly date his boss's daughter without incurring Elias's wrath. And she'd made it very clear that she didn't want promises or marriage anyway. So was this the clean, uncomplicated break that Nick was undoubtedly looking for?

I'm not ready to say goodbye. The sudden knowledge flooded her mind, along with panic. She couldn't possibly get attached to him again…she'd known it going into this fling. She didn't *want* to be attached to any man, even Nick. She'd had enough of answering to her father, then feeling guilt-ridden about Ari.

She wanted to go back to London and be free. But not yet. Not *now*. And not on Nick's orders. Her entire being rebelled.

He'd filled a suitcase and was opening more drawers. "Stop it, I said! I'm not going." She rushed over to the suitcase and began throwing things out of it again.

Nick caught her wrist and turned her to face him. "You *will* go, Helena."

"You just want to be rid of me!" The words spilled out before she could recall them and he jerked back as if she'd slapped him.

His gray eyes went even steelier and his nostrils flared while his mouth tightened to a grim line. "Is that what you think?"

She said nothing and his grip tightened on her wrist. Then suddenly he let go.

"If that is what you wish to tell yourself, then so be it," Nick said formally. "But you will pack and you will depart the ship tomorrow morning when we dock."

She made no move toward the suitcase.

He gazed at her coolly and said, "If you find yourself unable to gather your things personally, then I will be happy to see to it that you have valet service."

She hated that professional calm of his. She wanted to upset him as he had upset her. "Goodbyes never were your strong suit, were they, Nikolas?"

His only reaction was a tiny twitch at the corner of his left eye.

"We both know that you won't remove me publicly. My father would never stand for it."

Nick's gaze drilled into hers. "Fighting dirty, I see.

Invoking Papa's big name as my boss? I thought you never traded on your father's influence."

She looked away, feeling her cheeks flush. *Damn him!*

"But you're right, my love. I won't risk a public and melodramatic scene."

"I didn't think so." Satisfaction crept into her voice— her fatal error.

He noticed. "Helena, make no mistake. If you don't leave the ship tomorrow morning, I *will* have you quietly tossed into the brig."

Her mouth dropped open as he made his way to the door. "You wouldn't dare."

He opened it and stepped over the threshold before turning to face her. "You don't think so? You're wrong."

CHAPTER NINETEEN

NICK WAS IN the foulest of tempers when he left Helena's stateroom. How could she have accused him of forcing her to leave the cruise so that he didn't have to say goodbye?

It had made him so furious that he'd been on the verge of shaking her, or shouting at her, something he never did—and especially not to a woman. He'd sooner break down and sob on a public street.

He'd never even shouted at Linnea when things were at their worst between them. She'd castigated him for being a cold, emotionless bastard who'd never cared about her. She'd goaded him, slapped him, got right into his face and screamed until he'd just walked out the door.

Nick wouldn't play her game and he wouldn't give her the satisfaction. Not to mention the fact that by that point, five years into the marriage, he *didn't* have much feeling for her. They'd both known it was a mistake. He'd simply been relieved that they hadn't had children.

Goodbyes were never your strong suit, were they, Nikolas?

Helena could think whatever she liked about him, but by God he would keep her safe. He would never again let down a woman he cared about. Carolina's tragedy had taught him not to stand by passively.

Nick knew that Gideon would eventually find and close the loophole in security, whether it was human or technological or both. Gideon was the best. But in the meantime they had to minimize any risk to Helena.

Carolina's waxen face appeared in his mind, eyes staring, dull and lifeless despite their expression of pain and fear, and Nick raised an unsteady hand to his own eyes.

Helena said that he couldn't blame himself, but he'd been the one to find Carolina. He'd grown concerned because nobody had heard from her in over a week. He'd figured she was depressed and had stopped by to cheer her up....

Why couldn't he have stopped by three days before? Why had he been so goddamn self-absorbed, too busy for his own family?

I failed her.

Well, he wasn't taking any chances with Helena, no matter what she said or thought.

THAT EVENING before dinner, Nick stood for a long time in the shower. As the hot water cascaded down his body, he debated whether or not he should go to Helena's room in the morning to say goodbye.

Given the last scene between them, it was perfectly reasonable for him to avoid her. After all, why inflict himself upon a woman who clearly suspected him of trying to get rid of her for personal reasons?

He gritted his teeth. That still bothered the hell out of him. After what they'd shared together, after the confidences they'd exchanged, she could still suspect him of such a thing?

I once was ready to marry you, agape mou.

And yet, he had walked away. Would a different man have ignored her father's prominence and gone ahead and proposed with that tiny, pinhead of a diamond?

Had he been truly motivated by anger at her deception—or fear that she wouldn't say yes? Pride because he couldn't offer her the lifestyle she'd grown up with?

He braced his hands on the cool tiles of the shower stall and leaned his weight upon them, as if pushing the unwelcome thought away.

Then he rinsed the last traces of shampoo from his hair and shut off the tap. He stood there dripping and naked and all too aware….

Goodbyes never were your strong suit, were they, Nikolas? For the third damn time that day, the words echoed in his mind. He could be angry at Helena's comment, or he could acknowledge that there was some truth to it. He'd left and nursed his pride and his ego instead of putting them to the test.

What would she have said all those years ago? What might she say today, if they had a chance to do everything over again?

Nick opened the shower door and wrapped a towel around his lower body. He slicked back his hair with both hands. Then he went to the birch dresser that held his clothes and opened the third drawer. Under some casual collared shirts was a box his grandfather had carved for him when he was ten. He drew his fingers over the small waves and the tiny boat so lovingly etched into the lid. He traced the outline of the gull in the little swatch of sky.

Then he opened the box and removed a safety-deposit key, an ancient coin that he'd found in his teens while skin diving and a seashell from the coastal village of his birth in Greece.

Last, he tugged up a corner of the felt lining and pulled the fabric-covered piece of cardboard completely out.

Underneath was a small velvet pouch.

Nick untied the drawstring and shook out the object inside. It was a simple gold ring set with a diamond that looked almost microscopic. His mouth twisted. Only he knew that though the stone was tiny, it was of the finest quality and without a flaw—as white in color as nature made diamonds.

The ring had cost him all his savings: four months' salary plus a hell of a lot of overtime on Elias Stamos's freighter. He'd even helped unload the whole vessel to scrape together some more money. Fifteen years later, his muscles remembered the ache and strain and repetitive grind of the work. He'd injured his lower back and told Helena that he'd done it in a wrestling match.

Nick held the ring up to the light, the stone glittering at him. Still pure, still white, still encompassing the hopes and dreams of a silly kid.

I don't want promises, Nick. I'm not good wife material...I'm just a Gypsy.

A Gypsy like him. A Gypsy he'd ordered off his ship, to be on her way. Because he wanted her safe, and for no other reason. Nick put the ring back into the pouch and hid it under the lining of his box again. He couldn't believe he'd kept it all these years. But it hadn't seemed right to give it to Linnea, and he hadn't known what else to do with it. So he'd hidden the ring and tried to forget it was there.

He shoved the box back under his shirts and closed the drawer. What would she have said, if he'd only asked her?

The thought invaded his mind and took over. Marched through all the main roads of his consciousness. What would she have said?

And finally Nick knew. He knew without question what her answer would have been.

It would have been yes.

WHAT A BEAUTIFUL morning it was. Craig Peters paid little attention to the view of Valletta from his cabin. He clicked his fingers over the keyboard of his laptop, playing with a word here, changing a phrase there. He composed a long, florid letter mostly for his own entertainment, and then erased everything and started over. Best to keep this letter short and sweet.

My dear Helena,
We must further discuss the situation between us.
It is very important. Meet me in my stateroom at ten.
Nick.

There. That should be effective, and it was formal enough to sound like Captain Pappas. Craig's pulse spiked and his breathing quickened. He was taking a calculated risk by using Nick's room, yet there was a guard posted outside Helena's. He'd observed Nick for over a week now, and he'd never once returned to his room before lunch....

But if he did break the pattern, he'd get a nasty surprise—just a little earlier than scheduled.

Peters slipped on a pair of surgical gloves and printed out the note on shipboard stationery, folding it carefully. Now, how to get it to Helena Stamos with all of the heightened security? He thought he'd use the niece for that. They probably hadn't told her too much, considering her youth. And the silly little slut would likely enjoy the intrigue of passing along a love letter.

He picked up the glass of tepid water he'd set on the table next to him and ran his tongue back and forth along the edge.

You should never have interfered in my life, Mr. White Knight. Because now I am going to interfere in yours.

He felt like a child anticipating the arrival of Santa Claus. He simply couldn't wait to start the festivities.

GEMMA SIPPED her first cup of coffee and looked out at the port of Valletta and its magnificent skyline. Parts of the film *Munich* had been shot there, and Valletta's St. John's Co-Cathedral boasted the largest single work by the great painter Caravaggio.

As an architecture buff, thanks to her father, she wished fleetingly that she could go ashore to see some of the historic structures and Baroque buildings constructed by the Knights of Malta.

But she'd have plenty of opportunities to sightsee on a different cruise, one where she wasn't an intern.

Gemma turned at the tap on her shoulder and saw a

boy who couldn't be more than a couple of years older than she was. *Wow—he's tall, too. And good-looking.*

He was dressed in the white uniform of the ship's crew, and his dark hair was slicked back from his face, as if he'd recently showered and come on duty. He smiled at her and handed her a sealed envelope with Aunt Helena's name on it.

"I was told to give you this."

"By whom?" Gemma frowned.

"Another crew member, with the purser's desk."

"Oh. Okay." Why would they deliver a note with Helena's name on it to her niece? It struck Gemma as odd.

In response to her puzzled expression, the boy said, "He told me that it was personal and from the captain, to be delivered right away, and he wasn't able to locate Miss Stamos. He suggested you might know where she was?"

"Well…yes. I do, since I'm about to meet her for breakfast. So I'll give her the letter. Thank you."

The boy nodded. "I've seen you in the children's center during the day. You're great with the kids."

Charmed, Gemma blushed and stammered, "Th-thanks. See you around, okay?"

"Hope so." He smiled and waved goodbye.

Gemma found Aunt Helena in the Espresso bar, looking high-strung, as if she hadn't slept the night before. "Aunt H?"

Helena managed to produce a smile for her, and kissed her on both cheeks. "I wanted to say goodbye," she told Gemma. "I'm leaving the ship this morning. A limo will be at the dock for me just before noon."

"You're what? Why? Why aren't you staying for the rest of the cruise?" Gemma was dumbfounded.

"It's just best that I leave."

"Why?"

Helena shook her head. "It's that or the brig," she said lightly.

"The brig? What are you talking about?"

"Just kidding. Honestly, I'm getting a little stir-crazy aboard this ship and I need to get off."

Gemma narrowed her eyes at her aunt. "This has something to do with all the guards and security. Tell me what's going on. Is Captain Pappas making you leave because of those threats you mentioned?"

Aunt Helena's chin came up and her eyes flashed. "Captain Pappas cannot *make* me do anything."

"Uh-huh." Gemma watched her aunt play with the thin gold bangles on her wrists. They were funky and hand-hammered. Each one had a different-colored gemstone set into it somewhere along the diameter. Helena seemed upset and distracted. "You know what I think? I think you two had a fight."

"We did not have a fight." Helena stopped playing with the bracelets and fiddled instead with her tiny espresso spoon.

"You look like you were up all night."

"Slept like a baby, Gem." Helena's smile didn't reach her eyes.

"Well, if you did have a fight, maybe this is an apology." Gemma extended the envelope to her. "A crew member gave it to me to pass along to you. He said it's personal, from the captain."

Helena all but snatched it out of her hand, then stopped and bit her lip. "Thanks, Gemma." She looked at her niece ruefully. "You're right. I've been in a stew about Nick, and he did ask me to leave, and I'm not happy about it. Sorry."

"Are they making me leave, too?"

"No. The threats seem to be directed at me."

"Oh." Gemma drew her brows together, concerned. "Well, then it's probably a good thing that you're getting off the ship."

Helena scowled. "We'll see about that." She slipped her finger under the flap of the envelope. "This is all a big fuss over nothing."

Gemma nodded and watched as Helena pulled out the sheet of paper and scanned it quickly. She seemed to relax.

"So did he apologize?" She shouldn't pry, but she was curious.

"It sounds as if he's going to." Helena folded the note back up and shoved it into her pocket. She sat back and sipped at her espresso without fidgeting, like a normal person.

Her aunt had always been one of those small, hummingbirdlike people, full of nervous energy and darting around. But Gemma had rarely seen her in the state she'd been in this morning. "You must really care about him, Aunt H. Are you going to keep dating him?"

Helena's tiny cup clattered into her saucer. "No, Gem. Don't be silly. I live in London and he lives on *Alexandra's Dream.* I'm a creative type and he's a by-the-book, buttoned-up, ex-military type. It would never work out. Besides, I don't want to marry anybody. Been there, done that, got the T-shirt—as the Americans say."

Wow. That was a lot of excuses that had just come pouring out of her aunt H's mouth. Just one would have done the trick, Gemma thought as she sipped at her espresso. Suppressing a smile, she set down the cup. "Well. Sorry you're leaving. When will I see you again? Can I come to London in the fall and visit you?"

"Of course you can, sweetheart." Helena jumped up and put her arms around her. "But I hope we'll run into each other before that. And I want to tell you how proud I am of you. You're amazing with those children. Your mother would be proud, too. I can report to her that she's raised a daughter who's not only beautiful and kind, but great at her job."

Gemma hugged her aunt right back. "Thanks. Well, take care, okay?"

"Of course. I always do, Gem. Love you." And Helena blew her a kiss before walking away. Gemma watched as she ran a hand over the pocket with the note in it.

Gemma grinned. No matter what she said, Auntie H was in love with the handsome captain.

CHAPTER TWENTY

HELENA PICKED HER WAY between the packed suitcases to the mirror over the dresser in her suite. She'd put on a sleeveless, cherry-red silk blouse that tied at the waist, over the band of her long, navy-blue gypsy skirt. She'd chosen silver jewelry—the masks of tragedy and comedy suspended on a simple chain around her neck—and silver ballet flats. She finger-combed her hair and powdered her nose. She added just a touch of perfume behind each ear before dropping the bottle into her carry-on bag. Then she went into the bathroom to get her red lipstick.

It hardly mattered, since she was probably only saying goodbye to Nick. But she intended to leave a lasting impression on the man.

His note had been clipped and formal, just like him. So what else did he want to discuss about their relationship? The end of it? Or was he going to apologize? Would he ask to see her again? Perhaps he wished to visit her in London?

And was that a good idea? She didn't know. Now that she'd gotten over her fit of temper, she wasn't sure of anything at all. Except that she had disturbing feelings for Nick.

He'd claimed that with one glance at her, he'd fallen in love all over again. But was love enough when two people were so different? Did she love him back? And could she trust him?

Nick had walked out of her life fifteen years ago. Perhaps he had sent letters, as he claimed, but that didn't change the fact that without a word of goodbye, without waking her, he'd just disappeared.

At least today he'd say farewell in person. Perhaps that would make up for the past—and soften the future.

Helena opened the door, switched off the light and then fingered the note in her pocket as she headed for Nick's room.

As she took the elevator down to his floor and started along the hallway, she wondered why Nick hadn't just called her. It was a little odd…but the note had rung with Nick's formality, and had been hand-delivered to her niece by a uniformed crew member who'd said it was from the captain.

Helena passed the rooms of other officers and finally reached Nick's. She stared at the door, swallowed and raised her hand to knock. "Nick? It's me."

The door opened, but the room was dark inside. A masculine hand took hers. In the light from the hallway, Helena took note of the fact that it was smaller and paler than Nick's, and the knuckles were hairy. *Oh, dear God.*

She jerked back and opened her mouth to scream, but the male hand gripped her like a vise, yanked her into the room as if she were a rag doll and slammed the door. The man, whoever he was, knocked her against the wall and pinned her there by the throat. Then he pressed a cloth soaked in some chemical—ether?—against her face and everything went black.

HELENA AWOKE MUZZILY on a wave of nausea, accompanied by a dull headache. Her mouth felt as if it had been recently filled with sand. She might as well have been hungover. As she slowly returned to consciousness, she became aware that her shoulders and neck rang with pain, as did her wrists. They were tied behind her back and her hands were almost numb.

She lay on her side on the room's bed, and her skirt was rucked up almost to her waist, so that the man watching her from a chair across the room had a good view of her panties. He seemed to like that.

She didn't.

"Scream, and I'll kill you," he said. "I'll snap your neck like a chicken bone." Then he smiled at her, and Helena shivered.

His expression chilled her to the core. He was clean-shaven, with sparse sandy hair and a complexion like sautéed liver. He had a pinched nose too small for the rest of his broad features. His eyes, too, seemed undersize for his face: little, black, soulless holes. They looked like a shark's, except they weren't as alive. No, his eyes were like the old cigar burns she'd once seen on a bar counter in Athens.

"Did you sleep well, Miss Stamos?" the man asked, his voice overly polite. She focused on his mouth instead of his words. He had wide, fleshy lips that made her skin crawl.

"Answer me, you little whore." He got up and moved toward her, his white, hairy fingers flexing.

Petrified, she didn't know what to say. But he seemed to expect her to say something, since he looked more threatening by the second. She tried to free her sticky tongue from the roof of her mouth and watched in horror as he came closer.

Dear God, what is he going to do to me? She tried not to succumb to blind panic.

"I told you to answer!" he snapped. He fumbled with his belt buckle.

She swallowed a sob of sheer fear. "F-fine. I slept w-well." She hated the way her voice shook. "P-please don't hurt me. My father—he will pay anything you ask…."

"I don't want his money, you stupid little bitch. You don't have a clue as to why you're here, do you?"

She shook her head and struggled to sit up, sliding her legs over the side of the bed. She took some strange comfort from the contact of her bare feet with the solid floor, but she was unable to pull down her skirt, and his eyes drilled into the flesh of her thighs.

He made her feel dirtier with that one look than she'd ever felt in her life. "You were the one in my room."

"Yes." His lips stretched into another unpleasant smile, this one of satisfaction.

"Why?"

"Why not?" He dropped his hands from the belt buckle—thank God—and spread them, palms up.

He threw back his head and laughed, while she grew colder and colder inside.

"Look, you may have fixated on my picture from the society rags…"

His sneer became even more pronounced and he shook his head. "I am not fixated on you. You aren't much to look at, all skin and bones and little tits. Why the hell would I obsess?"

She stared at him, confounded.

He laughed. "Oh, you thought this was all about you? What a vain little whore you are."

"I don't understand." But a small kernel of relief began to blossom within her. He wasn't attracted to her. So that had to mean he wasn't going to rape her.

"Of course you don't understand." He walked to the small birch table near the cabin's sliding doors and picked up a decanter. He poured himself a tumbler full of what looked like whiskey.

"Then why…" She lurched to her feet, wobbling a little, but relieved that her skirt fell to cover her.

In an instant he'd crossed the room and in a flash of fleshy white, backhanded her. She fell across the bed, crying out, but he muffled the sound by crashing down on her and covering her mouth.

Helena, shaking, drew in as much air through her nose as possible, inhaling more of that hideous sweet, smoky musk. She wanted to cry and vomit at the same time.

His big, swollen body pressed hers down into the mattress, his flesh warm and damp, his breath unspeakable. She closed her eyes against his expression and tried to transfer her thoughts somewhere else.

"Don't you move or speak without my permission, or I'll make you sorry you were ever born."

Tears leaked from under her eyelids and she shook her head to let him know that she wouldn't make a sound.

He exhaled with satisfaction and heaved himself off the bed, leaving her sprawled there, her shoulders and arms and wrists in agony under her body. God alone knew what he would do next.

He settled himself back into his chair, drink in hand, and just stared at her.

"Why?" she finally asked, her voice still raspy from tears. "Why are you doing this?"

"I have my reasons."

She began to shake again. *What reasons? What did I ever do to deserve this?*

He held the glass to his lips and ran his tongue back and forth along the edge, like some kind of large, white lizard. He left a pasty trail of slime on the rim.

She wanted to lose consciousness so that she didn't have to think about this. But the ether was long gone and only the dull headache and dry mouth remained. Helena closed her eyes again.

"Look at me, bitch."

No telling what he'd do to her if she didn't. She focused on his fleshy face and evil, leering eyes.

"Yes, that's right. Take a good look, because I will be the last thing you ever see. But first, we will have some fun, you and I. And your pompous boyfriend is going to watch. Then I'll kill him, too."

She struggled upright, half gasping and half sobbing. *Nick? No, he can't hurt Nick.*

"Ah. I see that I now have your undivided attention. Excellent. Yes, the good captain is in for quite a show tonight."

He's going to rape me while he forces Nick to watch. A feeling of disbelief enveloped her. Surely nobody could be that evil.

She looked at the telephone sitting on the nightstand. Torture, pure torture, to have it next to her and not be able to dial it, get help.

"Who are you?" she whispered. "Why are you doing this?"

He considered her for a long moment, then shrugged. "My name is Manolis. That is all you need to know."

She'd heard the name before. Frantically she tried to think of where. And then it dawned on her. She remembered the phone ringing in Nick's quarters. *Hello, Mrs. Manolis,* he'd said. The unknown Eva who had called him to warn him. The woman had been right.

And Nick had shrugged off her warning, confident that the ship's security was sufficient to stop the man from boarding.

She looked around the room and saw…hair? On top of the dresser lay a whitish toupee and a mustache to match. A walker stood next to the dresser. Manolis had disguised himself as an older man. Probably he was traveling under an assumed identity.

Her thoughts darted back to the day she'd boarded *Alexandra's Dream.* A walker had jabbed her in the leg…. *Oh, I beg your pardon, madam….* Coincidence? It must have been, at that point, but it made her shiver.

He looked at his watch, growing impatient to get on with his horrible plan.

Helena had to find a way to warn Nick. She had to get out of here. But how? Her hands were almost completely numb, not to mention that they were bound.

The only weapons she had were her brain, her mouth and her looks, with which he was clearly unimpressed. *Think. Think, Helena.* "Mr. Manolis, please don't do this."

He laughed again.

"You don't want to go to jail, do you?"

"Shut up."

If she could only get him to free her hands, there might be some hope of escape. "If it's sex you want," she said, her voice shaking, "I will sleep with you. Just don't kill—"

"I told you to shut up, whore!" he snarled. His hands went to his belt again, ripped it from the loops. Then he hit her on the legs with the belt. She cried out, and he cursed, throwing his body on top of hers for the second time. His hand clamped over her mouth and nose and she couldn't breathe.

This is it. He's going to rape me and kill me. But at least Nick won't have to watch. That would destroy him.

Manolis dragged her off the bed in a headlock and over to the dresser. He wrenched open a drawer and snatched a pair of Nick's socks. Then he stuffed them into her mouth.

He threw her toward the bed again, but somehow she managed to get her footing. She scuttled past the nightstand and dove toward the bathroom, knowing even as she did so that it was no use.

He grabbed a fold of her skirt and ripped it. Then he swooped down and caught her around the middle.

Terrified, she couldn't make much of a sound because of the socks.

He hauled her upright and then hit her in the face again, this time opening a wound on her cheekbone.

Her eyes rolled back in her head from the force of the blow, and when she could focus again, she saw to her horror that he was hard. This *excited* him.

She shouldn't have been surprised, but the actual proof of how twisted he was stunned her.

And in that instant, she knew that if she was going to survive this day, she had to play possum. Manolis hit her again, catching her in the temple, and she forced her whole body to go limp, pretending to pass out. She slid in a boneless heap to the floor, forcing her face to remain expressionless even though her left shoulder screamed in agony and her head hit with a thump.

Dead. I am playing dead. Just like in the movies.

Her captor made a noise of disgust and kicked her in the ribs. Again, she forced herself not to respond, lying there like a wet towel.

He hauled her up from the floor and threw her on the bed once more. Then, mercifully, he seemed to buy her ploy and left her alone.

CHAPTER TWENTY-ONE

NICK HAD BEEN on the bridge since dawn, and it was now pushing ten. He would go to Helena and say goodbye. He was tempted to try to patch things up and ask her on a date on dry land sometime.

But what was the point? He belonged on water and knew it in his soul. He'd been born next to the sea and he would die next to it. The Thames wasn't going to cut it for him. And how could he ask her to give up the career she so obviously loved?

His mind in turmoil, Nick nevertheless kept his outer calm. It was what the captain of a ship did, no matter what the situation.

He walked to Helena's cabin, disappointed that Gideon hadn't been able to pinpoint the threat yet. He'd hoped for better news, hoped that they could have taken the guy down overnight so that she could stay aboard. But with the stalker still at large, he didn't want to risk her becoming a physical target.

Nick nodded at the guard and knocked on her door, but got no answer. "Helena?" he called.

"She left the room a few minutes ago, sir," said the guard.

Perhaps she'd gone for coffee. He'd try calling her from the bridge in half an hour or so.

He headed back up there, only to run into Gideon. "Sir!" the chief security officer said breathlessly. "I think we've got him. The immigration authorities in Valletta called me with suspicions of false papers on one of our passengers. He's traveling under the name of Craig Peters."

"And his real name?"

"Manolis. Kostas Manolis."

Nick went cold inside. Of course. Manolis had been on the ship for days under his alias, observing Nick. He'd have seen him with Helena, followed them. And so he'd targeted Helena as a way to get revenge on Nick.

"Get Helena Stamos off this ship immediately, Dayan. Her limousine isn't coming until noon, but I don't care. Get her another one. Then, once she's safe, pick up Manolis. Seal his room and stop any service to it."

"Yes, sir. Consider it done."

Nick went straight to the nearest courtesy phone. Even though he doubted she'd returned so quickly, he called Helena's room, letting it ring at least twenty times. She didn't answer.

He started to get concerned. *Oh, come on, Pappas. She went to get a cup of coffee and a Danish. Relax.*

But knowing that Kostas Manolis was on his ship ate at Nick, and he was now positive that the man was to blame for the incident in his office and the one in Helena's room. He'd been gathering information.

Restless, Nick checked the Espresso bar and the

American Grille in hopes of finding her there. He went up to the spa—maybe she'd gone for a manicure before departing. He checked the tearoom. No Helena.

Nick went back to the bridge and called Gideon. "She's not answering her telephone. I can't find her in any of the usual places. Has she already left?"

"No, sir. She's still aboard ship."

"And Manolis?" Nick asked sharply.

"Not in his room."

"Find him. Find him and hold him on a false documents charge."

"Sir, a search has been initiated for both of them."

Nick hung up, now close to frantic. Where the hell was Helena?

He actually jumped when the telephone rang next to him moments later. He picked it up and barked into it, "Pappas."

"Nick?"

Her voice was the sweetest sound he'd ever heard. He almost collapsed with relief. "Helena! I've been worried about you. Where are you?"

"I'm...I'm fine." But her voice caught and he knew instantly that she'd been crying.

"What is wrong, *agape mou?*"

"Nothing," she whispered. "I just don't want to say goodbye." She broke down.

Nick clenched the phone and took a deep breath. "I don't, either, Helena. But this is for your safety. Do you remember the woman who called to warn me? Eva?"

"Y-yes."

"Manolis, her ex-husband, is on board under an alias.

He is the man who was in your room—I am certain of it. I'm so sorry, Helena."

Her only response was a ragged breath, drawn in slowly.

"Where are you?" he asked again. "I have called your room again and again. I have looked for you."

"I just went out for some air. But, Nick, there are some things we need to talk about in private before I leave. Will you meet me at your stateroom? I can be there in five minutes."

"I'll be right there." Nick hung up and walked quickly to the elevators, so relieved to hear her voice that he felt weak in the knees.

KOSTAS TOOK the telephone receiver from Helena's nerveless hand and replaced it, with great satisfaction, in the cradle. She stared at it hopelessly, her eye throbbing where he'd hit her. The open wound over her cheekbone stung from the salt of her own tears.

She'd just completely and utterly betrayed Nick, set him up to walk into a trap. How could she have done it? Yet with a revolver pressed into her temple, what else could she have done?

Manolis kept the gun aimed at her head as desolation closed in on her. The black, menacing hole at the end of the muzzle reminded her of his eyes. She stared into it, seeking answers to riddles she'd never solve.

What made certain people merciless psychopaths?

How could sadists live with themselves? Why were some minds utterly empty of conscience or morality?

I don't understand, God. I simply do not understand.

But none of that changed the fact that she'd just deceived and entrapped Nick; that even now he was hurrying to his death because of her—and the pregame show Manolis had planned didn't even bear thinking about. She blocked that from her mind by focusing once again on her physical pain. She was fairly certain he'd cracked one of her ribs when he'd kicked her. It hurt to swallow, since he'd throttled her.

Her hands, which he'd finally untied when she'd begged to use the bathroom, were purplish and swollen. They crawled with thousands of invisible ants as the blood slowly began to circulate in her fingers again.

"You are a world-class liar, my dear," said her loathsome captor.

A compliment. How lovely. *Is this where I say thank you? Take a bow?* She inspected the ligature marks on her wrists and rubbed her chilled arms, which were covered with goose bumps.

"You'll bring Captain Pappas right to the door, and I'll do the rest."

Yes, such beautiful teamwork. If she thought it would do any good at all, she would have jumped him, beaten him with her fists, slammed her head into his jaw. But by now she knew that Manolis wouldn't hesitate to shoot her. Or with little effort, knock her—or strangle her—unconscious, and then she'd be of no help to Nick at all.

Think, Helena. Think!

"I don't know why I should be surprised by your skill," Kostas said. "All women are liars. Deceiving whores…" He poured himself another whiskey.

She shuddered and averted her eyes—or rather, eye.

The right one was now swollen shut. She sat propped against the headboard of the bed, her arms hugging herself and her head hanging low. Her chin almost rested on her chest.

Ever since he'd thrown water in her face and slapped her to force her to regain consciousness, she'd adopted a beaten, cringing posture. *Let him think I am weak, so he doesn't expect any resistance. Let him think that he's already broken my spirit.*

She was no student of psychology, but she was learning quickly from this experience. The more she'd resisted, the more Manolis had enjoyed himself.

Please, Nick. Put two and two together. Bring the whole security detail of Alexandra's Dream *with you. Don't come alone!*

But she hadn't been able to hint that she was in trouble, not with Manolis's revolver cocked and ready, pressed to her head.

I should have let him blow my brains out...but then he'd only shoot Nick down, too, when he came to investigate.

Manolis was doing that lizard thing again with his tongue and the rim of his whiskey glass. It made her sick, but that was the least of her concerns.

He set down the glass, licked his lips and checked his watch, a showy gold number. "Get up," he ordered. He retrieved the gun from his chair, then cocked the trigger again.

Slowly she swung her legs over the side of the bed and got to her feet.

"Quickly! Stupid bitch. Get over here." He strode to her, spun her around and clamped her neck into the crook of his elbow, hauling her against his chest. It was broad but curiously bony, and then he went soft at the stomach. She shuddered at the contact and at the sickening sweet, smoky stench of him. It mixed in her nostrils with his deodorant, and she felt faint.

Worse, she could feel his erection against her lower back and he rubbed himself against her, grunting. He propelled her to just inside the cabin door and they waited together in twisted, unhappy cohesion for Nick to arrive.

CHAPTER TWENTY-TWO

NICK WALKED to the elevators and rehearsed what he wanted to say to Helena. He nodded and smiled at other passengers and an attendant with a cleaning service cart in the corridor that led to his suite.

Helena wasn't there yet, but she'd be along shortly. He slid his key card into the door and pushed it open, only to freeze in his tracks.

She stood in front of him, inside his own room. She was shaking and gagged, her face tear-stained and bruised, her eyes full of terror and self-recrimination.

A man's arm was around her neck—and there was a gun at the back of her head.

"Come in, *Capitano,*" Manolis said in smug tones. "Please come in and make yourself at home."

As Nick recovered from his initial shock, his first instinct was to charge the man.

"I wouldn't, if I were you," said the bastard. His face was coated in a sheen of perspiration, his fleshy lips slick, but his hands appeared cool, dry and murderously calm.

"Step inside," he ordered Nick. "Slowly. Normally. Without making a sound. Or the brains of your little bitch, here, will splatter all over your pristine white uniform."

"Let her go," Nick said. But he had no choice but to do as Manolis told him.

"I'm sorry, Nikolas," Helena whispered.

"Shut up!" Kostas tightened his hold on her neck and ground himself against her spine. "But yes, you are sorry, you pathetic, bony whore. And I will make you sorrier."

"Don't call her that," Nick snapped.

"I will call her whatever I please, Pappas." Manolis backed slowly away from the door, dragging her with him. Then he inclined his head toward Nick. "Go and sit in that chair. Do it now. Stop to argue and I'll blow her ear off." He slid the nose of the revolver through her hair and jammed it against the cartilage of her right ear.

Nick's whole body went rigid. Screwed on to the end of the gun was a silencer. Nobody would ever hear the soft pop.

Trying not to think about it, he quickly scanned Helena from head to toe and began to vibrate with rage. The bastard had beaten her up, hurt her.

Fury raced through his veins along with his blood, sending the most primitive messages to his brain. *Kill Manolis. Kill him. Pound his head against the floor or the wall until he is dead. Break his neck.* He tried to reject the primal signals. After all, Helena was alive. He just needed to get her out of here, away from danger.

He looked at her again slowly, from her swollen right eye to the cut on her cheek, from the bruises around her neck to her torn skirt, which exposed bare thigh and a glimpse of her pale pink panties. Last, he saw the raised, red welts on her ankles, the man's belt lying on the floor. He didn't want to think about what else had been done to her.

And in that moment he knew that he truly could kill Manolis. That even if he wasn't given the chance, he would take it—courts and trials and civilization be damned. His captainship be damned. This man had hurt the woman Nick loved—and the entire purpose of his life boiled down to two goals. One, *get her out of here*. And two, *send Manolis straight to hell, where he belongs*.

He focused on the first goal for the moment. "Your issue is with me, and not with Helena Stamos. Let her go, and we'll settle this between us."

"Let her go, like you let Eva go?" Manolis shook his head and produced a nasty laugh. "I don't think so."

"She has nothing to do with this," Nick insisted.

"*Au contraire.* She has everything to do with this, *Capitano.* You stuck your nose in where it didn't belong. You interfered with my life and my woman. Now I'm going to interfere with yours."

Nick didn't know how to respond. *Should I deny that she's my "woman"? Tell him that I don't care at all what he does to her? Will he let her go then?*

Finally he said, "I interfered, as you call it, in your life because Eva asked me for help."

"My wife is a liar and a fantasist."

"Is that so. She imagined the bruises I saw on her? She beat herself? She had the posture of a frightened old woman because she was happy with you?"

Nick hadn't thought it was possible for those black eyes to get any darker. But they did, as Manolis's malevolence toward him expanded like a thundercloud.

Nick swallowed. When the cloud burst, he didn't want the man anywhere near Helena.

Kostas tightened his grip around her neck and dragged her over to the bed, where he sat and pulled her into his lap. She lay there pale and unmoving, like a porcelain doll—and that was what scared Nick more than anything.

Fiery, dramatic, colorful Helena did not behave this way. She threw off robes, made love as if the world would end in the morning. This waxen reproduction of Helena shook him to the core, reminded him all too much of Carolina.

"My wife belongs with me. She is my property. You stole her, Pappas. And now you're going to tell me where she is so that I can go and get her."

Nick stared stonily at him.

"You will tell me," Manolis repeated, tightening his hold on Helena.

Nick flinched.

She didn't.

"Where is my wife, *Capitano?*" Kostas demanded again, and Nick closed his eyes.

"She's no longer your wife, and she never was your *property.*"

In a single savage motion, Manolis ripped open Helena's blouse, laying her torso bare except for a pink lace bra.

Nick leaped to his feet and lunged forward, only to stop as Kostas punctuated his next words by tapping her chest with the gun. "Where. Is. Eva?"

"Goddamn it, shoot *me!* Kill me in cold blood, but leave her alone!"

"Wrong answer," Manolis snarled. He ripped the bra away from Helena's skin, and she couldn't help a small sound of protest. Her small pink nipples puckered in the sudden draft, and she covered herself with her hands.

Nick saw that they, too, were red and swollen—the bastard had obviously tied them. Hating himself, he broke. "Eva is in Ca—"

Kostas slapped Helena's hands down and nuzzled her breast with the gun.

Nick saw red and could barely keep from launching himself at the man.

"You were saying?" Kostas inquired.

"*California*. Now take your hands off her, you piece of *shit!*"

Manolis laughed softly. "Does this bother you, Pappas? Surely not. She's a whore. She was taking it from Tzekas behind your back."

Helena opened her eyes and shook her head almost imperceptibly.

Nick's heart nearly broke that in this horrible situation, she could possibly care what he thought. *I know. I would never believe his lies.* He tried to tell her that through his gaze, tried to steady her.

"Where in California, Pappas? I want a city. I want a street address. I want the name she's hiding under."

"I don't know that information, Manolis!"

"You know it," Kostas said grimly, his hand moving to the hem of Helena's skirt. He pulled it up.

Blood roared in Nick's ears. *No. Oh, God, no. This cannot happen. Not in front of my eyes. I will not let this happen.*

He shot forward.

"Sit down, Pappas!"

Nick stopped. The man had the gun muzzle between Helena's thighs. Tears trickled silently from under her closed eyelids and ran down her poor battered face.

The primal urge to kill hit Nick again. Just throw himself on Manolis, consequences be damned.

But the man would kill her for sure.

And Nick loved her too much to risk that.

Get a grip on yourself, Nikolas. Slowly, resenting every millimeter of retreat, he stepped backward until his knees came into contact with the edge of the chair. He sat, like a goddamn dog obeying its master. He sweated. He seethed.

"You're not cooperating very well, *Capitano.* Make a choice."

Some goddamn choice. Watch the woman I love be manhandled and probably raped—or watch her die?

"I don't have the information you want," Nick stormed. *"I. Don't. Have. It."*

"I don't believe you," said Manolis with cold malice. "Did Eva suck you off for your silence?"

"I never touched her!"

"Most likely, she sucked you off," Kostas mused, ignoring him. "Fine." He spread his thighs and pushed Helena forward so that she fell between them to the floor. "Time to get on your knees, whore."

"No!" Nick shouted. Without even being conscious of it, he was out of the chair again.

"Sit." Manolis hissed the word. "Or watch her die."

Helena still hadn't moved, remaining collapsed on the floor with her head dropped onto her arms.

"On your knees, whore. Don't make me say it again."

Slowly she raised her head and stared straight at Nick. The one good eye that he could see blazed with intention, and she raised her eyebrows.

Then she turned, eyes downcast and shoulders slumped, squatting at Manolis's feet as if begging for mercy.

A triumphant, unholy expression filled his face and he licked his lips. "On your knees and pull down my zipper."

No! Nausea rose in Nick's gut and he gripped the arms of the chair so tightly that he thought his fingers would stab through the fabric.

She hesitated.

"Pull it down!" Kostas slapped her with his left hand, keeping his right one on the gun.

Slowly, centimeter by centimeter, she took down the sick bastard's fly.

Impatiently, Manolis undid the button himself. "Now take it out."

She fumbled at his crotch among the folds of fabric there.

Bile rose in Nick's throat, threatening to choke him. He was going to be sick. *You're going to vomit? Think about her.*

Helena freed Kostas from the material, and Nick had never seen an uglier sight. Again, he wanted to launch himself at the man and pulverize him into nothing but bloody pulp.

Discipline. This is the only chance we're going to

get. He clutched the arms of the chair even more tightly, and noticed that sweat from his palms had soaked the upholstery.

Manolis leaned back and spread his thighs even wider. "You know what to do," he said.

Again she hesitated, and he turned his focus to yell at her. "Do it!"

She bent her head and Nick almost came unglued.

Then Kostas screamed in agony, shock and anger. She'd grabbed his testicles and twisted, hard.

Please—God—don't let him pull that trigger. Nick shot forward as Manolis grabbed Helena's hair in his free hand and yanked her head back. His knee slammed into her jaw.

Nick came from a diagonal and knocked Kostas flat onto the mattress. The man shrieked again and again. Helena was apparently yanking back and still twisting. Good girl!

The gun discharged with a muffled pop. Pain exploded in Nick's right arm. He didn't care. He grabbed Manolis by the neck and rained blows onto his face.

Helena finally let go and rolled out of the way. Nick saw that she was safe and still unleashed his rage on the son of a bitch who'd hurt and humiliated her, threatened to kill her.

Kostas tried to fight back, but Nick threw him off the bed and jumped on top of him.

Dimly he saw Helena at the phone. Then she was shouting at him and pulling him off Kostas. "Nikolas! Nikolas, stop! Stop it! I have the gun. Security is coming. Stop it! *No more.*"

Somehow she got through to him, despite the blood-lust, and he collapsed next to Manolis's prone body.

"You're bleeding," Helena said, kneeling next to him. "Oh God."

"Don't care," mumbled Nick as he crawled across the floor to her, tears running down his face. He threw his arms around her and held her tight. "I love you. God, I love you, Helena. Please forgive me." And despite all of his years in the navy and the four stripes on his shoulders, despite his legendary discipline, Nick broke down and cried like a baby because she was alive.

"Nikolas," she sobbed. "Oh, Nikolas."

He'd never known fear like that in his life. He was forced to let her go because nausea overcame him. He stumbled up and over to the sliding door, shoved it open and lurched outside. He braced his arms on the rail, hung his head over it and vomited.

She ran to the bathroom and wet a washcloth for him. He took it with thanks, mopped his face and breathed in great lungfuls of the ocean air while she clung to him, and he to her. Manolis was unconscious but breathing; there was no need to keep the gun trained on him.

Nick held Helena away from him and looked at her again, at her swollen eye, the open wound on her cheek, the awful bruise at her jaw. He framed her face with his hands, gently kissed each injury and then just gathered her into his arms again.

This is my fault—all of it. I let this happen to her.

"I'm so sorry," he said in ragged tones. He could barely form the words because of his shame.

"Nick, it's not your fault. You are not responsible for the actions of a madman." She rested her uninjured cheek against his chest.

"Yes, I am. I incited them, and I was warned." He gripped the rail so tightly that his hands went white.

If only he had taken Eva's call seriously. If only he'd thought about the possibility that Manolis might board the ship with false identification. If only he had watched over Helena himself.

I failed her just as I failed Carolina. What kind of man am I? In command of an entire ship and I cannot protect one woman from harm?

"Listen to me, Nikolas. You did not *incite* anyone. That's the most ridiculous thing I've ever heard. That man is *unhinged*. He considers women property. He's obsessive and violent, and it's probably only thanks to you that his ex-wife is still alive!"

Helena didn't know what else to say to make Nick stop blaming himself. He touched her face gently, the expression on his own full of guilt, regret, anger and so much more. His eyes filled with tears again, and it took her breath away that Nick, so normally buttoned-down and controlled, Mr. Military Discipline, was actually crying for her.

She, the emotional and dramatic one, was calm now that it was over. How strange.

Nick shook his head. "I was warned," he said again, wincing as he looked at her. "Oh, Helena, your eye…"

"Forget about my eye, Nick. Please. We're both alive and everything will heal. That's the important thing."

"I could have prevented this. God, Helena, I'm sorry. I'm so sorry."

"There's nothing you could have done! You were looking for a man in his early forties, not an octogenarian with a walker. And anyway, you had no reason to suspect that Manolis would target me—when it was you he wanted revenge upon."

"I failed you," was all he said. "Just like I failed Carolina."

"No, sweetheart. You didn't fail me. You were there and you stopped him."

But he didn't seem to hear her. He walked back inside and stood with his back to her, distant and unapproachable. Had he retreated emotionally again? Would she be able to reach him?

"Nikolas!" She felt desperate, angry now. "Get hold of yourself. And you have to stop taking the blame for Carolina's death. That was in no way your fault."

Nick slumped into the armchair near the door. "I could have prevented it."

"No, you couldn't have. You didn't know what was going on!"

"I knew," he said shortly. "I had a gut feeling that things weren't quite right. She had changed so much. She had let herself go, which wasn't like her at all. She no longer laughed…."

"A feeling isn't the same thing as knowledge, Nick. You can't continue to blame yourself—"

"I can," he said flatly. "Just as I blame myself for what happened to you today."

Helena put her hands on her hips and leveled her gaze on his. "Nick, what can I say to convince you?"

He drew in a ragged lungful of air and shook his head. "You can't say anything."

CHAPTER TWENTY-THREE

HELENA THREW UP her hands and quickly discarded her clothes for the terry robe hanging on the back of Nick's bathroom door. Her clothing was in an unsalvageable state of disrepair. She couldn't wait to take a shower and rinse the touch and the stench of Manolis off her skin. But Nick was more important, and his wound needed immediate attention.

She was taking his jacket off so that she could inspect his injured arm when several armed security officers burst into the room, closely followed by Gideon Dayan and the ship's medical personnel.

Their collective adrenaline was palpable, but there was nothing for them to do but to move out of the way as the medics loaded the now conscious Kostas Manolis onto a stretcher. He moaned as if in agony.

Helena couldn't dredge up any sympathy at all.

"Are you all right, Miss Stamos?" Gideon asked.

She nodded, self-consciously putting a hand up to her swollen eye. She must look a sight.

He turned to Nick. "Sir?" His eyes took in the state of the captain's hair, the wound in his arm, the blood all over his uniform. Then he swore in Hebrew.

"Gideon, you seem to be implying that I look less than my best."

The man ran a hand over his mouth and jaw. "I'm sorry, Captain—we couldn't find Manolis anywhere. He wasn't in his room, his ship card hadn't been used—" The usually stoic Dayan looked distressed.

"None of us anticipated anything like this, Gideon." The chief security officer assessed Helena. "I take full responsibility."

Nick glanced at him and shook his head.

"Just find out how he got that gun on board. And he's got some kind of master key—he entered my room and Helena's."

Gideon nodded soberly. "All baggage is scanned, so the gun must have come through food services or maintenance." He frowned. "As you know, the ship's security is the tightest in the industry—I have to believe he bribed a staff member. There's no other way. But we'll review procedure and do a full investigation. Maybe I can get Manolis to talk."

Helena stared at the two men. "Neither of you should blame yourselves for the actions of a deranged and twisted man."

She shuddered as she looked at the prone Manolis, even though at the moment he was more pathetic than frightening. But she didn't feel sorry for him—he was the embodiment of evil. Had Nick carried things too far? Probably. But a cold knowledge hit her: if their positions had been reversed, she wouldn't have hesitated to shoot Manolis dead to save Nick.

She hoped that Manolis stayed in prison for the rest of his life, though she knew that was unlikely.

He moaned on the stretcher. Then he spat out of his bloodied mouth. "*Eva*. Where is she, you bastard?"

Nick tore away from the man tending to his arm. He walked over to Kostas and eyed him grimly. "She's beyond your reach. You will never hurt her again."

Manolis told him to do something anatomically impossible.

Nick turned away, disgusted. "Gideon. Make sure you note for the record that this man is still obsessing about his ex-wife and trying to discover her whereabouts. The courts won't be impressed."

"Sit down, Nikolas, and let them take care of you." Helena touched his good arm.

He looked down at her, his gray eyes deepening as he caressed her uninjured cheek. "Nobody is doing anything to me until *you* are taken care of." He eyed the ship's doctor. "She needs a complete physical exam and the very best care."

"I'm fine," said Helena. "I need no such thing. Perhaps a bag of frozen peas for my eye. *He's* the one who needs a tourniquet! If he loses any more blood out of that arm we'll be able to paint the ship with it."

The doctor, a cool, competent, blond woman, nodded. "Sit down, Captain."

Nick gritted his teeth. "I told you to take care of her first, damn it!"

Helena rolled her eyes and poked him in the chest with her index finger. "Nikolas, be a good boy and stop disobeying Dr. Latsis. Now sit down."

Nick opened his mouth, probably to bark back at her. She doubted that anyone had spoken that way to him since he was eight years old, and never on board his ship. But under the bemused gazes of at least eight of his staff, Nick nodded meekly and sat.

Two of the ship's medical assistants wheeled Manolis out of the room, to Helena's relief.

"When you're done with his exam, handcuff him to the hospital bed," ordered Gideon. "And under no circumstances is he to be left alone."

As the room slowly began to clear out, Helena caught a glance at herself in the mirror above the dresser and recoiled.

Her hair was matted and tangled, one eyelid was swollen and purple, and there were bruises and scrapes everywhere.

Nick met her good eye in the mirror. Tears came to his. "I should have killed him."

"No, you are a better man than that." She grimaced at her reflection. "I'm a monster."

"You're not a monster. You're the most beautiful woman I've ever seen."

"Nikolas," she said, brushing his forehead with her lips, "you are a terrible liar."

A nurse hurried over to her. "Ms. Stamos, you must come to the medical center where I can do an exam."

The doctor nodded. "And in order for me to get this bullet out of his arm, Captain Pappas also needs to go to the medical center."

"Then I need you both in my office so that we can file a police report," added Gideon. "And we need this kept under wraps. Liberty Line and Argosy don't need any bad PR. We need to call Katherine Stamos immediately."

Helena met Nick's gaze ruefully. "It sounds as though we're going to have *such* an enjoyable afternoon."

AFTER ANOTHER disagreement with Dr. Latsis, Nick buckled under again and left his very capable staff captain in charge of *Alexandra's Dream* while he went to an unoccupied stateroom to rest. He refused to lie in a bed in the medical center near Manolis.

Alone and exhausted after the day's events, Nick stared stubbornly at the painkillers given to him by the doctor and refused to take them. The wound in his arm throbbed in time with his heartbeat, hurting like hell. But he didn't want to go all woozy or fall asleep—he had too many things on his mind.

First of all, he was one hundred percent in love with Helena Stamos, whether it was practical or not. And it made no difference whether or not she had once misrepresented herself to him.

He'd love her no matter who her father was, how much money she had, where she lived or how opposite they might be. He couldn't deny it and he couldn't help himself.

Seeing her almost die at the hands of that bastard had been the worst thing he'd ever been through, but also the most eye-opening.

I wanted to marry her once. I still do.

Helena, quite simply, came first. Before his career, before his adherence to rules and regulations, even before his reputation and his dignity. He didn't want her with "no strings attached." He wanted her all wrapped up in them, for good and for life.

But she'd made it clear what she thought of marriage.

Nick reminded himself that he'd thought he was done with it, too. Yet all it had taken was the right woman to change his mind. Could he be the right man for her, too?

He clearly remembered telling her that he loved her. *I love you. God, I love you, Helena. Please forgive me.* And though she'd clung to him, cried with him, she hadn't said, "I love you, too."

He knew that she cared for him. That he stirred up old feelings in her, that she was attracted to him. But did she love him back—or was it simply too late?

His thoughts and memories crowded against each other, jostling for space in his mind. Nick now almost wished he'd taken the damn painkillers so that he could experience a spot of peaceful oblivion.

He stared at the bottle, but left it where it was on the nightstand.

I have to know how she feels. I have to let her know how I feel—and not when she's in shock from having been manhandled and almost murdered. Once and for all, he needed to lay his emotions on the table.

Nick thought about the fact that she lived in London and was used to a cosmopolitan setting. She had a wildly successful career. She described herself as a Gypsy.

And yet…the ship stopped in many exciting ports and was filled with interesting people from all walks of life. When not on location or in planning meetings, she could work from *Alexandra's Dream*. She'd always loved the water. And what better circumstance for a Gypsy than a moving home that sailed around the world?

He rubbed absently at his arm, only to make the pain light him up. *Bad idea, Pappas.* While he waited for the nerves to stop screaming, his mind, now made up, went quietly to details.

He had a proposal to make.

Nick's thoughts then turned to Elias, her father and his employer. He had a strong suspicion that the old man had meddled once in their relationship—the disappearance of those letters couldn't be coincidental.

Would he try to meddle again? Fire the captain he'd hired for *Alexandra's Dream?*

Nick didn't know and didn't care. But the correct thing to do was to ask Stamos for his daughter's hand. Old-fashioned? Yes. But he'd appreciate being asked.

The bottom line was that Nick didn't give a damn what the man said—this was up to Helena, and her alone.

CHAPTER TWENTY-FOUR

HORRIFIED at what had happened to her aunt Helena, Gemma almost forgot that she was supposed to meet Chris that night, but she reluctantly made her way to the spot they'd agreed upon, on the Bacchus deck.

He was already there, lounging against the rail. He was off duty and had changed into a faded polo shirt and baggy shorts. He had long, thin legs covered with sparse blond hair.

He immediately drew her against him and tried to kiss her, but she turned her head and avoided his mouth.

"What's wrong?"

"My aunt was attacked," Gemma said. "And I feel responsible, because I gave her a note that turned out to be from the crazy guy who did it." Her chin trembled.

"Wow," Chris said.

Was she being unfair, or did his response seem woefully inadequate?

"That sucks."

Better and better.

"Yes, it does suck," said Gemma, a little tartly.

"Well, is she okay?"

"No. Her face looks like a punching bag and she's

pretty shaky. And I know they're not telling me everything that happened. I think the man may have tried to
rape her or something." She shivered.

"Wow," Chris said again. "That's...heavy."

Heavy?

"But, I mean, you didn't know the note was from the
crazy guy, right?"

She shook her head.

"Then why are you beating yourself up?" he asked.
"It's not your fault at all."

"I know I'm not responsible for what he did, but I
should have thought about the fact that it was strange
that someone would give *me* a note for *her*. I actually
did think about it, but I shrugged it off. And now I
know that the guy targeted me because I was the only
one probably dumb enough to actually give it to her
and not to security." She hunched her shoulders,
feeling sick.

Chris rubbed her back. It felt good for a moment,
until his hand dropped so low that it was almost on her
bottom. She sidestepped.

He grinned, looking a little sheepish.

Nice.

"Sorry."

She nodded indifferently.

"Want a beer?" Chris pulled two cans of Heineken
out of the pockets of his baggy shorts.

"No, thanks."

He shrugged. "Suit yourself." He popped one of the
cans open and guzzled about half of it. "You sure you don't
want one? It might relax you. You seem kind of tense."

No, really? "Well, how would you feel if one of your favorite relatives just got brutalized?"

He didn't seem to have a reply to that. But he did have a suggestion.

"So, I thought maybe we could go to your cabin and...you know. Mess around."

You have got to be kidding me. That's subtle. Suddenly she didn't find Chris nearly as good-looking as she had just a few days ago.

Had she really been thinking about sleeping with this insensitive jerk? Aunt Helena's words came back to her. *It's your body. But I'd urge you not to do anything just because of peer pressure or a feeling of not belonging to some "club." All right? And try to wait until it's someone you truly love.*

Gemma made her decision and pushed away from the rail. Instead of feeling embarrassed that she might be the only seventeen-year-old virgin in all the world, she felt just fine. When the right person came along, then maybe she'd consider sex. But Chris was definitely not a man worthy of being her first.

"C'mon, what d'you say, Gemma?" He grinned down at her, looking supremely confident that she'd jump at the chance to "mess around" with him.

She shook her head. "You know what, Chris? I'm really not in the mood."

"But—"

She patted his arm much as she would pat a dog. "You finish those beers and go party with your buddies. I'm going to check on my aunt."

CHAPTER TWENTY-FIVE

NICK STARED AT the telephone for several long moments before he actually dialed a number.

"Argosy Cruises," a woman answered. "May I help you?"

"I'd like to speak with Elias Stamos," Nick said.

"And may I ask who is calling?"

"Captain Nikolas Pappas of *Alexandra's Dream*."

"One moment, sir."

It was closer to five, but finally a gruff male voice came on the line. "Good morning, Pappas. To what do I owe the pleasure of your call?"

"Good morning, sir. I'm contacting you for several reasons. One, to let you know that your daughter Helena is safe, despite an unfortunate incident on board *Alexandra's Dream*."

Elias drew in a sharp breath. "What unfortunate incident?"

Bracing himself for an inevitable explosion, Nick relayed the events of the past few days. "I feel responsible, sir, because of my role in antagonizing Kostas Manolis."

"Nonsense," growled Stamos.

"I—"

"You did the right thing at Blue Aegean, Pappas. Word got to me about the incident. Why do you think I hired you to command *Alexandra's Dream* when no other company would put you in charge of a Jet Ski?"

Nick almost choked.

"The world needs more men like you, Captain. Men of honor and integrity."

"Thank you, sir. And yet, I offer you my sincere apologies that your daughter was endangered."

"I just thank God that she's all right."

"Yes, sir." Nick's response was heartfelt.

A pause ensued. Then Elias got straight to the point. "You say that this man targeted Helena because of your feelings for her?"

Nick didn't hesitate. "Yes, he did. And while I cannot apologize for loving her, I deeply regret that my love made her a target for a madman."

"Does my daughter return your feelings, Pappas?"

Nick took a deep breath. "I hope so, sir." He was gearing up for his next question when Elias pre-empted him.

"She could do worse."

"I beg your pardon?"

"You heard me."

"Sir, I want to ask your daughter to marry me. I've been in love with her for fifteen years."

"Yes," Elias said, "I know."

"You *know?*" Nick gripped the receiver tightly.

"Very little escapes me, where my daughters are concerned. I will admit that I was not pleased when she chose a deckhand on a freighter as her first love."

Nick fell silent, his jaw working.

"I felt sure that I knew what was best for her," Stamos continued after a pause. "I…arranged to have a word of warning put into the boy's ear."

Nick sat, breathing heavily as anger overtook him.

"He felt unworthy. He broke things off. My daughter was devastated."

Speechless, Nick almost hung up on the man.

"I was sure she'd recover in no time and find a more suitable man." Elias sighed. "But my wife was livid with me. It was Alexandra's dream that both of our children should find a love as magical, as powerful as ours. And I had interfered. What right did I have, when my own ancestors were hardly aristocrats?"

"My letters," Nick said. "You saw to it that they never reached Helena."

"Guilty as charged."

A strained silence hung between them.

"So it is I who owe *you* an apology. And I ask your forgiveness." Elias's irascible voice was uncharacteristically humble.

Nick exhaled harshly. "What you did was wrong, Stamos."

"Yes, well. Just you wait until you're a father one day, Nikolas. You may make a few mistakes of your own in trying to protect your children."

"Sir, I'd like your permission to marry your daughter."

"Well, then. If she'll have you, nothing would make me happier, Pappas. And perhaps my angel wife will forgive me today. For as I told you, in more ways than one, you are truly the captain of *Alexandra's Dream*."

THE SHIP HAD BEGUN its last leg of the cruise, sailing for
Civitavecchia and Rome. It was evening, and Helena
was at a loss. Nick had invited her to dinner—really
dinner this time—in his private dining room, but she
winced every time she looked into the mirror.

Her eye was less swollen, but still sported lovely
shades ranging from yellow to purple. She could open
it, but only partially. It gave her a sleepy, half-witted look.

The cut on her cheek and the bruise on her jaw she
covered with makeup, but she didn't know what to do
about the eye. Wear a patch over it? Cover her head
with a towel?

No, what she needed was some sort of hat that she
could tilt so that it dipped low over one eye. A veil
wouldn't hurt, either.

She had a straw hat that protected her face from the
sun, but it was hardly evening attire. Helena frowned at
it. Then she opened her closet and quickly flipped
through the hangers. She pulled out one of her gauzy
blouses and draped it over the hat. Hmm. Better.

She wasn't a costume designer for nothing. If she'd
created a princess costume out of a trash bag for little
Angela, then she could certainly come up with something for herself.

It took her about twenty minutes with nail scissors
and a few pins. When she'd finished, Helena had transformed the straw beach hat into an elegant confection
that coquettishly hid her right eye and complemented
the little black dress she wore over her broken rib. She
added lipstick to her mouth and swiped the lashes of her
left eye with mascara.

She decided against a necklace, because of the hat, but added Tahitian black pearl earrings and slipped the matching bracelet onto her wrist. Her hands she left bare.

She looked down at the welts on her legs. Nothing she could do about those. They would eventually fade.

Helena slid her feet into high-heeled black satin sling-backs with peep toes and checked her reflection in the mirror. Not bad. She looked a bit like a fifties film star attending the Kentucky Derby, but she'd do.

She nodded to passengers and staff she passed in the corridors as she made her way to Nick's quarters.

When he opened the door of his stateroom, her heart jumped into her mouth because he was so handsome. He held out a single red rose, and she saw that he wore a black dinner jacket and trousers, and a wry expression.

"You look stunning, Helena," he said as she accepted the rose.

"I look like a Cyclops attending a garden party, Nikolas. But you're sweet."

He touched the brim of the hat with a sad smile of comprehension. "A very lovely Cyclops."

He drew her inside and closed the door, and she took a good look at him and had to smile.

Like her, he'd had to get creative with his attire because the bandage around his arm wouldn't fit into the jacket sleeve. So he'd removed the sleeve entirely and messy little threads hung down over his shirt.

"You are not supposed to laugh at your knight in tarnished armor," he said with mock severity.

"I can't help it," she gasped. "Between the two of us, we look very, very odd."

"We're well matched." He smiled, took her hand and led her to sit on the sofa. "Pinot Grigio?" He handed her a chilled glass of wine. She was touched, again, that he remembered her favorite.

Behind them, the table was set with a white cloth, silver and china. Her eyes went to a spray of orchids in a crystal vase. And classical music played softly in the background.

Nick poured a glass of wine for himself and sat next to her. He took her hand and clinked her glass before he brought his own to his lips. "To you being safe." His hand shook slightly in hers and he squeezed her fingers.

"To *us* being safe," she said.

He nodded. "Are you…still in any discomfort?" He had shadows under his gray eyes, and he looked as if he were bracing himself to hear the answer.

"No, not really," she lied. "The doctor gave me salves and a painkiller. And besides, I'm tougher than I look." She set down her wineglass and laid her hand on his cheek, trying to comfort him.

He closed his eyes at her touch. "I'll never forgive myself," Nick said. But he set his glass down, too, took the hand against his cheek and brought her palm to his lips.

"Nick, I don't want to hear you say that."

"It's true. I allowed it to happen, and then—" He got up and paced to the balcony. "Then I couldn't protect you."

"You did protect me, love. When will you get that through your head?"

"But you acted first—I was helpless. God, do you know what that *did* to me?"

"I saw an opportunity and I took it. But if you hadn't been there and hadn't reacted so fast, we wouldn't be having this conversation."

Nick took a deep breath then walked back to her. "I know, Helena, that I'm not good at expressing my emotions. I've been accused by more than one person of having ice water running through my veins. But I don't want to be like that with you."

He took another breath, struggling for words. "Seeing you in his power, your life in his hands, I felt true fear as I have never felt it before. So many things rushed through my head that I couldn't make sense of. Mostly I just reacted. But if I focused on anything at all besides wanting to kill Manolis, it was my own stupidity at walking away from you all those years ago. Without a word."

"Oh, Nikolas…"

"Wait. Let me finish. You didn't deserve that. I should have confronted you, talked with you. I wasn't fair. You may have omitted to tell me who your father was, but what I did was worse. And I'm sorry. You said several nights ago that you've waited fifteen years for an apology. I want to offer that apology to you now."

Tears came to her eyes. "It's all right. It's done. Let's move on from there."

"I want you to know why, though. I was pulled aside by my supervisor on the freighter. He told me who you were, warned me off. I was devastated."

"My father," she said, and sighed. "Tell me that my father didn't have something to do with it."

Nick stayed utterly expressionless. "I don't know."

Helena looked up into his eyes and knew immediately

that he was lying. If she hadn't fallen in love with him again already, she would have done so right then and there. Nick, who held integrity above all things and who had probably never told a fib in his life, was flat-out lying to her so that she wouldn't be furious with her father.

She felt so tender toward Nick in that moment that she couldn't speak.

"Do you know how much I love you, Helena Stamos?"

The words warmed her like no others. "It can't be more than I love you, Nikolas."

His face lit up as if he hadn't been sure, the sweet, silly man. "I would argue the point, but I don't want to waste any more time than we already have. *Fifteen years,* Helena. Fifteen times three hundred and sixty-five. That's thousands upon thousands of days. And tens of thousands of hours. We have missed so much time together."

"Perhaps it wasn't wasted. Perhaps we needed that time to be certain…"

"I like the way you're thinking, *agape mou.*" He smiled at her. "Do you think, Helena, that you could end up with a man like me? Someone who makes his home on the water and only keeps an apartment on dry land because he has to?"

"Do you think you could end up with a Gypsy woman who travels constantly for work and for pleasure? Someone who sometimes paints like a madwoman in the middle of the night and isn't always logical? Someone who has a meddlesome father but who won't allow him to run her life anymore?"

Nick nodded. He dropped down to one knee. "I had meant to do this after dinner, with champagne. But I can't wait any longer. Fifteen years is enough." He reached into his pocket and withdrew a tiny blue-velvet pouch. Inside it was a gold ring with a tiny round diamond in a Tiffany setting.

Wordlessly she stared at it. Could it be…?

"I've kept it all these years," Nick said quietly. "I never knew why."

Tears slipped down her cheeks. "Oh, Nikolas."

"Will you marry me, Helena? Will you do me the honor of becoming my wife?"

In spite of all her past convictions about marriage, she didn't hesitate. "Yes," she whispered. "Yes, Nikolas, I will."

Then she frowned. "Wait."

His face fell almost comically. In fact, he looked stricken.

"I will marry you if you promise me that you will stop assuming the blame for both the incident with Manolis and Carolina's death."

Nick stared at her.

"I mean it," she said sternly.

He blinked. Then slowly he nodded. "If those are your terms, I will do my best. But then I have one of my own. You, Helena, will stop feeling guilty about your marriage to Ari. It's time for you to move past that."

She nodded. "I'll try."

"So you'll be my wife?"

"Yes. Nothing could make me happier, Nikolas."

His always steady hands trembled as he slid the ring onto the fourth finger of her left hand, then stood, pulling her up with him. "Maybe another baby?"

Swallowing a sob, she slipped into his arms.

"I can live part of the year with you in London," he said. "And maybe you can live on *Alexandra's Dream* for the other part, between projects?"

"Yes. We'll work it out."

He opened his mouth to continue, but she laid a finger across his lips. "Shh, Nick. Just kiss me, love. We can figure out all the details later."

So he did. He touched his mouth to hers and she opened to him gladly. He slid his arms around her waist and she slid her hands down his shoulders.

"Ouch," they said in unison. And ruefully, they laughed together. Intimacy was going to be a challenge with her battered rib and his injured arm. But somehow she thought they would manage. They had the rest of their lives, after all.

* * * * *

MEDITERRANEAN NIGHTS
*Join the glamorous world of cruising with the
guests and crew of* Alexandra's Dream—*the newest
luxury ship to set sail on the romantic Mediterranean.
The voyage continues in November 2007 with
BELOW DECK by Dorien Kelly.*

Mei Lin Wang has secrets, and she's hiding one of
them—her son—below deck on the cruise ship
Alexandra's Dream. A massage therapist in the ship's
spa, Lin has been on the run ever since her husband,
Wei, was killed more than a year ago.
Unsafe in her own country, she is determined to
protect their son from his father's enemies.
Gideon Dayan, the ship's chief security officer, is
intrigued by this woman of mystery. Gideon is also
haunted by tragedy, but hopes that both he and Lin
can let go of their pasts and face the future…together.

Here's a preview!

COMFORT. REST. NIGHT. A warm yet slightly rough hand settled against the side of her face, and a set of finger-tips rested at her throat. The clean, honest scent of soap and perhaps a whisper of sandalwood wafted over her. Another dream—it had to be. Lin embraced it.

Wei, my love.

The hand that had been at her face settled more firmly against her upper arm, its grip authoritative, yet not unpleasant.

"Miss Wang?"

She frowned, for the speaker used English, and his accent was distinctly un-Chinese. The hand shook her arm insistently, forcing her to rouse the rest of the way to consciousness.

She opened her eyes and focused on the man's face so close to hers. It was rugged, with a bold nose broken at least once in its owner's life.

"You fainted," he said.

Lin managed a nod.

He held a glass to her lips. "Drink."

A command, but this came as no surprise, since Gideon Dayan was doing the speaking. The ship's chief security officer was a man of few words, and all of them firm.

Following her line of vision, he looked over his shoulder. "That will be all," he said to the group.

They dispersed—even devoted Dima—a few saying "Glad you're okay" and "Feel better." For her part, she would have preferred that Dima or virtually anyone else among the spectators had stayed, and that Gideon Dayan had been on his way. He was the last soul on this ship she needed noticing her. Beyond that, he made her uncomfortable on some other level she'd much rather not consider, so she avoided him whenever possible. He had come to her for her services as a massage therapist, and on each of those occasions she'd been too aware of him…too uncomfortable, as she was now.

"I've paged for medical assistance," he said.

To wait for the doctor to confirm that she'd merely fainted, when Zhang waited for her with Wei?

Impossible. Any delay in their morning ritual would mean that Zhang would miss her opportunity to eat.

"That won't be necessary," she replied. "I'm much better now." She thrust the glass back at him, then worked her way to her feet.

His broad hand closed over her arm once again. Lin glanced up at his face, some six inches above her own, and subtly drew her arm away and made a step to skirt around him.

"Thank you for your help, but—"

He blocked her way. "The call to the doctor remains outstanding and will continue that way unless you let me see you to the medical center."

"I have no time. I'm due in the spa in minutes."
Alarm had crept into her voice. Again she mentally
chided herself for showing weakness. Lin drew in a
breath and calmed. "As you can see, I am well."

His gaze traveled down the length of her body.

"I can see that you're fit, but I have no way of
knowing that you are well," he replied, his voice level
and measured. "And I have also been told by Dima
Ivanov that you have yet to eat."

"Perhaps I ate before I saw Dima."

"And perhaps not. I'll cancel the medical page if you
come with me into the officers' dining room, where I can
personally be sure that you have breakfast."

"I'll take an orange or an apple," she said. "Whatever can be found that I can eat on my way to my
duties."

"If you insist," he said, then drew her into the crew's
dining room, where two of the waitresses nearly raced
to see who could reach him first.

"Could you please bring Miss Wang some fruit and
perhaps a muffin or other pastry?" he asked.

The winner of the race nodded enthusiastically.
"Anything else, sir?"

"Anything?" he asked Lin.

"Nothing," she replied.

"Bottled juice, too, if you can find some," he said to
the waitress.

"Yes, sir." She shot toward the service door as though
her future relied upon getting the requested items.

"Do you always receive this sort of response?" Lin
asked the man she refused to think of as her rescuer.

His mouth quirked into a slightly crooked smile, one that remained long enough for her to accept it as real.

"Definitely not," he said, and she realized he was referring to her blatantly unreceptive attitude.

"Then better to stay with those who appreciate you," she said, thinking that since he seemed the humorless sort, her dry comment might repel him.

Instead, he laughed. "But far less entertaining."

She had not measured her opponent properly. Sparking any interest at all was dangerous. It was far better that she be as bland as the sturdy blue carpet beneath their feet.

"I promise you I'll take my food to the spa and eat between appointments, sir," she offered in as meek a voice as she knew how to summon. "And I thank you for taking time from your morning to help me."

Ah, that seemed to have worked.

The chief security officer briefly frowned, then inclined his head in a nod. "As you wish, Miss Wang." He moved two steps toward the door and then turned back. "Take care of yourself."

After he was gone, Lin wondered why it was that those simple words sounded like a warning. She would take care, indeed.

HARLEQUIN®

Mediterranean NIGHTS™

*Not everything is above board
on Alexandra's Dream!*

*Enjoy plenty of secrets, drama and sensuality
in the latest from Mediterranean Nights.*

Coming in November 2007...

BELOW DECK

by

Dorien Kelly

Determined to protect her young son,
widow Mei Lin Wang keeps him hidden
aboard *Alexandra's Dream* under cover of
her job. But life gets extremely complicated
when the ship's security officer, Gideon Dayan,
is piqued by the mystery surrounding this
beautiful, haunted woman....

HARLEQUIN *Presents*

INNOCENT MISTRESS, VIRGIN WIFE

Wedded and bedded for the very first time

**Classic romances from
your favorite Presents authors**

Available this month:

THE SPANISH DUKE'S VIRGIN BRIDE

by Chantelle Shaw

#2679

Ruthless billionaire Duke Javier Herrera needs a wife
to inherit the family business. Grace is the daughter
of a man who's conned Javier, and in this he sees an
opportunity for revenge and a convenient wife....

Coming soon,

THE DEMETRIOS BRIDAL BARGAIN

by Kim Lawrence
Book #2686

www.eHarlequin.com

HP12679

REQUEST YOUR FREE BOOKS!

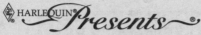 HARLEQUIN® *Presents*®

PASSION GUARANTEED SEDUCTION

2 FREE NOVELS PLUS 2 FREE GIFTS!

YES! Please send me 2 FREE Harlequin Presents® novels and my 2 FREE gifts. After receiving them, if I don't wish to receive any more books, I can return the shipping statement marked "cancel." If I don't cancel, I will receive 6 brand-new novels every month and be billed just $3.80 per book in the U.S., or $4.47 per book in Canada, plus 25¢ shipping and handling per book and applicable taxes, if any*. That's a savings of close to 15% off the cover price! I understand that accepting the 2 free books and gifts places me under no obligation to buy anything. I can always return a shipment and cancel at any time. Even if I never buy another book from Harlequin, the two free books and gifts are mine to keep forever.

106 HDN EEXK   306 HDN EEXV

Name _____ (PLEASE PRINT)

Address _____ Apt. #

City _____ State/Prov. _____ Zip/Postal Code

Signature (if under 18, a parent or guardian must sign)

Mail to the Harlequin Reader Service®:
IN U.S.A.: P.O. Box 1867, Buffalo, NY 14240-1867
IN CANADA: P.O. Box 609, Fort Erie, Ontario L2A 5X3

Not valid to current Harlequin Presents subscribers.

Want to try two free books from another line?
Call 1-800-873-8635 or visit www.morefreebooks.com.

* Terms and prices subject to change without notice. NY residents add applicable sales tax. Canadian residents will be charged applicable provincial taxes and GST. This offer is limited to one order per household. All orders subject to approval. Credit or debit balances in a customer's account(s) may be offset by any other outstanding balance owed by or to the customer. Please allow 4 to 6 weeks for delivery.

Your Privacy: Harlequin is committed to protecting your privacy. Our Privacy Policy is available online at www.eHarlequin.com or upon request from the Reader Service. From time to time we make our lists of customers available to reputable firms who may have a product or service of interest to you. If you would prefer we not share your name and address, please check here. ☐

HP07

HARLEQUIN *Presents*

Men who can't be tamed...or so they think!

If you love strong, commanding men,
you'll love this brand-new miniseries.

Meet the guy who breaks the rules to get exactly
what he wants, because he is...

HARD-EDGED & HANDSOME

He's the man who's impossible to resist....

RICH & RAKISH

He's got everything—and needs nobody...
until he meets one woman....

He's RUTHLESS!

In his pursuit of passion; in his world the winner takes all!

Coming in November:

THE BILLIONAIRE'S CAPTIVE BRIDE

by Emma Darcy
Book #2676

Coming in December:

BEDDED, OR WEDDED?

by Julia James
Book #2684

Brought to you by your favorite Harlequin Presents authors!

www.eHarlequin.com HP12676

HARLEQUIN Romance.

New York Times bestselling author

DIANA PALMER

Handsome, eligible ranch owner Stuart York knew Ivy Conley was too young for him, so he closed his heart to her and sent her away—despite the fireworks between them. Now, years later, Ivy is determined not to be treated like a little girl anymore…but for some reason, Stuart is always fighting her battles for her. And safe in Stuart's arms makes Ivy feel like a woman…his woman.

Winter Roses

Available November.

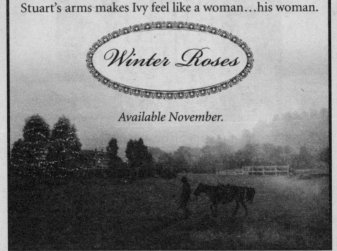

HRIBC03985